VILLAGE TEACHER

The Alternative School Logbook 1980–1981

Jack Sheffield

CORGI BOOKS

TRANSWORLD PUBLISHERS
61–63 Uxbridge Road, London W5 5SA
A Random House Group Company
www.randomhouse.co.uk

VILLAGE TEACHER
A CORGI BOOK: 9780552157889

First published in Great Britain
in 2010 by Bantam Press
an imprint of Transworld Publishers
Corgi edition published 2010

Addresses for Random House Group Ltd companies outside the UK
can be found at: www.randomhouse.co.uk
The Random House Group Ltd Reg. No. 954009

Penguin Random House is committed to a sustainable future for
our business, our readers and our planet. This book is made from
Forest Stewardship Council® certified paper.

Typeset in Palatino by
Kestrel Data, Exeter, Devon.

Printed and bound in Great Britain by Clays Ltd, St Ives plc

8 10 9 7

In fond memory of Vera Jane

Contents

Acknowledgements

I am indeed fortunate to have the support of my superb editor, the ever-patient Linda Evans, and the wonderful team at Transworld Publishers, including Nick Robinson, Madeline Toy, Lynsey Dalladay, Sophie Holmes and fellow 'Old Roundhegian' Martin Myers.

Special thanks go to my industrious agent, Philip Patterson of Marjacq Scripts, for his encouragement and good humour, and for proving that, even at five-feet-seven-inches tall, you can be a giant among literary agents!

I am grateful to all those who assisted in the research for this novel – in particular: Sarah Barrett, school nurse, Hampshire; Jenny Barrett, former secretary and Selectric typewriter demonstrator, Hampshire; Ted Barrett, retired senior manager, IBM, Hampshire; Patrick Busby, pricing director, church organist and Harrogate Rugby Club supporter, Hampshire; Janina Bywater, nurse and lecturer in psychology, Cornwall; Nick Cragg, chairman, Stafforce and Rotherham Rugby Club supporter, South

Yorkshire; Rob Cragg, ex-European director, Molex, Hampshire; The Revd Ben Flenley, Rector of Bentworth, Lasham, Medstead and Shalden, Hampshire; Kathryn Flenley, lay reader and schoolteacher, Hampshire; Clive Hutton, retired engineer and classic-car enthusiast, Hampshire; John Kirby, ex-policeman and Sunderland supporter, County Durham; Roy Linley, solutions analyst and Leeds United supporter, Unilever, Port Sunlight, Wirral; Sue Maddison, primary schoolteacher, Harrogate, North Yorkshire; Kerry Magennis-Prior, churchwarden, St Andrew's Church, Medstead, Hampshire; Sue Matthews, primary schoolteacher, York; Phil Parker, ex-teacher and Manchester United supporter, York; John Roberts, retired railway civil engineer, York; Zoe Roberts, museum explainer, York; Maureen Shying, Burradoo, NSW, Australia; Caroline Stockdale, librarian, York Central Library; and all the wonderful staff at Waterstone's, Alton, Hampshire.

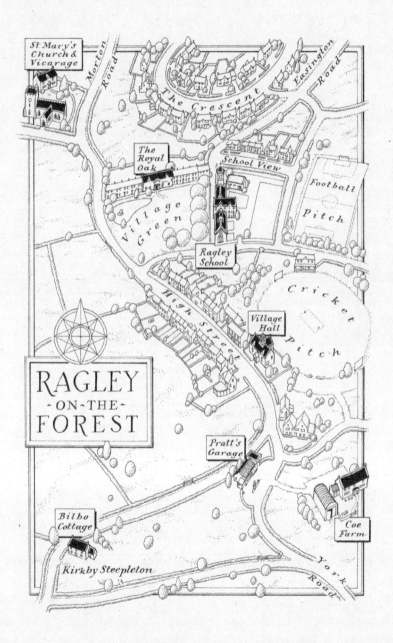

Prologue

Love is a fickle companion.

Six weeks ago I had it all . . . love of life, love of my school and, best of all, love of a woman.

Warm late-summer sunshine shone through the high-arched Victorian window of my office but, suddenly, I felt cold. I stared once again at the official-looking letter and shivered. I had been headmaster of Ragley-on-the-Forest Church of England Primary School in North Yorkshire for three years but it seemed unlikely I would complete a fourth. My days of being a village teacher were numbered.

It was Monday, 1 September 1980, and the school summer holiday was almost at an end. It had begun with the buying of a ring and hopes for a bright future. It was ending with news of school closures and the dashing of dreams.

I had asked Beth Henderson to marry me and, in spite of my previous entanglement with her sister Laura, to my delight she had said yes. Like me, Beth was a headteacher of a small village school in North Yorkshire and, at the end of July, we had packed quickly, jumped into my Morris Minor Traveller and driven down to Cornwall, where we found a quaint little cottage in the village of Summercourt. After two weeks of rugged scenery and cream teas, we returned to Yorkshire to plan our future together.

Beth and I walked down Stonegate, one of York's medieval streets, and stopped outside the bay window of Barbara Cattle's jewellery shop. One particular ring with its cluster of rose diamonds sparkled in the early August sunshine. The neat writing on the tiny label simply read: *Once owned by a Victorian lady.*

'It's beautiful, Jack,' said Beth quietly, 'but it's expensive – especially for a teacher.'

She was right. At £200 it represented a large slice of my monthly salary.

'It looks perfect,' I said quickly. Then I removed my Buddy Holly spectacles and began to polish them.

'Your teachers at Ragley say that's what you do when you're dealing with difficult parents,' said Beth, with a grin. 'You do it to give yourself thinking time.'

I hastily put them back on. 'You know me so well.'

'I certainly hope so,' she said. Her honey-blonde hair caressed her high cheekbones and her soft green eyes were full of mischief. She stretched up and kissed me on my cheek. 'Come on, Mr Sheffield,' she whispered in my ear, 'let's choose an engagement ring.'

*　　*　　*

As August drew to its close our attention turned back to our schools and to preparations for the new academic year. So it was on the first day of September I sifted through the holiday mail piled high on my desk. The letter from County Hall in Northallerton made it clear that some village schools were no longer economically viable and would have to close. We had fewer than ninety children on roll and I recalled that Beth had even fewer children in her school. Reluctantly, I pinned the letter on the office noticeboard and, with a sigh, unlocked the bottom drawer of my desk.

I took out the large, leather-bound school logbook and opened it to the next clean page. Then I filled my fountain pen with black Quink ink, wrote the date and stared at the empty page. The record of another school year was about to begin.

Three years ago, the retiring headmaster, John Pruett, had told me how to fill in the official school logbook. 'Just keep it simple,' he said. 'Whatever you do, don't say what really happens, because no one will believe you.'

So the real stories were written in my 'Alternative School Logbook'. And this is it!

Chapter One

A Smile for Raymond

*87 children were registered on roll on the first day of the
school year. A maintenance team from County Hall visited
school to free blocked pipework in the school kitchen. The
school photographer took photographs of all children and
classes.*

Extract from the Ragley School Logbook:
Thursday, 4 September 1980

'If it's like last year, Mr Sheffield, ah'll want m'money
back!'

Mrs Winifred Brown, our least favourite parent, had all
the charm of a Rottweiler with attitude. I took a step back
into the school office as she wedged her ample backside
in the door frame.

'Oh, I see,' I said . . . but I didn't.

'An' ah want my Damian t'be smiling this time, else
ah'll give that 'tographer what for.'

The penny dropped. At the end of last term, Vera

the secretary had typed a letter to parents to let them know the school photographer would be in school on the first Friday afternoon of the new school year. He had explained that he wanted the children to look suntanned and healthy after their six-week summer holiday.

I looked down at six-year-old Damian, who was picking his nose. 'I'm sure it will be fine, Mrs Brown,' I said, a little lamely, glancing down at her son's skinhead haircut and the remains of a KitKat bar smeared across his face.

'It'd better be,' she retorted as she stormed out into the entrance hall. 'An' ah'll be picking 'im up t'morrow just afore three o'clock,' she shouted as I closed the door. 'Ah've got business in York!'

I sat down at my desk, took a deep breath, removed my Buddy Holly spectacles and gave them a polish with the end of my outdated flower-power tie. Then I glanced up at the clock with its faded Roman numerals. It was 8.30 a.m. on Thursday, 4 September 1980, the first day of the autumn term. My fourth year as headteacher of Ragley-on-the-Forest Church of England Primary School in North Yorkshire had begun.

Anne Grainger, the deputy headteacher, walked into the office and glanced back at Mrs Brown. 'Happy days are here again,' she said. Anne, a slim, attractive brunette who looked nothing like her forty-eight years, was a wonderful teacher of the reception class and a loyal supporter of Ragley School. She also had the priceless qualities of patience and a sense of humour.

'Mrs Brown wants her Damian to be smiling on the class photograph tomorrow,' I explained.

'And pigs might fly,' retorted Anne. She glanced down at my feet. 'Like the new shoes, by the way,' she added mischievously.

I looked self-consciously at my new, trendy Kickers shoes peering out beneath my flared polyester trousers. Changing fashion had gradually crept up on us in Ragley village but the image of the new-look Eighties-man was clearly a far-off dream for me. The frayed leather patches on the elbows of my blue-checked herringbone sports jacket were not exactly at the cutting edge of fashion.

'Thanks, Anne,' I replied sheepishly. I glanced out of the window at the playground, which was filling up with excited children and the mothers of the new starters. 'I think I'll get some fresh air,' I said, 'and, hopefully, see a few friendly faces.' I unwound my gangling six-foot-one-inch frame from the wooden chair and attempted to flatten the palm-tree tuft of brown hair that refused to lie down on the crown of my head.

Anne grinned and glanced up at the clock. 'Don't be long, Jack. Vera will be giving out the new registers in a few minutes.'

The giant oak door creaked on its Victorian hinges and I hurried down the worn steps on to the tarmac play-ground surrounded by a waist-high wall of Yorkshire stone and topped with black metal railings. Mothers and children were walking up the cobbled school drive. I waved and they smiled in acknowledgement. They all looked relaxed with the exception of the furtive Mrs

Winifred Brown, who, to my surprise, disappeared suddenly round the back of the cycle shed and I wondered why she was going in that direction.

At the school gate, under the canopy of magnificent horse-chestnut trees that bordered the front of our school, eight-year-old Heathcliffe Earnshaw and his seven-year-old brother Terry stood staring up into the branches.

"Ullo, Mr Sheffield. Can we chuck sticks up t'get conkers, please?' asked Heathcliffe.

'I'm afraid not, Heathcliffe,' I said, with safety in mind, although I recalled that, as a boy, I had collected conkers in the same way. 'But I can reach the low branches, so we'll get some at morning playtime.'

'Thanks, Mr Sheffield,' said Heathcliffe. 'M'dad said 'e'd put some in t'oven tonight t'mek 'em 'ard.' Heathcliffe took his conkers very seriously.

Meanwhile, Terry looked up in admiration. In his eyes, Heathcliffe was Luke Skywalker and the Bionic Man all rolled into one.

I leant on the wrought-iron gate and looked across the village green. Morning sunshine lit up the white-fronted public house, The Royal Oak, which nestled comfortably in the centre of a row of cottages with pantile roofs and tall, sturdy brick chimneys. Outside, under the welcome shade of a weeping-willow tree, Old Tommy Piercy was sitting on the bench next to the duck pond, contentedly smoking a pipe of Old Holborn tobacco. He was watching the High Street coming alive. The village postman, Ted Postlethwaite, had just finished delivering mail to the General Stores & Newsagent, Piercy's Butcher's Shop, the Village Pharmacy, Pratt's Hardware Emporium, Nora's Coffee Shop and Diane's Hair Salon. Then he disappeared into the Post Office to enjoy his usual cup of tea with Miss Duff, the postmistress.

Off to my right, children were turning the corner of School View from the council estate and running towards school. Among them was eight-year-old Jimmy Poole. He was growing tall now but the mop of ginger curly hair, black-button eyes and freckled face were just as I remembered them.

'Good morning, Jimmy,' I said.

He stopped and looked up at me. 'Hello, Mithter Theffield,' he lisped. He pointed to the group of new starters standing with their mothers against the school wall. 'My thithter, Jemima, thtarth thchool today, Mr Theffield,' he panted.

Mrs Poole was clutching the tiny hand of four-year-old Jemima, whose long wavy ginger hair was neatly brushed and tied back with a blue ribbon.

'Well, I'm sure you'll look after her, Jimmy,' I said.

'Yeth, Mr Theffield,' shouted Jimmy as he ran off to discuss the forthcoming conker season with his friend Heathcliffe.

I looked back at the school and felt a pang of sadness. It was a solid Victorian building of reddish-brown bricks, high-arched windows, a steeply sloping grey slate roof and a tall, incongruous bell tower. Each year, for over one hundred years, the bell had rung to announce a new school year. In a huddle, by the stone steps of the entrance porch, stood seven mothers, each clutching the hand of a four-year-old new starter destined for

Anne Grainger's reception class. They were the new generation of Ragley children and, as I hurried back into school, I prayed they wouldn't be the last.

I wondered what the new academic year held in store.

For this was 1980. Over two million were unemployed, inflation had risen to more than twenty per cent and Margaret Thatcher was becoming increasingly annoyed by the antics of a certain Arthur Scargill. Stone-washed jeans were suddenly fashionable and Action Man had been voted Toy of the Decade. Intelligence was measured by the speed with which you could complete a Rubik cube and Phillips had released something called a compact-disc player. Meanwhile, an unknown group of children known as the St Winifred's School Choir were practising a song about their grandma.

When I opened the staff-room door, Vera was distributing a set of pristine school registers. Our tall, slim, elegant fifty-eight-year-old school secretary looked immaculate in her navy-blue pin-striped Marks & Spencer's business suit. 'Good morning, Mr Sheffield,' she said, 'and congratulations!' She gave me a knowing smile and handed over a beautiful Engagement card. It had been signed by all the staff.

'Jack, we're all so happy for you,' said Anne Grainger.

'Well done, Jack,' said Sally Pringle. She leant forward, gave me a peck on my cheek and glanced down at my new shoes, 'and I like the groovy footwear.'

Sally, a tall, ginger-haired thirty-nine-year-old who taught Class 3, the eight- and nine-year-olds, was wearing her usual loud colours. A voluminous bright-pink blouse hung loosely over her pillar-box red stretch cords. While the blouse clashed with her Pre-Raphaelite red hair, it comfortably hid her precious bulge. Sally was eighteen weeks pregnant and due to leave at Christmas, to be replaced by Miss Flint, our supply teacher.

She grinned wickedly and patted her tummy. 'And before long, Jack, it might be your turn to have a little one.'

'Oh no!' I exclaimed hurriedly. 'I don't think so . . . We've not even fixed a date for the wedding yet.'

'So when do you think it might be?' asked Jo Hunter. The diminutive twenty-five-year-old taught the seven- and eight-year-olds in Class 2. Jo was married to Dan Hunter, our friendly six-foot-four-inch local policeman, and was always full of energy. She was dressed in her new body-hugging tracksuit and Chris Evert trainers, with her long black hair tied back in a pony-tail.

'We're in no rush,' I said cautiously. 'It will probably be next year sometime.'

'Very wise, Mr Sheffield,' said Vera, peering at me over her steel-framed spectacles.

I smiled. Vera always insisted on calling me 'Mr Sheffield'. Only once had she ever called me by my first name and that was at the end of last term during a conversation that had changed my life. Vera had insisted I should tell Beth my true feelings. 'Go and find her, Jack. Don't let her go,' Vera had said. 'That happened to me once. I wouldn't want you to let it happen to Beth.'

I didn't ask Vera what she really meant and supposed I never would.

'Well, good luck, everybody. I'll go and ring the bell.'

So, on the stroke of nine o'clock, amid tearful farewells among the mothers of the new starters, the children of Ragley village wandered happily into school to begin the academic year 1980/81.

In my classroom, twenty-three ten- and eleven-year-olds were sitting at their hexagonal Formica-topped tables. In front of each child was a reading record card, a new wooden ruler, an HB pencil, a tin of Lakeland crayons, a rubber, a *New Oxford Dictionary* and a collection of new exercise books with different-coloured manila covers.

Predictably, I started off with something simple and we talked about what we had done during the school holiday. Soon all the class were writing and I was pleased to see ten-year-old Tracy Crabtree using her dictionary. Unknown to me, she was searching for the word 'steroids'. Twenty minutes later she placed her book on the pile on my desk for marking and moved on to some long multiplication. I picked up my red pen and read what Tracy had written:

'My dad bought some steroids in the holidays. My mam said he had to get them because she was fed up of him. She said he'd been putting it off for ages. So he got his hammer and fixed them to the stair carpet to stop it slipping.'

I underlined the word 'steroids', wrote 'stair rods' in the margin and 'Well done' at the bottom. Once again I reflected that teaching had its moments . . . particularly when I marked eleven-year-old Cathy Cathcart's book. Cathy had written, 'My gran was really poorly in the holidays. My mam said it was a terminal illness.'

I called Cathy out to my desk. 'I'm sorry to hear about your grandmother,' I said quietly.

'Oh, that's all right, Mr Sheffield, she's better now,' said Cathy cheerfully.

'But you wrote she had a terminal illness,' I said, pointing to the sentence.

'That's reight, Mr Sheffield. She were sick at 'Eathrow Airport.'

Shortly before morning assembly we had a discussion about the responsibilities of being in the 'top' class and I asked for volunteers for some of the responsible jobs we had to do each day. Two eleven-year-olds with sound financial sense, Simon Nelson and Carol Bustard, were put in charge of the tuck shop. Katy Ollerenshaw inevitably became blackboard-cleaning monitor. This job traditionally went to Ragley's tallest pupil and Katy had always been in the middle of the back row on class photographs. Cathy Cathcart, a fastidious timekeeper, became school-bell monitor and Darrell Topper became the 'letting teachers know that school assembly will start in five minutes' monitor as he was the fastest boy in school and for some strange reason was desperate for the job.

At morning break I collected a hot milky coffee and went out to do playground duty. It was a pleasure on such a lovely day and, as promised, I helped Heathcliffe and his friends collect a large pile of conkers. Soon, however, he was trying to teach the girls in his class how to wink and whistle. He was intensely proud that he could do both simultaneously.

*   *   *

After lunch we gathered in the staff-room. Vera was checking late dinner money and Anne and Jo were quizzing Sally about the trials of pregnancy.

I had spent twenty pence on my copy of *The Times* and scanned the news. Len Murray, the TUC General Secretary, wanted urgent talks with Jim Callaghan about incomes policy. Meanwhile, the BBC's recorded highlights of a Football League Cup match between Ipswich and Middlesbrough had not been screened last night because the Middlesbrough team had advertising on their shirts. The bright labels showing Middlesbrough's affiliation to Datsun Japanese cars was in contravention of the corporation's rules. Advertising was suddenly becoming big business in football and I wondered where it would end.

During afternoon school we had just begun our new project on the history of York when there was a tap on my door and Shirley the cook popped her head round the door. She looked anxious. 'I'm sorry to trouble you, Mr Sheffield, but can I have a word?'

I walked out into the corridor. Shirley Mapplebeck was a wonderful school cook and with her assistant, the formidable Mrs Doreen Critchley, worked wonders in her small kitchen. 'What is it, Shirley?' I asked.

'We've got a blockage, Mr Sheffield,' said Shirley, 'an 'ah can't get anything t'flush away.'

'Shall I have a look at playtime, Shirley?'

'Doreen 'ad a go before she left, Mr Sheffield. If she can't shift it, no one can.'

I nodded in agreement. Doreen Critchley had the forearms of a circus strong man. 'You'd better ask Miss Evans to ring County Hall, Shirley.'

By afternoon break, Vera had everything in hand in her usual unflappable style. 'Battersbys will be in first thing tomorrow, Mr Sheffield.'

'Battersbys?'

'Yes, Mr Sheffield, the Battersby brothers. They can un-block anything,' said Vera, with absolute certainty.

'Thanks, Vera,' I said. 'What would I do without you?'

She smiled and returned to typing a note to parents entitled 'School Photographs – Reminder' on her Royal Imperial typewriter.

It was after six o'clock when I climbed into my emerald-green Morris Minor Traveller and drove the three miles home to Bilbo Cottage in the sleepy village of Kirkby Steepleton.

I sat down in the lounge and began to write a report to the school governors about our new school library extension – now close to completion – while attempting to grill a pork chop. I was soon engrossed and only the smell of burning from the kitchen reminded me of my inability to multi-task. By 8.30 p.m. I needed a break so I switched on BBC 1 and settled down to watch *Yes Minister*. The brilliant Nigel Hawthorne was leading poor Paul Eddington his usual merry dance when the telephone rang.

'Had a good day?' asked a familiar voice. It was Beth.

'I wish you were here,' I said.

'Why?' said Beth. I imagined her green eyes twinkling with a hint of mischief.

'I've just cremated my evening meal.'

'Is that all?'

'Can you come round?' I asked hopefully. There was a pause and I knew she would be twirling a lock of honey-blonde hair between her fingers while she considered my proposal.

'Sorry, Jack – too much paperwork. Anyway, we can catch up at the weekend. I've got something interesting to show you.'

'Can't wait,' I said.

We said our usual goodbyes and, with the television for company, it was nearly midnight by the time I finished my report. Patrick Moore in *The Sky at Night* was wandering around a meteor crater in northern Arizona and looking as lonely as I felt when I switched off. Finally, in my quiet bedroom, I dispelled thoughts of blocked sinks and fell asleep wondering what life would be like when Beth was here.

The next morning bright autumn sunshine lit up the back road to Ragley village. At this time of year, my journey to school was always a joy in this beautiful corner of God's Own Country. Beyond the hawthorn hedgerow a field of corn swayed with the rhythm of the soft breeze and the breath of life. However, my peace was soon shattered when I drove up the cobbled school drive and heard the sound of hammering and loud voices.

In the car park was a filthy battleship-grey van covered in rust. A crude sign in white gloss had been painted on the back doors. It read: *Albert & Sidney Battersby – Blockages are our Business*.

The noise was coming from the other side of the cycle shed where two stocky unshaven men, dressed in filthy brown overalls, had removed a huge metal inspection cover. One of the pair was bald as a coot and peering down the hole. He was beating our Victorian drainage system with a club hammer and appeared completely unconcerned that he was up to his elbows in raw sewage. The other, sporting the thickest National Health spectacles I had ever seen and clearly the brains of the partnership, was issuing instructions.

'Good morning,' I shouted. 'I'm the headteacher, Jack Sheffield.'

''Morning, Mr Sheffield,' said the one with the spectacles. He peered at me myopically. 'Ah'm Bert an' this is m'brother, Sid.' Both of them were unmoved by the putrid smell.

'So, can you fix it?' I asked and wrinkled my nose.

Bert sucked air through his teeth and looked down at Sid. 'We've seen some blockages in us time, 'aven't we, Sid?' he said. Then he shook his head sadly as if someone had just died. ''Ow's it looking?'

'It's nine-inch solid down 'ere,' said Sid.

It was all becoming too graphic for me. 'It looks . . . terrible,' I said.

'Mebbe so,' said Sid, unconcerned.

'It might be shit t'you, Mr Sheffield, but it's our bread an' butter,' said Bert philosophically.

'Oh dear,' I mumbled, 'but can you help us, Mr Battersby?'

'There's only one thing for it, Sid,' said Bert.

'Y'don't mean . . .'

'A'h do,' said Bert. 'We've no choice.'

'Y'know what 'appened las' time?' said Sid ominously.

'If we don't use 'er, we've no chance.'

'Her?' I asked. 'Who do you mean?'

'Well, not 'xactly 'er, Mr Sheffield, it's more of a what,' said Bert.

'That's reight,' said Sid solemnly. 'You tell 'im, Bert.'

He looked me square in the eyes. 'We've no choice, Mr Sheffield. We'll 'ave t'use Big Bertha.' He announced it as if he'd just declared war on Russia.

'Big Bertha!'

'Best hinvention known to man or beast,' said Bert.

'If Big Bertha can't shift it, nowt can,' said Sid.

''Er pounds per square inch is frightening,' added Bert for good measure.

'Well, good luck,' I said hesitantly.

At twelve o'clock, Cathy Cathcart stood up to ring the bell. 'Posh van coming up t'drive, Mr Sheffield,' she said. Cathy had clearly become the new self-appointed 'announcer' for the class. A royal-blue van, spotless and waxed to a high sheen, pulled up in the car park. On the sides, under a distinctive coat of arms, blazed the words *Temple Photography* in gold flowing letters.

A tall, deathly pale, grey-haired and frail-looking man emerged and began to unpack his equipment. I went out and introduced myself.

'Good afternoon, Mr Sheffield,' he said, handing me

his card, which announced he was Raymond De 'Ath from Temple Photography in Thirkby.

'Oh, hello, Mr, er, Death,' I said.

'It's two syllables: De 'Ath,' he said in a tired voice. 'I'll set up in the school hall, shall I?'

It was soon evident that Raymond had lived a life of false enthusiasm. Over many years, countless crying babies and demanding mothers had finally ground down his mental resolve. His catchphrase, 'Smile for Raymond', was now a forlorn plea from the heart. As he picked up his tripod, he reflected that the last time *he* had smiled was when his wife had run off with a travelling salesman from Cleckheaton whose aftershave could stop a clock at ten paces.

By the time he reached the school entrance, his optimism was fading fast. Heathcliffe Earnshaw was holding open the door and smiling. At least, it was Heathcliffe's version of a smile. When Raymond saw the glassy-eyed stare, clenched teeth and contorted grimace he knew another tough day was in store.

'Ah've been learning t'smile all las' night,' said Heathcliffe cheerfully.

Raymond gazed back in horror. The boy's manic expression might have been that of an axe-murderer. Raymond nodded warily and hurried into the school hall, where, before setting up his camera equipment, he hastily swallowed two aspirins.

At afternoon break, Anne was on playground duty and Vera, who had taken charge of directing children from their classrooms to the chairs in front of Raymond's

screen in the school hall, was shaking her head in despair.
'If he says "Smile for Raymond" again, I'll scream,' she
whispered.

I decided to see how the Battersby brothers were pro-
gressing.

'Nearly done,' said Bert. 'We've set up Big Bertha.' The
brothers were admiring the ugly contraption as if it were
a thing of beauty.

It was then I noticed a gap in the school fence behind
the cycle shed. I frowned in dismay. Also, there were
cigarette stubs scattered on the ground. However, I was
soon distracted.

'Mr Sheffield,' said Sid suddenly, 'we've got a little bit
o' summat special.'

He beckoned me to the car park. Puzzled, I followed
the two brothers to the back doors of their van.

'Bit of a sideline, so t'speak,' said Bert. He smiled and
tapped the side of his bulbous nose with a filthy fore-
finger. Then he opened the doors and a repulsive smell of
decay floated out. On the floor was a collection of grubby
newspaper parcels. Sid selected one and opened it.

'We gerrit from a mate in Thirkby, Mr Sheffield,' said
Bert.

'Best lean bacon y'll ever see,' said Sid triumphantly,
holding up a rasher between his muddy brown finger
and thumb.

'Usu'lly a pound,' said Bert.

'But t'you, fifty pence,' added Sid.

After staying long enough to express polite interest, I
retreated quickly with a mumbled apology.

*　　　*　　　*

Back in the school hall, I mentioned the damaged fence to Vera.

'I'll ask Mr Paxton to fix it,' she said. John Paxton was Ragley's handyman.

'Perhaps he could plant a couple of shrubs as well to fill the gap, Vera.'

'Good idea. I'll arrange it,' she said.

'You know, Mr Sheffield,' added Vera thoughtfully, 'someone may be using it as a short cut from the council estate.'

'Smile for Raymond,' said the photographer once again. Vera visibly winced and hurried off to collect the last group of children.

At a quarter to three, Anne popped her head round the staff-room door. 'Excuse me, everybody,' she said. 'I'll keep all the children outside. Doctor Death says we're ready for the whole school photograph on the playground.'

Raymond De 'Ath ceremoniously placed five chairs in a line and ushered me to the chair in the centre. Anne sat on my right, Vera on my left, and they were flanked by Jo and Sally. Then he asked Katy Ollerenshaw to stand directly behind me, and the rest of the children were placed on either side, in descending order of height, to create a pyramid of faces. Anne's children sat cross-legged in front.

There was a long pause while Raymond disappeared like a furtive ostrich under his black cloak. 'Now assume a pose, please,' said a muffled voice.

'Damian Brown, don't forget to smile,' said Jo in a

commanding voice and I recalled my conversation with Mrs Brown.

'OK, Miss,' grumbled Damian, 'but m'face is 'urting.'

'Shall we say "Cheese", Mr Sheffield?' asked Tracy Crabtree.

'We said "Sausages" last year, sir,' said Darrell Topper helpfully.

Sally started to giggle and Anne joined in.

'Quiet now, please,' said Mr De 'Ath.

'Oh, for goodness' sake,' said Vera, losing patience.

'Are you ready?' he mumbled with a final twist of the lens.

Vera could stand it no longer. 'If he says "Smile for Raymond" once more I swear I'll—'

'OK, everybody . . . smile for Raymond.'

Then, in a split second, everything happened at once.

Behind the crouching photographer, round the corner of the cycle shed, Big Bertha cleared the blocked drain with a huge bang and a brown geyser of water plumed into the air. This was immediately followed by a loud scream and Mrs Winifred Brown appeared from behind the shed like a drowned rat with a damp cigarette hanging from her lips. Instantly, eighty-seven children, four teachers and one secretary burst into laughter and a camera shutter opened and closed.

Now, many years later, when I look at school photographs of times gone by, one stands out. In among the serious faces, teachers and pupils that have come and gone, there is one photograph that stands out from the rest. Above a neatly typed label, 'Ragley School 1980', it shows the happiest group of staff and pupils you could ever wish to meet.

They are united in one accord.

All of them are smiling for Raymond.

Chapter Two

The Brave New World of Vera Evans

Miss Evans received training on our new school typewriter. The Revd Joseph Evans took his weekly RE lesson. The PTA Annual General Meeting was followed by a 'Metric Mathematics' event to introduce our School Mathematics Project to parents.

Extract from the Ragley School Logbook:
Wednesday, 24 September 1980

Miss Vera Evans always made perfect scones.

In the vicarage kitchen all her utensils and ingredients were laid out neatly on the marble work surface. Having taken her faithful *Be-Ro Home Recipes: Scones, Cakes, Pastry & Puddings* from the pine shelf of cookery books next to her gleaming Aga cooker, she opened it to page 6, 'Be-Ro Rich Scones', and propped the stiff but well-worn pages against her ancient brass weighing scales. Her two-and-a-half-inch-diameter cutter, with which she would press out exactly twelve scones, sparkled in the autumn sunshine that streamed through the leaded panes of the arched kitchen window. Then she picked up her favourite wooden spoon, selected a spotless mixing bowl and began. Puccini's 'Humming Chorus' from *Madam Butterfly* was playing softly on her radio and, appropriately, she hummed along. It was Saturday morning, 20 September, and Vera was content in her world.

Vera had never married and she lived with her younger brother, the Revd Joseph Evans, in the vicarage on Morton Road. It was a beautifully furnished and spacious house and Vera took pride in keeping it spick-and-span. Her life was one of tidiness and order and even her three cats, Treacle, Jess and Maggie, were well-behaved. Her favourite, Maggie, a black cat with white paws, was named after Prime Minister Margaret Thatcher, Vera's political heroine. Hers was a quiet, serene life of church flowers, school administration and Women's Institute meetings.

However, little did she know it, but, at that very moment, changes were in store for the secretary of Ragley School. A revolution was about to take place and Vera's world would never be the same again.

A mile away in the Ragley School office I was looking at a typewriter, the like of which I had never seen before.

'It's an ergonomically designed, golf-ball head, IBM Selectric – and a bargain at three hundred pounds,' said Mr Joy, the salesman, with a voice like a machine-gun. He was clearly ex-army and looked very smart in his white shirt, grey suit and military tie. Unfortunately, his straight black, Brylcreemed hair, parted on the right, and his toothbrush moustache gave him an uncanny resemblance to Adolf Hitler.

'There's no carriage return,' I said, looking puzzled. 'So how will my secretary know how it works?'

'Don't worry, sir,' he said confidently, 'we have ways of making it work . . .' He was even beginning to sound like Hitler. 'The platen remains stationary, Mr Sheffield,' he added with a stony face. 'It's the golf-ball that moves side to side.'

'Platen?'

'The round rubber cylinder,' he explained, pointing. 'It's a state-of-the-art machine, Mr Sheffield, guaranteed to make your secretary's work the envy of the village.'

I nodded in agreement but secretly guessed Vera would have preferred her bramble jelly to be the envy of the village. 'The young lady at County Hall said, if I came in to school to receive delivery on Saturday morning, you would give a demonstration.'

'Ah, not exactly, sir. I'm the advance troops, so to speak.'

It felt like I was undergoing military manoeuvres. 'So will someone come to show our Miss Evans how it works?'

'Certainly, sir. Never fear, reinforcements will be here,' recited Mr Joy. 'Mr Grubb, our customer-service engineer, will visit next Wednesday at nine hundred hours precisely. He will provide installation and basic training.'

'Oh, well, thank you, Mr Joy,' I said, staring uncertainly at the strange machine.

He added a note in his diary and shook my hand firmly. 'So thank you for coming in at the weekend, sir. I'm sure you'll find everything to your satisfaction.' He locked his black executive briefcase and walked out to his car.

When he drove off, it occurred to me that Joy was an unfortunate name for a Hitler look-alike with no sense of humour.

I looked at the sleek, classic grey typewriter and decided to carry it through to the staff-room coffee-table ready for examination by Vera and the rest of the staff on Monday morning. Then I replaced Vera's Royal Imperial typewriter exactly where it had been on her highly polished desk, adjusted the photograph of her three cats, locked the school and drove home to Kirkby Steepleton.

On Monday morning we all gathered in the staff-room and stared at our new marvel of the modern world.

'It's fantastic,' said Jo, our resident scientist, who loved new technology. She was itching to get her hands on it.

'There's no carriage return,' said a bemused Anne, 'and it's not as tall as Vera's typewriter. Makes you wonder how they fit it all in.'

'It looks sort of . . . squashed,' said Sally reflectively, 'as if someone's sat on it.'

'Is there an instruction book?' asked the eager Jo.

'No, and we'd better not fiddle with it,' I said pointedly. 'There's an engineer coming on Wednesday to show Vera how to use it.'

We all looked at Vera, who shook her head. 'Progress,' she muttered and walked quietly down the tiny passageway to the school office. Everyone exchanged glances but said nothing. Soon we heard the familiar tap-tap-tap of Vera's trusty manual typewriter as she typed out the agenda for Wednesday's PTA Annual General Meeting, followed by the *ker-ching* as she swept the chromium arm of the carriage return. A few minutes later she wound out the Gestetner master sheet from the typewriter, smoothed it carefully on to the inky drum of the duplicating machine, peeled off the backing sheet and wound the handle to produce the copies of the agenda. It was a routine Vera could have done in her sleep. Sadly, routines change.

On Wednesday morning a watery sunlight filtered through the wind-torn clouds and cast a tapestry of flickering shadows on the land below. The drive on the back road from Kirkby Steepleton to Ragley village was always a pleasure on an autumn morning and I wound down the window as I trundled along. The last of the ripe barley, soon to be harvested, shimmered in the gentle breeze. Fields of russet gold swayed in sinuous rhythm in perfect harmony with the light and shade. It was a sight that lifted the spirit and satisfied the soul. However, while there was peace on earth, goodwill to all men was to be in short supply in the school office.

Vera frowned at the short, plump, prematurely balding man wearing a creased red polo shirt with a bolt of lightning logo that looked as if he was auditioning for a part in *Flash Gordon*. In Mr Graham Grubb's opinion, the gleaming new electric typewriter could virtually operate itself and he wasn't going to waste much time on this old dear who was looking at him as if he'd forgotten to do his maths homework.

'Right you are, Miss Heavens,' he said, 'first of all I'll switch it on and then you need to sit comfortably. Now remember: listen and you'll learn; don't and you won't.'

Vera took an instant dislike to this pompous young man with his well-rehearsed patter and complete lack of charm. 'It's Evans, not Heavens . . . and will you be sucking Polo mints throughout the entire demonstration?' said Vera in a cool, disarming manner.

'Er, no, Miss, er, Evans,' he mumbled and quickly placed his half-sucked mint into a grubby handkerchief.

Now that the pecking order in her office had been established, Vera glared at this newfangled contraption in its shiny case and wondered where the carriage-return handle was hiding. 'Very well,' she said regally, 'let us begin.'

Mr Grubb coughed nervously and recommenced. 'Well, Miss Evans, you feed t'paper in t'same way as y'manual and then 'old yer 'ands in a different position.' He held out his hands over the keyboard as if he were blessing it. 'So y'touch-typing will be a lot lighter on this 'un than on y'manual. Y'll notice t'print will be constant, like, and won't be light or dark like on y'old typewriter.'

Vera frowned again. *Her* typing was always constant.

'An' y'replacement ribbons are in a cartridge in a plastic container, so no more mucky fingers,' continued the young engineer. 'An', best of all, as there's no carriage return, 'cause y'typeball an' ribbon move from side t'side. A quick flick of y'little finger on t'return key an' t'golf-ball goes back to t'left 'and margin.'

This had an impact on Vera. If there was no carriage

41

return she could organize her desk differently. Her 'Flowers of England' coaster, a picture of lavender in full bloom, could now have a new home on the right-hand side of the machine. Things might not be as bad as they first seemed, even if this young man did drop his aitches.

'But you'll 'ave t'be careful, Miss Evans,' said Mr Grubb insistently, 'of not accidentally touching t'space bar.' He stared at Vera and nodded as if a problem had been solved. 'But *you'll* be OK,' he said reassuringly. 'It's jus' ladies with, er, large, er, y'know, big b-b-bosoms, when they lean forward,' he stuttered.

Vera's frosty stare switched from cool to glacial. 'Are we finished, Mr Grubb?'

'Y-yes,' he said, quickly switching off the typewriter and now eager to escape, 'so any problems, jus' ring IBM.'

'IBM?' said Vera.

'International Business Machines, Miss Evans – or, as they say in t'trade, "I've Been Married"!' He scurried away and shot off down the drive in his little white van.

Meanwhile, Vera's brother, Joseph Evans, had called in to take his weekly Religious Education lesson. He was teaching Sally's class and had begun to recap on how much the children remembered from last week's lesson about the Ten Commandments. Once again, he wondered why it was so difficult to communicate with primary-school children. In answer to the question 'Why did God give Moses two tablets?' Theresa Ackroyd said that he must have had a bad headache. Then, when he asked which commandment teaches us how to treat our little brothers and sisters, Heathcliffe Earnshaw had offered 'Thou shalt not kill'.

Finally, in despair, Joseph moved on to this week's Bible story. Everything seemed to be going well until he said, 'And God told Lot to take his wife and flee out of the city. But, sadly, boys and girls, his wife was turned into a pillar of salt.'

'An' what 'appened to the flea?' asked Amanda Pickles.

Joseph ran his long fingers through his thinning hair and wondered why God's work suddenly became so difficult with a class of eight- and nine-year-olds.

At lunchtime we gathered in the staff-room. Vera was looking preoccupied and Jo had made a list of all the metric measures equipment she needed for the parents' workshop that would take place after the evening meeting.

'Well, I'm all set for tonight,' said Jo, after ticking off her list.

'Metrication!' exclaimed Anne gloomily. 'After twenty-five years of teaching imperial measures.'

'Did you know that metrication began in France in the 1790s?' Sally said reflectively.

'Trust the French,' said Vera irritably.

'Everything's changing,' said Anne.

'It's a different world,' murmured Vera.

During afternoon school, back in my classroom Jonathan Greening, a ten-year-old farmer's son, was looking at an Ordnance Survey map of North Yorkshire as part of our

'History of York' project. The map was covered in grids of one-thousand-metre squares.

'These kilometre squares are puzzling, Mr Sheffield,' said Jonathan. 'We 'ave acres at 'ome.'

Jonathan was the fourth generation of his farming family and I thought of the life he would lead when he grew up. Metric measurements meant little to his world of bushels and pecks.

'Y'see, Mr Sheffield, acres are easy 'cause m'dad says everyone knows it's a unit of land measuring four thousand eight hundred and forty square yards.'

He bowed his head to his work and it occurred to me that he had a point.

In Jonathan's world it was always ten miles to York and when he went shopping for his mother the list would include half a dozen eggs, two pounds of minced beef, a pint of milk and, perhaps, as a special treat, four ounces of sherbet lemons.

At 3.45 p.m. Cathy Cathcart looked at her new wristwatch and rang the bell to announce the end of school. Since taking on this job, she had become a walking timetable.

'Thanks for a good day, Mr Sheffield,' said Cathy.

I was touched by her praise and general good humour.

'Thank you, Cathy, and what are you doing tonight?'

'Well, ah'm going 'ome for m'tea first, Mr Sheffield,' she said with another glance at her watch, 'an' then me an' Tracy are gonna watch *John Craven's Newsround* at five past five an' then *Blue Peter* at ten past.'

'So what's it about tonight, Cathy?' I asked.

'It'll be reight good tonight, Mr Sheffield,' said Cathy enthusiastically. 'Peter Duncan's washing Big Ben an' Peter an' Sarah Greene, who ah like, an' that Simon Groome, who Tracy thinks is too posh, are gonna learn square dancing. An' then ah'm gonna read up on m'metric.' She held up her School Mathematics Project workcard, gave me a big toothy smile and ran off.

At six o'clock I was alone in the school office when the telephone rang.

'Ragley School,' I said.

'Hello, Jack.'

'Oh, hello, Beth.'

'How about a drink after your PTA meeting?' she said.

'Good idea. See you in the Oak – say, around nine?'

'OK. 'Bye.'

Our calls were like that these days, short and sweet. Both of us were busy with our headships, particularly Beth, who was now beginning her second year as a village school headmistress. I glanced at my watch. It was six o'clock. In three hours I would be sitting opposite the woman I loved. With some effort I squeezed these thoughts from my tired brain and returned to my marking.

At seven thirty, Staff Nurse Sue Phillips, chair of the Ragley PTA, opened the Annual General Meeting and launched another year of activities that would raise much-needed funds for our school. All the teaching staff and Vera were there, plus a group of committee members, around a dozen eager mothers and a couple of serious-looking fathers.

'It's been an eventful past year,' said Sue, 'and we're all proud of the school extension that will be finished soon. The official opening will be on Saturday, the eighth of November, and Miss Barrington-Huntley, the chair of the Education Committee at County Hall, will be our official guest . . . So, well done, everybody!'

Everyone recognized this was a great achievement and Sue led a token round of applause. I joined in and caught Anne's eye. She smiled and I knew that, secretly, we were both hoping it might persuade the North Yorkshire County Council to save us from closure.

'Our next task is to fill our new library area with resources.' Sue took a deep breath and looked around in anticipation for support. 'So I propose this year's fund-raising is used for books and equipment.'

Approval was unanimous and Mrs Margery Ackroyd, the secretary, scribbled in her new spiral-bound note-book.

'And Mr Sheffield has said that a member of staff will attend the forthcoming Computers in Schools course at High Sutton Hall before we decide whether to purchase a computer for school.'

Jo's eyes lit up in expectation, while Anne and Sally suddenly renewed interest in their fingernails.

Sue, an attractive blue-eyed blonde, after the usual formal proceedings of voting in the new committee, brought the meeting to a speedy conclusion. 'And finally, Mrs Hunter has kindly displayed some examples of the new metric mathematics that form part of the school's scheme of work and we are all invited to have a go!' She gave a wry smile, closed the meeting and immediately the Baby Burco boiler was wheeled out from the kitchen and tea was served.

Around the sides of the hall, Jo Hunter had arranged the dining furniture and on each table she had displayed a 'metric mathematics' activity. Alongside the colourful School Mathematics Project boxes of workcards were litre measuring jugs, metre rulers and weighing scales. It was a busy, successful evening and I was in good spirits when, after locking up the school, I wandered into The Royal Oak.

Beth came into the lounge bar and all heads turned. Her beautifully tailored light-grey business suit and white collarless blouse emphasized her slim figure and she walked with natural confidence to my table near the bay window and sat down. Wisps of honey-blonde hair hung over her high cheekbones and her green eyes looked a little tired after her busy day.

'I bought you a white wine,' I said and placed the glass in front of her.

'Perfect,' she said and took a sip. 'Thanks, Jack.'

We chatted about the events of the day until, to my surprise, she pulled a *Times Educational Supplement* out of her shoulder bag and began to pore over the Primary Headships pages.

I was puzzled. 'What are you looking at those for?' I asked. 'You've only been at Hartingdale for a year.'

She didn't look up. Instead she took out a pencil and began circling some of the advertised headships. 'Just thinking ahead, Jack,' she murmured. 'After all, our schools might not survive the cuts.'

'Don't worry about that now, Beth,' I said. 'Put away your paper and enjoy your drink.'

She returned the newspaper to her bag, sat back and twiddled with her engagement ring, deep in thought.

'Would you like to come back with me to Bilbo Cottage . . . and perhaps stay over?' I asked hopefully.

Beth smiled. 'Tempting offer, Jack, but I've got a big assembly in the morning . . . and I need to be wide awake for that,' she added with a mischievous grin.

I was pleased her mood had lightened and the scent of Rive Gauche perfume lingered when I kissed her goodnight. My drive back to Kirkby Steepleton was filled with thoughts of how such a stunningly beautiful woman could have said yes to my proposal of marriage.

Thursday morning arrived and all was not well. Vera didn't bother reading her *Daily Telegraph* while she drank her morning cup of tea. The news that Margaret Thatcher, on her visit to Greece, blamed our present unemployment problems on 'world recession' passed her by. Nor did she appear concerned that Russia's President Brezhnev had warned of nuclear war. Vera had more pressing problems on her mind. Her typewriter wouldn't work and she didn't know why.

'Could you have a look at the new typewriter, please, Mr Sheffield,' she whispered in my ear at the end of morning break.

It didn't take me long to solve the immediate problem. 'It's not turned on, Vera,' I said. 'This one works on electricity.' I switched it on and a faint whirring sound indicated it had come to life.

'Oh dear, of course,' said Vera. 'How silly of me.' She sat down and put her head in her hands.

'Don't you worry,' I said, trying to be comforting.

She ran a long, elegant finger down the side of the hard plastic casing. 'I have an RSA Stage 3 typing certificate on my lounge wall, Mr Sheffield, but this morning I feel like a junior apprentice again.'

'Just take your time, Vera. There's no rush.'

She looked up at me and the strain was obvious. 'I know that things have to change and I can't live in the past . . . but some of this new technology leaves me cold.'

'Vera, you know I'd be lost without you. It's more important to me that you are happy in your work.'

She gave me a weak smile and nodded.

At lunchtime I spotted Sally tending her magnificent display of dahlias in the border outside her classroom window and I wondered who would look after them next year. I walked over to her and she stood up and rubbed her aching back.

'Should you be doing this, Sally?' I asked.

'I'm fine, Jack . . . Make hay while the sun shines.'

'Well, go carefully,' I said. 'I don't want you overdoing it.'

Sally smiled and patted her tummy. 'I'll be thirty-three weeks pregnant by the end of term and that seems a good time to finish.'

'It won't be the same without you,' I said.

'Miss Flint will be fine,' said Sally with a twinkle in her eye.

'Well, Vera has arranged with Miss Flint for her to come in earlier if needed.'

'How *is* Vera?' asked Sally. 'This new typewriter seems to be getting her down.'

'It is,' I said. 'She really needs something to cheer her up.'

Sally looked over my shoulder towards the school gate. 'I think your prayers might have been answered, Jack.'

Major Rupert Forbes-Kitchener, our sixty-two-year-old school governor and country gent, had emerged from a classic black Bentley and was walking up the cobbled drive. He waved his brass-topped walking cane in greeting and strode confidently towards the entrance door. As always, he looked smart in his country brown sports jacket, lovat-green waistcoat, regimental tie, cavalry-twill trousers with knife-edge creases, and sturdy brown brogues polished to a military shine.

I caught up with him and we walked into school.

'Hello, Jack. Jolly fine day, what?' he said.

'It is, Major,' I said. 'Good to see you.'

'Just checking on the news of school closures, Jack, from those chappies at County Hall,' he said. 'Got to make sure Ragley isn't for the chop.'

'I'm sure Miss Evans will bring you up to date, Major,' I said. 'I'm due back in class now.'

'Understood, old boy,' he said and patted me on the back.

I watched him tap gently on the office door and walk in.

'Good afternoon, Vera,' he said.

'Oh, Rupert!' Vera's cheeks reddened slightly.

'Please excuse the intrusion, Vera,' he said.

'Of course,' said Vera, quickly removing an error-strewn letter from the typewriter. 'Would you like a cup of tea?'

He took a large brass timepiece from his waistcoat pocket. 'I'm afraid duty calls, Vera. I only called in to catch up on the latest school closure news.'

Vera stood up and took a file from her beautifully organized filing cabinet. 'It's all in here, Rupert. Perhaps you can let me have it back next week.'

'Why not call round for tea on Saturday and I can return it then?' said the major.

Vera reddened again. 'Well . . . perhaps, Rupert. I'll let you know.'

The major stroked his neatly trimmed moustache thoughtfully, studied her strained appearance and quickly summed up the situation. 'My word, what's this?' he said.

'It's my new typewriter,' said Vera, 'and I'm afraid it's proving rather difficult to handle.'

'But, Vera, you are a remarkable woman.'

'That's kind of you to say so, Rupert,' she said.

'I am confident you can master this blighter, my dear.'

'Yes, of course, I shall do my best.'

'I know you will,' he said.

'It's just . . . you know . . . different routines and changes.'

He leant forward and held her hand. 'Vera, some things never change.'

She looked into his unwavering steel-blue eyes and felt like a young woman again. 'I know, Rupert.'

He stood up, opened the office door and looked back. 'So, then . . . tea on Saturday, what?'

Vera took a deep breath, gave the typewriter a fixed stare and replied softly, 'That would be lovely.'

The major closed the door and marched away.

Slowly, but with huge determination, Vera showed she would not be beaten and began to make progress. She forced herself to cock her wrists at a different angle and use the pads of her fingers rather than the tips. While her new typewriter was very sensitive and had a mind of its own, occasionally printing out a line of full stops, it also had the benefit of an extra ribbon to correct mistakes. Vera smiled. A world free of Tippex stretched out in front of her. By Friday afternoon, she was entirely competent in using the new typewriter and, apart from casting the odd wistful glance in the direction of her old machine, now consigned to the top shelf of the stationery cupboard, she had moved on in her life.

On my way home that Thursday I stopped on the High Street and called into Piercy's Butcher's Shop. The owner, Old Tommy, was chatting with the customers, and his grandson, Young Tommy, was busy serving them. The Ragley refuse collectors, Big Dave Robinson and his diminutive cousin, Little Malcolm Robinson, known locally as 'the bin men', were being served. Two farmworkers, Shane Ramsbottom and his younger brother Clint, were leaning on the counter, waiting for their weekly joint of beef.

"Ow's t'school, young Mr Sheffield?' said Old Tommy.

'Fine, thank you, Mr Piercy,' I replied.

'We've been 'earing about these killer-metres an' killer-grams y'learning 'em,' said Old Tommy. He pronounced the units as if they were in the same family as killer sharks. 'Ah don't 'old wi' it m'self.'

'I can understand that, Mr Piercy,' I said. 'It's just that the world is changing and children will need to understand metrication as they grow up.'

Old Tommy shook his head. He was a firm believer in the system of avoirdupois weights, traditionally used throughout the English-speaking world and based on sixteen ounces to the pound. 'Well, ah'll tell y'summat,' he said. Everyone in the shop looked with reverence at Old Tommy. 'Twenty-two yards will allus be t'length of a cricket pitch.'

'Y'reight there,' said Little Malcolm.

'Can't be owt else,' said Big Dave.

''Cause of 'istory,' said Clint Ramsbottom.

There was a pause while they all considered this meaningful comment by Clint. It had a certain gravitas they had never associated with a farm labourer who had highlights in his hair.

''E's reight is our Clint,' said Shane, flexing his muscles under his Status Quo T-shirt and cracking his huge knuckles.

Everyone agreed very quickly and I nodded hurriedly. It was important never to hesitate when agreeing with Shane.

'So what's it t'be, Mr Sheffield?' asked Young Tommy.

'Sausages, please, Tommy,' I said. 'Er, a pound's worth, please.'

Young Tommy weighed out the sausages. 'Anything else?' he asked.

'Yes, please. I'd like some lean bacon.'

'An' what weight would that be?' asked Old Tommy with a chuckle.

'About eight ounces, please,' I replied.

Everyone nodded. Old Tommy had made his point.

Saturday morning was a day of calm reflection and soft breezes. In the vicarage garden, bright plump blackberries filled the hedgerows and apples were turning rosy-red.

After the hectic week, Vera was finally back in her kitchen and at peace in her world. She glanced at the grandfather clock in the hallway and wondered what time she should leave to have tea with the major. It would be polite to take a small gift, she thought. Then she had an idea, picked up her Be-Ro recipe book and nodded to herself. She put her weighing scales on the worktop and lined up her brass imperial weights like a family of chesspieces. As Vera weighed out eight ounces of flour, she smiled. In this Eighties world of metrication and electric typewriters some things never changed.

She would make some scones . . . and they would, of course, be perfect.

Chapter Three

A Rose for Ruby

Mrs Smith, school caretaker, completed 10 years' service at Ragley School. We were informed that Richard Gomersall, Senior Primary Adviser, will be visiting school later this term.

Extract from the Ragley School Logbook:
Wednesday, 8 October 1980

'Ah love roses, Mr Sheffield, an' that's a real bobby-dazzler,' said Ruby the caretaker, sniffing the carmine-pink rose appreciatively.

I had put it in a tumbler of water next to the brass paperweight on my desk. It was Wednesday, 8 October, and late-afternoon autumn sunshine filled the school office.

'It's a Zephirine Drouhin from Beth's garden, Ruby – one of the last blooms of the season,' I explained.

Ruby Smith weighed over twenty stones and her extra-large double-X orange overall was straining to bursting point over her plump frame. Her cheeks were flushed bright-red and she pushed a few strands of damp wavy chestnut hair out of her eyes. 'That's a funny name,' said Ruby thoughtfully. 'Ah like a proper English rose m'self.'

She picked up the wickerwork basket from under my desk and emptied the crumpled carbon sheets and torn manila envelopes into her black bag. Then she dragged it towards the office door and paused, absent-mindedly polishing the door handle with a duster. 'Ah once 'ad roses, Mr Sheffield.'

'Did you, Ruby?' I said softly, looking up from my log-book.

She stared out of the office window, reflecting on happy times of long ago. 'On m'wedding day . . . They were yellow . . . an' smelt o' posh perfume an' new babies an' Christmas, all rolled into one. Ah'll never forget them roses.'

I put down my fountain pen and looked at her. On impulse I plucked the rose from the tumbler and held it up. 'Take this one, Ruby.'

'That's kind of you, Mr Sheffield, but ah'd better not if it were a present from Miss 'Enderson.'

I replaced the rose and smiled. 'Perhaps you're right.' Then a thought struck me. 'Maybe Ronnie will surprise you.'

'Huh, some 'opes,' said Ruby in disdain. ''E never 'as an' 'e never will. Y'know what they say, a leopard never changes its stripes.'

She sighed deeply and walked out into the corridor. As a parting riposte, she called over her shoulder: ''E'll allus be t'same, Mr Sheffield. 'E still eats peas off 'is knife.'

*   *   *

Vera came into the office, put the plastic cover over her new typewriter and tidied her desk. Then she picked up her handbag and gave me the familiar look that indicated she wanted a word.

In the entrance hall I could hear the clatter of Ruby's galvanized bucket and the sound of her singing 'Edelweiss' from her favourite musical, *The Sound of Music*.

Vera sat down in the chair opposite my desk, looking thoughtful. 'Mr Sheffield,' she said, 'on Friday it's Ruby's birthday and she's going to The Royal Oak with her family.'

'She'll enjoy that, won't she?'

'She will . . . but there's something else that I came across a while ago. This week Ruby will have completed ten years' service at Ragley.'

'I didn't know that.'

'She started when Mrs Trott retired. Mr Pruett appointed her because everyone in the village knew she was a hard-working cleaner and completely trustworthy.'

'So what are you suggesting, Vera?'

'We should celebrate it in some small way – perhaps tea and cakes after school on Friday.'

'Good idea. I'm sure Ruby would be thrilled.'

Half an hour later, Ruby packed away her dustpan and brushes. The school was quiet again and I turned my thoughts to the tough life of our cheerful caretaker.

Ruby had been blessed with six children. 'The first 'n' last were an accident but ah love 'em all,' she had once said. Her eldest son, twenty-nine-year-old Andy, was in the army and due to be home on leave soon, and her eldest daughter, twenty-seven-year-old Racquel, worked in the Joseph Rowntree chocolate factory. She lived in York with her husband, a factory storeman, and was trying for a baby with little success, much to her distress and Ruby's amazement.

'Ah've been trying t'get pregnant, Mam, but nowt's 'appenin',' she had confided to Ruby while sitting in her mother's kitchen. Ruby was puzzled. With Ronnie it had been as easy as falling off a log – in fact, six logs.

'Never mind, luv. It'll 'appen when t'times reight,' said Ruby with a consoling hug.

Ruby's other four children lived with Ronnie and herself in their council house at number 7, School View. Duggie, a twenty-five-year-old undertaker's assistant with the nickname 'Deadly', said his mother's full English breakfast on a Saturday would win a prize and he was happy sleeping on his little wooden bunk in the attic next to his Hornby Dublo train set and his collection of *Playboy* magazines. Twenty-year-old Sharon was considering getting engaged to the local blond-haired Adonis, Rodney Morgetroyd, the Morton village milkman; eighteen-year-old Natasha was an assistant in Diane's Hair Salon, and the baby of the family, seven-year-old Hazel, was a happy, rosy-cheeked little girl in Jo Hunter's class. Ruby often wondered if there would ever be a day when she didn't have to mop floors in order to feed them.

Back in her house, Ruby looked in the kitchen cupboard. The door had fallen off long ago and was now a shelf in Ronnie's shed, where he kept his racing pigeons. She selected a box of Cadbury's Smash and peered at the writing on the back. It said something about '16 servings of potato substitute' but Ruby knew her family had large appetites, particularly Duggie, so she tipped it all in a bowl and added some boiling water. 'That'll fill 'em up,' she murmured to herself and began to hum 'I am sixteen going on seventeen'.

After a lifetime of hard graft, Ruby had accepted her lot in life. Deep down she knew that the hapless, beer-swilling, unemployed Ronnie would never be like Christopher Plummer in *The Sound of Music*. But, one day . . . perhaps just for one day . . . she wished that she might be like Julie Andrews on an Austrian mountaintop, singing to all her children.

Suddenly the back door opened and in walked Racquel.

Ruby looked at her eldest daughter and shook her head sadly. Racquel was trying to earn some extra money as a representative for a couple of clothing catalogues, Kay's and Freeman's.

'Ah get commission, Mam,' she said with excitement in her eyes: 'a pound f'every ten pound in orders.'

'Give it 'ere,' said Ruby with a sigh and a shake of her head. 'Let's 'ave a look . . . Ah need a new pinny.'

On Thursday morning at nine o'clock, the enthusiastic Simon Nelson was waiting for me by my desk. The previous evening he had asked for homework and he proudly gave me his book for marking. He had completed a piece of writing about his namesake, the English admiral Horatio Nelson.

'Well done, Simon,' I said, putting a tick next to his final sentence, which read, 'He died at the Battle of Trafalgar on 21 October 1805.' 'You got the date right.'

Simon looked up at me and grinned. 'My mam told me, Mr Sheffield. She said it's easy to remember 'cause it's exactly a week after Cliff Richard's birthday.' It occurred to me that I could learn a lot from Mrs Nelson about teaching history.

Vera worked half-days on Tuesdays and Thursdays, so it was lunchtime when she arrived from her weekly Cross-Stitch Club in the village hall. She looked preoccupied and was clutching a copy of a newspaper. Apparently, the ladies had downed needles while attempting to solve the final clue in Vera's weekly labour of love – namely, the *Yorkshire Post* prize crossword. Sadly, they were unsuccessful.

'Just one left, everyone, and it's tricky,' announced Vera.

'What's the clue?' asked Anne.

'Nineteen across, nine letters: confused or perplexed,' recited Vera. She knew it off by heart.

'What letters have you got?' said Sally, taking her notebook and pencil from her shoulder bag.

'It's something-L-something-something-M-something-X-something-D.'

Sally wrote it down and stared intently.

'Sure about the X?' asked Jo, looking over Sally's shoulder.

'Yes, if TAXES is right,' said Vera, staring sadly at her almost completed crossword.

Everyone racked their brains for the solution but, while we had enough degrees, certificates and essay prizes between us to sink a ship, the solution was not forthcoming and Vera folded up the newspaper. 'How frustrating,' she said. 'We just need someone who's brilliant at crosswords. Perhaps I'll ring the major later.'

When the bell rang a slightly deflated group of cross-word-failures wandered back to class.

It was just before afternoon break when Cathy Cathcart looked up from her poster colour painting of York Minster and announced, 'Mr Smith's coming up t'drive, Mr Sheffield.' Ruby had often described Ronnie as 'no more than seven stones dripping wet' and in his crumpled baggy suit and his Leeds United bobble hat he certainly looked it.

When I walked through the school hall, Anne's reception class was deeply involved in a dramatic production of the epic tale 'The Three Billy Goats Gruff'. However, Jemima Poole, delighted to be given the part of the wicked troll, had not entirely grasped its carnivorous nature.

'Would you please stop all that clipetty-clopetty on my bridge . . . 'cause it's hard to concentrate?' said the polite Jemima in a sweet voice.

Meanwhile, in the entrance hall, Ronnie had not got past Checkpoint Vera.

'Mr Smith would like a word with you, Mr Sheffield,' said Vera coldly.

'Ah'm wond'ring abart this *do* after school,' said Ronnie.

'It should be fine, Ronnie. Miss Evans is looking after it.'

Ronnie glanced nervously at Vera. 'Well, do ah need t'do owt?'

'How about a nice surprise for Ruby?' I said.

'Bit awkward, Mr Sheffield. Ah've no money t'spare.'

I racked my brains. 'You could tidy up your front garden, Ronnie. Ruby's always on about that . . . Mind you, she'd probably have a seizure.'

Ronnie was confused. He thought a seizure was a Roman emperor. All the same, 'M'back's been playin' up,' he said quickly.

Vera looked at him with cool appraisal. 'Ronnie, you really *ought* to do that for Ruby.'

'Er . . . yes, ah s'ppose, Miss Evans.' He knew when he was cornered.

When he finally left, Ronnie felt as though he had just gone ten rounds with Henry Cooper.

At the end of school, I was at my desk in the school office and Vera was doing some filing when Anne walked in.

'We're all set for tomorrow,' she said. 'Shirley and Mrs Critchley are in charge of refreshments and Ruby's family have been invited.'

'Thanks, Anne,' I said.

Suddenly, mop in hand, Ruby appeared at the door with her latest announcement. 'Our Duggie's got a new girlfriend, Miss Evans,' she said, with a note of disapproval in her voice. 'Y'know t'type: butter wouldn't melt in 'er mouth.'

'Who is she, Ruby?' asked Vera.

'She's called Julie an' she works in t'X-ray department in t'hospital . . . But ah saw through 'er straight away.'

'I suppose you would if she worked in the X-ray department,' I quipped.

Anne frowned at me and Ruby pressed on, oblivious to the joke.

'An' ah don't know what's got into my Ronnie. 'E's tidying t'garden an' going at it like a fiddler's elbow.'

Vera gave me a knowing look.

'Ah'm absolutely flabbergasted,' said Ruby and she wandered off to mop the entrance hall.

Friday dawned cold but clear. The season was moving on and as I drove to school I could hear in the distance the deep-throated chugging of a tractor. Shane and Clint Ramsbottom were ploughing in Twenty-Acre field. They were supervised from the neighbouring treetops by the dark brooding shapes of rooks, their beady eyes searching for a juicy breakfast among the ruler-straight furrows.

When I walked into the school office, Vera plucked the rose from the tumbler of water on my desk and held it up. 'Mr Sheffield,' she said, 'have you got any roses left in *your* back garden?'

'I think so, yes. There are a few on the Peace floribunda bush next to my garden seat.'

Her eyes crinkled into a smile. 'Then, please meet on the stroke of twelve, Mr Sheffield. We have an errand to run, if that's OK.'

At twelve o'clock I left Anne in charge while Vera and I drove to Kirkby Steepleton. In the garden of Bilbo Cottage we found the last half-dozen of my yellow, beautifully scented roses and Vera wrapped their woody stems in a clump of damp tissues. When we returned to school she hid them in Shirley's kitchen sink and then broke the news to Ruby about the tea and cakes in the school hall at four o'clock.

'That's very kind, Miss Evans,' said Ruby, dabbing away a tear. 'Ah'll put m'posh frock on under me overall when I come back at t'end of school.'

At half past four I was enjoying a slice of Shirley's magnificent treacle tart and a cup of tea. Anne, Sally and Jo were chatting with Ruby's daughters, Ruby was trying to persuade Ronnie to remove his bobble hat and, all the while, Vera was deep in conversation with the major.

The hall was full of light-hearted chatter and it died down when I asked for quiet. I made a short speech about how much we all appreciated Ruby's work and asked Anne to present a 'Thank you' card, signed by all the staff and governors, along with a Co-op token.

Then, at a signal from Vera, Ronnie stood beside Ruby and murmured, 'Ruby, luv, there's summat else.' He pointed towards the hall doors. 'Our 'Azel's got summat f'you.'

Vera was holding Hazel Smith's hand and whispering in her ear. The little girl looked bright as a new pin in a gingham frock, brown leather sandals and short white ankle socks. Her big sister Sharon had braided her long hair and tied it with a bright-pink ribbon. She was also carrying a yellow rose.

'This is for you, Mam,' said Hazel.

Ruby knelt down in front of Hazel, took the rose and gave her a big kiss.

'When ah grow up ah'll 'ave a garden wi' roses, Mam,' she said.

'That's lovely, 'Azel.'

'An' then y'll allus 'ave roses,' said Hazel.

Ruby crouched down and hugged her. Tears began to stream down her face.

'Why are y'crying, Mam?' said Hazel.

'Don't fret, luv,' said Ruby almost to herself. 'It's jus' roses. They do that sometimes.'

Then Racquel, Duggie, Sharon and Natasha each presented Ruby with their rose. Ruby dried her eyes on the hem of her skirt, stood up and held Hazel's hand.

'Do you want to say anything, Ruby?' asked Vera.

'Ah can't, Miss Evans,' said Ruby. 'Ah feel proper flummoxed.'

'Ruby!' exclaimed Vera. 'I'm so glad you do!' She hurried over to the piano, picked up a newspaper from under her handbag and waved it triumphantly in the air. 'Nineteen across, nine letters: confused or perplexed,' announced Vera.

'Ah don't understand, Miss Evans,' said Ruby.

'FLUMMOXED!' exclaimed Vera. 'You've solved our prize crossword!' Then she gave Ruby a big kiss on the cheek and filled in the missing letters.

Suddenly, Anne sat down at the piano and played the opening bars of 'My Favourite Things'.

'C'mon, Mam,' urged Duggie, 'give us a song.'

Racquel took her mother's hand and led her to the piano and Ruby began to sing 'Raindrops on roses', at which

Sharon and Natasha burst into applause. Meanwhile, Vera and the major were whispering conspiratorially in the corner of the hall.

An hour later it was a happy group that arrived back at number 7, School View. Ronnie opened the gate proudly and pointed to the tidy garden. Ruby kissed his bobble hat and enveloped him in a rib-crushing hug.

'Ah'm glad y'pleased, Ruby luv,' gasped Ronnie and hurried into the house.

Ruby kissed each of her five children as they walked past her into the crowded lounge. Then she turned and walked, alone, back down the garden path. The noisy chatter of her family spilled out into the street and Ruby smiled. She was pleased they were all safe and together for a brief time.

Then she looked down at her roses and sniffed them appreciatively. Finally, she touched each one lightly with a dumpy work-red finger and remembered a morning long ago when the young Ruby had stood on this very spot with a bouquet of yellow roses.

Back in school, the hall had been cleared and all was quiet. Only the ticking of the old clock, echoing in the Victorian rafters, disturbed the silence. I jumped when the telephone rang.

'Hello, Jack, how are you?' It was the distinctive voice of the chair of the Education Committee at County Hall.

'Oh, hello, Miss Barrington-Huntley. Good to hear from you,' I said quickly.

'Jack, I'll get to the point. I've asked Richard Gomersall,

Senior Primary Adviser, to call in to see you later this term. He's visiting all the schools in the Easington area to gather information for a follow-up document to "The Rationalization of Small Schools in North Yorkshire".'

'Yes, it obviously caused us some anxiety,' I said, wondering where Vera had filed it.

There was a long pause.

'Jack, we're at the beginning of a long and difficult process,' said Miss Barrington-Huntley, clearly weighing her words. 'All I can say at this stage is: hope for the best but prepare for the worst.'

'I see,' I said cautiously.

'And I note from my diary that I shall be with you on Saturday, the eighth of November for the opening of your new library area.'

'Yes. We're looking forward to your visit.'

'So am I. Thank you, Jack . . . Goodbye.'

I replaced the receiver and to my surprise it rang again almost immediately.

'How did the presentation go?' It was Beth.

'Oh, hello, Beth. Yes, it went well and Ruby loved it.'

'I've got a PTA event on tonight but I could see you later?'

'Well, Ruby asked me to call in at the Oak on my way home.'

'Shall I see you there, say, about nine?'

'Perfect. See you then.'

The Royal Oak was busy when I walked in. Ruby and Ronnie were sitting in the place of honour on the bench seat near the dartboard. Racquel and Sharon were at the same table and Natasha had stayed at home to watch *Charlie's Angels* and look after Hazel. Duggie was mingling with the Ragley Rovers football team.

'What's it t'be, Mr Sheffield?' said Sheila Bradshaw, the landlady.

I glanced at the menu on the chalkboard. 'Just half of Chestnut and minced beef and onions in a giant Yorkshire pudding, please, Sheila.'

'Ah like a man wi' a good appetite.' She was wearing a bright-pink boob tube and a black leather miniskirt. I averted my eyes from her astonishing cleavage and stared at the bottled shandy on the shelf behind her. 'We've been 'earing about this metrication that y'teaching 'em,' said Sheila. 'Our Claire's doing it as well at t'big school.' Sheila's teenage daughter, Claire Bradshaw, had been in my class when I first arrived at Ragley. 'Ah think it's wonderful what y'teach 'em in school these days.' She leant provocatively over the bar and fluttered her enormous false eyelashes. I could almost feel the draught. 'We never 'ad no teachers like you when ah were at school.'

Her husband, Don, ex-wrestler and built like a fork-lift truck, shouted from the other end of the bar, 'Matriculation, did y'say, Mr Sheffield? Is it legal?'

'Shurrup, y'big soft ha'penny,' said Sheila. 'It's all that Frenchified stuff about weights an' measures. One day we might b'serving beer in litres.'

'Lads won't like it, luv,' said Don, nodding towards the inebriated football team. 'They like beer in tankards.'

Team captain Big Dave Robinson leant on the bar. 'Usual, Don,' he said, and Don began to pull thirteen pints of Tetley's bitter for team manager Ronnie, the team, plus the twelfth man, Stevie 'Supersub' Coleclough.

'An' that wants switching off,' said Big Dave to Don, pointing to the television on the high shelf above the bar. 'We don't want no southerners 'ere wi' puffy 'airdos.'

Noel Edmonds was presenting *Top Gear* at the Paris Motor Show. It was clear that the new range of Rolls-Royce cars, the latest Ford Escort and the turbo-charged Renault held little interest for these sons of Yorkshire.

Don switched it off and nodded towards three strange men in sparkly suits. 'Entertainment's jus' arrived f'Ruby's party,' he announced, 'an' they smell o' fish.'

Troy Phoenix, lead singer and local fishmonger, otherwise known as Norman Barraclough, had teamed up with two of his friends who sold fish in Whitby. One had learnt three chords from his *Bert Weedon's Play-in-a-Day Guitar Guide* and the other played the drums, or, to be more precise, a drum.

'We booked a trio,' shouted Shane Ramsbottom in disgust from the far end of the bar, 'an' three of 'em 'ave turned up!'

Stevie 'Supersub' Coleclough, proud of being the only member of the football team with any academic qualifications, spoke up. 'No, Shane, a trio is . . .' and then stopped when he saw Shane frown. Stevie had remembered it was never wise to disagree with a muscular psychopath who had the letters H-A-R-D tattooed on the knuckles of his right hand.

'Who are they?' asked Big Dave.

'Troy Phoenix and the Whalers,' said Don.

'Ah've 'eard 'em,' said Chris 'Kojak' Wojciechowski, the

Bald-Headed Ball Wizard. 'All they do is bloody wail,' and he laughed at his own joke.

Little Malcolm Robinson and 'Deadly' Duggie Smith came to help carry the frothing pint pots to the thirsty footballers.

'Ah've 'eard you've gorra new girlfriend, Duggie,' said Sheila.

'She lives in a posh 'ouse in Easington,' said Duggie proudly. 'She's even gorra gazebo in 'er garden.'

Big Dave and Little Malcolm looked at each other in amazement.

'Bloody 'ell!' exclaimed Big Dave. 'If that David Hattenb'rough knew, e'd be round there in a flash.'

'Y'reight there, Dave,' agreed Little Malcolm.

I found a seat near the bay window and enjoyed my piping-hot food. The troubles of school life waned in the happy atmosphere and I had the prospect of a weekend with Beth ahead of me. When she walked in, heads turned and, as always, she looked a perfect English beauty in her white blouse and a classic pin-striped trouser suit.

She paused at Ruby's table and gave her a kiss on the cheek. 'Happy birthday, Ruby. Sorry I couldn't make your presentation but Jack will tell me all about it.'

'Thank you, Miss 'Enderson,' said Ruby, 'an' please can y'show our Racquel an' Sharon y'engagement ring?'

After a few admiring glances Beth joined me and squeezed my hand, 'Good to see you,' she said. I bought her a gin and tonic and she took a sip, rubbed the ache out of her neck and stretched luxuriously. 'Bliss,' she murmured: 'the weekend at last.'

'Busy day?' I asked.

'Very,' said Beth, taking another sip and pushing a few stray strands of hair behind her ears. 'I even had Miss B-H telling me not to worry but to be prepared for any eventuality.'

'So did I.'

Beth looked round as Troy Phoenix and his aptly named Whalers began to sing 'House of the Rising Sun'. 'Shall we go?' she said with a grin.

'Let's,' I said and we finished our drinks.

We waved goodbye to Ruby, who pointed to her roses and gave me a big smile. It looked like her day was complete. But when Beth and I walked out into the cold night air I realized it wasn't.

On the far side of the village green, a classic black Bentley had just pulled up and Major Rupert Forbes-Kitchener was standing next to it. From the rear of the car emerged an army sergeant, who jumped to attention and saluted. The major returned the salute, climbed back in and drove away. Andy Smith looked smart in his uniform. Taller than his father, he had the same wiry build but when he smiled there was no mistaking he was Ruby's son.

Beth and I followed him in to see Ruby's reaction.

Ruby stopped singing along and stared, barely able to believe her eyes.

'Andy . . . my son, my son!' And with that she burst into tears and hugged her eldest child as if she never wanted to let him go.

It was a scene I'll never forget but what made it special was that Andy had a gift for his mother.

In his hand he held a flower . . . It was the sixth yellow rose.

So it was that later that evening, in the crowded front room of 7, School View, Ruby was granted her wish and she sang to her children . . . all six of them.

Chapter Four

Jane Austen's Footsteps

School closed today for the one-week half-term holiday with
86 children on roll.

Extract from the Ragley School Logbook:
Friday, 24 October 1980

The purple-grey sky began to darken and I could smell rain on the autumn wind. It had been a long drive to Hampshire.

Dusk was drawing in and Beth and I were keen to arrive at her parents' home before nightfall. We slowed as an old wooden signpost came into view. It read LITTLE CHAWTON 2.

'We're nearly there, Jack,' said Beth and she leant over and squeezed my hand. Her excitement was obvious, whereas I felt a knot of apprehension in my stomach as our meet-the-family weekend drew near.

It was Saturday, 25 October. We had left North Yorkshire after breakfast and gradually the miles sped by. A coffee break in South Yorkshire was followed by a relaxing lunch in a friendly roadside pub in the Midlands and afternoon tea near Oxford. Finally, as darkness began to fall, we meandered through a cluster of classic English villages bordered by water meadows and breathtaking forests. Hampshire was truly a beautiful county. However, my mud-splattered Morris Minor Traveller was beginning to groan in protest as we descended a hill beneath an avenue of giant trees. Above our heads their branches arched like a bridge of fingers across the narrow road and formed a dark tunnel that shut out the sky. I gripped the steering wheel a little tighter.

Soon we were following an ancient tractor down the main street of Little Chawton. The bright amber lights of the Cricketer public house pierced the gloom and I pulled up alongside an old cast-iron hand pump at the edge of the village green. Ahead was a church with a square Norman tower and a row of neat thatched cottages fronted with red brick and Hampshire flint.

Beth pointed ahead. 'Turn left at the church, Jack, and drive to the top of the rise.'

A few spots of rain had begun to fall as we parked outside the last cottage. It was a mellow brick-and-beam building, expertly thatched, with sloping window frames and not a right angle in sight. I breathed a sigh of relief that we had arrived safely.

'This is it, Jack: Austen Cottage,' said Beth excitedly. 'Drive down to the far end of the driveway next to Dad's shed.'

Lights appeared at the front door and a tall, athletic man with steel-grey hair and a relaxed smile strode out to meet us. It was John Henderson, Beth's father, dressed in a country-checked shirt, warm woollen waistcoat and thick cord trousers. He was fifty-seven years old but looked much younger.

Beth opened the passenger door, jumped out and gave her father a big hug. 'Good to be home, Dad,' she said.

'Thank God you're here, Beth,' he said with a grin. 'Your mother's been stirring her precious watercress soup for the past hour.'

Beth gave him a kiss on the cheek. 'She doesn't change, then!'

He grabbed Beth's overnight bag and stretched out his hand to me in greeting. 'Good journey, Jack?'

'Fine, thank you . . . Mr Henderson,' I replied hesitantly.

He grinned. 'Call me John. No formalities here, Jack . . . particularly for my future son-in-law.' His handshake was firm. At six feet tall his eyes were on a level with mine and he gave me a warm smile.

In the warmth of a huge terracotta-tiled kitchen, Diane Henderson looked less relaxed. She glanced up from stirring a large pan of soup and, in a blue-striped apron that emphasized her slim figure, she pushed a strand of soft blonde hair behind her ear. Her high cheekbones, clear skin and green eyes reminded me of Beth . . . *and Laura*.

Next to me, on an old Welsh dresser, was a small television set. Alan Titchmarsh was happily presenting his gardening guide and, on the shelf above, alongside a collection of the novels of Jane Austen, were many framed photographs. One was dated 1958 when the twelve-year-old Beth and ten-year-old Laura had waited excitedly outside the Salisbury Gaumont to see Buddy Holly and the Crickets. Others showed the two sisters riding ponies, dressed as girl guides, playing college hockey and enjoying skiing holidays.

Beth saw me looking at the photographs. 'Oh, Mother!' she exclaimed. 'These are *so* embarrassing.'

Diane took the soup off the hob, walked over to Beth and gave her a hug, and I thought that, side by side, they looked more like sisters.

'Welcome home, Beth,' she said, holding her elder daughter's hands and then taking a step back to appraise her. 'Come and sit down, you must be tired.'

Then she turned down the sound on the television set and looked up at me with a small smile. Her steady gaze appeared cautious. She smoothed her hands down the sides of her apron, stretched up and gave me a peck on the cheek.

'Hello, Jack . . . I hope you're hungry,' she said. 'I've made enough soup for an army.'

'Yes, please, Mrs Henderson. It certainly smells appetizing,' I said.

'Jack . . . *do* call me Diane.' She surveyed me with a calm gaze again and I wondered what thoughts were passing through her mind.

On the table was a veritable feast: a cured ham, boiled potatoes, large red tomatoes, fresh beetroot, a towering sponge cake and a bottle of home-made cowslip wine. Diane began serving her watercress soup, a local Hampshire speciality, with crusty fresh-baked bread rolls, and we all tucked in.

'When's Laura coming?' asked Beth.

John put down his spoon and wiped his mouth with a snowy-white napkin. 'She rang this afternoon . . . said she'll be here for Sunday lunch and staying for the afternoon before going back to London.'

'Is she bringing Desmond?' asked Beth.

'Yes,' said Diane simply.

I looked up and she was staring at me.

'Sounds like she's pretty keen on him,' said Beth.

'Well, you know Laura,' said John: 'no half-measures.'

I felt the knot in my stomach tighten.

Beth smiled and returned to her meal, while her mother glanced at me again before offering second helpings of the delicious watercress soup.

Gradually we all relaxed with the good food and potent home-made wine. There was lively banter between Beth and her father while Diane Henderson cleared the dishes. I offered to help but she was insistent I remain at the table. My thoughts drifted to Beth's younger sister. The dynamic, vivacious and attractive Laura always lived life to the full. During her time as manager of the fashion department of Liberty's in York we had spent a lot of time together. To me she was an exciting friend but Laura had seen our relationship in a different way. Eight months ago, on Leap Year Day, she had joked about it being the day when women could propose to men. My cool response to the idea ended a blossoming relationship and Laura had returned to London and resumed her old job at Liberty's in Regent Street. We hadn't spoken since.

Later that evening, we sat in the low-beamed lounge by a crackling log fire and Beth and I related stories of our lives as village school headteachers. Finally, over a second bottle of home-made wine, we shared an old album of photographs taken on John's ancient Kodak No. 2 automatic Brownie camera. Their Isle of Wight holiday in 1949 brought back many happy memories for them.

Only charred embers remained in the fire grate when the album was closed. John set off to lock up the house and Diane returned to the kitchen to make some hot milky bedtime drinks.

Beth closed the lounge door and whispered, 'I'm in my old room, Jack, and you're in the spare room.'

'Of course,' I said with a smile.

We walked through to the kitchen, collected our drinks, and I browsed through the copies of *Pride and Prejudice*, *Mansfield Park* and *Emma*.

'We named the cottage after Jane Austen,' said Diane, 'but this is my favourite.' She picked up a well-thumbed copy of *Sense and Sensibility*, opened it to the first page and scanned the familiar introduction to the Dashwood family. 'It's really two love stories . . . of two sisters.' She looked up and I wondered if there was a hint of hidden significance. 'Have you read it, Jack?'

'A long time ago,' I said, 'for A Level English.'

'Bedtime reading,' she said and passed it to me.

'Thanks, Diane.'

She opened the door, paused in the doorway and looked back as if there was something on her mind. Whatever it was she decided not to share it. Then she looked me up and down. 'Goodnight, Jack . . . Sleep well,' she said, and walked out into the hallway, leaving the door open for me to follow.

*   *   *

The small single bedroom was quiet and cosy. I sat up in bed and looked around at the rough-plastered, white-washed walls, the ancient beams above my head and the framed pictures of steam engines and pretty watercolour views of Hampshire villages.

I was soon engrossed in *Sense and Sensibility* and full of admiration for Jane Austen's acute perceptions of human nature and her wicked sense of humour. Finally, to the sound of the whispering of the thatched roof in the evening breeze, I fell into a deep sleep.

It was a chill dawn and even the cock crowing in the far distance sounded mournful. I looked out of the window upon my strange new world. On the south wall of Austen Cottage, an espalier pear had been trained to perfection and, in the hedgerow, blackberry briars trailed in among the berries of hips and haws. Beneath me, chrysanthemums were like burnished gold in the slanting October sunshine and Virginia creeper spread its leaves of autumn fire across the flint-studded walls.

I dressed quickly, made my way down the creaking stairs in stockinged feet and sat in the stone-flagged entrance porch to put on my shoes. The kitchen door was unlocked and I walked outside into the yard and made my way up the well-worn pathway to a sturdy wooden fence.

John was walking towards me with an old enamel bucket and gave me a cheery wave. 'Lovely morning, Jack,' he shouted. He opened the five-barred gate and set down the bucket. I peered inside. Nestling on a handful of straw were six large brown eggs. He followed my gaze. 'Breakfast,' he said. 'You can't beat fresh eggs.'

We both leant on the fence and stared into the distance. A traditional patchwork of the fields of rural England stretched out before us in the morning mist. In a fertile valley of shimmering watercress beds, a classic English village appeared frozen in time. Next to the ancient church, a pond fed by local streams was a home for mallards and moorhens and, in among the tall trees, an old schoolhouse, faced with undressed flint, had a bell tower just like Ragley School. I smiled at the memory.

'You have a lovely home, John,' I said, 'and Hampshire looks a fine place, gentler than North Yorkshire.'

'Yes, we like it here,' mused John. 'It's a simple life. Since I retired from the RAF, I potter along. We sell milk and eggs, raise a few pigs, and I help out on the Watercress Line.'

'Watercress Line?'

'Steam engines, Jack. Every man has his passion.'

I glanced at his weather-beaten face and we stared out upon this perfect autumn morning.

'I'm a lucky man, John,' I said, breaking the silence. 'I never thought Beth would say yes.'

He nodded thoughtfully.

'You have two wonderful daughters . . . both beautiful and talented.'

'And both very different,' he added. Then he gazed into the distance. 'Laura . . . ah, Laura,' he mused. 'She was always the light and shade of my life – sometimes happy, then sad, often in the same moment.'

'Laura is always great fun, John,' I said, 'and she's clearly going places in the fashion world, by all accounts.'

'I just hope it lasts,' he said. 'A lot of her projects have often come crashing down round her ears.' His expression gave no hint of hidden meaning. 'She was very fond of you, Jack . . . but you must know that by now.'

I turned to face him. 'It's always been Beth for me, John. There was never any other. I'm sorry if I made Laura think otherwise.'

He put his hand on my shoulder in a fatherly way. 'Well, I wish you luck. If you have half the happiness I've had, then you'll be truly blessed. But remember: Beth is like her mother – a very independent woman. She's used to organizing life *her* way. There'll have to be some give-and-take.'

'I understand, John.'

After breakfast, Beth was keen to show me the local market town of Alton.

'You two go, Beth,' said Diane. 'Your father and I have a few jobs to do.'

'I'll take you in, if you like,' said John.

'No, you won't,' said Diane firmly. 'You can stay and help me.'

John grinned. 'This is what you've got to get used to, Jack.' He rummaged in his pocket and gave Beth a set of keys. 'Take the Land-Rover, if you like.'

'Thanks, Dad. We'll only be an hour.'

We clambered into the Land-Rover and Beth took the wheel. On the way we slowed up outside the house where Jane Austen spent the final eight years of her life with her mother and her sister Cassandra.

'This is where she came to live in 1809,' said Beth, 'and where she wrote *Pride and Prejudice, Sense and Sensibility, Mansfield Park, Emma* and *Persuasion*.'

When we reached the outskirts of Alton, Beth suddenly pulled up alongside a huge triangular grassy area flanked by an avenue of horse-chestnut trees known as the Butts. She jumped out, set off quickly to the centre of the green and looked back at me. Then she raised her voice in the crisp morning air.

'Jack, you're walking in Jane Austen's footsteps,' said Beth. 'That's what my mother used to say to me when I came here as a child.'

The branches above me sighed with the weight of memories and I tried to imagine the young Jane Austen, unaware she was destined for greatness. She would walk from her home, perhaps to this very spot, and reflect on early-nineteenth-century life and the comedy of manners being acted out around her.

Then Beth took my hand and, as leaves of russet and gold twirled round our heads, we walked into Alton's High Street. In the pretty market square Beth pointed to a line of black cut-out witches on their broomsticks hanging from the striped canopy above a greengrocer's. The shop was doing a roaring trade selling jars of local quince jam and bright-orange hollowed-out pumpkins with leering, toothy grins in preparation for Hallowe'en.

Next door was a tiny coffee shop. Beth tugged at my sleeve. 'Let's go in. There's something I want to talk to you about.'

We ordered two milky coffees and sat down.

'I've been thinking, Jack,' said Beth, stirring her coffee.

'About what?'

Beth looked thoughtful, weighing her words. 'Our future – or, to be more precise, your future.'

'Aren't they the same thing?' I asked.

She looked up at me and then resumed stirring her coffee.

'What's on your mind?' I asked.

She put down the spoon, picked up the mug of coffee, blew on the surface and took a sip. 'Jack, you must realize that the future of Ragley School is uncertain.'

'Surely the same could be said of Hartingdale?' I countered.

She shook her head as if disappointed by my response. 'No, don't you see? It's different because of its location. I'm the only school in my area that caters for the children of three small villages plus Hartingdale itself. You're close to the large primary school in Easington, so Ragley children could easily be transported there.'

'So are you saying there's a good chance Ragley may close?'

'No, Jack, I'm just saying that . . . you're vulnerable.'

'So what are you suggesting?'

'Jack . . .' Beth gave me a level stare, 'I think you should look for another headship.'

We drank our coffee in silence.

Back at Austen Cottage, a bright-red 1977 Triumph Spitfire 1500 pulled into the gateway ahead of us and John and

Diane came out of the house on to the gravelled driveway.

Desmond Dix, manager of Liberty's in London, climbed out in a haze of cigarette smoke. He was a short, stocky man in his early forties with thinning black hair and a designer suit that would have cost more than I made in a month. The top three buttons of his white silk shirt were not fastened, revealing his hairy chest and a thin silver chain with the letters *DD* interlinked. He stubbed out his cigarette with the heel of his expensive ankle-high leather boots and walked confidently over to John and Diane.

'Hi there,' he said.

John's face was impassive as he shook hands.

Laura stepped out of the car like a film star. She was wearing skin-tight stone-washed jeans and a black leather jacket that accentuated her catwalk-model figure. Her pink lipstick exactly matched her polo-necked sweater. She looked sensational.

Diane gave her a hug, then stood back and critically surveyed her younger daughter. 'You're skin and bone, Laura. I hope you're eating properly.'

'Stop worrying, Mother,' said Laura and turned to her sister. 'Hi, Beth. Let's see the ring.' She nodded in exaggerated approval. 'Good choice,' and gave her sister an air-kiss. She walked over to me. 'And how's the village teacher?'

'I'm fine, Laura,' I said simply.

She tugged the sleeve of my old herringbone-pattern sports jacket. 'Dear me, Jack, I remember this old thing.' She reached up and straightened my crumpled lapels.

'You need to take him in hand, Beth – or hasn't Eighties fashion arrived yet in the frozen north?'

'How are you, Laura?' I asked.

Laura looked at me curiously. 'Fine,' she said. 'This is Desmond, by the way.' I shook his hand; it was soft and fleshy. 'And this is Jack . . . Beth's fiancé.' She seemed to emphasize the word *fiancé*.

'Hi,' he said briefly. 'What age do you teach?' he asked curtly.

'Primary-school children . . . up to elevens.'

He looked surprised. 'Oh, so when will you be qualified to teach at secondary school?'

'It doesn't work like that,' I said.

'Come on, Desmond,' said Laura, grabbing his hand. 'Take no notice of him, Jack, he's only teasing.'

John had booked a table for lunch in the Cricketer and we all squeezed into the Land-Rover. When we walked in, I was reminded of The Royal Oak in Ragley. At the corner table, a group of farmers was arguing loudly about food production.

'Thart young man be roight,' said a ruddy-faced old-timer, pointing to an article in the *Maltings Echo*. Apparently, Peter Walker, Minister of Agriculture, Fisheries and Food, had predicted big changes in the way food would be produced and that so-called 'convenience foods' were just around the corner. Incredibly, four out of ten homes now had a freezer, but, on a teacher's salary, I doubted I would ever own one.

After a drink in the lounge bar, when I experienced a strange local beer that looked like flat cider, we all settled down to enjoy a good Sunday lunch. I was surprised to see squirrel soup on the menu and I wondered what the children back in Ragley School would have made of it, particularly those in the Tufty Club. Apparently, according to John, local delicacies such as squirrel and bacon casserole and even squirrel pasties had been very popular during the Second World War. However, when I saw a main course option of rook pie, I decided that maybe the soup was not so bad after all.

To my relief, roast beef and Yorkshire pudding was also on the menu and, although the Yorkshire puddings were strange, tiny creations, the local beef was excellent. The sweet course of white chocolate with mint and watercress mousse suggested that watercress was a staple part of the Hampshire diet.

After the meal, Desmond took out a pack of Peter Stuyvesant luxury-length filter cigarettes. They were longer than King Size and I looked at them with curiosity. He selected one and lit it. On the side of the pack was a warning: THINK FIRST – MOST DOCTORS DON'T SMOKE. Desmond saw me reading it. 'Good job I don't want to be a doctor,' he said, expertly blowing a smoke ring in the air.

When we finally returned to Austen Cottage the light was fading and soon it would be dusk. Diane and Beth walked inside, absorbed in animated conversation about wedding dresses, while Desmond lifted the bonnet of his sports car so John could try to solve the mystery of a strange knocking noise. Grateful for the peace and quiet, I walked to the fence that surrounded the large paddock.

A few minutes later Laura, with light quick steps like a fawn in the forest, suddenly appeared.

'Oh, hello, Laura,' I said. 'Is it fixed?'

'It was boring so I left them to it,' she said dismissively. She looked me up and down. 'You don't change, do you?'

'Pardon?'

'Still wearing these old spectacles?' She reached up and took them off. Her touch was gossamer soft and I reacted to her cool fingertips. 'There . . . that's better,' she said, smiling.

'Laura . . . earlier this year . . . I'm sorry if I upset you.'

In an absent-minded way, she began picking at the loose threads on the frayed edges of the leather patches on the elbows of my sports jacket.

'Pity you didn't let me smarten you up . . . new Eighties spectacles, new suit.'

'I never was a knight in armour, Laura . . . just a village teacher.'

The soft breeze lifted a few strands of her long brown hair and she flicked them behind her ears in the same way as Beth. 'I thought you said you weren't the marrying kind.'

There was a slam of a car bonnet in the distance. 'You've got Desmond now, Laura.'

'I know,' she said softly.

'He'll give you whatever you want.'

'Will he?' There was a hint of sadness in her green eyes.

'I don't understand.'

She smiled and replaced my spectacles. 'You never did, Jack . . . That's part of your charm.'

Her high-heeled boots crunched on the gravel as she walked quickly back to the house. I leant back on the fence and glanced up at the house. A still figure was looking down at me from Beth's bedroom window. It was Diane.

When Desmond and Laura roared off back to London, she gave a fleeting wave but didn't look back. That evening Diane and Beth laid out a cold supper buffet of fresh-baked bread, ham, pickles, beetroot, carrots, a potato salad and a magnificent Victoria sponge with butter icing. The conversation inevitably returned to possible school closures and wedding plans.

'I think you're wise to wait,' said Diane; 'so much is uncertain at present.'

That night, when I finally turned out the light and lay back on my pillow, I wondered if Diane Henderson had ever compared Beth and Laura to Austen's contrasting sisters in *Sense and Sensibility* – the cool, sensible Elinor and the passionate, idealistic Marianne. It wasn't difficult to work out which was which.

On Monday morning, we said our goodbyes and it was time to head home. The miles rolled by and, finally, in the far distance, the bulk of the North Yorkshire moors lay heavy on the horizon. The purple swathes of heather had long gone now, replaced by a golden haze as the bracken turned. The season had changed and I was back in God's Own Country. It was good to be home.

That night, after saying goodnight to Beth outside her cottage in Morton, I sat by a log fire in Bilbo Cottage and reflected on the weekend and the fate of two sisters.

While I had played a part in their destiny, deep down I knew our journey had just begun.

We had walked in Jane Austen's footsteps . . . but the final chapter was still a long way off.

Chapter Five

The Ashes of Archibald Pike

Miss Barrington-Huntley, chair of the Education Committee, will be our official guest for the opening of the school extension on Saturday, 8 November. Miss Evans has offered to prepare a time capsule to be inserted in the new wall. The school choir will be singing at the Remembrance Day service at St Mary's Church on Sunday, 9 November.

Extract from the Ragley School Logbook:
Thursday, 6 November 1980

'Let's have a time capsule!' exclaimed Anne.

It was four o'clock on Thursday, 6 November, and we were enjoying a welcome cup of tea in the staff-room prior to our impromptu staff meeting to discuss the official opening of the school extension.

Jo looked up from the article 'Domestic science for infants' in her *Child Education* magazine. 'Did you say *time capsule?*'

'Yes,' said Anne. 'The builder said it's all the rage and he's left a space in the cavity wall behind where the official plaque is to be mounted.'

Vera sipped her tea thoughtfully. 'What a good idea,' she said. 'It could be a record of the life of Ragley School.'

'That's right, Vera,' agreed Sally. 'We could get the children involved.'

'With writing and drawings,' added Jo, warming to the idea.

'And a school photograph,' said Vera.

'Then let Miss You-Know-Who put it in the cavity space at the opening ceremony,' said Anne, 'and my John can screw the plaque on the wall.'

Everyone seemed to be talking at once. 'Hang on a minute,' I asked, 'where are we going to get a time capsule?'

There was silence.

Suddenly Vera jumped up. 'I know just the person,' she said, and hurried out to the telephone in the office.

Three miles away in the Easington Progressive Working Men's Club, Big Dave Robinson and his cousin Little Malcolm each put a fifty-pence piece into the red plastic bucket on the trestle table in the seedy, smoke-filled entrance hall. The label on the side of the bucket read IN MEMORY OF ARCHIBALD PIKE.

The club was a ramshackle building that had once been a bottling factory on the outskirts of Easington, and Big Dave and Little Malcolm went there once a fortnight to drink John Smith's bitter instead of their usual Tetley's.

However, the main attraction for Big Dave was that it was a 'men only' club so Little Malcolm's girlfriend, Dorothy Humpleby, couldn't come with them. The only women allowed in were the ones who worked there.

Behind the table sat the chain-smoking man-and-wife team who comprised the club's entire social committee; namely, Caesar and Lilly Trickey. They were both in their sixties and had been members for as long as they could remember.

'Thanks, lads,' said Lilly. ''E were salt o' the earth were Archie. Been a T'anic member for nigh on forty years.' The club had been opened on the day the *Titanic* sank on 15 April 1912 and, in consequence, had been nicknamed the T'anic ever since.

'So tell us, Lilly, what 'appened to old Archie?' asked Big Dave. It was pointless asking Caesar a question because Lilly always answered for him.

'Well, ah'll tell y'summat f'nowt,' said Lilly: ''e 'ad a wonderful death.'

''Ow come?' asked Big Dave.

''E came in last Friday . . . an' 'Arry, with 'is tin leg, were taking t'money on t'raffle.'

'Then what?' asked Big Dave.

''E sat down with 'is pint o' John Smith's an' 'is ticket an' 'ad a funny turn.'

'A funny turn?' echoed Caesar.

'Shurrup!' said Lilly. 'Ah'm telling t'tale.'

'Sorry, luv,' mumbled Caesar apologetically.

'Yes,' said Lilly. ''Arry came over, with 'is tin leg, an' said that Archie 'ad been tekken badly,' she took a puff on her cigarette, '. . . in fact, very badly.'

'Oh 'eck,' said Little Malcolm.

'An' when ah went t'look ah saw 'e 'ad a pint in one 'and an' a winning ticket in t'other.'

'A winning raffle ticket!' exclaimed Big Dave.

'Yes . . . an' 'e were dead as a doornail,' said Lilly.

'That's terrible,' said Big Dave.

'Y'reight there, Dave,' agreed Little Malcolm.

'It were a shock, ah can tell you,' said Lilly.

'Fancy that . . . a dead body . . . So what did y'do?' asked Big Dave.

'All we *could* do, Dave.' Lilly took a last puff of her cigarette and lit another from its glowing tip. 'We drew t'raffle again an' Betty behind t'bar were thrilled. She won six free snooker lessons.'

Vera parked her spotless Austin A40 in Easington, outside a distinctive Victorian red-brick house. The elegant hand-painted sign over the porch read 'S. B. Flagstaff, Funeral Director'. The door sported a new coat of jet-black gloss and the brass door knocker, handle and letterbox gleamed after its weekly polish.

Vera rang the bell and walked in. A faint smell of Brasso, wood glue and linseed oil hung in the still air of a reception area that resembled a Dickensian drawing room. Appropriately, looking like a character from *Nicholas Nickleby*, a plump, grey-haired man in his sixties wearing a black three-piece suit walked into the room. Septimus Bernard Flagstaff, known as Bernie to his friends, was president of the Ragley and Morton Stag Beetle Society and famous for his collection of pressed flowers.

He took his large brass timepiece from the pocket of his

waistcoat and nodded in satisfaction. 'You're a punctual lady, Miss Evans. Ah've always said punctuality comes afore godliness.' He raised his voice. 'Isn't that right, Douglas?'

Our caretaker's son, Duggie Smith, appeared from the back room in a haze of cigar smoke. He looked flustered as he secreted a half-smoked Castella behind his left ear. Fortunately his Boomtown Rats hairstyle hid the evidence.

'Y'reight there, Mr Flagstaff,' agreed Duggie: 'punctuality comes afore, er . . . what y'said.'

Septimus nodded in satisfaction. 'Can you get one of t'spare urns, please, Douglas?' He turned to Vera. 'This time-capsule idea you mentioned on t'telephone sounds very interesting, Miss Evans. Ah presume it's one o' your charitable notions, no doubt.' It appeared Septimus was a secret admirer. 'You're a very fine lady, Miss Evans, if ah may be so bold.'

'She certainly is, Mr Flagstaff,' said Duggie from the back room. He selected one of the urns from the dark oak cupboard and placed the large screw-top metal cylindrical canister on the counter. It looked like an outsize vacuum flask.

'Here y'are, then, Miss Evans,' said Septimus.

'Thank you very much indeed, Septimus,' said Vera. 'This will be perfect.'

'We are 'ere t'serve, Miss Evans,' he said with a bow as he opened the door for Vera.

On Friday morning when I drove into the school car park, a familiar Austin A40 pulled up next to me. Vera climbed out of the passenger seat and a very tense-looking Joseph drove off quickly.

'Hello, Vera,' I said. 'Joseph is in a hurry.'

'He's got Archibald's funeral this morning and it's been a bit hectic for him. The poor man had no family, you see . . . No wonder he's stressed.'

'Archibald?'

'Archibald Pike, Mr Sheffield,' said Vera, 'the church bellringer.'

We walked into school and, in the staff-room, Anne was waiting for us. 'Hello, Vera. What's happening about the time capsule?'

'It's at the vicarage, Anne,' said Vera, taking four cardboard tubes from her bag, 'and these fit in nicely. I made them last night. There's one for each class to fill. Give them back to me later today and I'll pack up the capsule neatly this evening and bring it in tomorrow.' Vera had clearly worked it all out. We all took our tubes as if we were at the start of a relay race.

'Well done, Vera,' I said, relieved it was one job less for me to do.

'You're an angel,' said Anne.

'Impressive,' said Sally.

'Thanks, Vera,' said Jo, peering through hers as if it were a telescope.

By lunchtime we handed our cardboard tubes to Vera. All were filled with photographs, writing and drawings. However, a few of the sentences written by Anne's children about friends and family had to be rejected for more appropriate ones, including:

My mummy is a lollipop lady. She makes traffic jams.
My mummy is lovely and wears black underwear.
My mummy has a tall voice. My daddy is the second boss
of our house.

Meanwhile, Vera had other things on her mind. She held up the front page of her *Daily Telegraph*. 'He's very handsome, don't you think?' said Vera. 'I'm sure Margaret will like him.'

Under the headline 'Landslide win for Reagan' was a photograph of the ex-movie star Ronald Reagan, who had become President of the USA and was heading for the White House. The Republicans had swept cowboy Ronnie and his running mate, George Bush, into power and control of the Senate.

Sally looked up from her magazine. 'Do you realize,' she said, 'that a man who boasts never to have read a book in his life is now the most powerful man on earth?'

'I heard he'd read the Bible,' said Jo, putting down her *Rules of Netball* on the coffee-table.

'Oh well, that's all right, then,' said Vera.

I peered over Vera's shoulder. 'It says here that his mind is clear of intellectual clutter and at sixty-nine he's the oldest man ever to be inaugurated as US President,' I added.

'Hmmm . . . I still think Margaret will like his rugged good looks,' said Vera.

Sally couldn't think of a polite answer and returned to her November 1980 issue of *Cosmopolitan* to consider the merits of two of her favourite men. Did she prefer Richard Gere, the 'classically sexy man', or Sting, 'the cool hero in today's laid-back liberated times'? It was a tough choice and one thing was for sure: cowboy Ronnie didn't get a look-in.

During afternoon school, I called into Jo's classroom to borrow her copy of *Stig of the Dump* to read to my class. Large grey waterproof plastic cloths covered each table top, and children, wearing outsize back-to-front shirts to protect their clothes, were painting with poster colours and large brushes on A3 paper.

'Looks interesting,' I said. Unlike Sally and Anne, teaching art was not one of Jo's strong subjects.

'We're doing Picasso,' whispered Jo, 'so if the children's paintings don't turn out right, nobody will know!'

However, this indisputable logic was quickly forgotten when a heated argument broke out on a nearby table. 'Give us a paintbrush, Vicky,' shouted Terry Earnshaw to Victoria Alice Dudley-Palmer, Class 2's paintbrush monitor.

Victoria Alice looked in dismay at her ungrammatical friend. 'No, Terry, *please* give *me* a paintbrush,' she said with great emphasis.

Terry looked puzzled. 'But you've already got one.'

I hurried to my classroom secretly relieved I had the ten- and eleven-year-olds to teach.

When the bell rang for the end of school, all was ready for the big day. The small extension to the school entrance hall had been completed and a large audience of parents, children and villagers was expected on Saturday afternoon at the grand opening. Miss Barrington-Huntley had confirmed she would be our official guest, and Sue Phillips, our PTA chairman, had rushed into Coney Street in York before her late shift at York Hospital to buy a new dress from Leak & Thorpe. Vera had telephoned the local reporter at the *Easington Herald & Pioneer* to confirm the event would be photographed and recorded for posterity.

Joseph looked harassed when he came to collect Vera, so she sat him down in the staff-room and gave him a cup of her herbal tea.

'How did the funeral go, Joseph?' I asked when I walked in.

'I've arranged for his ashes to be scattered at the foot of the bell tower on Sunday after the Remembrance Day service. Sadly, because he had no family, it will be just his fellow bellringers.'

'So who was Archibald Pike?' I asked.

Vera gave me that look I knew so well and I settled down in a chair to hear about the bellringer of Ragley and Morton.

Archibald and his fellow campanologists had taken their job very seriously. Every Wednesday was practice night and for two hours Archibald had put them through their paces. St Mary's Church had what bellringers would call a 'ring' of six bells, with a tenor in E that weighed the best part of a ton. Cast long ago by Taylor's of Loughborough and hung above the west end of the church, they had marked many great occasions including the end of the World Wars in 1918 and 1945. Also, it was a tradition in the village that the sonorous tenor bell would toll alone to mark the passing of a villager, with one toll for every year of the deceased's life. In Archibald's case there were eighty-eight.

Once each month, Archibald would climb the seventy-six stone steps to the ringing chamber in the tower, where the air was dusty and a colony of pipistrelle bats had made their home. He would clamber up through the trapdoor and lean against the bells, splashed white with owl droppings. Then he would look down at the villages of Ragley and Morton, laid out below him in perfect miniature, and, in his private space, he would watch the world go by.

Archibald's routine was always the same. The bell ropes, each one with a fluffy end tricked out in red, white and blue stripes, were tied off neatly with a half-hitch. He would start with the treble bell until it rolled over, past the vertical, and swung round. Then the next five ropes would snake down and fly up to the ceiling through the pulley holes. He would yell 'One, two, three, four, five, six,' keeping the rhythm even. Only once, in 1963, when his braces snapped and his trousers fell round his ankles, was Archibald's perfectly synchronized sequence ever disturbed.

When Joseph and Vera finally drove off, I sat down at my desk in the office and reflected on the interesting life of a man I had never known.

An hour later I needed a hot drink and a change of scenery so I drove out of school and pulled up outside Nora's Coffee Shop in the High Street. When I walked in, Kate Bush was singing 'Babooshka' on the old red and chrome juke-box. Dorothy Humpleby, the twenty-four-year-old, peroxide blonde, five-foot-eleven-inch coffee-shop assistant and would-be model, was leaning on the counter and filing her nails. She was dressed in a skin-tight white polo-neck sweater, plush velvet hotpants, a wide white belt and her favourite bright-red, high-heeled, Wonder Woman boots, complete with white vertical stripes made from insulation tape.

'Ah love Kate Bush,' said Dorothy, swaying to the music, 'an' she wears this black bodysuit when she's singing it,' she added, a dreamy look in her eyes. 'It's reight good.'

On the other side of the counter, her boyfriend, the five-foot-four-inch bin man Little Malcolm Robinson, looked up at Dorothy like a lovesick puppy. As he stared over the plate of slightly stale, and aptly named, rock buns, he wondered why he had an ache in his stomach. It was obviously indigestion but he had read in the *Reveille* that he might be in love.

'What's it t'be, Malcolm?' said Dorothy.

'Two mugs o' tea, please, Dorothy,' said Little Malcolm, 'an' ah've got summat f'you,' he added in a whisper. He passed a small box over the counter.

'Come on, laughing boy, 'urry up wi' them teas,' shouted Big Dave from a nearby table, and gave Little Malcolm his big-girl's-blouse look.

Malcolm reeled under the gaze but recovered quickly and pressed on. 'Woman in t'chemist said it were f'gorgeous, sexy young women . . . an' ah thought o' you, Dorothy.'

'Oooh, Malcolm, ah love it when y'romantic.'

As Malcolm began to heap three spoonfuls of sugar

into each mug, the owner, Nora Pratt, looked up from the frothy coffee machine. Forty-three-year-old Nora was the president of the Ragley Amateur Dramatic Society and her complete inability to pronounce the letter 'R' had not prevented her from always getting the star part in the annual pantomime.

'Look, Nora,' said Dorothy. 'Malcolm's bought me some Charlie perfume spray by Revlon.'

'It's a weally lovely fwagwence,' said Nora knowingly. The short, stocky Nora considered herself to be an authority on most things.

Little Malcolm picked up his two mugs of tea. ''Ello, Mr Sheffield,' he said. 'Ah've jus'seen Duggie. 'E says 'is boss fancies Miss Evans.'

'Does he?' I said.

''E's a strange man is Duggie's boss, Mr Sheffield,' said Dorothy.

'Oh, why's that, Dorothy?' I asked.

'He's psychic 'cause 'e's seventh child of a seventh child, so Mrs Ackroyd says, an' she knows about these things. She told me 'e were born with super-unnatural powers,' said Dorothy. 'He comes in wi' Duggie sometimes an' once 'e gave me a sort of look an' 'e told me ah were gonna meet a tall dark stranger.'

Nora and I both glanced at Little Malcolm sitting at a nearby table.

'An' 'e were reight – excep' for t'tall bit, o' course – and, er, well, ah s'ppose ah've known Malcolm all m'life,' she added. 'But 'e's definitely psychic an' 'e sez everyone 'as a sort of box inside 'em an' 'e jus' sort of opens it up an' reads what's there.'

'Ah don't want 'im weading my box,' said Nora defiantly.

Everyone looked at Nora but, wisely, said nothing.

'So what's it t'be, Mr Sheffield?' asked Dorothy.

'A coffee, please, Dorothy.'

'Fwothy coffee coming up, Mr Sheffield,' said Nora, 'an' 'ow about a wock bun, fwesh in yesterday?'

On Saturday morning I peered through the leaded panes of my bedroom window and looked down at my neglected vegetable patch. The last of the onion crop, forgotten now and gone to seed, waved their fluffy heads in the chill autumn breeze. My garden needed some tender loving care and I sighed. I knew how it felt. I was missing Beth. Her suggestion that I look for another headship flickered through my mind . . . but not for long.

On my journey into school I called in to Victor Pratt's garage at the end of Ragley High Street. As usual, Victor, elder brother of Nora Pratt, was not in good humour as he served me from the single pump.

'How are you, Victor?' I asked.

'Ah'm not 'appy, Mr Sheffield,' said Victor mournfully.

'I'm sorry to hear that.'

'In fact, it's a long time since ah were 'appy.'

'And when was that?' I asked, racking my brains to recall the last time I had seen Victor smile.

'During t'winter o' discontent, Mr Sheffield. 'Appy days them was,' said Victor, screwing up my petrol cap. 'Ah sold more paraffin than y' could throw a stick at.'

'So what's the problem now, Victor?' I asked, handing over a ten-pound note.

'Ah've got plumbago,' said Victor.

'Oh dear,' I said, suppressing a smile. 'That sounds painful.'

'Y'reight there, Mr Sheffield. An' me pipes are playing me up again, if y'tek mi meaning.'

As I drove away I guessed there was a peculiar symmetry in having plumbago and pipe problems.

By two o'clock we were ready and a large crowd of villagers had gathered outside our new school extension. Sue Phillips, striking in her new dress, was chatting happily with the imposing Miss Barrington-Huntley. Beth had found a spare maypole ribbon in the store room of her school and she and Anne had stretched it across the school porch. Meanwhile, Ruby was very proud to be in charge of the large pair of dressmaker's scissors, courtesy of the Cross-Stitch Club, for the tape-cutting ceremony.

'It gives me great pleasure to declare Ragley's new school extension officially open,' said Miss Barrington-Huntley. Cameras clicked and the chair of the Education Committee knew she looked the part in her dramatic new hat from Brown's in York.

In the library area, Anne's husband, the bearded John Grainger, was standing with screwdriver in hand ready to replace the brass plate that covered the hole where the time capsule would be placed.

'Joseph,' said Vera anxiously, 'you said you'd bring the time capsule from the car.'

'Sorry,' said Joseph absent-mindedly and rushed off to the car park.

Miss Barrington-Huntley had recently purchased a pair of gold-rimmed spectacles and she peered over the top of them in surprise at the sight of our vicar running towards her like Seb Coe with a vacuum flask.

Speeches were made and, finally, Miss Barrington-Huntley posed for the official photographer while holding the time capsule as if it was the World Cup.

'Well done, Jack,' said Miss Barrington-Huntley when the ceremony was over and we were in the car park. 'It's a wonderful achievement.'

'Thank you,' I said. 'It was good of you to give up your time.'

She climbed into her car and wound down the window. 'And thank you for not pressing me about possible school closures, Jack. This wasn't the time.'

She drove off and I stood there, relieved it was over and that nothing had gone wrong.

Back in the library area, John Grainger screwed the plaque in place and confined the time capsule to decades of darkness.

'I wonder when that will see the light of day again,' I said.

'Let's hope it's another hundred years,' said Vera.

That evening Beth and I sat in the Odeon Cinema in York watching *The Life of Brian* and we both relaxed after a busy week.

'I'm pleased it went well for you today, Jack,' said

Beth sleepily as she rested her head on my shoulder.

Her hair was against my cheek and I closed my eyes. We were coming to the end of a perfect day.

Remembrance Sunday dawned with a reluctant light. It was an iron-grey morning and a thick mist lay heavy on the silent fields.

At ten forty-five Beth and I joined Vera, Anne and John Grainger outside St Mary's Church midst the silent, soberly dressed, still crowd, all with our own private thoughts and memories. The church bell tolled mournfully as we gathered round the tall stone war memorial that had been erected in 1948. It was beautifully maintained and set in a small cordoned-off area on a mound of manicured grass. On its sides were carved the names of the fallen of two World Wars from the villages of Ragley and Morton.

Albert Jenkins, retired railway worker and school governor, was there in his dark-grey three-piece suit and thick woollen scarf. 'For whom the bell tolls; it tolls for thee,' he recited quietly with a gentle smile. 'Seems strange that Archibald isn't ringing the bells,' he said, looking up at the bell tower.

Beth squeezed my hand as Major Rupert Forbes-Kitchener, a row of medals gleaming on his black Crombie overcoat, read out the names of those who gave their lives. There was an occasional stirring in the crowd as the name of a loved one was recalled.

Then the major read the famous extract from Laurence Binyon's 'For the Fallen', composed on the cliffs of Cornwall in 1914:

'They shall grow not old, as we that are left grow old:
Age shall not weary them, nor the years condemn.
At the going down of the sun and in the morning
We will remember them.'

The church clock struck eleven and young Alan Broadbent, of the Ragley and Morton Scout Troop, raised his bugle and sounded the Last Post.

Then there was silence, the like of which happened only once each year. It always felt as though it lasted more than two minutes as we counted the heartbeats and thought of those who had fought bravely for our freedom and would never again stand by our side. I remembered my grandfather, killed at the age of twenty-one, on the first bloody day of the Battle of the Somme.

Only the sound of the birds in the high elms and the stirring of russet leaves at our feet disturbed the silent tableau.

Then the major broke the silence. 'When you go home, tell them of us and say, "for their tomorrow, we gave our today".'

Reveille was sounded and, after a prayer, we filed quietly into church behind the colour parties of scouts, guides, cubs and brownies. A rousing hymn was followed by the national anthem and Joseph's blessing, then finally parents, grandparents and children walked out to resume their busy lives and the church was silent again.

Beth and I were saying our goodbyes to Anne and John when Vera said, 'Shall we scatter the ashes now, Joseph?' A few of the bellringers were hovering in the far corner of the churchyard. Joseph opened the boot of their car. 'No, it's in the well of the back seat,' said Vera.

'No, it isn't,' said Joseph with a vacant smile, 'it's here.'

'But that's where I put the time capsule, Joseph.'

He lifted the canister out and held it up.

Vera stared in horror. 'Oh, please, it can't be!'

We all gathered round as Vera unscrewed the top of the canister and peered inside. It contained four cardboard tubes.

'Oh dear,' said Joseph.

'Oh, Joseph!' exclaimed Vera.

John Grainger leant over and whispered in my ear, 'Don't worry, Jack, I've got a screwdriver in the car.'

A week later, Jo pinned up a cutting from the *Easington Herald & Pioneer* on the staff-room noticeboard and we all gathered round to look at it. I noticed Vera and Anne exchange a private glance and a secret smile. Under the headline 'Time capsule for Ragley School' was a photograph of the elegant and dignified chair of the Education Committee standing in front of the new Ragley School library extension.

Miss Barrington-Huntley was smiling serenely and cradling a metal canister, blissfully unaware that she was holding the ashes of Archibald Pike.

Chapter Six

Captain Kirk and the Flea Circus

Mr Richard Gomersall, Senior Primary Adviser, visited school to gather information for the Education Committee's follow-up document to 'The Rationalization of Small Schools in North Yorkshire'. The PTA organized a visit to Billy Batt's International Circus in Easington.

Extract from the Ragley School Logbook:
Wednesday, 26 November 1980

'Ah'm worried about our Mary, Mr Sheffield,' said Mrs Scrimshaw. 'She's not been 'erself lately.'

It was after school on Tuesday, 25 November, and Peggy Scrimshaw, the wife of the local pharmacist, had called in to the school office. It had been a tough day. Our first rehearsal for the Christmas play had not gone well and I had a thumping headache.

'Come in, Mrs Scrimshaw,' I said wearily, 'and tell me about it.'

'Well, ah know that Mrs 'Unter is a wonderful teacher

and ah've spoken to 'er about it an' she says she'll keep an eye on 'er.'

Six-year-old Mary Scrimshaw had shown great enthusiasm when she first started in Anne's reception class, but during the past weeks she had become subdued.

'Mary is a lovely girl, Mrs Scrimshaw,' I said. 'I'm sure we can get to the bottom of it and you've done the right thing letting us know.'

Mrs Scrimshaw gave me a strained smile and got up to leave. 'Thank you for y'time, Mr Sheffield, an' if y'don't mind me saying . . . y'looking a bit peaky.'

'I've got a bad headache,' I said.

'Call in on y'way 'ome, Mr Sheffield,' she said, 'an' ah'll give y'some tablets t'get shut of it.'

As she left, the telephone rang. It was Beth.

'Jack, some news for you: Richard Gomersall is coming your way,' she said. 'He's doing his audit of village schools for this school closure business. I caught sight of his list and it's Ragley tomorrow morning.'

'Oh no,' I groaned.

'It'll be fine, Jack,' she said with slightly false enthusiasm.

'So how did it go?' I asked.

'Not sure really. He just wandered around school making notes and with a sort of *strained* expression on his face.'

'Oh, well, thanks for letting me know,' I said.

'OK, Jack, and are we still on for the circus trip tomorrow?'

'Yes,' I said. 'Vera's got the tickets for the staff and their partners, so I'll pick you up around six thirty.'

'See you then. 'Bye – and good luck.'

I admired her boundless energy and stared at the telephone. Then I rubbed my aching head and wondered if women got headaches the same as men did. It was just that I had never heard them complain about it.

As I walked into the Village Pharmacy, Mrs Earnshaw was being served.

Next to her, Heathcliffe and Terry had their noses pressed against the glass counter and one-year-old Dallas Sue-Ellen Earnshaw, sitting up in her push-chair, was red in the face and making strange noises.

'Peggy'll serve y', Mr Sheffield, while ah get Mrs Earnshaw's prescription,' said Eugene Scrimshaw. He assumed a dramatic pose at the foot of the back stairs. 'To boldly go, Mr Sheffield,' he said with a chuckle. The Ragley village pharmacist was fond of his split infinitive. 'Beam me up, Peggy,' he yelled and, with high-pitched laughter, he disappeared.

'Ah know where ah'd like t'beam 'im,' muttered Peggy and glowered in my direction. 'If 'e asks me to give 'im another Vulcan salute ah'll tell 'im where 'e can stick it.'

Eugene, a small, prematurely balding man in his late thirties, had the thickest wire-rimmed spectacles I had ever seen. They made him look like a startled owl. He was also a huge *Star Trek* fan and he had converted his attic into the flight deck of the Starship Enterprise. For, in the strange world of Eugene Scrimshaw, he loved acting out his role as James Tiberius Kirk, Captain of the *USS Enterprise*.

He had recorded the opening soundtrack of *Star Trek*

on his Grundig reel-to-reel tape recorder. When he pressed the start button he would transport himself into the twenty-third century with his imaginary First Officer, the cool, analytical, logical Mr Spock.

Around him were life-size posters of his crew, including Lieutenant Sulu at the flight controls; chief engineer Lieutenant Commander Scott; chief medical officer Dr Leonard McCoy and the attractive, long-legged communications officer Lieutenant Uhura.

The diminutive chemist in his over-long white coat reappeared with a dark-brown glass bottle of murky-looking medicine. 'Here y'are, Mrs Earnshaw. This'll get Mr Earnshaw's bowels shiftin'. This stuff's better than Dyno-Rod.'

'Thank you, Mr Scrimshaw. Yurra star,' said Mrs Earnshaw.

Heathcliffe fiddled with the cap of the bottle. 'Ah can't get t'lid off, Mam,' he said in frustration.

'Y'not s'pposed to,' shouted Mrs Earnshaw, removing the cap with a confident twist and smelling the medicine. 'It's one o' them new child-proof caps.'

Terry looked in amazement at the bottle. 'But how does it know it's 'Eathcliffe, Mam?'

'C'mon, let's get 'ome,' said Mrs Earnshaw.

'Go forth an' prosper,' recited Eugene. He raised his right hand, palm facing outwards, and, with some difficulty, he separated his second and third fingers and gave Mrs Earnshaw his V-shaped Vulcan salute.

Mrs Earnshaw smiled politely and stared wide-eyed in the direction of Peggy. It had been a long day and Peggy was clearly not impressed. She held up her right hand,

pretended to throttle an invisible foe, and then proceeded to unpack a box of Erasmic aftershave foam. Had he
known, Eugene would have been impressed. Peggy had
clearly perfected Mr Spock's Vulcan nerve-pinch.

'I called in for those headache tablets, Mrs Scrimshaw,'
I said.

'Oh yes, sorry, Mr Sheffield,' she said, looking distracted.
'Ah've got 'em 'ere,' and she selected a packet of extra-
strength aspirins from behind the counter. 'There y'are:
these'll do t'trick.' I put a pound note on top of the ancient
till. Mrs Scrimshaw dropped the tablets into a small white
paper bag and gave me my change. 'Y'know, Mr Sheffield,
ah met 'im in toiletries in Boots the Chemist,' said Peggy
with a wistful glance. 'Ah thought 'e were normal then.
Anyway, our Mary will be seven tomorrow and we're all
off to t'circus. She's real excited. Let's 'ope it cheers 'er
up.'

'Thanks,' I said, 'and I hope you have a lovely time.'

As I left she turned her attention to stacking boxes of
Setler's indigestion tablets but, sadly, in her case they
were not bringing instant relief.

On impulse, I turned left past Pratt's Hardware Emporium
and walked into Nora's Coffee Shop. Dorothy Humpleby
was standing behind the counter, fiddling with her pen-
dulous earrings and swaying to Randy Crawford's 'One
Day I'll Fly Away'.

Dorothy regarded me dispassionately. 'Y'looking down
in t'dumps, Mr Sheffield.'

'I've got a headache, Dorothy,' I said.

Nora Pratt walked in from the back room, carrying her

coat and scarf. She was also clutching her script for the forthcoming Ragley annual pantomime. This year it was *Jack and the Beanstalk*.

'Please could I have some water, Dorothy?' I held up the packet of aspirins. 'I've just got these from the chemist.'

'OK, Mr Sheffield, coming up,' said Dorothy and she put a glass of water on the counter. ''E's a right one is that chemist,' she added and resumed fiddling with her earrings.

''E loves 'is *Star Twek* does Mr Scwimshaw,' said Nora as she stuffed her script in her shopping bag.

I put two tablets in my mouth and swilled them down.

'By the way, Mr Sheffield, Nora gorrit reight about that murderer,' said Dorothy.

'Pardon?' I gulped.

'Y'know . . . about who shot JR.'

'Oh, I see.'

Nora beamed with false modesty as she pulled on her coat. She was delighted she had been the only person in the village to guess correctly who had shot J. R. Ewing in *Dallas*. A week ago the whole country had been glued to their television screens to discover it was Kristen who had shot television's greatest villain.

'Ah told yer it was Kwisten,' said Nora. 'Ah was weally sure.'

'Well done, Nora,' I said.

'Well, it couldn't 'ave been that Victorwia Pwincipal,' said Nora. 'It 'ad t'be Bing Cwosby's daughter.'

And with that she marched out, leaving the door

jingling behind her. In the darkness she began to sing the Neil Diamond song that was moving up the charts and was due to be a real tearjerker in the forthcoming pantomime. As she crossed the High Street, Nora looked up to the heavens and, in a piercing voice, sang, 'Love on the wocks . . .'

Meanwhile, Little Malcolm walked to the juke-box, put in his five-pence piece, selected F13 and stood by the counter to wait for Dennis Waterman's 'I Could Be So Good For You'. 'Two more teas, please, when y'ready, Dorothy,' he said, '. . . an' this record's f'you,' he whispered.

'Ooh, Malcolm. Ah love it when y'surprise me,' said Dorothy, loud enough for every customer to hear.

Little Malcolm blushed furiously and rummaged in his donkey jacket for some more change.

'Gerra move on, lover boy,' shouted Big Dave from one of the far tables. 'It's like waiting f'Christmas.'

'So what's it t'be, Mr Sheffield?' she asked.

I surveyed the tired-looking display of pies and cakes. 'A coffee and a bacon sandwich, please, Dorothy.'

A large mug of bubbling foam appeared on the counter. 'Here y'are, Mr Sheffield. Ah'll bring y'buttie straight over,' she said, while fluttering her false eyelashes at Little Malcolm.

I walked over to an empty table where a copy of the *Easington Herald & Pioneer* had been left behind. The editor was proud of his eye-catching headlines and this one, 'An end to castration', was no exception. Next to a photograph of a young pig that looked as if it was about to burst into tears, the paragraph read, 'The British Veterinary

Association called for an end to the castration of young pigs. In the past it was done because of the lingering smell that occurred in mature boars. Now pigs are slaughtered so young that the smell no longer occurs.'

A moment later, Dorothy arrived. ''Ere's y'bacon sandwich, Mr Sheffield,' she said.

I stared at it, glanced back at the photograph of the tearful pig and winced. Suddenly I'd become a vegetarian.

Next door, in Pratt's Hardware Emporium, Vera was deep in a conversation about fleas with Timothy Pratt. Timothy was the younger brother of Nora and, owing to his fanatical need for order and symmetry, was known as Tidy Tim.

'Obviously my little darlings haven't got fleas, Timothy. They're not the type. But I just want to make sure.'

'Well, Miss Evans,' said Timothy, 'these are t'latest thing f'getting shut o' fleas. It's t'new range o' Sherley Flea Bands.' Timothy selected one from his alphabetical display.

'It would have to be the best you've got, Timothy,' said Vera emphatically.

'These are top o' t'range, Miss Evans,' said Timothy, taking care to align the cardboard package so it was parallel with the edge of the counter. Tidy Tim liked parallel lines.

'I see,' said Vera, opening the box and examining the neat little cat collars.

Timothy read from the side of the packet. 'It says 'ere "treated with a virulent insecticide", Miss Evans.'

'I'll take three, please,' said Vera. Nothing was too good for Vera's cats.

He took Vera's pound note, counted out the change and then rearranged the remaining cat collars so the boxes were exactly in line. Tidy Tim also liked *straight* lines.

On Wednesday morning, the first frosts had arrived and, in the tiny porch of Bilbo Cottage, a perfect spider's web, sprinkled with frozen droplets, sparkled in the sharp sunlight. Sadly, I was not in the mood to appreciate the wonders of nature. A visit from the Senior Primary Adviser beckoned and I prayed it would go well. The future of Ragley School might depend upon it.

I pulled up outside the General Stores & Newsagent, where the owner, Prudence Golightly, was deep in conversation with Vera. It appeared that Margaret Thatcher and her Chancellor, Sir Geoffrey Howe, were clearly having a tough time.

'I'll change to an *Express* this morning, Prudence,' said Vera, shaking her head indignantly at the range of head-lines in the morning newspapers.

The *Daily Mail* had been a devoted supporter of the government but its headline 'Maggie must do U-turn' suggested a change of heart. The *Daily Express* appeared to be the only tabloid newspaper supporting Mrs Thatcher and it complained bitterly about its 'fairweather friends'. 'The Lady's not for burning', it proclaimed. 'We stand right behind Mrs Thatcher.'

I bought my usual copy of *The Times* and then wished I hadn't. It featured the complaint that teachers have an easy life and, according to the results of a dubious survey, we enjoyed an average teaching week of only twenty-two hours. I wished the reporter could come and work alongside me.

Just before nine o'clock, Richard Gomersall, the Senior Primary Adviser from County Hall in Northallerton, arrived. A short, slightly-built man in his late forties with a magnificent mane of long wavy reddish-brown hair, he was renowned for his immaculate sartorial elegance. He was wearing a purple corduroy suit with wide lapels and flared trousers and his shirt sported loud vertical salmon stripes and a stiff white collar. A flower-power tie and brown leather Cuban-heeled boots completed the ensemble. Strangely, however, he kept hitching up his trousers with a pained expression.

'Good morning, Jack,' he said. 'I'm here for a brief fact-finding tour.' He gripped his clipboard tightly in front of him and there were beads of perspiration on his fore-head.

'Hello, Richard,' I said. 'Well, I'm teaching this morning, of course, but Miss Evans will assist if there's anything you need.'

'Perhaps Mr Gomersall would like to sit down and have a coffee before he begins,' said Vera cautiously.

Richard Gomersall looked gratefully at Vera and accepted with some relief. 'Thank you,' he said breathlessly.

A few minutes later Vera popped her head round my classroom door. 'I'm just taking Mr Gomersall to the chemist, Mr Sheffield. He's a little unwell. I'll be back soon.'

True to her word, she soon returned. Cathy Cathcart looked up from her diagram of an isosceles triangle and announced, 'Miss Evans coming up t'drive, Mr Sheffield.' I peered out of the classroom window to see Vera sitting primly in her Austin A40 and, beside her, was a smiling and relaxed Richard Gomersall.

He was soon busy making copious notes, visiting each classroom and talking to the children. One of them was Mary Scrimshaw.

'Mrs Hunter, I've just had a chat with little Mary,' said Richard.

'Yes, it's her birthday today,' said Jo.

'I know,' he said. 'I asked her what she wanted for her birthday and she said she wanted her daddy to stay at home and not fly away. She sounded really worried.'

'That's interesting,' said Jo.

Five minutes later Jo and Mary were deep in conversation.

At morning break I was on playground duty and the children were excited at the prospect of going to Billy Batt's International Circus. The travelling company of performers had set up their big top, thanks to the major, on the land near Old Morton Manor House. Conversations around me were dominated by the strange world of acrobats, clowns, trained animals, trapeze artists, tightrope walkers, plate-spinning jugglers, a human cannonball and, even, a flea circus.

Richard Gomersall walked out on to the playground with Anne. 'Thanks for everything, Jack,' he said and tapped his clipboard. 'I've got all I need. Everyone has been helpful, especially Miss Evans, and we shall, of course, keep you informed.'

I knew if he had anything to say about school closures he would tell me. This obviously wasn't the time. We shook hands and he walked to the car park.

'Well, let's hope we've survived,' I said.

Anne gave me a probing look. 'Jack, I've just spoken to Jo and we think we know what's wrong with Mary Scrimshaw.'

Two minutes later I smiled. Everything was clear.

'Don't worry, we'll deal with it,' said Anne. 'I'll have a word with Mrs Scrimshaw when she collects Mary.'

At the end of school Vera was handing out the tickets for the circus when Mrs Scrimshaw tapped on the office door. I stepped out into the entrance hall.

'What a relief, Mr Sheffield. Mrs Grainger an' Mrs 'Unter 'ave told me what was troubling our Mary, so ah'll 'ave a word wi' Eugene. 'E means well with 'is stargazing, ah s'ppose. Mary just took it t'wrong way.'

'I'm pleased we found out in the end,' I said.

'An' ah got m'circus tickets from Miss Evans when she called in today. She 'ad a poor man with 'er who's 'aving a 'ernia operation next week.'

'Oh, I see,' I said, suddenly realizing why Richard Gomersall had looked so distressed. 'Did he need pain-killers?'

Mrs Scrimshaw laughed. 'No, 'e needed a new surgical truss. 'Is elastic 'ad gone on 'is old one!'

*   *   *

119

When I walked into the office Vera was just replacing the receiver.

'That was Mr Gomersall ringing to say thank you for accommodating him today, Mr Sheffield. He was very complimentary and said that visiting Ragley had proved to be . . .' she glanced down at her spiral-bound pad with a hint of a smile, 'an uplifting experience.'

At seven o'clock I was sitting next to Beth in a huge striped marquee. Tiered seating surrounded a circus ring that had been liberally covered with sawdust, and a ringmaster in his red coat and black top hat was cracking his whip and telling us we were about to see the finest entertainment on earth.

It lived up to expectations, with Vera and Joseph almost leaping out of their seats as the clowns pretended to throw water over them. Dan Hunter was invited to test the strength of the iron bars before the circus strongman bent them and Sally said she felt her baby kick when the human cannonball was fired across the arena. Meanwhile, Anne sat up and took interest in the blond-haired horse trainer who had a strong resemblance to David Soul.

The ringmaster cracked his whip again and announced, 'Please welcome Professor Potts and his amazing flea circus.'

A tall gentleman in a black frock-coat and a stovepipe hat walked to the centre of the ring, pushing a large box on wheels. In bright paint on the side it read: PROFESSOR POTTS PHANTASMAGORICAL CIRQUE DE PUCES.

'*Cirque de puces*?' I said.

Beth whispered in my ear, 'It's French for flea circus.'

The professor had learnt his trade at Jeffries Flea Circus at Bingley Hall in Birmingham in the 1950s and his claim to fame was an appearance on the British *Pathé News* at the cinema. He opened his box and arranged a miniature gun carriage and a collection of tiny carts.

'Ladies and ze gentlemen *et les enfants*, my fleaz will now perform ze amazing feat for you.' Everybody clapped. 'A volunteer, *s'il vous plaît*. Iz eet a birthday for *un enfant* in ze audience?'

Eugene Scrimshaw, on the front row, waved and a very excited Mary and her mother went to stand alongside the flea circus.

'Sadly, my fleaz from Florida, zay 'ave all died from ze cold.' There was a communal sigh of disappointment, although it was noticeable that Vera did not join in. 'So I now use ze Yorkshire fleaz,' he announced triumphantly.

This was greeted with huge applause and a standing ovation from the Ragley Rovers football team on the back row.

'Y'can't beat Yorkshire f'fleas,' shouted Big Dave Robinson. 'We breed 'em tough up 'ere.'

'Y'reight there, Dave,' mumbled Little Malcolm through a mouthful of candy-floss.

It was a strange act as the fleas were too small to be seen. We could only presume that Mary saw them as she encouraged them to pull carts up a ramp. At the end Mary waved goodbye to her tiny friends, Professor Potts got the biggest cheer of the night and we all went home, tired but happy and ready for an early night. All, that is, except Vera, who inspected her cats very carefully and made sure their flea collars were perfectly secure.

At the end of school on Friday I was chatting with Anne, Sally and Vera in the staff-room when Jo came in, clutching a sheet of paper.

'Jack,' said Jo. 'Have a look at this. It's exceptional. Mary Scrimshaw's suddenly coming on in leaps and bounds again with her writing. And she's developing a wonderful imagination.'

Jo handed me a sheet of A4 paper and I smiled as I read the large, neat, infant printing. Mary had written:

Daddy and Mummy took me to the circus.
It was my birthday.
I am 7.
The best bit was the man with the fleas.
The man loved them like Daddy and Mummy love me.
When I grow up I will have fleas and I will love them too.
But I will always love Mummy and Daddy best.
When they kiss me good night Mummy smells of nice soap.
Daddy says one day he will take me to the stars.
I'm glad I'm me.

I pulled on my duffel coat and old college scarf, picked up Mary's writing, and walked across the High Street. It was the time of the dying of the light and dusk settled like a purple cloak over the rooftops of Ragley village.

The pharmacy was quiet and Mrs Scrimshaw was

tidying the shelves. 'Mrs Hunter wanted you to see this,' I said.

Minutes later she dabbed her eyes as she read her daughter's words. 'It's wonderful, Mr Sheffield. Thank you for showing it to me.'

There was a scamper of feet on the stairs and Eugene appeared with Mary. 'Hello, Mr Sheffield,' he said. 'We've jus' been looking at t'stars through m'telescope.'

'I can see where Mary gets her imagination from,' I said with a smile.

He lifted up Mary in his arms and opened the door for me. Peggy came to stand beside them and smiled. 'Thank you, Mr Sheffield. We're all right now.'

As I walked across the forecourt Mary called out, ''Bye, Mr Sheffield.' Then she raised her little right hand, separated her second and third fingers into a V-shape and gave me a passable imitation of Mr Spock's Vulcan salute. Eugene and Peggy laughed and, in perfect unison, they raised their right hands and joined in.

It was an image I shall always remember – the three of them standing together in the brightly lit shop window. Beneath the twinkling stars and the silent, inky-black world of space, they were a family again.

Chapter Seven

Jilly Cooper and the Yorkshire Fairies

Rehearsals went ahead for the school Christmas enter-tainment. County Hall requested a copy of our scheme for mathematics for their 'common curriculum' working party.

Extract from the Ragley School Logbook:
Friday, 5 December 1980

'It's usually something boring,' said Sally with a tired grin. She leant against the staff-room door and rubbed her aching back. She had now passed the thirtieth week of her pregnancy and standing in front of a class was taking its toll.

'Yes. I know what you mean,' said Anne. 'My John's just the same. He bought me a toolkit last year.'

It was Friday lunchtime, 5 December, and Christmas preparations were beginning in earnest. I stopped winding the handle of our Roneo spirit duplicator. On the master sheet on the cylindrical drum was Cathy

124

Cathcart's drawing of a fat robin for our Christmas entertainment programme and it occurred to me that it wasn't only Sally who looked pregnant. 'What's boring?' I asked.

'Colin's Christmas present,' said Sally. 'It's always cheap perfume or a jumper that's too small. Still, he means well.'

Vera was recording late dinner money in her register. 'He may surprise you,' she said with a reassuring smile but slightly false optimism.

Sally shook her head. 'Unlikely. You know Colin.'

'My Dan bought me underwear last year,' announced Jo, without looking up from her 'How to make a Christmas snowflake mobile' article in our monthly *Child Education* magazine, 'and it fitted perfectly.'

Anne, Sally and Vera looked at Jo with a mixture of amusement, appreciation and horror . . . and in that order.

'I don't think John would know where to start with a present like that,' said Anne. 'Anyway, you won't believe what he's giving me for my Christmas treat.'

Suddenly, I was interested. 'What's that?' I said. 'I could do with a few ideas for Beth's present.'

'Well, you know John loves his steam trains, don't you?' said Anne. 'The Keighley and Worth Valley Railway are running "Santa Steam Specials" every Sunday in December. So we're going this weekend!'

'That sounds great,' I said, warming to the idea.

'I think Anne was hoping for something a little more romantic, Jack,' said Sally.

'Too right,' retorted Anne.

Vera frowned and stirred her Earl Grey tea noisily.

'Dan's going on the train to Leeds tomorrow to buy my present,' said Jo. 'Why not ask John and Colin to go with him? Should be a good day out for them and Dan would enjoy the company.'

'Mmm, yes, good idea,' said Sally. 'I'll mention it. Dan might point him in the right direction.'

'So what are you giving Beth for Christmas?' asked Anne with a mischievous grin.

I gathered up the pregnant robins, stacked them on the coffee-table and pondered for a moment. 'Not sure yet, Anne . . . but maybe a trip to Leeds would be a good idea.'

During the afternoon my class made good progress on our huge 'Twelve Days of Christmas' frieze. Apart from Cathy Cathcart painting two tortoises to represent two turtle doves and Carol Bustard decorating the three French hens with rather fetching navy-blue berets and a string of onions, it turned out fine.

At afternoon playtime, Sally was looking tired.

'Come and sit down,' said Jo, jumping up and grabbing her coat and scarf. 'I'll do your playground duty.'

'Thanks, Jo,' said Sally, collapsing into the nearest chair. 'You're an angel.'

Sally was soon engrossed in an article in Vera's December 1980 issue of *Yorkshire Life*. 'It says here that Jilly Cooper is on tour in the north of England to publicize the launch of her latest novel, *Class*,' said Sally. 'Pity I won't see her. I don't think she's coming to York.'

'I love Jilly Cooper,' said Anne.

'I'm reading *Bella* at the moment,' said Sally.

'What's it like?' asked Anne.

'Brilliant!' said Sally. 'It's about this sexy actress called Bella Parkinson and she meets a rich, handsome guy called Rupert Henriques who fancies the pants off her.'

'Oh, dear,' said Vera disapprovingly and, with a noisy clatter of crockery, she began to collect the teacups.

Sally leant over to Anne and whispered conspiratorially, 'I'll pass it on to you when I've finished.'

Anne nodded and grinned. While David Soul in *Starsky and Hutch* would always be her heart-throb, Rupert Henriques sounded to be a sufficiently interesting diversion from yet another tale of John's woodcarving exploits.

That evening over a fish-and-chips supper, I watched the BBC news with Beth.

It featured Queen Elizabeth, the Queen Mother, playing snooker at the Press Club in London as part of her eightieth birthday celebrations and another complaint about the behaviour of the Press towards Lady Diana Spencer. Meanwhile, Anna Ford informed us, with suitably repressed humour, that Ian Botham, the twenty-five-year-old England cricket captain, had been banned from driving for a month and fined eighty pounds after being chased in his Saab by the police up the M5 motorway for 17 miles. Mr Hywell Jenkins for the defence had informed the court he was 'a little excited at being made captain'.

Suddenly, the phone rang. It was Dan Hunter.

'Jack, I'm going into Leeds tomorrow to buy a Christmas present for Jo. Do you fancy coming?'

'I'd better check with Beth,' I said.

'Don't bother, Jack. She's going into York with Jo. Colin and John are tagging along as well.'

'Sounds like a good day out.'

'I'll pick you up around nine. See you then.'

'So, you're going Christmas shopping with Dan?' said Beth with a smile. 'I hope you select some appropriate gifts.'

'Is there anything in particular you want?' I asked hopefully.

A straight answer was too much to hope for. 'Surprise me,' said Beth coyly. 'I certainly intend to surprise you.'

For the rest of the evening I racked my brains but no inspiration was forthcoming.

On Saturday morning at nine o'clock a two-tone-green Wolseley Hornet pulled up outside Bilbo Cottage. Dan was at the wheel and Colin and John were on the back seat. We parked in York railway station and queued up for a newspaper. I bought my usual *Times*; Dan bought the *Sun*; John spent twelve pence on a *Daily Mail* and Colin bought a *Do It Yourself* home improvement magazine and four KitKats.

After working with women every day it made a change to be in the company of men and I relaxed in the instant camaraderie. The platform was crowded and we followed the huge figure of Dan as the train eased its way into the station. It was the hourly service from Newcastle to Liverpool and the eight blue and grey carriages were covered in thick grime. John, the train buff, informed us they were hauled by a Class 47 diesel electric locomotive but we were more concerned to get a seat. Dan quickly found four seats with a table and we settled down with our newspapers, magazines and a welcome KitKat each.

I opened my *Times* and frowned. Under the headline 'Oil battle looms in the Falklands', a report indicated there was trouble brewing with Argentina. Mr Nicholas Soames, Minister of State for Latin America, had visited the Falkland Islands after Argentina had claimed these islands and begun a dispute over who owned drilling rights. I couldn't see us backing down on the issue of sovereignty and I wondered what the outcome might be.

On a lighter note, on the back page was a photograph of Steve Davis, a new snooker star, who had just won in one week more than I earned in a year. Apparently the tall, slim, ginger-haired twenty-three-year-old had begun to play at Pontins Holiday Camp at the age of twelve. I recalled that when I was twelve this would have been regarded as a misspent youth but now I wasn't so sure.

At eleven o'clock we walked out of the station into Leeds City Square and stood on the steps of the Queen's Hotel, staring at the busy scene of traffic and shoppers.

'Hey, look at this!' exclaimed Dan. Outside the hotel entrance was a large sign, 'JILLY COOPER – Book Signing, 12 noon to 1.00 p.m.'

I recalled the conversation in the staff-room. 'Colin, that would be perfect for Sally. She was on about Jilly Cooper yesterday.'

'Jack's right,' said Dan. 'A signed copy would be special.

She'd be really impressed on Christmas morning. In fact, we could all get one!'

'Who's Jilly Cooper?' asked a bemused John. I was beginning to see why Anne fancied David Soul.

Colin lit up an evil-smelling roll-up cigarette and inhaled deeply. 'I fancy something to eat before all this shopping.'

'And maybe a pint afterwards,' added John hopefully. He'd already forgotten about Jilly Cooper.

Dan looked at his watch. 'OK, how about over there?' He pointed across the road to a grubby café on Boar Lane. The name 'Buddy's' was emblazoned across the window above a picture of Buddy Holly. 'Then we can come back here for the book signing.'

I liked simple solutions and suddenly remembered why I enjoyed shopping with men.

When we walked in we realized there was a 1950s theme and, suddenly, my black-framed spectacles were back in fashion. Buddy Holly's 'That'll be the Day' was blasting out on the juke-box and the waiter, leaning against the counter, looked the part in his drainpipe trousers, brocade waistcoat, bootlace tie and brothel-creeper shoes. He stubbed out his cigarette, combed his greasy Tony Curtis hairstyle and yelled 'Peggy Sue . . . customers!'

A tough-looking waitress in a short pink skirt with a net petticoat and bobby socks came over to our table. The name 'Peggy Sue' was stitched on her white blouse and a red-and-white checked scarf was knotted cowboy-style round her neck. She fingered her platinum-blonde pony-tail, took a final puff of her cigarette and removed the pencil from behind her ear.

'Yeah?' she said, taking out a notepad.

'Is there a menu?' I asked.

'It's on t'board,' she said, looking at me as if I couldn't read.

We looked at the chalkboard on the wall next to the peeling pictures of Elvis Presley, Bill Hayley and, incongruously, Hughie Green in a scene from the television show *Double Your Money*. Hughie was looking suitably tense as he asked a contestant a question for the top prize of thirty-two pounds.

'Mek up y'minds,' grumbled Peggy Sue. 'Ah've got a thirty-seven bus t'catch at 'alf past eleven!'

This was clearly a long way from the Dean Court Hotel in York.

'What do you recommend?' asked Dan.

'Burgers an' Coke,' said Peggy Sue, eyeing up the tall, handsome Dan.

Everyone nodded. 'For four, then, please, er . . . Peggy Sue,' said Dan.

'S'not m'real name,' she said with a brown-toothed smile. 'Ah'm Marlene from Gipton.'

For four men on a shopping trip, eating is a purely functional activity and no one complained that the burgers were like cardboard; however, when the drinks arrived, John stared sadly at his Coke. 'There's ice in here!'

'Giz it 'ere, y'soft ha'porth,' said Peggy Sue as she fished out the ice cubes with her fingers and threw them in the ashtray.

We only left a modest tip.

*   *   *

The Queen's Hotel with its opulent 1930s Art Deco interior was a perfect venue for a celebrity book signing and a large crowd had gathered for one of Yorkshire's adopted daughters. Women of all ages and from all walks of life were chatting together.

'She started out with a piece on young wives for the *Sunday Times* in 1969, you know,' said a large lady in a tweed suit, 'and then moved on to a regular column,' she added in a loud voice as if she was announcing the runners and riders for the three-thirty at Cheltenham.

Her tall willowy friend in a lilac bouclé knit dress, determined not to be outdone, replied in a high-pitched, squeaky voice, 'Well, I heard that when she was asked how she relaxed, with reading or sex . . .' Everyone around her stopped speaking and immediately listened in. '. . . Jilly said that reading's the thing because sex isn't relaxing, you have to concentrate too hard!'

The lady in the tweed skirt blushed slightly and sought to change the subject quickly. 'I do like the pretty chenille trim on your cuffs, my dear.'

The queue was huge and we found ourselves near the back of it. Jilly Cooper was clearly very popular. When I looked around I noticed we were the only men. The four of us stood there feeling a little embarrassed while the conversation around us continued to be animated.

'Her great-great-grandfather was Liberal MP for Leeds,' said a knowledgeable woman in front.

'And she was brought up in Ilkley,' said another Yorkshire lady, with a hint of pride.

There was a tap on my shoulder. 'Have you read

Harriet?' asked a strange little lady behind me in a quaint hat. 'It's my favourite.'

'I'm afraid not,' I replied. 'I haven't read any Jilly Cooper novels . . . But my fiancée thinks they're wonderful,' I added hastily, fearing that those ahead of me would turn into a literary lynch mob. They were holding up novels with titles that reminded me of upper-crust first names such as Imogen and Prudence.

There was a cheer as Jilly Cooper arrived, looking stunning and full of *joie de vivre*. Elegant and slim, with long wavy hair cascading around her shoulders, she was certainly an English beauty. Her rosy cheeks shone with health and her eyes crinkled with laughter.

Finally, it was our turn and Dan and John got their books signed. Dan in particular made a significant impression and I imagined Jilly thinking he would make the perfect hero for her next novel. Colin nervously proffered his copy of *Class: A View from Middle England*.

'It's for my wife,' muttered Colin.

'Jolly good,' said Jilly cheerfully, 'and what's her name?'

'Sally,' said Colin, 'and, er . . . she's expecting.'

'Oh, jolly super,' said Jilly, scribbling away, 'and when's it due?'

'Early next year,' gulped Colin.

'I'm sure it will be a beautiful baby,' said Jilly, passing over the signed copy and shaking his hand.

'Er, thank you and . . . er, lovely to meet you,' said Colin.

Then it was my turn. I put a copy of *Octavia* on the desk and gave Jilly a nervous glance.

'Hello. I'm Jilly,' she said with a toothy smile.

'Oh, hello, I'm Jack . . . Jack Sheffield, and this one's for my fiancée, Beth, please,' I said.

'Super name,' said Jilly, scribbling again. She wrote 'To Beth', signed it with a flourish and looked up at me. 'Oh, how absolutely jolly,' she said, 'and when's the big day?'

'Oh, er, probably next year,' I said hesitantly.

'And what do you do, Jack?' she asked.

'I'm a village schoolteacher,' I said. 'Well, actually, the headteacher,' I added, forsaking all modesty. 'It's an interesting life.'

'Sounds like a jolly good story,' said Jilly with a twinkle in her eyes and handed me the signed copy.

'Yes, perhaps it is,' I said. 'Well, thank you and it's a pleasure to meet you – and I promise to read one of your novels,' I added and then felt rather foolish.

Jilly rummaged in a bag at her feet and pulled out a dog-eared paperback entitled *Bella*. 'Here, try this,' she said. 'It's about an actress and you might find it fun.'

'Oh, thank you,' I said, quite taken aback by this turn of events.

'Super!' she exclaimed and turned her attentions to the lady in the quaint hat.

At the far side of the huge foyer, a stall had been set up and two women were offering a gift-wrapping service. The four of us had our books beautifully wrapped in red crêpe paper with a pink bow and a Christmas gift tag. The book signing had finally ended when Jilly's Auntie Gwen arrived. A sensible-looking, tweed-clad lady from

Ripon, she apparently played a star role in *Class* and was, the story goes, the only sensible person in the book.

As we walked out of the Queen's Hotel I glanced back at this monumental building with its Portland stone façade and admired its Victorian grandeur. We hurried across a zebra crossing into Leeds City Square, towards the magnificent piazza and its huge centrepiece, the majestic 1903 statue of the Black Prince on horseback. Then we strode out towards the Town Hall, with its stone lions standing guard in timeless repose, and I revelled in being back in the great northern city of my birth. Leeds was teeming with shoppers scurrying here and there under the bright Christmas lights in the grand stores on Briggate and in the magical arcades with their high-quality jewellers' and stationers. This really was a wonderful place for Christmas shopping.

Then we walked up the Headrow towards Lewis's department store. The Christmas window displays were, as always, quite splendid. A large banner, lit up with fairy lights, beckoned us in to 'Meet Father Christmas in his *Wind in the Willows* grotto and toy fair on the third floor'.

We stopped in the entrance and surveyed the scene. 'So, what's the plan?' asked John nervously. Everywhere we looked, confident women shoppers were walking purposefully around the store.

'Why don't we split up into pairs?' said Dan. 'I'll go with Colin. It shouldn't take more than half an hour to buy one or two gifts and then we can have a pint.' Dan was rapidly becoming a New Age Eighties-man.

'OK,' I said, looking up at the huge sign at the foot of

the escalator. 'So let's meet at Santa's grotto,' I said. 'We should be able to find that easily.'

So, with our matching parcels under our arms, we set off somewhat irresolutely to seek the Christmas present of our partners' dreams.

'This looks good,' said John, picking up a 'Make-your-own-handbag kit'.

'No, John,' I said. 'It's not romantic enough.'

'Well, how about one of these?' He pointed to a Steadfast Screwmaster ratchet screwdriver. 'For when she needs one when I'm out at Camera Club,' said John earnestly.

I began to realize why Dan had picked Colin as his shopping partner. Finally, I gave up when he said, 'How about some Bonjela? She gets mouth ulcers occasionally and . . . there's a really good book on woodcarving I've seen.'

Meanwhile, the other intrepid duo was doing well. The poster in the cosmetics department proclaimed that 'the new range of Perlier skin products nourish and protect your skin with pure honey and virgin bees' wax'.

'I wonder how they know the bees are virgins,' said Colin with a smile.

An assistant who smelt like a perfume factory held up jars of moisturizing cream, cleansing lotion and skin toner. 'With Perlier skin products you can enjoy the feel and look of natural beauty,' she recited.

'I'll take one of each,' said Dan confidently.

He picked up his bag of cosmetics and turned through

three hundred and sixty degrees. At six-feet-four-inches tall he could see every display of products.

'Come on, Colin, I've spotted just the thing for you.'

Colin looked thoughtfully at the hair-styling brush and blow-dryer. On the box it claimed: 'The way to beautiful hair can be yours with this hot styler.'

'I'll take this. She's always fiddling with her hair,' said Colin knowingly to the assistant, who gave him a fixed smile but kept her thoughts to herself.

I was beginning to despair. John was standing under a sign, PUT GRASS CUTTINGS IN THEIR PLACE – IN THE GRASS BOX, and staring lovingly at a Mountfield Vacuum-flo lawnmower, winner of the Special Garden Machinery Award 1980. 'Isn't she a beauty?' he said. 'I wonder—'

'No, John,' I said hurriedly and steered him to a cosmetics counter. 'How about this?' I said. The label read: 'With '*Crème Progrès de Lancôme, Paris*, retain that healthy and glowing look for longer.'

John stroked his curly beard with his huge wood-carver's hands and nodded.

'Anne would be really impressed,' I said imploringly.

After a while he relented. 'OK, Jack, but I think I'll get that ratchet screwdriver as well . . . It'll come in handy.'

I bought some cosmetics as well for Beth and then browsed around the record department. I selected the LP record 'Moments', featuring a few of Beth's favourites including Cliff Richard's 'Miss You Nights', Peter Sarstedt's 'Where Do You Go to My Lovely' and David Soul's 'Let's Have a Quiet Night In'.

Then, feeling pleased with our purchases, we went up the escalator to find Santa's grotto.

The familiar *Wind in the Willows* characters, including the mild-mannered Mole, relaxed Ratty, conceited Mr Toad and the gruff Mr Badger, were all in costume. They were surrounded by an assorted cast of extras comprising little girls from the local dancing school dressed as otters, weasels, stoats and foxes.

At the back of the grotto Dan and Colin were waiting next to a semicircle of picket fencing that divided the shoppers from an open shed covered in fake polystyrene snow.

'How's it gone?' asked Dan.

'Fine,' I said. John held up his new screwdriver. 'Well, apart from that.'

Colin looked at it appreciatively. 'Nice screwdriver, John.'

We piled our Jilly Cooper novels on a table just inside the fencing and then gathered round our carrier bags. Instantly we became a mutual appreciation society.

'Perfect,' said Dan, admiring John's cosmetics.

'Excellent,' I said, fully appreciating the superior merits of Colin's hair styler.

'Have we finished?' said John plaintively. 'I fancy a pint.'

'Good idea,' said Colin, 'and I know a great William Younger's pub in Briggate.'

We picked up our carrier bags and headed for the escalator.

Outside, we crossed the Headrow, walked down

Briggate and were soon enjoying a pint of excellent beer.

'Sally will like the tongs,' I said, supping contentedly.

'And the Jilly Cooper book,' said Dan draining the dregs. 'Who's for another?'

'Bloody hell!' said Colin. He looked around at our carrier bags. 'We've left the books behind!'

'You're right,' I said. 'On the table next to Santa's grotto.'

'Come on,' said Dan and we rushed out.

Under a large wooden sign that read SANTA'S WORKSHOP stood two bored-looking women dressed as fairies, listlessly wrapping presents. One fairy was short and plump and the other tall and skinny. They looked to be in their twenties and were dressed in sparkly one-piece white bathing costumes, white tights, pink ballet shoes and cheap tiaras. Their cardboard wings had been painted with matt emulsion but not sufficiently well to cover up the words THIS WAY UP.

'Excuse me,' I said. 'We've lost our presents.'

The little plump fairy looked up in disbelief. 'You tryin' t'pull my ding-a-ling?' she said.

'No,' said Dan. 'We all put a present on this table and now they've gone.'

The tall skinny one looked at Dan adoringly. 'Ah've not seen you round 'ere before. Ah'm Tracy an' ah get off at five.'

'An' ah'm Sharon an' so do I.'

Both of them looked at Dan as if he was a Greek god.

'So can you help us to find them?' I asked.

They were still staring at Dan.

'Where do the presents go when you've wrapped them?' asked Colin.

'We give 'em t'Santa,' said Tracy.

'Yeah – in 'is grotto,' added Sharon.

'How do we get in there?' asked Dan. 'There's no door.'

'Round t'front. Y'll 'ave t'queue,' said Tracy.

'Can you go for us?' asked Colin.

'No. We 'ave t'wrap Santa's bloody presents,' said Sharon.

''Old on,' said Tracy, 'did they 'ave a pink bow on top?'

'Yes, they did,' said Colin.

'Cos we've not got no pink bows, 'ave we, Tracy?' said Sharon.

'Please will you go and find them for us,' implored Dan.

'We'll wrap these presents for you while you're looking,' I pleaded.

'OK,' said Sharon and Tracy and they ran off.

So, for the next five minutes we became Santa's little helpers and struggled to keep straight-faced at the strange looks from the shoppers.

It was a relief when the fairies returned with the four presents still neatly wrapped and labelled and with their pink bows still intact.

'Thank you,' we all said in unison, much relieved.

Then, much to Dan's surprise, the two fairies both stretched up and kissed him.

We beat a hasty retreat and soon we were drinking William Younger's best bitter.

'I don't know why women make a fuss about shopping,' said John.

We all nodded and supped contentedly.

'It's easy if you're organized,' said Colin, with a distinct lack of modesty.

'It went like clockwork,' said Dan.

'And we've all got perfect gifts,' I said.

We all drained our glasses. 'Another?' I said. Everyone nodded, deep in his own thoughts.

'There is one thing,' said Dan. 'I do my sergeant's exams next year.'

'So?' I said.

We all looked at Dan curiously.

'Well . . . y'know . . . being kissed by fairies won't go down well at the station.'

We were still laughing when we got back on the train.

On the journey home Colin and John were poring over an article on how to make perfect mitre joints in Colin's DIY magazine and Dan was studying the football results in the late sports paper and wondering why Kevin Keegan wanted to play for Southampton.

Meanwhile, I took the copy of Jilly Cooper's *Bella* out of my pocket and started to read. After a few minutes I smiled and wondered what Beth might like to do after her Christmas shopping.

Chapter Eight

An Apple for Rudolph

*School closed today for the Christmas holidays with 87
children on roll. On Christmas Eve children from Class 1
and Class 2 will be taking part in the 2.30 p.m. Christmas
Crib service at St Mary's Church.*

Extract from the Ragley School Logbook:
Friday, 19 December 1980

'Would you like some apples, Mr Sheffield?' asked
Prudence Golightly.

It was Christmas Eve morning in Ragley village and I
was in the General Stores & Newsagent. My shopping
bag was weighed down with potatoes, parsnips, carrots,
satsumas, dates and a box of Paxo stuffing . . . but there
was room for a few shiny apples.

'Yes, please,' I said.

Miss Golightly put three in a brown paper bag on the
ancient weighing scales; then, as an afterthought, she

selected a huge bright-red apple. 'And one for Rudolph,' she said with a smile.

On the high shelf behind her, Jeremy, her teddy bear and lifelong friend, was sitting next to a tin of loose-leaf Lyon's tea and an old advertisement for Hudson's soap and Carter's Little Liver Pills. Prudence made all his clothes and, on this festive day, he wore a hand-knitted bobble hat and matching red scarf, with a white shirt, cream hand-knitted cardigan, cord trousers and mint-green wellington boots. 'Good morning, Jeremy,' I said, 'and a happy Christmas, Miss Golightly.' The doorbell jingled as I walked out into the High Street.

On the other side of Ragley village, at 7 School View, eight-year-old Hazel Smith was looking out of her bedroom window and wondering where Santa's sleigh was going to land.

The narrow street on the council estate was crowded with old cars and vans. She stared up at the steep slope of the pantile roof and the tall brick chimney that leant perilously. Then she looked directly below her window and her gaze lingered on her father's wooden outbuilding. Ronnie Smith was proud of his pigeon shed and guarded it fiercely behind a high fence of closely woven chicken-wire. Hazel stared at the large flat roof and smiled. It was perfect for a safe sleigh landing.

Above her bed, Hazel's latest painting was taped to the wall. During the last week of term in Jo Hunter's class, in bright poster colours Hazel had painted Santa's sleigh pulled by his reindeer. She pointed a small dumpy finger at each one in turn and recited slowly the names she had learnt so well: 'Dasher, Dancer, Prancer, Vixen, Comet, Cupid, Donner, Blitzen . . . and Rudolph.' Hazel touched his red nose and then stared out of the window again. Finally, a smile lit up her face. She knew exactly where to put Rudolph's carrot.

In the High Street my breath steamed in front of me and I turned up the hood of my duffel coat and tightened my old college scarf. Cold as iron, still as stone, Ragley village was frozen in its cloak of fresh snow. Slanting grey wisps of wood smoke rose from the cottage chimneys and etched diagonal pathways across a steel-blue sky.

Outside Piercy's Butcher's Shop, the local church choir had begun to gather round a flaming brazier of burning logs. It was traditional for them to sing carols in the village on Christmas Eve morning between ten and eleven o'clock. Any passing villagers were invited to join in and, with frequent breaks for complimentary mince pies and Old Tommy Piercy's famous hot Yorkshire punch, it was always a welcome attraction. The punch was made from a recipe given to Old Tommy by his mother just after the Second World War. The addition of the remains of a bottle of Cointreau, along with liberal doses of brandy and dark rum, ensured the resulting potent concoction had a kick that could be measured on the Richter scale.

Old Tommy staggered out with another steaming pan.

'How are you, Mr Piercy?' I asked.

'Fair t'middlin', young Mr Sheffield,' said Old Tommy.

'That smells good,' I said, sniffing the air appreciatively.

'Then you must 'ave some,' he said, scooping up a generous cupful. 'Y'need t'keep warm.' He nodded towards the frost-covered hedgerows. 'Look at t'berries – it's a sign of 'ard winter t'come.'

I sipped Old Tommy's concoction and, as a fireball hit my stomach, a familiar voice chirped up beside me.

'Hello, Mithter Theffield,' lisped Jimmy Poole, his ginger curls sticking out of his hand-knitted balaclava. 'Thanta's coming to our houthe tonight.'

'And we're going to give 'im some supper,' added his little sister, Jemima.

'Yeth,' agreed Jimmy; 'a minth pie an' a glath of therry, but . . .' he looked anxiously at his mother, 'what about Rudolph?'

I rummaged in my bag and pulled out the large red apple. 'How about giving him this?'

Mrs Poole gave me a knowing smile. 'That's very kind,' she said. 'Say thank you, Jimmy.'

'Thank you, Mither Theffield,' said Jimmy.

Suddenly, Jemima tugged her mother's sleeve. 'Mummy, my teeth are coughing.'

'That's a new one,' I said.

'She means she's got hiccups,' said Mrs Poole with a smile.

'An' I've got a thiny apple,' said Jimmy as they wandered off up the High Street.

'Good morning, Jack.' The Revd Joseph Evans, resplendent in an incongruous bright-red bobble hat, white clerical collar and black duffel coat, waved a greeting. He was encouraging passers-by to pick up a carol sheet and sing with the choir. In the butcher's shop, villagers were queuing for their Christmas turkeys, joints of ham, sausages and streaky bacon. Joseph popped his head round the open doorway. 'Any requests?' he asked.

'A small piece of gammon, please,' croaked ninety-four-year-old Ada Cade, Ragley's oldest inhabitant, fiddling with her hearing aid.

Her daughter Emily gave Joseph a nervous smile. 'Perhaps "Hark the Herald", vicar,' she said.

'Our pleasure,' said Joseph and rejoined the hardy band of members warming themselves round the crackling logs while supping vast quantities of Old Tommy's punch and becoming more inebriated by the minute.

The exception was Joseph's teetotal sister. 'Won't you join us, Mr Sheffield?' said the elegant Vera, handing me a carol sheet. As always she looked immaculate in a stylish checked tweed overcoat from Schofield's in Leeds, with a matching navy-blue knitted scarf and hat and warm leather boots, lined with lambswool.

'Thanks, Vera,' I said. 'I'd love to but I'm not sure I'll add much to your bass section.'

'I rather think they're past caring, Mr Sheffield,' said Vera.

We launched into 'Hark the Herald', 'Once in Royal David's City' and 'We Three Kings'. Villagers paused to throw their spare change into the red plastic bucket that was trimmed in tinsel and propped against the trestle table on which a tray of piping-hot sausage rolls had been placed by Young Tommy Piercy, Old Tommy's strapping nineteen-year-old grandson. Finally, I picked up my shopping and said farewell to the red-nosed choir. 'See you at the crib service,' shouted Joseph. Some of our youngest children from Ragley School were appearing in the nativity play and I had promised I would be there.

My car was in the school car park so I walked up the High Street and round the village green. Every fleur-de-lis on the railings on top of the Yorkshire stone walls that surrounded our playground was rimed with diamond-white crystal and the arched Victorian windows were dusted with frost patterns. In the low morning sunshine, Ragley-on the-Forest Church of England Primary School looked like a Christmas card.

I walked up the cobbled school drive, breathed on my car key to warm it and unlocked my Morris Minor Traveller. After putting my shopping in the back, just for the fun of it I walked across the playground and felt that familiar thrill at making the first footprints in the crisp white snow.

Suddenly, to my surprise, Ruby the caretaker appeared from the entrance porch holding up a broom handle, attached to which was a curved steel blade. She looked like Britannia in a headscarf.

'Morning, Mr Sheffield. Ah've jus' called in for m'snowshifter,' she said. 'Our front path's like the Harctic.'

'Can't your Ronnie do that, Ruby?'

'Y'know what Ronnie's like on Christmas Eve,' she said. ''E spends all day in T'Royal Oak.'

'Oh well, good luck, Ruby,' I said.

She walked off down the drive and, as an afterthought, called out, 'Anyway, our 'Azel's real excited, Mr Sheffield. She can't wait f'Santa an' Rudolph t'come.'

As I drove home to Kirkby Steepleton I peered towards the distant Hambleton Hills. More snow was coming. The landscape was fading now, sky and hills blurred like a child's pastel drawing. A mist, like a cotton-wool shroud, covered the distant fields. Only a tall elm tree pierced the low cloud and, from the perch of its highest branches, a parliament of rooks surveyed their ghostly dominion with unforgiving, beady eyes.

Bilbo Cottage looked welcoming with its holly wreath hanging on the front door. When I walked in, wintry sunshine gleamed on the leaded panes and lit up the hallway in a blaze of light. Beth was spending Christmas with her parents in Hampshire, while I remained in Yorkshire with my regular Christmas visitors: my little Scottish mother, Margaret, and her sister, May.

Aunt May had just finished making her annual cannonade of stuffing balls. 'Ah dinna want t'blow my own crumpet, Margaret,' she said, looking at them in admiration, 'but these are wee beauties.' There was no denying my aunt had her own version of the English language, but it was perfectly understandable.

'Y'nae canna have too much of a good thing,' said my mother.

Where Aunt May's cooking was concerned, she was nothing if not loyal. I looked at the platter of stuffing balls in dismay.

'But they're nae like that Gordon Blue cookery,' said Aunt May modestly.

She was right. It was possible to play two rounds of golf with one of these spherical offerings without ever damaging its rock-like surface.

Suddenly, there was a loud knocking at the front door and Margaret and May scurried from the kitchen to be the first to open it.

'Ah've a Christmas pheasant f'Mr Sheffield.'

I recognized the voice as I walked into the hallway. It was Deke Ramsbottom's. His council snow plough was parked outside.

'Come in out of the cold, Deke,' I said. 'What's this about a Christmas present?' I asked, thinking I had misheard.

To everyone's surprise he held up a huge pheasant by its neck. 'It flew into m'snow plough jus' outside Kirkby an' died,' said Deke by way of explanation. 'It needs plucking,' he added as he passed it to Margaret.

'Ye have come to the right place, laddie,' said my mother gratefully.

'Och aye,' said May. 'Me and Margaret are the queen's knees at plucking pheasants.'

After a lunch of carrot and parsnip soup followed by a slice of Christmas cake with a generous wedge of crumbly Wensleydale cheese, we set off for the Christmas crib service at St Mary's Church. On the way into Ragley I drove into the forecourt of Victor Pratt's garage to fill up with petrol from his single pump.

While it was the season of goodwill, Victor adhered to

a different calendar. He never smiled as he plodded his weary way through life.

'M'pipes are playing up again,' he said mournfully. For a brief moment I wondered if Victor meant his cast-iron heating system in his dilapidated garage or something more personal. 'An' ah think ah've got agoraphobia,' said Victor. 'Ah read abart it in t'*News o' t'World*.'

'I'm sorry to hear that, Victor.'

As we drove away, May looked back at the huge, oil-smeared garage mechanic and shook her head sadly. 'Y'would nae think a great lump of a Sassenach would be frightened o' wee spiders,' she said.

On the Morton Road a crowd of parents and grand-parents were making their way towards St Mary's Church with an assorted collection of tiny shepherds, angels and Roman soldiers. The Christmas Eve crib service was one of the most popular events in the festive calendar and, in the crisp layer of snow, a crushed ribbon of scumbled footsteps wound its way from the church gates to the haven of the entrance porch. The church was filling up quickly.

The Revd Joseph Evans was standing next to the empty straw-covered crib and looking forlornly at a shoebox full of tiny hand-painted clay figures. After being passed from house to house during recent weeks, as was the tradition, Mary and Joseph had arrived back much the worse for wear. Gradually a hush descended as the organist, Elsie Crapper, who had obviously taken her tablets, sat at the organ and played a Valium-sedated and calming version of 'White Christmas'. Next to her a string of coloured lights stretched over the crib and above the nave. Joseph ascended the three steps into the pulpit and pointed a long bony finger at the deserted crib.

'Joseph and Mary have not arrived yet,' he said with an all-knowing look and a beatific smile.

'Why?' shouted Jemima Poole.

'Shush!' whispered Mrs Poole.

'Thuth,' echoed Jimmy. 'You're thupothed to lithen.'

'Why?' repeated Jemima fiercely.

Joseph battled on regardless while, at the foot of the choir stalls, three small and very lively Roman soldiers, all between five and six years old and in full plastic armour, were given a sword in one hand and a large sign on a stick in the other. The signs read ANGELS PLEASE, SHEPHERDS PLEASE and KINGS PLEASE and their job was to walk up the aisle and inform the relevant cast members when it was their turn for stardom.

After a shortened version of 'Little Donkey', two five-year-olds stepped on to the stage block at the front of the nave. Sonia Tricklebank looked the part as a demure Mary and spoke her lines beautifully, while Barry Ollerenshaw, as a reluctant Joseph, had clearly no intention of holding hands with a girl.

'They're bonny wee bairns, May,' whispered Margaret.

'Och aye, Margaret,' said May, nodding in agreement.

'An' the wee lassie, Mary, speaks well.'

'Och aye, Margaret. She must have had electrocution lessons.'

They both sat back wiping tears from their eyes until Angel Gabriel arrived to announce the birth of baby

Jesus. No one commented on the fact that, although she looked beautiful in her coat-hanger halo and white fairy wings, her big rubber wellington boots did rather lessen the overall angelic appearance. After all, outside on the Morton Road, it had begun to snow again.

Then, while we sang the first six verses of 'While Shepherds Watched', seven-year-old Terry Earnshaw, as an unlikely shepherd in a dressing gown and York City football socks, pointed urgently at the tinsel star on top of the Christmas tree and then gave his brother, Heathcliffe, and little sister, Dallas Sue-Ellen, a thumbs-up.

All seemed to be going relatively smoothly until six-year-old Benjamin Roberts announced, 'We bring you gold, Frankenstein and myrrh!' and a bemused Elsie Crapper launched into the first five verses of 'We Three Kings'.

Suddenly, there was confusion at the back of the church. Mrs Buttle had left the kings' presents in her car. Fortunately, Mrs Ackroyd, on the back pew, rummaged in her shopping bag and came up with an instant solution. She thrust three items into the hands of the anxious kings.

So it was that on that snowy Christmas Eve in St Mary's Church, the packed congregation watched the Three Kings present baby Jesus with a jar of pickled gherkins, a tin of Heinz baked beans followed by, appropriately, a box of Setlers indigestion tablets.

We finished with Anne Grainger leading all the little ones in a rendition of 'Silent Night' and then the vicar invited parents and grandparents to take photos.

After the blessing, a closing prayer and a brief hiatus

when the three Roman soldiers began an impromptu sword fight over who should get the blame for opening the final window of the brownies' advent calendar, we all filed into the church hall for mince pies and mulled wine.

'Ah think Jesus were lucky, Mr Sheffield,' said Heathcliffe Earnshaw thoughtfully. "Is dad being a carpenter an' all. 'E could knock up a decent cot an' a playpen an' a few shelves in two shakes of a lamb's tail.'

There was no doubt that the Christmas story had made an impact on the ever-practical Heathcliffe.

It was dark when we came out of church and snow had begun to fall.

Jimmy Poole was standing beside me and pointing upwards. 'Look, Mr Theffield, look!' he exclaimed.

Moving steadily across the vast black sky was a winking red light. 'I can see it, Jimmy,' I said.

'What's that in the sky?' said Jemima.

'It'th Thanta'th thleigh,' said Jimmy.

'But what's that red light?' said Jemima.

'It'th Rudolp'th red nothe,' explained Jimmy with absolute certainty.

Back in Kirkby Steepleton, Margaret and May settled down with a cup of tea to watch *All Star Record Breakers* with Roy Castle and I jumped back in the car to drive to Easington. The spacious cobbled square was a perfect place for a Christmas market and the bright lights of the tall Christmas tree next to the war memorial shone down on the colourful stalls. The market attracted lots of last-minute shoppers from the nearby villages and all the shops around the edge of the square were brightly lit. The Easington town crier in his three-cornered hat and ceremonial frock-coat looked like Gulliver as he rang his bell and chanted, 'Oyez! Oyez! Oyez!'

Suddenly, out of the darkness emerged the huge frame of our local bobby, PC Dan Hunter.

'Hello, Dan,' I said. 'How are you?'

He blew on his cold hands. 'I'm going home for my greatcoat, Jack,' he said. 'It's late duty in Ragley tonight and it looks like being a cold one.'

'Well, good luck . . . and a happy Christmas.'

'You too, Jack,' and he strode off as snow began to fall again.

I bought a bag of roast chestnuts and wandered off to look at the stalls. Over the loudspeaker system, the Christmas number one record, 'There's No One Quite Like Grandma' by the St Winifred's School Choir, was blasting out for the hundredth time and all the adults groaned while the children sang along.

Outside the window of W. H. Smith, a group of girl guides, holding bright lanterns on tall broom handles, sang 'In the Bleak Mid-Winter' and added to the festive spirit. Meanwhile, little Benjamin Roberts was staring in the window at a range of Corgi Matchbox toys. Under the heading 'British at its Best' was a model 3500 Rover police car at £2.65, but, with appropriate patriotism, he finally settled on a model Austin Mini Metro at £1.79 and his mother walked in to buy it. In contrast, Mrs Ackroyd had more modern presents in mind for her children. She bought an Electronic Mastermind for £9.99 and a Space Invaders Breakout game for £19.99 and it occurred to me that Christmas toys had come a long way from the clockwork trains and cowboy cap guns of my boyhood.

An annual treat at the Easington Fayre was Winston Eckersley and his most treasured possession, a 1905 Gasparini street organ. Built in Paris, it had somehow found its way to Holland during the Second World War. It was there that Winston had spotted the street organ of his dreams and he bought it for a few pounds. Riddled with woodworm, it was in a poor state, but for Winston it was a labour of love and he set to in his garden shed to restore it completely. He installed twenty-four new bass pipes and a new rank of violins. Then he decorated it beautifully and it became a feature at all the local village fêtes throughout the Sixties and Seventies, playing the 'Dam Busters March', 'Morning Has Broken', 'Lord of the Dance' and his George Formby selection. Appropriately, on this frosty Christmas Eve, he was playing 'Rudolph the Red-Nosed Reindeer' and the shoppers were singing along.

At the foot of the giant Christmas tree the Easington & District Rotary Club had set up their usual Santa's grotto in a cordoned-off area and parents and children were queuing to enter the magical garden shed lit up with twinkling fairy lights. Members of the Rotary committee, dressed as elves, if slightly ageing and portly ones, collected money for charity in their bright-yellow buckets.

As usual it was doing a roaring trade as excited children took their turns and I leant on the picket fence to watch. Ruby Smith had just come out with Hazel and they gave me a wave. Mrs Poole was next in line with Jimmy and Jemima.

Santa looked up from the article 'Cheap flights to America' in his *Easington Herald & Pioneer* and moved smoothly into role with his new customers.

'Ho, ho, ho,' said Santa, 'and what would you like for Christmas?'

'Ah'd like a Thpit, pleath,' said Jimmy with conviction.

'A spit?' said Santa in surprise.

'Yeth, pleathe,' replied Jimmy.

'You'd like a spit?' asked Santa, looking anxiously at Mrs Poole.

''E means a Spit the Dog puppet, Santa,' she explained. ''E's seen it on telly wi' that ventriloquist.'

Santa recalled seeing Bob Carolgees with his puppet and thought he had a lot to answer for.

'It'll be a friend for Thcargill,' said Jimmy sincerely. Scargill was Jimmy's lively Yorkshire terrier and Jimmy loved him dearly, a feeling not shared by the Ragley postman.

'Well, I'll have to ask my little elves to look in their workshop,' said Santa cautiously.

Mrs Poole nodded and then pushed Jemima forward.

'Ho, ho, ho, and what would you like, little girl?' asked Santa.

'Ah'd like a boyfriend, please, Santa,' said Jemima confidently.

'A boyfriend!' exclaimed Santa.

'Yes, please,' said Jemima politely, 'an' 'ave' y'got any black ones?'

For a moment Santa just stared. He couldn't even muster a 'ho, ho, ho'. Finally he said: 'Pardon?'

'It's for my Barbie doll, Santa,' explained Jemima. 'She's one of t'new black ones an' ah think she'd like a black Action Man.'

'Oh, well . . . I'm, er, sure she would,' stuttered Santa.

It was clear that Barbie and her boyfriend Ken, or the more macho Action Man, were not the main topic of conversation at Rotary Club meetings. However, in 1980 they were the rage among small girls and boys. The little plastic dolls also sported a huge and lucrative range of clothing, including horse-riding gear, pop-star costumes, outfits for the beach, office and party wear. The versatile Action Man could also perform over fifty different military activities, while Ken, in his smart sports jacket and open-top car, merely looked the perfect boyfriend.

'I'll tell my elves to look in their toy factory,' said Santa guardedly.

Mrs Poole nodded again and smiled at him. 'Thank you, Santa,' she said, 'an' we'll leave a mince pie and a glass of sherry in t'usual place f'you tonight.'

'Ho, ho, ho, and thank you,' said Santa.

'An', Thanta,' said Jimmy, 'Hazel Thmith hath left an apple f'Rudolph.'

Outside, in the marketplace, Mrs Poole crouched down and looked at Jimmy curiously. 'Ah thought *you* were leaving an apple f'Rudolph, Jimmy,' she said.

'No, Mam,' said Jimmy. 'Ah thwapped it with Hazel Thmith for a carrot.'

Mrs Poole stood up and scanned the market square. Five minutes later she was whispering something in Ruby Smith's ear.

At ten o'clock whirling snowflakes pattered against Hazel Smith's bedroom window. Though still excited, she was close to falling asleep.

"E won't come if y'stay awake,' whispered Ruby as she tucked her in.

'OK, Mam,' murmured Hazel with a big yawn, 'an' 'ave y'left Santa 'is mince pie?'

'Yes luv,' said Ruby with a smile.

'An' 'is sherry?'

'Yes, luv,' repeated Ruby and gave her a goodnight kiss.

'An' don't worry, Mam, ah've left Rudolph 'is apple.'

Ruby stopped in the doorway and turned. She'd forgotten the apple. 'Oh . . . an' where did y'leave that, luv?' she asked hesitantly.

'Out o' t'window, Mam,' and with a final yawn she fell asleep.

Ruby crept over to the window, peered through the curtains and her eyes widened in surprise. There below her, right in the centre of the roof of Ronnie's shed, was a large apple.

'Oh, bloomin' 'eck,' muttered Ruby.

In Bilbo Cottage, Margaret and May, in matching tartan dressing gowns, kissed me goodnight and picked up their mugs of Horlicks. I pulled on my duffel coat, scarf and gloves ready for the journey to St Mary's Church and midnight mass. The service was due to start at half past eleven and it was always a very special occasion in the local village calendar.

'Dinna y'go skidd'ng in that car o' yours,' said Margaret. 'Stay alert.'

'Nae fear, Margaret,' said May, 'your Jack's always had guid reflections.'

The journey on the back road into Ragley was silent and eerie. Flakes of snow drifted weightlessly in the sharp glare of the headlights and the moonlight lit up the snow-covered trees. As I drove up the High Street, to my surprise I saw Ruby the caretaker and PC Dan Hunter walking across the village green from the council estate. They were each carrying a wooden ladder.

I pulled up, wound down my window and waved at Ruby, while Dan stacked the ladders in the back yard of The Royal Oak. 'Everything all right, Ruby?' I shouted.

'Yes, thank you, Mr Sheffield,' replied Ruby. 'I 'ad a problem but it's been sorted, thanks to that nice young PC 'Unter.'

'OK, well . . . merry Christmas, Ruby.'

'And t'you, Mr Sheffield,' and she hurried off back home.

Dan reappeared, gave us both a wave and climbed back into the warmth of his little grey van. Puzzled, I drove off.

Whirling snowflakes pattered against the giant door of St Mary's Church as I walked in. Soon all the pews were filled and, in spite of the late hour, excitement crackled like electricity. The wide ledges of the stone pillars were all trimmed with glossy green holly, bright with red berries, and on each ledge a candle flickered.

'Away in a Manger' was being played very softly on the organ and then, at half past eleven, the church bells stopped ringing, the ancient door was closed and quiet descended on the congregation like a soft blanket. Mary McIntyre, the leader of the choir and the most wonderful soprano, sang the first verse of 'Once in Royal David's City' and the choir entered, each member carrying a candle.

Gradually, our little village church was filled with music. I looked around me and thought how good it was to be part of a Yorkshire Christmas. Farmers with lusty baritone voices complemented the sweet singing of the ladies of the Ragley and Morton Women's Institute. It was a wonderful service but around me, on this occasion, there were only adults. The children were tucked up in bed . . . all except one.

Hazel Smith woke up, rubbed her sleepy eyes and tip-toed to the window. She peered down at the roof of the shed and smiled. The apple was still there but something had happened . . . something very special.

In the crisp white snow were two deep parallel grooves that began at the edge of the roof and ended abruptly in front of the apple. Santa's sleigh had landed exactly where Hazel thought it would. Then she stared at the apple, from which a huge bite had been taken.

After all, thought Hazel as she got back into bed and closed her eyes, *Rudolph has big teeth*.

Chapter Nine

The Barnsley Ferret-Legger

County Hall requested early attention to the annual Form 7 giving details of anticipated admission numbers for 1981. The Governing Body gave permission for 30 school chairs to be lent to the Village Hall Committee prior to the performance of Jack and the Beanstalk *by the Ragley Amateur Dramatic Society on New Year's Eve.*

Extract from the Ragley School Logbook:
Tuesday, 30 December 1980

"E's a martyr to 'is ferrets is Uncle Kingsley,' said Timothy Pratt.

'Really?' I said, but my thoughts were elsewhere. I put a tin of Crown matt white emulsion paint on the counter of Pratt's Hardware Emporium. 'So who's Kingsley?'

'M'uncle, Mr Sheffield. 'E's from Grimethorpe an' 'e's coming this afternoon with 'is ferrets f'New Year. An' he's gonna 'elp me with t'lights for t'panto.'

'Oh, yes,' I mumbled as I rummaged in my pocket for a

pound note. 'Well, I expect I'll see you in the village hall, Timothy. I'm helping Peter Miles-Humphreys paint the scenery.' It was the morning of New Year's Eve and another Ragley pantomime was in store. The local Amateur Dramatic Society were about to put their own personal stamp on the familiar tale of *Jack and the Beanstalk*.

Timothy handed me my change. 'Well, ah'll see y'later, Mr Sheffield.'

I stopped in the doorway as a thought struck me. 'Timothy, did you say you have an uncle called Kingsley who breeds ferrets?'

'Jus' Simone an' Garfunkle.'

'Simon and Garfunkle?'

'No, Mr Sheffield, it's *Simone*. She's a girl ferret,' explained Timothy. 'Uncle Kingsley called 'em Simon an' Garfunkle an' then 'e found out one of 'em were a girl.'

'Oh, I see,' I said. I opened the door and the bell jingled madly.

'Mr Sheffield,' Timothy called after me, 'ah'll introduce you t'Uncle Kingsley. 'E's a clever man, bright as a button, an' 'e got a scholarship when 'e were a lad. In our family 'e's definitely the most intelligent Pratt.'

I shook my head in wonderment and walked out into the freezing High Street. Stan Coe's mud-splattered Land-Rover was parked across the road, outside the village hall. A burly figure I didn't recognize was in the passenger seat and his sister, Deirdre Coe, was glaring at me through the rear window.

Stan wound down his window and shouted, 'Judgement Day, Sheffield. Y'won't be so 'igh an' mighty when y'school is shut down.' He dropped off his passengers and roared off down the High Street and back to his farm.

I had hoped my problems with Stan Coe would have gone by now and I knew he would be pleased to hear about the news of the possible closure of our school. Ever since he was removed from the school governors in my first year as headteacher, he had continued a vendetta against me. I was saddened by his vindictiveness and ignored him as I wedged the tin of paint in the boot of my car behind my tool-box and petrol can.

'Well, if looks could kill . . .' said a familiar voice. It was Ruby, a warm scarf wrapped round her headscarf and her cheeks rosy-red in the cold. 'A reight pair, Mr Sheffield, an' up t'no good, ah'll warrant. One day ah'll give that Deirdre Coe a piece o' my mind,' said Ruby.

I followed her gaze. Across the High Street, Deirdre Coe was deep in conversation with a heavily built man who looked like a younger version of Stan Coe, the landowner and local bully.

'Who's that with Deirdre?' I asked.

'That's 'er little brother, Gerry. 'E's a builder in Thirkby an' another villain. Ah wouldn't trust 'im as far as ah could throw 'im.'

'What's he doing in Ragley I wonder?'

'Haven't you 'eard?' chuckled Ruby. 'Deirdre's been trying f'years t'get a part in t'pantomime an' this year's she's finally got one. She's front end o' t'cow and Gerry's 'ad 'is arm twisted t'be t'back end.'

'Should be worth seeing, Ruby,' I said with a grin.

'Y'reight there, Mr Sheffield, an' ah'll be there wi' Ronnie on t'front row as usual. But ah'll tell y'summat, we won't be clapping *'er.'* And with that she hurried off towards the General Stores.

Meanwhile, Diane's Hair Salon was still and quiet. Diane Wigglesworth had reserved a special morning appointment for her friend and next-door neighbour, Nora Pratt. She knew Nora wanted to look like a film star on the biggest night of her year.

'So who's it gonna be this year, Nora? Another one o' them Charlie's Angels?'

'No, ah'm fed up wi' Fawwer Fawcett,' said Nora. She pointed to a photograph in the *Radio Times*. ''Ow about Julie Chwistie?'

'No problem,' said Diane. For her, achieving the impossible with the ladies of Ragley village, plus a few of the more adventurous young men, was a daily challenge. However, with her state-of-the-art accelerator that cut down drying time for highlights, along with her new range of Silver Minx and Deep Slate setting lotions, she oozed confidence. Even so, while most of her customers wanted to be New Age Eighties women, Diane knew that some of her traditional procedures would stay with her for ever. So, as usual, she sprayed Yorkshire Pale Ale on Nora's hair as a setting lotion before attaching her outsize plastic rollers and then wheeling out the ancient hair dryer.

In the reassuring cocoon of her little private world, Nora relaxed under the blast of the dryer and began to rehearse her songs. 'Ah'm dweaming of a white Chwistmas,' she sang as Diane, with a sympathetic smile on her face, swept the floor for the last time in 1980.

*   *   *

Big Dave Robinson and Little Malcolm had just parked their refuse wagon outside Nora's Coffee Shop and they both gave me a cheery wave.

'Fine morning, Mr Sheffield,' shouted Big Dave cheerily.

'Good morning, Dave. 'Morning, Malcolm,' I replied.

'Time for our 'ot drink,' said Little Malcolm, striding quickly towards the door of the Coffee Shop. It sounded a good idea and a better prospect than painting Dame Trott's pantomime kitchen.

When I walked into Nora's Coffee Shop, 'There's No One Quite Like Grandma' was drowning out the hubbub of conversation, for, I hoped, the last time. Little Malcolm was waiting patiently at the counter.

Dorothy emerged from the back room and sat on the high stool behind the counter. As she began to flick through a magazine she fluttered her eyelashes at the love of her life. 'Oh, 'ullo, Malcolm.'

''Ullo, Dorothy,' said Little Malcolm, his cheeks reddening. ''Ow's it going?'

'Bit fed up wi' this record, Malcolm,' she said, glancing over at the chrome and red juke-box. 'Ah reckon John Lennon should 'ave been number one wi' "Starting Over". Terrible shame t'poor man got shot.'

'Y'reight there, Dorothy,' said Little Malcolm sadly.

'Ah loved them Beatles,' said Dorothy.

'So did I,' echoed Little Malcolm.

He had that pain in his chest again. In the *News of the World* it said that it was because (a) he didn't exercise enough, or that (b) he had indigestion, or (c) he could be in love. As Little Malcolm was built like a weight-lifter after hefting heavy bags of rubbish all week and had the constitution of an ox, he reckoned it was likely to be the latter. He looked up into Dorothy's eyes and wondered why they always looked so perfect. Then a loud voice jerked him from the pleasant image that was forming in his mind's eye.

'C'mon, Casanova,' shouted Big Dave gruffly as he sat down at a nearby table. ''Urry up an' get teas in.'

As Dorothy poured two large mugs of tea and heaped three spoonfuls of sugar into each, Nora walked in sporting her Julie Christie look, which had been already severely ruffled by the stiff breeze on the High Street.

'Nice 'air-do, Nora,' said Dorothy, glancing up. 'Ah like Kate Bush.'

Nora gave her a lofty look and went to hang up her coat. I took a deep breath and attempted to engage Dorothy in conversation. This was always a journey into the unknown.

'So, good morning, Dorothy. Have you got any plans for the holiday?' I asked politely.

'Ah'm gonna watch that film tomorrow night wi' Malcolm, at 'alf pas' six on ITV, Mr Sheffield,' recited Dorothy. 'It's *Doctor Chicago* – 'bout them Russians in love. We're looking forward to it, aren't we, Malcolm?'

Little Malcolm blushed furiously while Big Dave gave him his famous big-girl's-blouse look, perfected since his diminutive cousin had started his incongruous relationship with the five-foot-eleven-inch would-be fashion model.

Nora Pratt, stacking a pyramid of two-day-old chocolate

éclairs at the other end of the counter, was still smarting from the Kate Bush comment. 'It's not *Chicago*, Dowothy, it's *Zhivago*,' she said, 'wi' that 'andsome Omar Shawif and that weally beautiful Julie Chwistie.'

It occurred to me that this was a good idea for the first evening of 1981. Beth Henderson together with David Lean's superb production of the epic Russian love story sounded a great combination.

'It's a wonderful film, Nora,' I agreed.

'Ah love a good womance,' said Nora. 'Ah wemember when ah went t'see *The King and I* with Yul Bwynner.'

'Did you?' said Dorothy. 'Ah went wi' Madge from t'Co-op.'

Not for the first time, Nora wondered what went on in the alternative universe inhabited by her well-meaning but strangely vacant Coffee Shop assistant.

As I waited for my frothy coffee, I opened my copy of *The Times*. The headline 'New Year's Honours List ignores British medal winners in Moscow Olympic Games' reflected the government's attitude to their official appeal not to compete being ignored by the athletes. Meanwhile, Robin Day, the popular television journalist and interviewer, was given a knighthood.

I shared a table with Ragley's favourite bin men, drank my coffee, picked up my newspaper and said my good-byes.

'Well, good luck tonight, Nora,' I said. 'It's time for me to paint some more scenery.'

Nora glanced up at the clock. 'Oh dear, ah'll 'ave t'wush. Ah've jus' wemembered, ah've got to pwactise "White Chwistmas". It was wubbish at the wehearsal.'

She rushed upstairs and Dorothy stared after her, looked up at the huge poster of *Jack and the Beanstalk*, shook her head and returned with a secret smile to her *Smash Hits* magazine and a full-page picture of David Essex.

Meanwhile, Ruby had followed Deirdre Coe into Piercy's Butcher's Shop. 'Now then, Mr Piercy,' said Deirdre in a loud voice, 'ah want two big pork pies f'me an' our Gerry. We've gorra keep us strength up for t'dress rehearsal this afternoon.'

'So is Gerry one o' them actor-types, then?' asked Old Tommy, while Young Tommy reached for two family-size pork pies from the front-window display.

''E's allus 'ad a touch o' t'thespian about 'im, 'as our Gerry,' said Deirdre pompously. 'My Uncle Albert, who worked be'ind t'scenes at t'Theatre Royal in York, allus said thespianism runs in t'family.'

Ruby was confused and wondered how Gerald Coe could be a thespian. She thought thespians were women who sat together on the back row of the Odeon cinema on Saturday nights and held hands when the film started.

When I walked into the village hall with my tin of paint and a four-inch paintbrush, Felicity Miles-Humphreys, the producer, in her flowing black kaftan and scarlet bandanna, was having problems with her beanstalk.

'Higher, please, darling,' screeched Felicity. 'The beanstalk simply must be taller than the giant.'

Her long-suffering husband, Peter, the bank clerk with

the unfortunate stutter, cast a nervous glance in her direction and winced visibly.

'OK, F-F-Felicity,' said Peter, 'I'll t-t-tie it to the c-c-c . . .'

'Cloud,' added Nigel, his thirteen-year-old son who was adept at finishing his incomplete sentences.

Felicity's elder son, twenty-year-old Rupert, who had always got the starring male role since she had been artistic director, was staring in a full-length mirror and making minute adjustments to his hair. He'd used a mixture of sugar and water to make it stand up in spikes.

'That's wonderful, darling,' said Felicity. 'It did need that active and dynamic-with-a-hint-of-surprised look.'

Rupert put a hand to his fevered brow in an artistic pose and sighed with relief. He was completely unaware that his mother secretly believed her gangling son, with the sparrow legs and never-ending acne, looked as if he'd just been electrocuted.

I had just finished whitewashing Dame Trott's kitchen, or, to be more precise, a sheet of eight-by-four hardboard, when Timothy Pratt walked in with a lean, wiry man wearing a flat cap and the baggiest three-piece suit I had ever seen. He looked as if he'd just called in from a P. G. Wodehouse grouse-shooting party. Tidy Tim was carrying a step-ladder and his highly polished metal tool-box in order to do the lights for the pantomime.

'This is Mr Sheffield,' said Timothy, 'our 'eadteacher ah were telling you about.'

Kingsley removed his flat cap and gently put down his wooden cage containing two excited ferrets. 'Ah'm

Kingsley an' this is Simone an' Garfunkle,' he said. 'Ah never go nowhere wi'out 'em.'

We shook hands. 'Pleased to meet you,' I said, 'and . . . hello to you too,' I added, glancing down at the ferrets. They looked at me as if I was their next meal.

'Ah've 'eard good things abart thee from our Timothy, Mr Sheffield,' he said. He put a finger and thumb into the pocket of his thick tweed waistcoat. ''Ere's my card.'

Surprised, I took the unusual business card from his gnarled hand. It was one of those produced on a printing machine at the railway station. It read 'Kingsley Pratt, C.I.D.'

'C.I.D?'

'That's reight, Mr Sheffield. Stands f'Confidential Information Destruction.'

'Oh, what does that mean?' I asked.

'Ah tear up waste paper an' tek it t'tip in Grimethorpe,' said Kingsley.

At lunchtime I took a break from painting and called into The Royal Oak and ordered a half of Chestnut and a meat pie. As usual, the taproom was the place where the topics of the day were aired.

'There's that new breakfas' telly,' said Kojak. 'Ah reckon it might catch on.'

'Ah'm not sure,' said Stevie 'Supersub' Coleclough, holding up a copy of the *Yorkshire Evening Post*. The headline read 'Breakfast TV – 3 hours of woe'. 'It says 'ere that fifty-six per cent aren't interested 'cause they 'ave no time t'watch it.'

'Ah'm not surprised,' said Big Dave. 'Ah don't want that David Frost wi' m'cornflakes.'

'Y'reight there, Dave,' said Little Malcolm. ''Cept mebbe if it's Angela Rippon and Anna Ford.'

The football team considered this unexpected addition to the debate.

'That Angela Rippon, she's got lovely legs,' said Sheila from behind the bar. 'An' that Anna Ford's always got a smashing 'air-do,' she added for good measure.

There was a chorus of approval from the village football team as each member grappled with his own personal fantasy of alluring newsreaders. In doing so they reaffirmed the view that men think of sex every eight seconds.

It was during this period of contemplation that Kingsley Pratt walked in. He introduced himself and his ferrets while Don pulled a pint and Sheila selected a pie from the kitchen. Then he put the cage under a table and sat down to talk to the football team.

Sheila looked concerned. 'Ah'm not keen on ferrets in our taproom, Don.'

'They're safe enough,' said Don. ''E's gorrem in a cage.'

'They look evil little buggers t'me,' said Sheila.

'Don't let 'im 'ear y'saying that. 'E sez' 'e's a ferret-legger,' said Don with a sense of awe.

'What's that s'pposed t'be?'

'Dunno, luv, but looking at t'teeth on that one 'e calls Garfunkle ah wouldn't want t'find out.'

'Here y'are,' said Sheila as she served Kingsley with a pork pie and two pickled onions. 'That'll put 'airs on y'chest.'

171

Kingsley picked up one of the pickled onions and studied it as if he was a jeweller examining a flawed diamond. 'Ta, luv,' he said thoughtfully, 'but in Grimethorpe we 'ave pickled onions as big as y'fist.'

We all nodded in acknowledgement at this little-known but very significant fact.

Kingsley soon found a welcome audience and explained that the ancient sport of 'ferret-legging' – namely, popping a ferret down a trouser leg and starting the clock – was his favourite pastime. Generations of Yorkshire miners had done this to thwart unfriendly gamekeepers and Kingsley was keen to keep up the tradition.

Apparently, a certain Mr Reginald Mellor, soldier, steeplejack and miner, had slipped one down his trouser leg while being interviewed by Brian Glover, the Barnsley playwright and actor. Mr Mellor had been disdainful of the pretenders to his crown. According to *The Guinness Book of Records* the longest time for keeping a ferret down your trousers had been recorded at an impressive forty seconds. Mr Mellor claimed his best time was over five hours.

'So are there any rules f'this ferrets-down-yer-trousers stuff?' asked Don as he pulled Kingsley's third pint of Tetley's bitter.

'Tha's got to 'ave rules, tha knaws,' said Kingsley gravely. 'Y'trouser bottoms 'ave t'be tucked into y'socks for a start-off, so t'ferret can run from one leg to t'other.'

'That meks sense,' said Big Dave.

'It does that,' agreed Little Malcolm.

Everyone nodded and winced at the indisputable logic.

'An y'can't use tranquillizers t'mek 'em dozy,' said Kingsley, supping deeply on his pint.

'Ah never thought o' that,' said Shane.

Clint considered this and reflected that no ferret with an ounce of sense would ever dream of biting his psychopathic brother.

'An' y'can't tek 'em y'self t'dull t'pain.'

We all blinked at the thought.

'Ah never thought o' that, neither,' said Shane.

Everyone nodded. It was always wise to agree with Shane, even with a double negative.

'An' they've purra stop t'filing a ferret's teeth t'mek 'em less sharp,' added Kingsley with gravitas.

And for the first time in my life I felt an empathy with ferrets.

On my way out I bumped into Stan Coe. As he weighed sixteen stones I came off worse.

'Watch where y'going, Sheffield,' he said gruffly.

'I usually do, Mr Coe,' I said.

He barred my way, not letting me pass.

'Excuse me, please,' I said.

'Not looking quite so good now f'you, Sheffield,' he said with a brown-toothed leer. 'From what ah 'ear, y'days are numbered.'

'You're mistaken,' I said abruptly and walked away quietly seething.

* * *

The dress rehearsal was a disaster. The beanstalk kept falling down, the giant couldn't see out of his papier-mâché head and Daisy the Cow kept tripping up over her huge dangling udder.

'Ah think ah've put m'back out,' complained Gerald Coe to his red-faced sister as they sat at the side of the stage.

'Shurrup, Gerry,' shouted Deirdre. She looked up at me as I rushed to put the finishing artistic touches to the giant's castle. 'An' soon you'll be laughin' on t'other side o' y'face, Mr 'Eadteacher.'

It was almost six o'clock when I called in for petrol at Victor Pratt's garage. He was just shutting up for the holiday.

'Hello, Victor,' I said. 'I've just met your Kingsley.'

"E's allus been a character 'as Uncle Kingsley,' said Victor.

'Oh, yes?'

"E were kiss o' death, were our Kingsley, during World War Two.'

'Why was that?' I asked.

"E were a Desert Rat . . . Arrived on a Sunday an' captured on Monday.'

'Oh, that's unfortunate,' I said.

'Word 'ad it that t'Germans gave 'im back on Tuesday,' added Victor gloomily. "E were too much bother.'

It concerned me that Victor was always such a pessimist. 'Victor,' I said, 'did you know that optimists live longer?'

'Hmmf . . . serves 'em reight,' muttered Victor and with that he took my ten-pound note and shambled away.

*　　*　　*

Back in the kitchen of Bilbo Cottage, a pleasant surprise awaited me and thoughts of Stan and Deirdre Coe were quickly forgotten. My kitchen, disorganized since the departure of Margaret and May for their Hogmanay in Scotland, sparkled and everything was tidy once again.

'Beth, you're a wonder,' I said.

She looked great in hip-hugging jeans, Chris Evert trainers and a white polo-neck jumper.

I caught the aroma of appetizing food. 'That smells good,' I said.

'There's a casserole in the oven,' she said, drying her hands on her apron. I gave her a kiss and she grinned. 'You need a shower and your spectacles are covered in paint splashes.'

'Can I eat first?' I said.

'Yes, but hurry,' she said glancing at her watch. 'The panto starts in an hour. I'm going to get changed.' She hung her apron on the back of the door, grabbed a Leak & Thorpe carrier bag from the hallway and rushed upstairs.

Beth had visited Coney Street in York during the afternoon and selected a New Year's Eve outfit from the 'Ladies Pride' selection. Apparently, the outfits were all half price with sizes ranging from 12 to 22. I recalled Laura telling me she was a size 12 but I had no idea what it meant in inches. As Beth occasionally swapped dresses with her sister, I guessed Beth must be the same size.

Forty minutes later, well-fed, showered and in my best grey suit with flared trousers and wide lapels, I stood in front of the hallway mirror trying to flatten the palm tree of brown hair on the crown of my head. Beth came downstairs looking stunning in a new light-grey dress with a tight-fitting bodice and a delicate lace choker. She stopped on the bottom step so that we were the same height and I held her in my arms.

'Marry me . . . tonight,' I said.

She smiled, checked her earrings and looked pre-occupied. 'I want to, Jack,' she said softly, 'but not tonight . . . not yet.'

I had learnt from past experience not to push too hard, so I helped her into her long leather coat and waited while she made adjustments to a scarf that exactly matched her green eyes.

The village hall was packed. Ruby was on the front row with a reluctant Ronnie and an excited Hazel. Joseph and Vera were on the third row, as Vera wanted to keep her distance from the 'rowdy element' at the back, namely, the Ragley Rovers football team, and had saved two seats for Beth and myself. Timothy, Victor and Kingsley Pratt had arrived early and secured the three seats close to the door that led backstage. Disconcertingly, Kingsley was on his hands and knees and clearly looking for something.

The pantomime was similar to previous years' with uncoordinated dance routines, the curtains opening during scene changes and occasional shouts of 'Speak up!' from disgruntled members of the audience who wanted value for their fifty-pence tickets. However, the first act was the one destined to be remembered for many years to come. At the last minute, Gerald Coe complained he'd 'put mi back out' and couldn't perform. A reluctant

Stan Coe had been press-ganged into the rear end of the cow by the formidable duo of his sister and Felicity Miles-Humphreys.

So it was that when the character Jack walked on stage with Daisy the Cow he looked puzzled. According to the script, Daisy's only line was 'Moooo'.

'There's summat in yer udder,' came a gruff voice from the back end.

'Shurrup,' hissed the front end.

'It's wriggling abart,' shouted the back end.

'Aaaaghh!' screamed the front end. 'Ah've been bitten! Aaaaghh!'

The audience roared with laughter and Daisy the Cow leapt in the air and ran off the stage. The prompter, Amelia Duff, looked at her script in surprise. It definitely said, '*Daisy – exit stage left.*' However, on this occasion, the front end had exited stage left and the back end stage right.

Suddenly, Kingsley Pratt leapt to his feet. 'Garfunkle, Garfunkle!' he cried and rushed backstage through the side door.

Fortunately normal service was soon resumed, although Jack received five magic beans for a cow that was apparently grazing in a nearby field. In spite of Giant Blunderbuss's head falling off when he attempted to climb the beanstalk, the pantomime limped successfully to its conclusion.

Finally, true to tradition, Nora Pratt was given the biggest round of applause . . . even when she sang 'I Have a Dweam' and the football team on the back row joined in. Like Nora, and much to the amusement of the audience, they sympathetically dropped the letter 'r' from the entire Abba hit record.

Predictably, the Coe family did not return for the traditional New Year's Eve party that immediately followed the pantomime. They left with Gerald holding his aching back, a red-faced Stan carrying a cow costume and Deirdre rubbing a ferret bite on her ample backside.

In complete contrast, life was wonderful once again for the ferret-legger from Grimethorpe. Garfunkle, his prodigal ferret, had returned. After escaping from his cage just before the performance he had found a comfortable hiding place in Daisy's udder. The rest of the story was already part of Ragley folklore.

At midnight, when Clint Ramsbottom tuned in his ghetto blaster to the chimes of Big Ben and balloons fell from the football goal nets attached to the ceiling, I held Beth in my arms. Around us a curious group gathered to sing 'Auld Lang Syne'. It comprised Anne and John Grainger, Jo and Dan Hunter, Vera and Joseph Evans, the complete Pratt family, and, thankfully secure in their cage, two ferrets by the name of Simone and Garfunkle.

It was easy to tell which was which: Garfunkle was the one with a piece of Deirdre Coe's knickers in its teeth!

Chapter Ten

New Brooms

*Miss Valerie Flint, supply teacher, will take over from
Tuesday, 6 January, as full-time teacher in Class 3 during
Mrs Pringle's maternity leave. A new telephone will be
installed this week in the school office with an extension in
the staff-room.*

Extract from the Ragley School Logbook:
Monday, 5 January 1981

Wood smoke hung over Ragley village like a pallbearer's
overcoat. Black and heavy, it tumbled over the pantile
roofs. The Clean Air Act of 1956, following the Great
Smog of 1952, had not yet been adopted by the villagers
of Ragley. They preferred burning logs to smokeless fuel
and Deke Ramsbottom dropped off another trailer load
at the General Stores.

I sat at my desk, filled my fountain pen with Quink ink
and shivered. Above my head, a mosaic of frost patterns
etched the windows of the school office in their Victorian

179

casements. Outside, the winter earth was frozen and no life or sound penetrated its hardness. Nature was gripped in an iron fist and the villagers of Ragley huddled round their log fires.

I took the school logbook from my bottom drawer, opened it to the next clean page and wrote the date, Monday, 5 January. The record for 1981 in the history of Ragley-on-the-Forest Church of England Primary School had begun.

It was early morning on the day before the start of the spring term. I leant back in my creaking leather-covered wooden chair and stared across the room at the neat rows of framed photographs on the office wall, mostly black and white but more recently in a colour fixative that, sadly, appeared to be fast-fading. My predecessor, John Pruett, had begun the collection in 1946 when he became headteacher and I had continued the tradition. So it was that, each year, all the pupils and teachers of Ragley School gathered in front of the entrance porch and were all captured at a moment in time – their time.

Now it was my turn to do my best for our village school. I didn't want to be the headteacher who closed the school gates for the last time. The signs were not promising. Another letter had arrived from County Hall, informing me that a decision about the future of Ragley School would be considered by the Education Committee during the coming months. The word 'considered' rattled round my tired brain. The letter was signed by Miss Barrington-Huntley but on this occasion there was no personal postscript to lighten the import of the message. I guessed Beth had received the same letter.

Also, there was another pile of mail requesting information about our scheme of work for reading and writing. Some form of common curriculum for the nation's schools appeared inevitable. As I pondered the outcome, suddenly the telephone on my desk rang. It was my first call of 1981 and I wondered who it could be on this bleak morning. I was surprised . . . the voice sounded almost hysterical.

'If y'don't 'urry up, on your 'ead be it.'

'Who's speaking, please?' I asked.

'Y'know very well who's speaking.' She had a high-pitched voice that sounded vaguely familiar. 'Are y'comin' t'clean my chimney or not?'

'Chimney?' I asked. 'What chimney?'

'*My* bloody chimney, y'soft ha'porth,' she screamed. Suddenly she started coughing. 'Oh no, there's soot everywhere! If y'not 'ere in five minutes, ah'll get a proper chimney-sweep.'

With that she rang off and I put down the receiver. It was clearly a wrong number. Then, still a little confused, I picked up my pen and began to write, 'Miss Valerie Flint, supply teacher, will take over from Tuesday, 6 January, as full-time teacher in Class 3 during Mrs Pringle's maternity leave.'

I sat back and stared at the page. Ragley School wouldn't be the same without Sally. Times were changing.

By mid-morning I recalled a piece of advice given to me by John Pruett when I had started at Ragley. He said, 'Remember to *walk the job*, Jack. Don't get bogged down in your office.' All the teachers were in their classrooms, mounting displays of work and tidying cupboards, so I decided to see how they were getting on.

I began in Sally's classroom, except now a new label had been pinned on the door. It read: 'Miss V. Flint'.

Valerie Flint was an imposing figure and renowned for her excellent classroom management and strict but fair discipline. We were clearly fortunate to get such a 'safe pair of hands' to take charge of Sally's eight- and nine-year-olds. When I walked in, Valerie was setting up a fish tank on Sally's nature table.

'Oh, good morning, Jack,' she said with a confident smile.

'Hello, Valerie,' I said. 'Can I help?'

'No, it's fine, thanks. I'm just preparing a new home for Tarzan and Jane.'

'Tarzan and Jane?'

'My goldfish, Jack. I thought they would add some interest to my nature table.'

My nature table . . . There had been a subtle shift of power.

To her credit, Sally, now eight months pregnant, had come in to help. "Morning, Jack,' she said cheerfully. She was at the sink, washing paint palettes and bristle-haired brushes. Her face was flushed with the effort.

'Let me help,' I said.

She grinned. 'I'm not an invalid – just pregnant.' She patted her tummy and Valerie Flint gave her a wistful glance. 'I thought I'd help Valerie get off to a good start.'

'Thanks, Sally,' I said, 'but do be careful.'

'I keep telling her the same,' said Valerie, looking concerned.

I decided to leave them to it. The classroom looked different already – tidy and well organized. 'I'll put the heater on in the staff-room,' I said. 'We could meet for coffee at half past ten.'

'Vera will probably prepare it,' said Valerie. 'She phoned me this morning.'

I recalled that Vera and Valerie were both long-standing members of the Women's Institute, so I presumed they knew each other well. I looked back at Valerie as she confidently introduced Tarzan and Jane to their new home. At six feet tall, she had been an outstanding netball player in her younger days and, although now in her late fifties, she cut a slim, elegant figure in a beautifully tailored trouser suit, her favoured style of dress. While the traditional Vera still frowned at female staff wearing trousers, Miss Flint had become a firm ally on my first day at Ragley when I dismissed this particular outdated restriction on female clothing upheld by my predecessor.

Next door, Jo looked relaxed in her classroom and had just finished making an anemometer out of wooden off-cuts and four plastic beakers. 'Hi, Jack. What do you think?' she said, proudly spinning it round like a horizontal windmill.

'Brilliant!' I said and then looked around her classroom. It was like walking into the Science Museum. Jo's displays were always full of interest with their magnets, prisms and pulley systems.

Then I wandered across the school hall and into Anne's reception class. She was on her hands and knees in the Home Corner, trying to repair the mini-kitchen. The cooker door had fallen off. 'Hello, Jack. I knew John's

Christmas present would come in handy,' she said with a wry grin and a final twist of her ratchet screwdriver. 'I've seen the letter from Miss High-and-Mighty from County Hall, by the way.' She stood up and closed the classroom door. 'Jack,' she said quietly, 'I read in the *Pioneer* that possibly four out of the seventeen village schools in this area could close.' She looked around her bright and busy classroom, a world of sand trays, Plasticine and powder paint. 'It would be sad to lose all this.'

I recalled Beth's words, 'You're *vulnerable*.'

'You know I'll do everything I can,' I said.

Anne nodded. 'I know you will, Jack.' She gathered her brown hair into a pony-tail at the nape of her neck and, with a practised twist, attached an elastic toggle. There were a few grey hairs I hadn't noticed before.

At half past ten, like creatures of habit, we all gathered in the staff-room. The heater was on full-blast and Vera served mugs of piping-hot milky coffee and the remains of her Christmas cake. Everyone had read the latest 'school closure' letter on the noticeboard but we had all decided to press on regardless. I looked around the staff-room and realized how lucky I was to have such a dedicated team, none more so than the incomparable Vera, without whom I would be lost.

Anne and Vera were deep in conversation, checking a note to parents requesting that they write their child's name clearly inside their wellington boots. Vera had also suggested we ask for any old wallpaper books, as our communal stock cupboard was now devoid of A3 sugar paper for the children's painting lessons. Anne had reckoned that, following recent cuts in school expenditure, our capitation was now nine pence per child per day. However, she had chosen not to mention this to Vera, who was delighted that Mrs Thatcher was firmly in charge of the nation's handbag.

I recalled that Jim Callaghan had used the word 'accountability' in relation to schools in a speech in 1976 but it was Mrs Thatcher who had reinforced the value-for-money theme.

Meanwhile, Jo was admiring Sally's new Sony Walkman. Two million had been sold in the previous year and Sally was now playing classical music via her headphones to her unborn child. Valerie was peering with gimlet eyes over her half-moon spectacles at the list of after-school clubs for the new term. With great deliberation she added her name and slowly I was coming to realize that, while losing Sally was a blow, Valerie was bringing a new impetus to our work that I hadn't anticipated. The list read:

> Country Dancing, Choir (AG)
> Netball, Science (JH)
> Football, Chess (JS)
> Recorder, Pottery (VF)

'I'm afraid I can't do Sally's guitar club, Jack,' said Valerie, 'so I thought Pottery might be interesting and I can get the children's claywork fired in the kiln at the comprehensive school.'

'Thanks, Valerie,' I said. I was impressed – and even more so with Valerie's next offer.

She came to sit beside me and put a few photographs on the coffee-table. 'Have a look at these, everybody. I know of an excellent place in the Yorkshire Dales to take a party of children,' she said, and we all gathered round.

'It's that lovely village they use in the television series *All Creatures Great and Small*,' said Anne in surprise.

'Darrowby?' said Jo quizzically.

'Yes, but it's really Askrigg,' said Sally. 'It's a lovely place. Colin and I drove through it on our way to Aysgarth Falls last summer.'

'That's right,' said Valerie, pointing to a photograph of a large building, 'and this is a mill conversion called Askrigg Low Mill Residential Youth Centre. I went there when I did supply teaching at Easington Primary. I could write to them for details, if you like.'

'Thanks, Valerie,' I said. 'A wonderful idea. Please do.'

When everyone returned to their classrooms, Vera collected the mugs and cake plates and smiled up at me. 'New brooms, Mr Sheffield . . . new brooms.'

I stayed late at school and gusting snow smoothed the cobbles of the school drive when I eventually clambered into my frozen car. The welcoming bright-orange lights of The Royal Oak together with the promise of warm food on such a bitterly cold night made an attractive proposition.

For once, the conversation in the taproom wasn't about football, sex or beer. In the news that morning, Sweden had become the first country to legislate against aerosol sprays on the grounds that they harm the atmosphere.

Stevie 'Supersub' Coleclough raised the topic. 'They're banning aerosol sprays in Sweden,' he said.

The rest of the football team were perplexed.

'What's that in aid of?' asked Big Dave. 'Meks no sense.'

'No sense at all,' agreed Little Malcolm.

Don the barman stopped wiping glasses and put down his York City tea towel. 'So 'ow do women stop sweating?' he asked.

'We don't sweat, we *perspire*,' retorted Sheila tartly, hitching up her sparkly boob tube and folding her arms, with difficulty, in annoyance.

'It's 'cause o' that ozone layer,' said Stevie, not to be deflected.

'That's reight,' said Kojak. 'Ah 'eard it on t'news.'

'What ozone layer?' asked Big Dave.

'It's up in t'sky,' said Kojak.

Everyone looked out of the window at the vast black sky. Dark clouds scudded across the moon.

'Mebbe it's too dark t'see it,' said Shane.

'Well, what's it look like?' asked Clint.

'Y'can't see it . . . It's just there,' said Stevie.

'Well 'ow d'you know it's there?' asked Big Dave.

''Cause o' that feller on telly,' said Stevie.

There was a prolonged silence while they all supped on their Tetley's bitter. Finally normal service was resumed when Clint spoke up.

'Ah went out wi' a Swedish girl once.'

'Did she smell nice?' said Shane.

'Yeah, but she were from Pontefract.'

'There y'are, then,' said Big Dave. 'She prob'ly used an aerosol.'

As this weighty environmental issue had reached its inevitable conclusion, Sheila opened up a new topic of conversation. She surveyed Clint Ramsbottom from his baggy white shirt with lace cuffs to his tight stone-washed jeans and Doc Marten boots. 'What y'dressed like that for, Clint?' she asked.

'Ah'm a New Romantic,' said Clint proudly.

'Well, y'certainly don't look romantic t'me,' said Big Dave.

'Y'reight there, Dave,' said Shane. ''E looks like a big jessie.'

Clint's face flushed and this did little to enhance the subtle bronze and crimson highlights in his David Bowie feather cut. Wisely he said nothing.

'It's futurism,' said Stevie 'Supersub' Coleclough. 'Ah read it in a magazine in t'doctor's.' Stevie always liked to sound superior to his less qualified friends.

'That's reight,' agreed Clint, pleased that someone was on the same wavelength. He had also been in the doctor's surgery and read the same article. 'It's an antidote t'punk,' he recited.

Shane looked puzzled. He couldn't recall having an Auntie Dot.

'Well, ah don't get it,' said Big Dave. 'What's wrong wi' jus' looking . . . y'know, normal?'

As they nodded in agreement and returned to their beer, little did they know it but new brooms were sweeping out the old. The year 1981 had a few surprises in store for the Ragley Rovers football team. A world of frilly shirts, pixie boots, fingerless gloves and black eyeliner was just around the corner.

Meanwhile, Sheila served me with a giant Yorkshire pudding. It was perfect: slightly crisp at the edges, filled with mince and onions and smothered in delicious gravy – a feast on a freezing Yorkshire night.

On the other side of the lounge bar, Geoffrey Dudley-Palmer was sitting at a table in the bay window. He had just ordered Sheila's special 'belly buster' mixed grill and he sat back, puffed on his Tipalet cigar and stared out of the window at his new Volvo. For the huge sum of £8,501 he had purchased an exclusive THOR, one of a limited edition of only 450 in the UK. It sported automatic transmission, tinted glass, black cloth upholstery, alloy wheels, a spoiler, rear seat head restraints, a sunroof and a gleaming black finish. Geoffrey was content – well, almost. He was hungry. In fact he was ravenous.

Two weeks ago, a Breville sandwich toaster had seemed an ideal Christmas gift for his wife. While he could never imagine using it, he knew Petula would love this addition to her state-of-the-art kitchen. The young salesman at Lewis's department store in Leeds had informed him that the unique action cut sandwiches in half and then sealed the edges.

However, since then, every meal for Geoffrey Dudley-Palmer was wedged between two slices of bread, sealed round the edges and heated to one thousand degrees centigrade. He was unimpressed that this labour-saving phenomenon was popular with teenagers who created sandwiches named 'Nuclear Afterblast' and 'Biochemical Warfare'. He was also thoroughly sick of cheese-and-tomato sandwiches and having to scrape the charred remains from the 'non-stick' hotplates. It was time for a clear-out and the sandwich toaster was about to join the waffle iron and soda stream in the garage.

So, when his 'belly buster' special turned up he picked up his knife and fork like a man who hadn't eaten a decent meal for a week – which, of course, he hadn't.

When I left, Ronnie Smith, the team manager, was talking tactics with Big Dave and Little Malcolm. As usual he was using a tomato-ketchup bottle and a salt cellar to represent the team's two great stalwarts. Sadly, the diminutive Malcolm was fed up. Every time Ronnie demonstrated tactics, he was always the short, stumpy salt cellar.

Even so, he kept his misgivings to himself as Big Dave still hadn't forgiven him for going with Dorothy to the Refuse Collectors' Annual Fancy Dress Ball in York. They had dressed up as Sonny and Cher, while Big Dave, in protest, had simply put on his wellies and gone as Alan Titchmarsh.

On Tuesday morning, outside the frosted window panes of Bilbo Cottage, a robin, its red breast stark against the snow, perched on the handle of my garden spade. Its bright eyes stared forlornly at a white world devoid of life. Then it sang a wistful, melancholic song that matched my mood.

My thoughts were elsewhere. Beth's wise words were like the flurries of snowflakes – briefly touching my consciousness and then gusting away into the dark recesses of my mind. *You're vulnerable*, she had said, and I knew it was so.

However, it was business as usual when I turned into the school gates and pale sunlight shone weakly on the frosty car park. Ruby, in a headscarf and old overcoat, had brushed away the snow from the entrance steps and was sprinkling them with salt.

"Urry up, Mr Sheffield. Y'll catch y'death o' cold out there,' she shouted. 'An' a 'appy new year,' she added as an afterthought.

At exactly nine o'clock Cathy Cathcart pulled on the school bell rope and announced the beginning of the spring term 1981. With a self-satisfied glance at her wristwatch, she attached the rope to the cast-iron cleat on the wall and walked into my classroom. Another year had begun.

Cathy, a keen little girl, was soon hard at work in her English exercise book. I was pleased she was using her dictionary but, sadly, it was not always to good effect. In answer to the instruction 'Use the word *judicious* in a sentence', Cathy, presumably with the Fairy Liquid commercial in mind, had written: 'Hands that judicious can be soft as your face.' Also, when asked to describe the meaning of a 'turbine' she had written: 'What an Arab wears on his head.' Not for the first time it occurred to me that you needed a sense of humour to survive as a teacher.

At lunchtime, on this bitter winter's day, I marvelled at the beauty of Ragley School. The railings were etched in frost and each fleur-de-lis was topped with an arrowhead of fresh snow. A smooth curve of crusted white rime formed a repeated pattern on each pane of glass in the tall arched windows. The sound of the children's games was muffled and their breath formed tiny clouds of vapour in the still, icy air.

Meanwhile, in the staff-room, Vera was reporting the latest news. 'We're getting a new telephone in the office,' she said, 'and an extension line in the staff-room. It appears there's been some fuss about our phone number and I assured the young lady it ended in three zero.'

'I wonder if it will be one of the new push-button telephones,' said Jo.

'Yes,' said Vera, consulting a pink maintenance form on her clipboard. 'It's one of those new Trimphones.'

Jo's eyes widened in excitement: she loved new technology and knew that before the end of the year the school would own a computer.

Vera picked up her *Daily Telegraph* and scanned with relief the story that the Yorkshire Ripper had finally been brought to justice for the killing of thirteen women. He had been arrested last week in Sheffield after driving with false number plates. Then she spotted a story that did not appeal to her.

'Ridiculous!' she exclaimed, tossing the newspaper on to the coffee-table.

'What's wrong, Vera?' asked Valerie.

'Just look at that,' said Vera, pointing at the headline.

It read: 'Should the Queen retire?'

'Just because she's fifty-three,' said Vera, 'and Charles is now thirty-one.'

'I agree, Vera, it's scandalous,' said Valerie, who, much to Vera's approval, was another ardent royalist. 'Queen Victoria reigned until she was eighty-two.'

'Quite right, Valerie,' said Vera. 'The monarchy is secure and solid.'

'Respected and popular,' added Valerie for good measure, 'and the new girlfriend for Charles is a real beauty.'

'Oh, you mean Lady Diana Spencer?' said Anne, looking up from marking her children's writing books. Jemima Poole had written, 'I love my mummy even when she is grumpy.'

'Yes,' said Valerie. 'She's the granddaughter of Lady Fermoy, you know, who was a lady of the bedchamber to the Queen Mother for thirty years.'

'Yes, she's definitely got the right background, but don't you think she's rather young?'

'I thought Charles would have tied the knot with her older sister, Sarah, a couple of years ago,' said Anne. 'She seemed to be the royal flame at the time.'

'It's possible his father's selected this one,' said Vera as she locked the metal money box for late dinner money.

'You may well be right,' said Valerie and she collected her dinner register and set off back to her classroom.

'Yes . . . well, let's just hope they're happy,' said Vera quietly to herself.

Just before afternoon break I called briefly into Valerie's classroom. All the children were working hard. Miss Flint had written on the blackboard, in beautiful cursive script, *The quick brown fox jumps over the lazy dog*, a sentence that includes all the letters of the alphabet, and the children had copied it in their very best handwriting in their writing books. Nine-year-old Sarah Tait had added *and the farmer was not pleased*, clearly determined to cast judgement on the worthiness of the dog. It struck me as a very formal exercise and a long way from Sally's style of teaching, her so-called 'integrated day'.

Valerie's slate-grey eyes never wavered as she looked at me steadily. It was as if she knew what I was thinking. 'It's not just facts and knowledge, Jack,' she whispered in my ear. 'They're important . . . but I try to give my children *wisdom*. That will be much more important in this broken world.'

There was more to Valerie than met the eye and it occurred to me that I could learn a lot from this experienced lady.

At the end of school I was walking out of the building with Vera and Valerie when a small white van pulled up in the car park and a short, stocky man with a sooty face and gleaming white teeth climbed out. On the side of the van it read: *Kelvin Froggat, Chimney-sweep*, with a telephone number underneath that looked familiar. It was the same number as Ragley School!

He obviously knew Vera. ''Ello, Miss Evans,' he said breathlessly. 'Ah'm real sorry, there's been a mix-up wi' phone numbers. Ah were given t'wrong one. Las' two digits are t'wrong way round. Ah'll gerrit changed straight away.'

'Thank you, Kelvin. I'm sure it's not your fault,' said Vera graciously. After all, Kelvin cleaned the vicarage chimneys every year and was always tidy.

I recalled the strange telephone call. 'I took a message

yesterday morning from a lady who sounded worried about her chimney.'

'That were Deirdre Coe,' he said. 'She weren't pleased. An' t'make matters worse, 'er chimneys were in such a poor state m'brooms got stuck an' ah've 'ad t'get a new set.'

'I'm sorry to hear that, Mr Froggat,' I said.

He drove off, followed by Valerie in her 1971 Vauxhall Viva Estate. Whirling flakes of snow filled the frozen sky and danced like ghostly moths in the flickering beams of their headlights.

Vera stood beside me as we watched their red tail lights disappear.

Then she smiled up at me. 'As I was saying, Mr Sheffield . . . new brooms.'

Chapter Eleven

The Problem with Men

All staff began to prepare mid-year reports for distribution at half-term. Our outdoor education weekend in early June for the children in Class 4 was booked.

Extract from the Ragley School Logbook:
Monday, 2 February 1981

Colin Pringle looked in his briefcase and knew his life had changed for ever.

On his way home from work he had called into Woolworth's in York. He stared intently at a bottle of Johnson's baby shampoo. For 59p it promised 'no more tears' on the label. He looked up at Sally, who nodded in approval. As an afterthought, he had also bought some Johnson's baby oil for 69p, a large tube of Aquafresh toothpaste for 25p and a bottle of Silvikrin shampoo for 39p.

'These are for your hospital bag,' he said and Sally gave him a strained smile. The time was getting close.

Sally was finally fed up with pregnancy and wanted it all to be over. Ruby had suggested long walks and pineapple chunks to hurry things along, whereas a voluble Mrs Ackroyd in the General Stores had sworn by spicy foods and herbal tea. Sally had tried all these but her backache was worse and she couldn't sleep at night. The midwife had told her the baby's head was engaged, and going to the toilet had become an uncomfortable experience. Sally had also begun to experience fake contractions but kept it to herself. Sharing this news with the nervous Colin would probably give him a heart attack. She looked at him sadly. He had given up smoking and was sucking giant humbugs as if there was no tomorrow. Still, she thought, it wasn't his fault. After all, he was just a man.

Meanwhile, three miles away, Sheila Bradshaw was making an announcement. 'T'problem wi' men is they're only good f'one thing an' most of 'em are useless at that.'

Don the barman looked sheepishly at me and then glanced nervously at his buxom wife. He pulled a half pint of Chestnut Mild. 'Here y'are, Jack,' he said and then added in a conspiratorial whisper, 'and good luck when y'finally get married.'

It was Monday evening, 2 February, and I had arranged to meet Beth in The Royal Oak. The members of the Ragley Rovers football team stared at Sheila as she fiddled with the controls of the television set in the taproom. The sight of Sheila in a skin-tight micro-miniskirt and halfway up a step-ladder was a welcome distraction from their mournful analysis of last Saturday's heavy defeat to the Thirkby United Colts XI. A group of fifteen-year-old boys had put six goals past them.

'It were too frosty t'tackle 'em,' muttered Clint Ramsbottom.

'Y'reight, Nancy. Pitch were like glass,' agreed Shane.

Clint winced when his big brother called him 'Nancy' but, as always, he nodded in acknowledgement. No one in their right mind would ever disagree with Shane.

'Them kids were like Torvill an' Dean out there,' said Big Dave.

'Y'reight there, Dave,' said Little Malcolm. 'We should 'ave worn skates instead of football boots.'

Everyone nodded even though most had never heard of Jayne Torvill and Christopher Dean, the new European ice-dancing champions.

'An' that's another thing wi' you men,' said Sheila: 'Yer allus complaining.'

Meanwhile, Colin was still anxious. Sally, to take her mind off her increasing discomfort, had persuaded him to read the instructions for their new Hotpoint automatic top loader washing machine. The salesman had told Colin and Sally that at £289.95 it could cope with a 10-pound wash load, had a no-tangle action and an impressive 1,050 rpm spin speed. Colin had simply looked perplexed and Sally had taken the initiative.

'We'll take it,' she said, 'and Colin . . .' she fixed him with a stern expression, 'you will have to learn how to use it.'

Colin was dumbstruck. It hadn't occurred to him that

having a baby would have such far-reaching and life-changing implications.

However, at that moment, Sally glanced at the clock on the mantelpiece and began to time her contractions. They were now five minutes apart and each one lasted almost one minute.

'Colin,' she said quietly, 'put the hospital bag in the car. It's time to go.'

Colin sprinted like a headless chicken to the car, ran back for the bag, returned once more for the car keys and finally roared off like Jackie Stewart in the Monaco Grand Prix.

Beth walked into the lounge bar and, as always, she looked stunning, even after a long day at school. She reached up to kiss me on the cheek, slipped off her sheepskin coat and woolly scarf and sat opposite me at the table by the bay window. She was wearing a smart two-piece outfit in jade with slightly padded shoulders, a suede-look embroidered waistcoat and a straight skirt.

'Gosh, I need a drink, Jack. That governors' report took an age.' She rubbed her neck and stretched.

'G and T?'

'Perfect,' said Beth.

Soon we were sipping our drinks and, eventually, Beth launched into what was on our minds. 'Any news about Ragley?' she asked quietly.

I put down my drink. 'Nothing concrete . . . just rumours. I've heard they may close Morton School to coincide with Miss Tripps' retirement.'

'That's a blow for Morton but good for you, Jack. The

Morton children would come to Ragley. There're only about thirty of them, I think.'

'We'd need another classroom,' I said.

'You'd get one of those mobiles. We had a couple of those when I was at Thirkby. They erect them in a day. The only problem is water. There's no supply and art work becomes a bit of a pain. But there's plenty of spare land near your cycle shed. I expect they'd put it there.'

I pondered this strange new scenario. 'Sad for Morton, though, Beth,' I said.

'Maybe, but it would make economic sense and Joseph is chairman of governors of both schools, so if it meant this was the only way to save Ragley he would have to go along with the closure of Morton.'

Her words 'economic sense' reverberated in my tired brain. The world was changing and Mrs Thatcher's new cost-efficient society had a hard edge to it for public servants. I was also seeing the tough side of Beth. There was steel there I hadn't noticed before. Deep down, I didn't want to benefit from Morton's loss and I had a great affection for Miss Tripps. It would break her heart to oversee the closure of her beloved village school. Thoughtfully, I supped on my Chestnut Mild as the strains of Abba's 'The Winner Takes It All' drifted through from the taproom juke-box.

'There is another way forward, Jack.'

Beth leant under the table, opened her leather shoulder bag and took out a well-thumbed copy of the new issue of the *Times Educational Supplement*. She opened it to the Primary Appointments page, where she had circled a number of advertised posts. She pointed to one of them. 'There's a large school in Bridlington, Jack . . . a much higher salary . . . You may want to think about it.'

'I'm not sure, Beth. I wouldn't be a class teacher any more.'

'But surely it's your next logical step, isn't it?'

I took a deep breath and quickly scanned the text of the advertisement. 'Following the retirement of .'. . a new headteacher required for September 1981 . . . 350+ children on roll . . .'

'We could sell up and move to somewhere in North Yorkshire between Hartingdale and the coast,' added Beth.

It seemed as though she had worked it all out.

'But I thought you would want to move in with me at Bilbo Cottage.'

'Did you?'

'And I love teaching, Beth. I'd miss not having a class of my own.'

'Would you?'

'And . . . I love Ragley . . . the school, the village, the people. I feel at home here.'

'Ah . . .' said Beth. She picked up a menu from the table, then glanced at the special of the day on the blackboard above the fireplace. Predictably it was shepherd's pie. Beth leant over and squeezed my hand. 'Shall we order some food?' she said simply.

At the bar I ordered two specials while Sheila was serving Clint Ramsbottom with his chicken and chips in a basket.

'Give us a knife an' fork, please, Sheila,' said Clint.

'Didn't they teach y'no grammar at school, then?' Sheila asked him, winking at me.

"Ow d'you mean?' asked Clint.

'It should be please give *me* my knife and fork.'

Clint shook his head in puzzlement. 'But ah ain't got none.'

Colin was now in a state of panic. The roads were freezing over as he skidded through the entrance of Fulton Maternity Hospital. It looked like an old wartime army camp with a collection of single-storey buildings scattered round a large Victorian edifice with a huge chimney.

He pulled up outside the main entrance and a nurse in a starched apron hurried down the stone steps to help. Colin grabbed the heavy bag out of the boot while the nurse took Sally's arm. She led her into an entrance hall of bare cream and green walls. A large sign with an arrow pointing to the right read WARDS; another, with an arrow to the left, read DELIVERY ROOMS.

They turned left down a corridor of polished tiles, and the nurse's black lace-up shoes tapped out a brisk rhythm that exactly matched Sally's heartbeat.

In the delivery room, the matron held Sally's hand. 'Sally,' she said in a calm, reassuring voice, 'don't worry. Everything looks normal.'

Sally looked at the three other women in the ward, who appeared to be in their early twenties. 'I feel ancient here,' she breathed. 'Is it safe at my age?' There was a hint of uncertainty in her voice.

The matron put a cooling hand on Sally's forehead.

'You're a healthy woman. There's no cause for concern.' She glanced into the corridor, where Colin was down to his last humbug. 'Shall I ask your husband to come in?'

'Not just yet, thanks. Perhaps later,' whispered Sally.

'I understand,' said the matron – and she did.

The conversation in The Royal Oak had drifted back to the bitterly cold weather.

'It's from Siberia, all this snow,' said Kojak.

'Bloody Russians!' said Big Dave in disgust. 'We don't want no Russian snow 'ere.'

'Y'reight there, Dave,' agreed Little Malcolm. 'We want proper Yorkshire snow.'

Everyone nodded in agreement and supped thoughtfully until Sheila broke the silence. 'Ah knew a Russian once,' she said, staring wistfully at a bottle of vodka, 'name o' Stan something.'

Don gave her a sharp glance.

''E never put no sugar in m'tea,' continued Sheila in a little world of her own. 'Said ah were sweet enough.'

'Huh!' said Don. He grabbed a pint pot and wiped it vigorously with his York City tea towel.

'Like ah said, y'can't trust Russians,' said Big Dave.

''Ere, 'ere,' said Little Malcolm. 'Nowt worse.'

From out of a haze of Old Holborn tobacco smoke at the end of the bar, Old Tommy Piercy spoke up. Old Tommy tended to say very little but when he did everyone listened. ''Owd on, 'owd on, not so 'asty, young Malcolm,' said Old Tommy. He tapped his pipe on the bar for order. 'Y'forgettin' southerners.'

In Old Tommy's politically incorrect but perfectly

formed world, southerners always ranked below Russians, Germans, French onion-sellers, Australian cricketers, teetotallers and vegetarians. Everyone nodded in agreement at his words of wisdom and proceeded to sup in silence. The oracle had spoken.

'Mrs Pringle, we have three trainee midwives who would like to attend the birth . . . if you have no objection.'

Sally blinked through her perspiration and nodded. The question had appeared rhetorical anyway.

The matron beckoned them in and they stood there in a line, two slim young women and a youthful dark-haired man with an attempt at a first moustache who looked as though he had just been let out of school for the day. He blinked nervously and stared in apparent horror at the scene before him.

They observed with varying degrees of emotion. The two young women seemed to take it in their stride. However, the young man suddenly found himself in a nightmare world of starched caps, white wellies, red rubber aprons and pregnant women with their legs in stirrups. By the time the midwife used a hook to break the waters he was having second thoughts about his choice of career.

Suddenly, the pace of events increased.

By now Sally had begun to scream so loudly the walls rattled. Also, much to Colin's dismay, she yelled that if he even considered trying for another baby she would personally castrate him with his new mole-grip pliers.

'You tell 'im, luv,' muttered one of the female trainee midwives.

'Use this, Sally,' said the midwife. 'Gas and air – it'll help.' Two cylinders were fixed on a trolley alongside the bed. Sally held the black rubber mask to her face and breathed the welcome gas in.

Colin had gone grey, then green, and was now chewing the inside of his face mask.

'The head's out . . .' said the midwife. 'The shoulders are out . . .' Colin slipped gently on to the floor. 'And the husband's out!'

This was followed by the cries of the two female trainee midwives. They were supporting their male colleague under his armpits and dragging him out of the room. He had fainted as well.

'Men!' muttered the midwife as she proceeded calmly.

She was a large, experienced, formidable woman with hands like coal shovels but with the dexterity of a seamstress. After cutting the umbilical cord and checking the baby's breathing, everything seemed well. The child was wrapped in a green cloth and given to Sally.

The midwife's demeanour softened for a brief moment and she smiled. 'Sally,' she said softly, 'you have a beautiful baby girl.'

What happened next was a blur to Sally. She simply felt so tired. From the delivery room, she soon found herself in a ward with other mothers and their babies.

Baby Pringle reappeared, washed clean and wearing a small white nightie open at the back and a terry-towelling nappy held together with a large safety pin. She was so tiny, a little bundle of humanity on a cellular blanket in what looked like a Perspex fish tank. The pink tags on her wrist and ankle announced that she weighed seven pounds and one ounce and that she had been born at 4.00 a.m. on 3 February 1981.

Sally looked at Colin, who was now recovered. 'We have a daughter,' she said.

Colin was about to add, 'With ginger hair,' but thought better of it. After all, he was a New Age Eighties-man and he knew he had to be sensitive.

On Tuesday morning a monochrome world of winter stretched out before me. A tracery of silver frost rimed every twig on the still, frozen trees, while rooks and starlings settled on the parallel shadows in the distant ploughed fields. However, in the far corner of my garden, aconites and snowdrops lifted the spirit and gave hope of warmer days to come.

I was further cheered to see nine-year-old Debbie Clack carrying a large armful of furry willow catkins for Valerie Flint's nature table. Her mother, Mrs Cynthia Clack, was hurrying up the drive with her and I remembered I had asked her to call in to see me.

'It was about your Debbie's PE kit, Mrs Clack,' I said in the school entrance hall.

''E's 'opeless, is my Charlie, Mr Sheffield,' said Mrs Clack as she rummaged in her shopping bag. 'Anyway, 'ere's some PE kit for our Debbie. Ah went to t'Co-op.'

'Well, I'm really pleased, Mrs Clack. Debbie loves the netball lessons with Mrs Hunter and I was a bit concerned when I received this note from your husband.' I took it from my pocket. It read: 'Please excuse our Debbie from netball but we can't afford the PE kit.' I gave her the scruffy piece of paper. 'And it didn't help that it's been written on the back of a betting slip, Mrs Clack.'

'Don't you worry, Mr Sheffield,' said the determined Mrs Clack, 'ah'll give 'im what-for when 'e comes home.'

At that moment, and blissfully unaware that he wouldn't be getting his usual Tuesday night pie, chips and mushy peas followed by jam roly-poly pudding and custard, Charlie Clack, Ragley's finest car salesman, was in full flow with a browbeaten bank clerk in the Ford garage in Easington.

'This is Britain's best-selling small car,' recited Charlie, 'the fantastic Ford Escort that goes from thirty to fifty in eleven-point-three seconds, an' wi' its thirteen 'undred engine, square headlights, matt-black grill an' 'ound-stooth up'olstry, y'looking at t'car of the Eighties.' Charlie gave his customer a glassy-eyed stare of holier-than-thou sincerity while at the back of his mind he was desperate to know the result of the three-thirty from Market Rasen.

I walked with Mrs Clack to the main entrance door and opened it for her. As she stepped out into the frozen world, she shook her head and growled at the mothers sheltering under the porch, 'Men . . . who needs 'em?' and all the mothers nodded vigorously in agreement.

I stepped back in alarm. Above my head the spikes of silver icicles hung from the porch like shark's teeth and I made a mental note never to get on the wrong side of Mrs Clack.

*　　*　　*

Suddenly the office telephone rang and Vera seemed to be asking a barrage of questions. 'Thank you, Colin, and congratulations. Send Sally our love and we'll visit tomorrow evening.'

Ruby was polishing the handle of the office door and had heard every word. 'It's a girl,' she shouted to me, 'Mrs Pringle's 'ad a baby girl,' and she dashed off to tell Shirley and Doreen in the kitchen and then Anne, Jo and Valerie.

We all gathered in the office and Vera gave us chapter and verse of the night's events.

Throughout the day it dominated our conversations and, eventually, at the end of school Ruby came into my classroom and began to sweep the floor.

'Good news about Mrs Pringle, Mr Sheffield,' said Ruby, leaning on her broom.

'Wonderful news, Ruby,' I said, looking up from my marking.

'Teks m'back t'me an' Ronnie,' said Ruby with a faraway look in her eyes. 'Ah were proper smitten with 'im, Mr Sheffield. Ah thought 'e were real 'andsome. Then ah fell for a baby an' that were that.'

'How did you meet Ronnie?' I asked.

'It were m'sister, Rose, Mr Sheffield. She introduced me to 'im.'

'I didn't know you had a sister, Ruby,' I said.

'Oh yes, Mr Sheffield. Lovely lass, is our Rose. She 'as a knicker stall on Thirkby market, an' 'er 'ouse is allus spotless wi' lovely crisp sheets an' them nice toiletries what she pinches out o' 'otels.'

'Sounds a lovely lady,' I said.

'Y'reight there, Mr Sheffield,' said Ruby and wandered off into the corridor, assuming she had finished sweeping my classroom floor, which, of course, she hadn't.

Meanwhile, by Wednesday lunchtime Sally was learning how to breast-feed.

Dr Davenport had called in to check the stitches and he was followed by 'Booby-Sue', the resident expert.

'What Booby-Sue doesn't know about breast-feeding isn't worth knowing,' said Matron. She was correct.

Gradually, Sally learnt to alternate, left then right.

Back in the Ragley staff-room, a strange sight met my eyes. Dan Hunter was stretched out on the carpet with his legs in the air, while Jo was shaking his trouser leg as if her life depended on it.

'Sorry, Jack,' said Dan, looking up at me and clearly very embarrassed. 'I just called in and I know this looks odd . . . but needs must, as they say.'

'I'll come back later,' I said, hurrying to close the door.

'No, Jack,' explained Jo, very red in the face, 'it's really quite simple. We need money to buy a present for Sally's baby and it's too late for either of us to go to the bank. There's some change in Dan's truncheon pocket and the only way to get it out is through gravity!'

With a final shake, fifty-pence pieces and other small coins began to trickle out one by one from the long, narrow pocket.

'Spare a copper?' said Anne, who had arrived at that

moment and seemed completely undeterred by the demonstration of police gymnastics.

Shortly before visiting time we all descended on the hospital waiting room. I was clutching a bag of grapes and Beth had wrapped up a beautiful Babygro outfit in white tissue paper. Vera was showing Anne Grainger a little white cardigan she had knitted; Dan Hunter, rather self-consciously, was holding a soft toy bunny rabbit and Jo was taking the price tag off a plastic changing mat. Ruby had crocheted some tiny bootees and adorned them with pink ribbons, while Valerie had a large envelope containing a voucher for baby clothes.

From where we sat, we were able to hear an interesting conversation in the ward beyond. A lively five-year-old girl, holding her grandmother's hand, walked confidently up to her mother's bed and sat down. Looking at her grandmother's lined face, in a loud voice, she asked, 'How old are you, Grandma?'

'I'm too old to remember,' she replied.

'Well, Grandma, if you can't remember, all you have to do is look in the back of your pants. Mine say five to six.' She nodded sagely, then turned to her mother. 'Mummy, if you're very good will the nurses let you bring him home?' she asked.

A nurse pulled shut a curtain around the bed, but we could hear the continuing conversation.

'Yes, darling. This is your brother and he'll be coming to live with us.'

There was a pause. Then, 'What's Mummy doing now, Grandma?' asked the little girl.

'She's feeding your baby brother with milk,' said her grandmother gently.

'Yesterday Mummy was feeding him with the other one.'

'Yes . . . Your mummy can choose which one,' came the cautious reply.

'Oh, I see,' said the little girl. 'So is one for hot milk and the other for cold milk?'

It was a happy group that took turns to see Sally and her baby, who, surprisingly, hadn't got a name yet. Eventually, after much cooing, examining fingers and toes and agreeing there is nothing softer than a baby's skin, we drove home. Occasionally, I glanced across at Beth and wondered if she was thinking the same.

After the regulation ten days in hospital, Sally was allowed to leave. Colin parked the car outside the entrance and helped her down the steps and into the back seat. Meanwhile, a self-assured nurse followed with the baby, warmly dressed in a Babygro outfit with press-studs, a white shawl wrapped over her head, and passed her to Sally. The tiny girl had a name now, a beautiful name: it was Grace.

As they turned on to the A19 and drove out of York, Colin looked anxious and sucked a humbug furiously.

'Are you all right, Colin?' asked Sally.

'Sort of,' mumbled Colin.

'What is it?' Sally asked firmly.

'Well, you know the washing machine . . .'

'Yes?'

'I've done some washing.'

'Oh, yes?'

'And I've read the instructions,' he said with an air of desperation. 'In fact, quite a few times.'

'And?'

'I can't seem to be able to open the door to get it out.'

'How long has the washing been in there?' asked Sally evenly, trying not to hyperventilate.

'Five days,' said Colin forlornly.

Sally said nothing.

That was the problem with men, she thought. They were, well, just men.

Chapter Twelve

Beauty and the Blacksmith

School closed today for the one-week half-term holiday with 88 children registered on roll. The hinges are broken on the main entrance door and Miss Evans arranged for repairs to be completed while school is closed.

Extract from the Ragley School Logbook:
Friday, 20 February 1981

'No one does fleur-de-lis like Virgil,' said Vera knowingly.

Ruby looked puzzled. She thought Fleur-de-Lis was a French film star. Nevertheless, 'Lovely man is Virgil,' she said, polishing the handle of the staff-room door, her usual task when listening in to our conversations. ''E mended our coal scuttle las' week.'

'He's certainly a craftsman,' said Valerie Flint, blowing on the surface of her boiling-hot milky coffee and lowering herself gently into a chair. 'I heard that he's done work for York Minster.'

Jo looked up from her *Nuffield Book of Environmental Studies*. 'I pass his smithy on my way to school, Jack,' she said. 'When I drive past I usually wave and he waves back but, come to think of it, he never looks particularly happy.' She returned to the diagram of how to make a weather station. 'My Dan said he did a great job repairing our lawn mower,' she added as an afterthought.

'An 'e did that weathercock on t'top o' village 'all,' said Ruby, still polishing the door handle.

'In fact your Hazel did a lovely drawing of it in her Weather project folder,' said Jo.

Ruby smiled in appreciation. 'She teks after me, Mrs 'Unter. Ah allus loved art.'

Appropriately, no one mentioned the fact that Hazel's interpretation of our local weathercock looked more like Orville the Duck.

It was Friday morning playtime, 20 February, and we were about to break up for the one-week half-term holiday. Our Victorian school boiler was working overtime and the ancient hot-water pipes creaked and groaned as they expanded with the sudden rush of heat. The staff-room gas fire was on full blast and we had all gathered for a welcome hot drink, with the exception of Anne, who was on playground duty. The world outside was a frozen wasteland but the rosy-cheeked children seemed impervious to the cold and were busy rolling snowballs and building snowmen. Meanwhile, the entrance hall was like an icebox as the icy draughts whistled through the gaps between the front entrance door and the cracked door frame.

'The repairs to the door need to be completed as a

matter of urgency, Mr Sheffield,' said Vera insistently. A hundred years of use had taken its toll and I knew this was an important job. It was also clear that Vera wanted a decision. 'Joseph said that the governors have sanctioned the work as long as the costs are reasonable . . . And there's no problem with Virgil.' She held up a large brown envelope. 'He dropped this in to the vicarage last night.' Inside, in beautiful copperplate, was the blacksmith's handwritten estimate for a set of new cast-iron giant hinges for our huge school entrance door, plus the labour costs to rehang it.

I made up my mind. 'I'll call in after school and ask him to do the job.'

'You won't be disappointed, Mr Sheffield,' said Vera, with a satisfied smile.

'I'm looking forward to meeting him,' I said.

'It's jus' that 'e never smiles, does 'e, Miss Evans?' said Ruby, finally giving up the pretence of polishing the door handle.

'That's right, Ruby,' said Vera pensively; 'he's not smiled for a long time.'

She and Ruby exchanged a glance I knew so well. They knew something I didn't.

'An' y'know who's come back, don't you, Miss Evans?'

Vera nodded. 'Yes, Ruby. I heard your Beauty was back from Australia.'

'That's reight,' said Ruby with a shake of her head. 'It didn't work out, so ah 'eard.'

'I'm sorry to hear that, Ruby.'

'Well, ah'm not . . . begging y'pardon, Miss Evans.' She

gave the door handle a final polish, walked out into the corridor and pulled the door shut after her.

I looked up at Vera, puzzled by Ruby's final remark. 'Beauty?'

'She's Ruby's niece, Mr Sheffield. Lives in Thirkby . . . Must be in her mid-thirties now.' Then she gave me that familiar knowing look.

It was obvious there was a story here and I presumed that, in time, Vera would relate it to me. Little did I know it but the opportunity was destined to arrive sooner than expected.

At the end of the school day I drove slowly up the frosty Easington Road out of Ragley to a small well-kept cottage on Chauntsinger Lane. This was the home and workplace of Virgil Crichton, the local blacksmith, where he lived alone. As I parked on the snowy forecourt of his huge stone-built outbuilding, it occurred to me this would make a wonderful educational visit for my class. The sign above the ancient doors simply read *The Forge* and I stood in the darkness watching Virgil at work.

Although he was a great bear of a man of immense strength, he was known to be quiet and gentle. He still repaired and sharpened scythes and bill-hooks but, with the modernization of farm machinery, making horse ploughs had become a forgotten art. While he missed the giant shire-horses of his childhood, he still enjoyed looking after the major's horses, making sure they were shod to his daughter's exacting standards.

There was a steady pattern to Virgil's work and his life. When the embers in his furnace were glowing fiery red,

Virgil would take a ready-cut piece of metal and place it in the fierce heat and then pump the long handle of the bellows. In his massive right hand he would handle the heavy tongs and pick out a red-hot piece of iron. Finally, when it glowed like a setting sun, he would take it to the anvil and shape a perfect horseshoe.

On this dark, winter night, under a bright light, he was kneeling on the concrete floor, battering a broken pig trough with a hammer. Business was steady for Virgil but it was also slow. Once his giant hammer had beaten out a regular rhythm. Now there was only a broken lawnmower to repair or perhaps a set of fire irons for Old Tommy Piercy. It was sad that on most days the anvil was now strangely silent. Perhaps that was why he never smiled.

My footsteps crunched across the forecourt and Virgil looked up, took off his leather apron and extended a huge hand in greeting. I noticed his leather braces were fastened to his thick cord trousers with a couple of horse nails.

He looked up and nodded as if he was expecting me. 'Hello, Mr Sheffield. Good of you to drop by,' he said and we shook hands. Like me, he was in his thirties but perhaps two or three years older. However, while we were both about the same height, he must have been four stones heavier and his huge muscular shoulders resembled those of a weightlifter. In the sharp lights of the forge, his eyes of steel-grey stared back at me, guarded and steady.

'Please call me Jack,' I said. 'Good to meet you.'

'I'm Virgil,' he said simply.

I held up his written estimate. 'Thanks for this, Virgil. It looks fine . . . so please start the job when you can. You certainly came highly recommended from Miss Evans.'

He nodded and his huge mane of black wavy hair tumbled over the collar of his faded denim shirt. 'She's a fine lady is Miss Evans,' he said. He gestured at the collection of broken and twisted metal and a dusty tea chest full of old horseshoes. 'There's not a lot going on, as you can see,' he said simply. 'I'll finish this job and then start tomorrow – say, about eleven o'clock.' Virgil clearly didn't waste words. He was also one who kept all emotion hidden from the outside world.

I nodded and drove back through the frozen night to Kirkby Steepleton.

Saturday was an important day for Vera and the St Mary's Church social committee. It was the occasion of the annual church jumble sale. In the villages of Ragley and Morton it was a popular event because, as Vera reminded us, it had a better class of jumble. Instead of the battered Monopoly games, broken Action Men and Starsky and Hutch annuals that were a feature at the school jumble sale, the church jumble sale attracted the higher echelon of local society. Antique vases, complete dinner services and brass candlesticks were the norm, along with lawnmowers and trailers that had been replaced with top-of-the range models by their wealthy owners. I had promised Vera that Beth and I would look after the bookstall.

At eleven o'clock I drove into the school car park. Virgil's van was already there. I took out my huge bunch of keys, unlocked the great oak entrance door and handed him the spare key.

'I'll be in from time to time during the day, Virgil, and I've asked Ruby to call by and make you a pot of tea.'

'There's no need,' said Virgil quickly, 'but I appreciate the offer,' he added.

'Ruby will be here anyway, Virgil,' I said. 'She often does a couple of hours on a Saturday.'

Virgil said nothing. He just turned and set to work to remove the broken hinges.

An hour later I had set up the bookstall in the church hall. Beth had said she would be along later and, on a creaking trestle table, I piled gardening books in one box, do-it-yourself in another, and then I stacked the paperbacks in alphabetical order. When I returned to school, Virgil had already replaced the warped door frame.

'That's looking a lot better now,' I said. 'Thanks, Virgil. I'm really grateful.'

'It'll be finished this afternoon, Jack,' he said.

I looked at my watch. 'I'm hungry,' I said. 'How about breaking off for a bite to eat?'

Virgil thought for a moment and stared at me as if weighing me up. Then he gave a brief nod. 'Good idea, I'll just make the door secure and we can call in at Old Tommy's for a pie, if you like.'

'That's fine by me,' I said.

We trudged through the snow across the High Street, our breath steaming in the air. 'Interesting name . . . Virgil,' I said, recalling my rudimentary Latin. 'He was a famous Roman poet, wasn't he?'

'That's right, Jack. My grandfather was a reader and he loved his Virgil. He taught me all about Publius Vergilius Maro. That was his real name and, of course, he wrote the *Aeneid*. It turned out to be my favourite book.' Virgil was suddenly animated. Clearly this was a topic that interested him greatly. 'He was a great man, Jack,' he continued, 'born on the fifteenth of October in seventy BC and died in nineteen BC. That's a short life for so many wise words.'

There was a lot more to this man than met the eye but, as we walked into Piercy's Butcher's Shop, the delicious scent of warm pies put all thoughts of Roman poets far from our minds.

'Two growlers, please, Mr Piercy,' said Virgil.

I looked curiously at Virgil. 'Growlers?'

'My treat, Jack,' he said simply. 'I'm grateful for the work.'

Old Tommy passed over two of his much celebrated pork pies.

'These are magnificent pies, Mr Piercy,' I said gratefully.

'That they are, young Mr Sheffield, an' ah'll tell y'summat f'nowt. Ah learnt 'ow t'mek pork pies when ah were apprentice butcher wi' m'Uncle Randolph Piercy in 'is little shop in Kirkstall Road in Leeds.'

So it was that Old Tommy continued to make his famous pork pies by forcing a mixture of meat, fat and gristle into cold-water pastry. But it was the seasoning, perfected during his apprenticeship and now a family secret, that made his pies such a treat.

'Here y'are, young Virgil,' said Old Tommy. He handed

over a small carton. 'A bit o' mint sauce will go just nicely,' he added with a grin.

Sitting by the old pine table in the school entrance hall we ate our pies and our stomachs rumbled with pleasure. 'And that's why they're called growlers, Jack,' said Virgil reflectively but still without a hint of a smile.

The church jumble sale was about to begin when I walked in. Beth had already taken charge of the bookstall and was in conversation with Vera, who looked animated as she held up her *Daily Telegraph*.

'Oh, I must share this with you,' she announced triumphantly and began to read: 'It is with the greatest pleasure that the Queen and the Duke of Edinburgh announce the betrothal of their beloved son the Prince of Wales to the Lady Diana Spencer, daughter of the Earl Spencer and the Honourable Mrs Shand Kydd.'

'Good news, Vera,' said Beth. 'You always wanted him to settle down with a lovely young girl and he seems to have found one.'

'I certainly hope so,' said Vera. 'She looks perfect for him – and so beautiful. I can't wait for the wedding.'

'Neither can I,' I said and gave Beth a knowing look, but she appeared not to notice.

Vera hurried off to look after the crockery stall with the doctor's wife, Joyce Davenport, and immediately launched into a description of the classic lines of a Hornsea pottery teapot with Mrs Dudley-Palmer. Throughout, Vera showed commendable restraint. After all, it was difficult to take seriously a woman who loved Angel Delight, fondue sets and shag-pile carpets. Fortunately

Vera was entirely unaware that Petula Dudley-Palmer played 'Chirpy, Chirpy, Cheep, Cheep' on her Sony Walkman when she donned her Fame leg warmers and went out with the Ragley ladies jogging group.

Joyce Davenport smiled wistfully at her dearest friend. The young Joyce Duckham and Vera Evans had been in the same class throughout their teenage years and she had often wondered why the tall, slim, attractive Vera had never found the man of her dreams. Then she noticed that, on the other side of the hall, Virginia Forbes-Kitchener was examining some horse-livery equipment. However, her father was disinterested. He was looking in *their* direction and it appeared he had eyes only for Vera. The major had been a widower for many years and Joyce began to wonder.

By mid-afternoon, Beth and I had almost sold out. Margery Ackroyd had bought the last Jilly Cooper novel and Mary Hardisty had purchased an Alan Titchmarsh gardening book, 'but only because he's a Yorkshireman', she explained hastily. 'My George wouldn't read it otherwise.'

I looked at my watch. 'I'd better call round at school again to see if the work on the main door has been finished,' I said.

'Fine, Jack,' said Beth. 'Come back for me in half an hour. I'll clear up here.'

Suddenly Ruby, clutching a cardboard box of crockery, appeared. With her was a tall, slender woman I had never seen before.

"Ello, Mr Sheffield, Miss 'Enderson,' said Ruby. 'This is

our Beauty. She's visiting t'day from Thirkby.'

Ruby's niece was a long-legged natural beauty with shoulder-length wavy chestnut hair. She gave me a shy smile and extended her hand in greeting. 'Hello, Mr Sheffield. Our Ruby 'as told me all about you,' said Beauty with a smile that must have broken many hearts and a peculiar mixture of a Yorkshire accent mixed with an Australian lilt.

'Pleased to meet you, Beauty,' I said hesitantly.

'That's m'nickname, Mr Sheffield. M'mother an' our Ruby allus called me that,' she said with another smile that lit up the room. 'An' ah prefer it t'Beverley.'

I looked at Ruby's heavy box of crockery. 'I'm calling into school, Ruby, so I can give you a lift home if you like.'

'Thank you, Mr Sheffield,' said Ruby. 'That's reight kind.'

Beauty's eyes lit up. 'Ooh, can ah 'ave a look round t'old school, Mr Sheffield?' she said enthusiastically. 'It's years since I left 'ere. It would be lovely t'see it again.'

'Of course,' I said. 'We'll call in on the way back.'

Virgil had just cleared up and was giving the giant hinges a final oiling when I stopped outside the school gates.

'Virgil!' exclaimed Beauty, staring as if she had seen a ghost.

'Beauty,' said Virgil, and the colour drained from his ruddy cheeks.

Ruby put her hand on my arm. 'P'raps we can give 'em a few minutes, Mr Sheffield . . . There's 'istory between these two.'

223

We climbed back in the car as Beauty walked towards Virgil. It was time for a story and I settled back into my driver's seat while Ruby told me the sad tale.

After a whirlwind romance, Beauty, an assistant on the cosmetics counter in Boots the Chemist in Thirkby, had surprised her family and run off in 1963 with her manager, Clive Turner. He had been offered a job in Australia as chief chemist in a new pharmaceutical factory in Sydney and decided an attractive girlfriend would be an asset in his drive to the top of his profession.

They had taken advantage of the ten-pound assisted passage and boarded a plane that, with stops in Rome, Bombay and Darwin, took forty hours to arrive in New South Wales, where Beauty, looking like Audrey Hepburn in high heels, white gloves, dark-blue two-piece suit and matching leather handbag, walked confidently into Sydney airport. They were met by Clive's chief executive in his pale-green Holden F J and whisked off to a smart hotel.

They were married in November 1963, the weekend before the assassination of President John Kennedy, and moved into a spacious rented house at Mona Vale on the northern peninsula in sight of the sea. Beauty loved the open air but soon discovered she was not allowed to change into her swimsuit on the beach and that only one-piece costumes were allowed. Also the shark patrols made her even more nervous than the funnel-web spiders. Every week she wrote to her mother on blue airmail paper and told her all about the sights and the sea and plans for the new Opera House – but never about how she felt, lonely and far from home.

For the first few years all seemed well, then Clive had his first affair. They were guests of the Royal Agricultural Society at Sydney showground for the Royal Easter Show. The blonde wife of his colleague was both irresistible and available.

By the mid-Seventies, Beauty couldn't stand Clive's bullying and womanizing any longer and she sought a divorce. Clive was glad to oblige. Beauty had served her purpose.

She moved into a spare room in a girlfriend's house and, eventually, there came a morning a few months ago when she knew it was time to leave Australia. The postman had pushed the mail into the mailbox at the end of the driveway and blown his whistle. Then the delivery boy had thrown the local Sydney newspaper on to the front lawn. She had collected the mail, picked up the newspaper and then stared out to sea. It was time to return to her home and family.

Beauty looked up at the rugged features of the giant blacksmith. 'Clive told me you were going out wi' that Alice from t'bakery in Easington,' said Beauty.

Virgil looked shocked. 'I never went out with her, but I think we both know why he would say that.'

'But ah saw y'going into 'er house,' said Beauty sadly, 'and ah was coming to see you.'

'I was doing some work for her father,' said Virgil. 'I was repairing his trailer as a favour.'

'Oh, ah see,' said Beauty.

'When you didn't turn up I thought you'd lost interest. After all, just look at me, Beauty,' said Virgil. 'I'm no oil painting.' His face was etched with the memory of that day. 'Then I saw you and Clive in his flash car about a week later. I could never compete with that.'

'Ah should 'ave known,' she said.

A few days later the weather had changed and the snow had finally gone. There was a shift in the wind and hopes of warmer days for the shoppers on Ragley High Street. Outside the village hall I met Albert Jenkins, school governor and a wise friend. He pointed up the street.

'Now, there's a sight for sore eyes,' he said.

On the opposite pavement Virgil and Beauty were walking hand in hand and deep in conversation but what was extraordinary was the fact that Virgil's face was wreathed in smiles.

'Good to see, isn't it, Jack?' said Albert. 'I haven't seen Virgil smile in years.'

'I did wonder why he always appeared so reserved, as if he didn't want to let his feelings out,' I said. 'I'm pleased he's found a bit of happiness at last.'

'Virgil's grandfather was a great friend to me, Jack, but, sadly, he's passed on now. He loved his Latin and he introduced me to the *Aeneid*, the Roman Empire's national epic.'

'Yes. Virgil mentioned it to me. He's a big fan.'

'There were some great lines in it . . . "*Audentes fortuna iuvat*".' I smiled at Albert's animated expression. 'Fortune favours the brave. Book ten, line two hundred and eighty-four.'

'It's one to remember,' I said.

'This may surprise you, Jack, but Virgil was actually christened *Isaac* Virgil Crichton.'

'Isaac?'

'That's right. He was such a cheerful baby and his mother was a great Bible reader.'

'I still don't follow, Albert,' I said.

Virgil and Beauty had stopped outside Nora's Coffee Shop. After being awarded an OBE by the Queen, Cliff Richard was in the top ten in America with 'We Don't Talk Any More'. It was on full volume as Virgil opened the door. Beauty whispered something in his ear and he laughed out loud.

'Jack . . . *Isaac* is Hebrew for laughter,' said Albert.

Finally I understood and smiled. 'So Virgil was right,' I said.

We watched them walk into the shop with the confidence of lovers.

Albert nodded and gave me a knowing look. '*Omnia vincit amor*. Book ten, line sixty-nine,' he murmured quietly.

The translation was surprisingly easy and I smiled. 'Love conquers all,' I said.

Above our heads, a parliament of rooks ceased their debate and flew off into a powder-blue sky. It was time to move on and Beth had promised warm soup back at Bilbo Cottage.

Chapter Thirteen

The Last Rag-and-Bone Man

Every child made a pancake today. The school cook, Mrs Mapplebeck, demonstrated how to mix the ingredients and, throughout the day, assisted by parents, each class took turns to use the single-ring electric stove in the school hall.

Extract from the Ragley School Logbook:
Tuesday, 3 March 1981

'You 'ave t'make one revelation every ten yards, Mr Sheffield,' said Ruby as she emptied my waste-paper basket into a black bag. 'It says so on t'poster outside village 'all.'

'Pardon?' I looked up from my *Yorkshire Purchasing Organization* catalogue. The price of HB pencils was causing me concern.

'It's t'annual pancake race on Saturday, Mr Sheffield,' said Ruby. 'They allus 'ave it t'Saturday after Pancake Day on t'village green.'

'Oh, I see. So are you entering, Ruby?' I asked.

'Well, our 'Azel wants me to 'ave a go.'

'I remember you winning the ladies' egg-and-spoon race, Ruby, so I'm sure you would be good at pancake racing.'

Ruby flushed with modesty at this reminder of a great day in her life three summers ago. 'Mebbe so, Mr Sheffield, an' ah'm good at making revelations.'

'Revelations?'

'That's reight,' said Ruby as she walked out of the office, dragging the black bag behind her. 'Y'ave t'keep flippin' y'pancake . . . one revelation every ten yards. Teks a lot o' skill, does that.'

I returned, bemused, to my stationery order and the price of pencils. We would have to make economies somewhere unless Mrs Thatcher relented on her public sector cut-backs. I chuckled to myself. Now, that would be a revelation.

Out of the window I watched the children arriving at school, all looking relaxed and happy and some carrying aprons and small frying pans. It was early morning on Shrove Tuesday, the last day before Lent and the final chance to indulge in fat, butter and eggs before a time of abstinence. Our school cook, Shirley Mapplebeck, was already preparing the ingredients in her kitchen for the marathon pancake-making event of the year.

Two more cars pulled up outside the school gate, followed by Mrs Dudley-Palmer's Rolls-Royce, and children piled out on to the pavement. I was puzzled why this was so as, in our tiny village, everyone lived within walking distance. It occurred to me there could be a safety problem if more parents started this unusual habit. We might even have to request some warning signs or painted lines on the road immediately outside the gate and I decided to raise the issue at our next governors' meeting. In the meantime, it was back to the HB pencils.

My first lesson was going well. You could have heard a pin drop.

'There's five senses, boys and girls,' I said with a voice of absolute authority: 'hearing, touch, sight, smell and taste. Human beings need these senses to understand the world around us.' I picked up a stick of white chalk and wrote the names of the senses on the blackboard.

Soon the children were in five groups, each one exploring a different sense. On the 'hearing' table I had set up the Grundig reel-to-reel tape recorder, on which I had recorded a variety of sounds that the children had to identify and write down. On the 'taste' table I had bicarbonate of soda, salt, sugar and sherbet, and on the 'touch' table there was a 'feely' box. I had cut a circular hole in the top of a grocery box and filled it with objects, including a tin, a jar, a toothbrush, a pack of sausages, an apple, a piece of sandpaper, leaves, a ceramic tile, a gobstopper, marbles and some tree bark. The children took turns to try to identify the objects while blindfolded.

As usual, the discussion didn't always go in the direction I had anticipated. Cathy Cathcart was waving her hand in the air. 'Mr Sheffield,' she said with a grin, 'why do noses run an' feet smell?'

It occurred to me that, although teaching might not be well paid, at least it was interesting.

*   *   *

At lunchtime in the staff-room Anne was scanning the front page of her *Yorkshire Post*. 'Hooray!' she cried. 'Inflation's gone down to thirteen per cent!' These were turbulent times in politics. The 'Gang of Four', Dr David Owen, Shirley Williams, Roy Jenkins and William Rogers, had launched the Social Democratic Party, there were real fears of a national miners' strike and Michael Foot, Leader of the Opposition, had asked Mrs Thatcher what she intended to do.

However, Vera and Valerie had more important things on their minds. They were poring over Delia Smith's cookery book and discussing soup recipes for the forthcoming series of Lent lunches.

'Seems early this year for pancakes,' said Jo.

Vera looked up. 'Shrove Tuesday is always forty-seven days before Easter Sunday, which this year is on the nineteenth of April,' she said with absolute certainty. The church calendar was always at Vera's fingertips.

Throughout the day each class went into the school hall to make their pancakes, supervised by teachers and parents. Shirley the cook described each step of the process and the day was a great success. Even though the one I made stuck to the pan and finished up looking like shredded bladderwrack, all the children were sympathetic and recognized that this was Shirley's day. She was definitely in charge, with the reliable Ruby as her second-in-command. I wondered if there was any correlation between pancakes and personality: Ruby's was large and fluffy, whereas Vera's was slim, even and perfectly symmetrical.

'That were a good day, Mr Sheffield,' said Darrell Topper as everyone left at the end of the day. I smiled in acknowledgement. It wasn't the moment to insist on correct grammar.

Saturday morning dawned bright and fair. The recent heavy rain that had cleared away the snow had gone now and early spring sunshine lifted the spirits. On my Bush radio, at nine o'clock on Radio 2, David Jacobs faded out The Byrds singing 'Mr Tambourine Man' to allow the newsreader to reassure us that the recent serious flooding of the River Ouse in York was only likely to occur once in every four hundred years.

Later, I was sitting with Beth in Nora's Coffee Shop, eating a Wagon Wheel and drinking a frothy coffee. At the counter, Dorothy was telling the teenagers Claire Bradshaw and Anita Cuthbertson why pixie boots were every young girl's dream. These wrinkly pull-on boots kept your feet warm and Dorothy had just bought a new pair that went up to her knees.

Beth seemed quiet, pursing her lips and blowing on the surface of her coffee . . . *just like Laura*. She was more quiet than usual, as if something was on her mind. In the background John Lennon's 'Imagine' was playing softly on the juke-box.

'Beth . . . would you like to go for a walk?'

She smiled and picked up her scarf and gloves. 'Good idea,' she said, but there was a hint of sadness in her eyes.

We walked across the High Street and up the well-worn

path towards the ramshackle cricket pavilion. I swung open the five-barred gate and our footsteps crunched on the gravelled car park until we reached the grassy path alongside the white picket fence that surrounded the cricket field. Beyond the hedgerow to our left was a dense wooded area that separated the track from the football field, from which came the distant cries of children.

I put my arm round her shoulders and we stopped next to a smart, newly varnished wooden bench next to the ancient cricket scoreboard. Screwed to the backrest of the bench was an engraved brass plaque that read, 'In fond memory of our most faithful supporter, HERBIE BARRETT, who left this boundary in 1976 after a good innings of 86.' We sat down and stared across the field to the woods beyond.

Suddenly the clouds cleared as if washed by a William Turner sky and sunlight burst through the bare twigs and splashed on to the woodland floor. It was a time of new life and new beginnings. Soon the coppice of hazel, lime, ash and chestnut would send up a mass of new shoots. In among the new grass, primroses, the first 'rose' of spring, provided a bright carpet of colour. It was a sight to lift the spirits and I looked at Beth. She was unmoving, deep in thought.

'Beth, I love living here . . . Don't you?'

She stared, unfocused, into the distance. 'It's fine, Jack, but . . .'

'But what?'

'Perhaps we have different ambitions.'

This wasn't the answer I had expected. 'Beth . . . I have hopes and dreams like any other man.'

'But where do you see us in five years' time or, say, at the end of the Eighties?'

'Well, I suppose I had hoped we would live together at Bilbo Cottage. It would make a lovely home – particularly if we considered having children.'

Beth nodded slowly but continued to stare into the distance. 'I see,' she said.

'Are you all right?' I asked softly and stroked her hand.

She gave me a faint smile. 'I'm fine, Jack. Don't worry about me. It's just the thought of our schools closing and what would happen then. It's so unsettling.'

'Beth, we'll be fine. I'm sure it will work out.'

She looked into my eyes as if seeing me for the first time. 'I never thought you might want to be a village teacher all your life, Jack. I just assumed you'd move on . . . that we would *both* move on,' she said, almost to herself.

'Beth, I love you . . . I'll be what you want me to be.'

She leant over and kissed me on the lips. 'And I love you, Jack.'

We sat there in the chilly silence, both deep in our own thoughts, until I heard the ringing of a distant handbell.

In Ragley High Street all eyes turned. A grey gypsy cob with a long shaggy forelock and mane clattered along, drawing a brightly painted cart. Tom Kettle, the local rag-and-bone man, was making his monthly visit to Ragley village. 'Rag-oh-bone, rag-oh-bone,' was the familiar cry, followed by the clip-clop of a horse's iron-shod hoofs.

Tom knew there would be a large crowd on this special day when the villagers of Ragley assembled on the village green for the annual pancake race. Seb Coe in the Moscow

Olympics could not have enjoyed a more partisan crowd. In this little corner of North Yorkshire, Olympic gold medals came a poor second to the Ragley Pancake Day trophy. It was a small silver cup on the base of which the names of the winners of past years were inscribed. The 1981 race, due to commence at midday, was destined to be one that would go down in Ragley folklore.

It was eleven o'clock and Tom Kettle's faithful horse, Silver, trotted at a steady pace up the High Street and his brightly polished harness clinked with the rhythm of his hoofbeats. Tom flicked the reins more out of habit than necessity. Silver knew the routine: pull, pause and rest. Outside the village hall, Silver came to a halt next to the grassy mound at the side of the road and he bowed his head and chomped contentedly.

Deirdre Coe was driving past in her Land-Rover on her way home to collect her frying pan and she pulled up sharply. 'Y'want t'keep moving on. We don't want your kind 'ere!' she bellowed.

Tom looked up nervously. Both Stan and Deirdre Coe had always given him a hard time. Silver gave Deirdre a baleful glare as she drove off, cursing. Unlike Tom, he didn't mind showing his true emotions.

Katy Ollerenshaw and Cathy Cathcart, after watching Noel Edmonds and his *Multi-Coloured Swap Shop*, were walking down the High Street and had observed the whole incident.

'Mr Kettle,' asked Katy politely, 'do horses have feelings?'

'My Silver,' said Tom, 'well, 'e knaws if tha's a good person or a bad person.'

'How does he know?' asked Katy.

''E jus' does,' said Tom. ''Orses are clever, tha knaws.'

'Mebbe 'e 'as an extra sense,' said Cathy, reaching up and stroking Silver's muzzle. 'We've been doin' about senses in school.'

Tom grinned, pulled out his trusty brass bugle, licked his dry lips, gave three sharp blasts and, for good measure, in a loud voice he shouted, 'Any ol' iron, any ol' iron.'

Tom and Silver were popular local characters. Tom was in his mid-sixties and had spoken of retirement in recent years. He wore a cloth cap, checked shirt, leather waistcoat, old thick corduroy trousers and boots with steel toe-caps.

Silver was seventeen years old and beginning to find the strain of pulling the heavy cart a little more difficult as the years rolled by. Tom climbed down and patted his dear friend's stocky neck, at which Silver peered round his large leather blinkers and gave Tom a knowing look, as if he was sharing the same thoughts of retirement.

Tom was married to a travelling woman with weathered brown skin. She walked from house to house around the local villages, selling lucky heather and clothes pegs made from coppiced hazel, and if you crossed her palm with silver she would tell your fortune. They lived in a caravan next to a tumble-down stable near the old forest on the outskirts of Easington, while Silver was left to graze on a spare acre of land that nobody seemed to want. It was a quiet, lonely existence but it suited Tom and he eked out a simple living.

His only neighbour was a strange man. Arthur

Backhouse, an occasional gravedigger, who preferred to be known as Archdruid King Arthur Greatdragon. He lived alone in the next field, in a mobile caravan that he referred to as his 'proto-druidic megalith', and each winter equinox his fellow Druids called in for their annual party. After consuming a few giant cans of Watney's Party Seven Draught Bitter, Arthur and his fellow revellers would dance round a blazing campfire and chant prayers for the return of sunshine.

The highlight of the evening was Arthur drinking a yard of ale and then attempting to cry out a sacred magical call to Lugh, the Sun God. Sadly, the urgent need to be violently sick in the nearby hedgerow lessened the impact of this season-changing recitation.

Fortunately for Arthur, however, his Druid girlfriend, Margery – a Smarties packer in the Joseph Rowntree factory – otherwise known as Airmid, the Goddess of Herb-lore, was always there to provide relief. She immediately offered Arthur a potent herbal mixture of ground ivy and mugwort from the leather pouch round her neck. However, on reflection, he decided to go for the Alka-Seltzer in his kitchen cabinet. Then, in the early hours of the morning, the Druids would make their way home, except, of course, for the Goddess of Herb-lore, who always stayed the night. So, for Arthur, his prayers were answered and the earth continued to move.

Beth and I arrived back in the High Street as a stream of children, tugging adults behind them, gathered round the horse and cart. While the children patted Silver, their parents arrived with armfuls of old clothing and pieces of unwanted furniture. It was the flotsam of their life that Big Dave and Little Malcolm couldn't remove in their bin wagon. In exchange, Tom would give each child a blue balloon and a length of baling twine.

Soon a crowd of children were making their way up the High Street towards the village green with their balloons floating on the brisk breeze.

'Ronnie!' shouted Ruby. 'Go and get that old iron bedstead from our back garden.'

'M'back's a bit painful, my luv,' said Ronnie, more in hope than expectation.

'Tell our Duggie t'give you a 'and,' commanded Ruby, 'an' then our 'Azel will get a balloon.' We watched Ronnie walk slowly back home. "E's a lazy so-an'-so is that one,' said Ruby, shaking her head.

At twelve o'clock it seemed the whole village had surrounded the village green. Dan Hunter had provided some plastic cones from the back of his police van to mark out the track and Albert Jenkins read out the strict rules to the twenty competitors who had assembled on the forecourt of The Royal Oak.

Most had come for the fun of it and it was an incongruous group of ladies who chatted, giggled, admired each other's pancakes and, in some cases, exchanged recipes. Petula Dudley-Palmer had made her pancake very carefully that morning. After consulting page 139 of her *Good Housekeeping's New Picture Cookery* book she had created an impressive layered pancake filled with whipped cream and jam. The thought of flipping her creation horrified her.

The vivacious Madame Jacqueline Laporte, the French teacher from Easington Comprehensive School, always celebrated Mardi Gras and had covered her pancake with a hot sauce of caramelized sugar, orange juice and lightly grated orange peel. The pièce de résistance was a splash of Grand Marnier. While the resulting flambéed crêpe Suzette was perhaps a little too cordon bleu for Ragley Pancake Day, it was generally agreed that the attractive French woman with the Bridget Bardot looks repeatedly produced the crème de la crème of pancakes. The watching menfolk also noted that, in her figure-hugging, pencil-slim black skirt, she would never win a pancake race in a month of *dimanches*.

Deirdre Coe's pancake looked like a fossilized cowpat. Brown and inedible, it displayed little of culinary or artistic merit. However, such was its consistency, Deirdre could flip it with unerring accuracy like a leather placemat. After practising for an hour in her brother's cowshed she had only dropped it twice in the festering cow muck that covered the concrete floor. However, after a quick wipe with a dishcloth, it was as good as new. By the time she had arrived at the start line the local punters had her down as the marginal favourite.

Ruby walked to the start line with her frying pan gripped in her hand. She had made her batter, fried it in a pan, sprinkled the resulting pancake with a little caster sugar, and she was ready.

Deirdre Coe took a last puff of her cigarette and sneered at Ruby. 'Judgement Day, y'big lump.'

'Y'll gerra clout if y'don't shurrup!' retorted Ruby.

'Get lost, caretaker-skivvy. See you at t'finish,' said Deirdre.

Albert fired his starting pistol, the crowd cheered the competitors and they were off.

After a lifetime of mopping floors Ruby had wrists like a Canadian lumberjack and she held her frying pan in a vice-like grip. With unerring accuracy she flipped her pancake every ten paces, to the satisfaction of the pancake race judge, Albert Jenkins, and by halfway round the track she had taken the lead.

'C'mon, Mam,' yelled Ruby's daughters.

'Come on, Ruby,' shouted Joseph and Vera Evans, forgetting all sense of decorum.

What Deirdre Coe lacked in fitness and technique she made up for with devious cunning. A nudge here, a shove there, and her rivals fell by the wayside one by one. Coming up to the last bend by the duck pond at the side of the village green there was only Ruby to beat. Ruby had hugged the inside lane and there was no way Deirdre could overtake unless she went to the outside of the track. The crowd held their breath as Deirdre made her move. It was now or never.

As she dug her elbows into Ruby's ample frame and, with a last desperate lunge, tried to pass her on the outside of the track, she beheld a fiercesome sight. Tom Kettle had parked his cart under the weeping-willow tree at the side of the duck pond and Silver was grazing nearby, unmoved by the noise and the charge of the pancake brigade. Unmoved, that is, until Deirdre Coe came flying by and something stirred in the cob's memory.

Silver stretched out his broad head towards her. His ears turned back and the whites of his eyes glared in a manic stare. With gums stretched back to reveal his tombstone teeth, he snarled and grabbed Deirdre's pancake as she flipped it for the last time.

'Hi-ho, Silver,' yelled Deke Ramsbottom, waving his cowboy hat.

'Ru-bee, Ru-bee,' chanted the Ragley Rovers football team.

Deirdre finished up on her backside in a muddy patch by the duck pond, while Ruby roared up the home straight like Red Rum in the Grand National.

'Ruby, my luv,' shouted Ronnie, surprisingly removing his bobble hat and throwing it in the air.

'My mam's a winner,' shouted Hazel, clutching her blue balloon.

Ruby was presented with the trophy, the crowd cheered and everyone went home to eat their pancakes. It was another memorable day.

As Tom led Silver back to his cart he whispered in his ear and patted him gently.

Cathy Cathcart tugged my sleeve. 'You can tell he loves his horse, can't you, Mr Sheffield? It's like when my mam tucks me in at night.'

'You're right, Cathy,' I said.

'P'raps it's another one o' them senses . . .' called Cathy as she disappeared into the crowd.

Perhaps it was.

Chapter Fourteen

A Boy and a Kite

*A 'Reading Workshop' will commence next Monday in
the school hall at ten o'clock. A letter went out inviting
parents, grandparents and friends to support the scheme
aimed at promoting reading throughout the school.*

Extract from the Ragley School Logbook:
Friday, 27 March 1981

The curtains were closed; they always were.

Violet Tinkle sat in her high-backed armchair, fingered
her string of pearls and stared blankly at the flickering
beams of light that pierced the gap between the heavy
velvet curtains.

She was seventy-one years old and a resident of the
Hartford Home for Retired Gentlefolk, an imposing red-
brick Victorian building that hid behind a tall yew hedge
set back in two acres of private land beyond the Ragley
cricket pitch. It had once been a military hospital during
World War Two where soldiers, sailors and airmen had

their tired and broken bodies nursed back to health.

Outside her window the late March wind was strength-
ening. It rattled the grey roof slates and shook the tall
chimneypots. Suddenly a strong gust blew back the curtains and – through the glass doors, beyond the balcony
– Violet saw something that would change her life. It was
a boy and a kite.

'Ah've lost it, Mr Sheffield,' said eleven-year-old Darrell
Topper. He looked close to tears.

'Lost it?' I repeated in surprise. 'But it's bright yellow
and as tall as you.'

'Ah know, Mr Sheffield, but it went over that 'igh 'edge
where them old people live an' ah daren't go in there.'

I looked across the Ragley cricket field. A sturdy wood-
en gate was set into the hedge like a castle portcullis.

Jo Hunter walked over to me. 'One's gone over the
hedge, Jack,' she said. 'Do you want me to go and ask for
it back?'

It was Friday lunchtime, 27 March, and Jo and I had
taken the children in my class into the village to test out
their new kites as part of our Flight project. Earlier in the
week we had enjoyed an exciting art and craft lesson
making weird and wonderful kite creations of all shapes
and sizes, each with a long tail of streamers that looked
like a string of bow ties. Timothy Pratt had provided a
collection of garden canes for the framework and a huge
ball of fine garden twine. After using up all the left-over
crêpe and tissue paper from Christmas, twenty-three kites
had been launched successfully but now only twenty-two
were in the air.

I looked at the formidable hedge. The other side was unknown. 'No, I'll go. You take over, Jo, and I'll be back in five minutes.'

Darrell walked with me to the gate. I looked up and there on the first floor, leaning over a wrought-iron Juliet balcony, was an aristocratic lady with grey hair tied in a neat bun, a warm cardigan covering a smart cream blouse, a calf-length tweed skirt, thick stockings and smart leather brogue shoes. The string of pearls around her neck sparkled in the bright sunshine.

She waved a delicate hand. 'Hello,' she said with a weak smile.

'Good afternoon,' I shouted up to her. 'I'm Jack Sheffield, the village school headteacher. A kite belonging to one of my pupils has blown over the hedge.'

'Yes, I can see it,' she said.

'I wondered if I might be allowed to collect it?'

'Yes, of course. I'll come down.'

She reappeared a few moments later at the French windows that led from the house to the garden. The kite was tangled above our heads halfway up the high hedge.

'There's a pair of step-ladders in the gardener's store.' She pointed to an old brick outbuilding. The large wooden doors were open and gardening tools were stacked neatly inside.

After collecting the kite, I returned the step-ladders. 'Thank you,' I said. 'Darrell will be thrilled to get it back.'

'I'm Mrs Tinkle, by the way, Mr Sheffield – Violet Tinkle,' she said with a gentle smile. 'I do believe I'm the only Violet in the village,' she said proudly.

'I'm delighted to meet you, Mrs Tinkle,' I said.

She looked around her as if it was a new experience. Snowdrops were like pearls in the sunshine. 'I'd almost forgotten how beautiful springtime is,' she said. Young sprouting leaves of hawthorn had brought new life to the skeleton hedgerows and spears of daffodil buds, surrounded by their blue-green leaves, thrust their heads above the grass.

'Would you like to meet Darrell?' I said. 'I'm sure he'd like to say thank you.' I beckoned to him to join us.

'You have a fine kite, Darrell,' said Violet.

'Thank you,' he said, looking relieved.

'I used to make kites when I was a girl,' she said.

Darrell looked in surprise. 'Did you?'

'And . . . are you working hard at school?' she asked.

His cheeks flushed. 'Ah'm trying m'best but reading's 'ard,' he replied with refreshing honesty.

Violet smiled, we said goodbye and she went back inside. Suddenly, a tall athletic young woman in a Cambridge-blue polo shirt, with a Hartford oak tree logo, jeans and trainers, came out carrying a clipboard. She smiled at me in recognition.

'Oh, hello, Mr Sheffield. I'm Janet Ollerenshaw, one of the carers here. My sister Katy is in your class.' She looked at Darrell's kite and grinned. 'Can I help?'

'Pleased to meet you, Janet,' I said as we shook hands. 'We've just retrieved Darrell's kite. Mrs Tinkle helped us find a ladder.'

'That's a good sign,' Janet said thoughtfully. 'Her curtains are open at last.'

'She's a nice lady,' said Darrell.

'She is,' said Janet. 'Just a bit lonely since her sister passed on.'

'I'm sorry to hear that,' I said.

We walked to the gate and looked out on to the cricket field. Jo had gathered all the children together with their kites ready to walk back to school. Janet waved to her sister and the tall willowy Katy waved back. The likeness was striking.

'She's like I was,' said Janet reflectively. 'I was netball captain just like our Katy when Mr Pruett was headteacher.'

Darrell and I joined the end of the straggling line of kite-bearers.

'I could write 'er a thank-you letter, Mr Sheffield,' said Darrell. 'That might cheer 'er up.'

I looked at him in surprise. Writing wasn't his favourite pastime. 'Well done, Darrell,' I said enthusiastically. 'That's a great idea – let's do it this afternoon.'

Back in school, Vera was typing a notice for parents entitled 'READING WORKSHOP – Monday, 30 March'.

At the last staff meeting, Valerie Flint had come up with the idea. It was aimed at promoting reading throughout the school and everyone decided to give it a try. Ruby agreed to put out the dining tables in the school hall at ten o'clock each day and parents, grandparents and friends of Ragley School would be invited to come and listen to children read. On a card inside the book they would note down the number of pages read and any words that had caused difficulty. Then the class teacher would check this information on their return to the classroom. We thought it would be good for the children, increase the frequency of reading and further develop our school as a centre of the village community.

At the end of school I was in the office, completing my governors' report, when the telephone rang. It was Richard Gomersall, Senior Primary Adviser from County Hall.

'Hello, Jack. Glad I've caught you. I have something to tell you that may be of interest,' he said.

'Yes?'

'Barry Prior, headteacher at Gorse Manor Primary School in Scarborough, is retiring at Christmas. It's a large school, Jack – four hundred and fifty rising to five hundred.'

'Yes. I know Barry,' I said. 'I've met him on various courses – a lovely man.'

'That's right, Jack . . . but the school is ready for taking forward into the Eighties. We'll be advertising next term.'

'I see,' I said. 'Well, I hope Barry will be very happy in his retirement.'

There was a pause and I heard a riffling of papers. 'You see, Jack, I'm at High Sutton Hall leading the curriculum course and, as you know, Beth is here.'

'Yes?' I was surprised at the direction the conversation was taking.

'She mentioned you were thinking of a move to a bigger school.'

'Did she?' I was shocked.

'So I thought I'd bring this to your attention, particularly with the fate of some of our smaller schools uncertain at present.'

I was determined to cover up my surprise. 'Well, I appreciate your letting me know, Richard.'

'You've built up a good reputation, Jack, and we always like to develop and promote our own, so to speak.'

'I see.'

'I'll call in when I can.'

'Thanks, Richard.'

The line went dead and I was still staring at the receiver when Vera walked in.

'Anything urgent, Mr Sheffield? You looked concerned,' she said as she filed away the latest reading test results.

'No, Vera,' I replied quickly, perhaps a little too quickly, and she looked at me curiously.

On my way home I delivered Darrell's letter for Mrs Tinkle but my mind was buzzing after the telephone conversation. I needed to speak to Beth – in private.

On Sunday morning I gave my Morris Minor Traveller a quick polish. It was Mother's Day, Beth had returned from High Sutton to her home in Morton and Diane Henderson had driven up from Hampshire to spend the weekend with her. We had agreed to attend the Mothering Sunday service at St Mary's followed by lunch at The Royal Oak.

As I drove out of Kirkby Steepleton I sensed a faint stirring of wind and soil. The season was turning. Cow parsley had begun to invade the verges at the side of the back road to Ragley village and blackbirds were making their nests. Above me, among the purple elm buds in the high branches, the high-pitched cawing of rooks shattered the silence whenever a precious twig was stolen to repair a nest. The nearby woods were carpeted with primroses and soon the children of Ragley would be excited by the first signs of frogspawn.

After a lovely service we pulled up outside The Royal Oak. Beth held my hand as we walked in and the slim, elegant Diane Henderson looked stunning in a cream two-piece trouser suit. As always, they turned heads and I felt good to be accompanied by two such beautiful women.

Sheila's Sunday roast dinners were always a treat and both bars were filling quickly as we found a table.

Diane glanced at the pile of Sunday newspapers on the reception table. 'I see the wedding date has been confirmed,' she said.

I looked at her in surprise. 'Pardon?'

Beth grinned. 'Mother means the *royal* wedding, Jack.'

'Yes,' said Diane. 'It said in the paper that Charles and Diana will marry on the twenty-ninth of July.'

'Just after the end of the summer term,' said Beth.

'Good job we didn't pick that date,' I said.

'Beth was saying it will probably be next year,' said Diane.

'You know, Jack . . . when things are more settled,' added Beth a little hurriedly.

I stood up. 'I'll order, shall I?'

Big Dave and Little Malcolm were staring up at the television above the bar and watching highlights of the first London Marathon organized by Chris Brasher, the former Olympic steeplechaser. The American Dick Beardsley and Norwegian Inge Simonsen had shared first place by crossing the finishing line holding hands in a little over two hours, eleven minutes. Joyce Smith was the winner of the ladies race in just under two and a half hours and, remarkably, eighty per cent of the seven-and-a-half-thousand competitors completed the course.

'It'll never catch on,' said Big Dave.

'Y'reight there, Dave,' said Little Malcolm.

'Did y'see who won?' asked Clint Ramsbottom.

'It were a dead 'eat,' said Stevie 'Supersub' Coleclough.

'A dead 'eat!' exclaimed Big Dave. ''Ow can it be a dead 'eat after twenty-six miles?'

'It were won by two fellers an' one were a Norwegian,' said Stevie.

'They were 'olding 'ands,' added Chris 'Kojak' Wojciechowski knowingly.

'Y'know what they say about Norwegians,' said Big Dave darkly and everyone nodded.

'Y'reight there, Dave,' agreed Little Malcolm, although, apart from Norwegian seamen knitting their own socks, he didn't entirely follow his giant cousin's train of thought.

'Ah don't see much point in it,' said Shane Ramsbottom, 'jus' running.'

'Y'spot-on there, Shane,' said his brother Clint. 'It's not like y'running *for* summat . . . like a bus.'

'Or running *away* from summat,' added Kojak, '. . . like a woman.'

'Women are no good at running,' said Nutter Neilsen with authority. 'They're not built t'same as us.'

Puzzled, everyone looked at Nutter, who usually added very little to their conversations.

Sheila rose to the challenge. 'An' what's wrong wi' women running?' Her sequinned boob tube stretched tight under the strain of her risen chest. At that exact moment every man around stared at her prodigious bosom and, unaware everyone else was thinking the same thought, considered it was a good thing that women weren't built the same as men.

'Well, ah've 'eard they'd lose weight from all t'wrong places,' explained Nutter hastily.

Sheila glanced down at her main asset. 'Oh, ah see,' said Sheila. 'Well, Nutter, mebbe y've gorra point there.'

'Anyway, ah'd speed it up,' he continued.

''Ow?' asked Big Dave.

'Ah'd give 'em all a ten-minute start an' then ah'd set t'major's 'ounds after 'em. Y'wunt want t'be in t'back o' one o' them pantomime 'orses then, ah reckon.'

Everyone nodded, impressed at Nutter's new-found ability for divergent thinking.

Beth was sitting alone when I returned to our table with three glasses of red wine.

'My mother has gone to get something from the car,' she said.

I plunged in. 'Richard Gomersall said you had told him I was thinking of another headship.'

Beth sipped her wine and looked at me steadily. 'Yes, I did.'

'It came as a bit of a surprise.'

Beth seemed unflustered. 'It seemed a good opportunity to mention it,' she said.

'It's just that I have never said I wanted a bigger headship and I felt a bit . . . awkward.'

'I was just trying to help, Jack. Come the summer term, decisions will have to be made, whether we like it or not. If you're not proactive you may miss your chance.'

I was becoming increasingly aware of a steely resolve to Beth that until recently I hadn't realized was there. It wasn't a comfortable feeling.

Diane came back in, carrying a large creased envelope. 'Sorry to be so long.' She pulled out a Mother's Day card and pointed to the handwritten message. 'Here it is, Beth,' said Diane. 'Laura says she's coming up to see you at Easter.'

Sheila served us with roast beef and Yorkshire pudding and I sat back and drank my wine. My appetite had disappeared. Life was becoming more complicated.

On Monday morning Vera was on the telephone when I walked into the office.

'Yes, of course, Janet,' she said. 'It's a wonderful idea and it will be good for Violet to get out again at last.' She put down the receiver and looked at me. 'Good news, Mr Sheffield,' she said. 'That was Janet Ollerenshaw. She's bringing Violet Tinkle to the reading workshop.'

'And I know just the person who would like to read to her,' I said.

It was during morning break that Vera told me the story of Violet Tinkle.

*   *   *

Violet was born in Portsmouth in 1909 and, twenty years later, had married William Tinkle. They had two sons, John and Edward. In October 1940 Violet and her boys had listened to the wireless and heard the sixteen-year-old Princess Elizabeth's broadcast to the children of Britain and the Empire. It was to be the last night she spent with her sons. Of Portsmouth's seventy thousand homes, sixty-three thousand were damaged by German bombs. The sound and the fury of the blast lived with Violet for the rest of her life and she grieved that she had been spared while her sons had been killed instantly. William never returned from the war and she didn't remarry.

So it was that Violet came to live with her sister, Mavis, in a little cottage on the Morton Road and soon the pair of them were immersed in the war effort. They coordinated the local Dig for Victory campaign during the time German U-boats in the Atlantic were preventing food imports from reaching our shores from other parts of the Empire. Then they taught children how to garden and began a pig and poultry club. The children performed plays to raise money for the war effort and collected scrap metal and silver paper to help the government make more Spitfires.

Evacuees continued to arrive from the cities, each child carrying a cardboard box containing a pair of spare shoes and socks, a change of underwear, pyjamas, towel, soap, toothbrush and a warm coat. Brothers and sisters were kept together, and they never forgot the day Mrs Tinkle took them to see Judy Garland in *The Wizard of Oz*. Very soon they called her Auntie Violet.

*   *   *

At ten o'clock, Violet was sitting at a table in the school hall. Darrell was reading to her from his *Ginn Reading 360* book. At first he struggled, but slowly, his confidence increasing, he made progress.

Violet looked carefully at Darrell. 'Don't worry,' she said quietly. 'Those who have never failed have never really tried.'

Darrell nodded, not fully understanding.

'Tell me,' said Violet, 'what do you like reading?'

'Ah love football, Mrs Tinkle, speshully Roy Race.'

'Roy Race?'

'Yes,'e's in t'*Roy of the Rovers* comic every Monday. 'E's player-manager of Melchester Rovers an' they're 'aving a tough time.'

'Oh, are they?'

The bell went for morning break and I joined Darrell and a few of his friends at Violet's table. Alongside her was a battered Cadbury's Milk Tray box.

'What's that for, Mrs Tinkle?' asked Darrell.

'I keep all my memories in a chocolate box,' said Violet simply. Inside were photographs of her past life, including one of a young and beautiful woman. It was a long-ago world of long dresses and starched collars, a time of uncut loaves and creamy milk, of brass bands and gramophone records – and a time of war and countless soldiers who never came home.

More children gathered round and were fascinated by Violet's memories of Bisto and Bovril, Ford and Austin, Lyons Corner Houses and tea dances. Anne, Vera and Valerie came and sat down beside me to enjoy the company of this remarkable lady. There was grace and lightness to her movements and the raven hair that had once cascaded around her shoulders was now a tight silver-grey bun on the top of her head and held in place by a bird's nest of metal hair grips.

'We were told to Dig for Victory,' said Violet, 'and if one and a half million homes saved a small bucket of coal each day it would provide enough fuel to build a destroyer.'

Shirley came out of the kitchen and looked at Violet's old ration book.

'We never wasted our vegetable water,' she said to Shirley. 'Instead we used it to make soup the Oxo way and I learnt how to make a cake without eggs.' Shirley's eyebrows shot up in surprise. 'We used saccharine instead.' She held up an old savings book. 'I used to buy National Savings Certificates at the Post Office. If I saved fifteen shillings, after five years it would be worth seventeen shillings and sixpence,' she said proudly. 'We were also told that life would be wonderful after the war. The drawings in my *Good Housekeeping* magazine showed a land of high-rise flats, new shopping centres and Rufflette tape for new curtains to brighten our windows after the blackout.'

By the time Violet left she had answered a hundred questions and had promised Darrell she would be back every Monday to hear him read.

I walked out with Violet and we stood by the school gate. 'Thank you for coming in, Mrs Tinkle,' I said. 'The children have loved your stories and I know Darrell will look forward to your next visit.'

'No: thank *you*, Mr Sheffield. This has brightened up my life. Since my sister passed on it's been a silent world, just shadows and dust . . . shadows and dust,' she repeated softly.

It was the following Monday morning when I met Violet again. We were in the General Stores and, much to the surprise of Miss Golightly, she had just spent fifteen pence on a *Roy of the Rovers* comic.

'Good morning, Mrs Tinkle,' I said.

She smiled. 'Good morning, Mr Sheffield. This is for Darrell.'

I looked puzzled.

'You may not be aware, Mr Sheffield, but Roy Race, the manager of Melchester Rovers, is having a difficult time at present,' and with that she walked out.

It was an unlikely duo but Violet and Darrell were destined to remain friends in the coming years. In our next craft lesson, Darrell made a gift for his reading workshop partner. It was a teapot stand made out of off-cuts. Even though it had a distinct wobble, Violet was destined to keep it for the rest of her life.

The next time the children in my class flew their kites on the Ragley cricket pitch I stared into the distance. Beyond the high yew hedge and a Juliet balcony was a particular window and I smiled.

Something was different now.

The curtains were open; they always were.

Chapter Fifteen

Agatha Christie and the Missing Vicar

School closed today for the Easter holidays. End-of-term reports were sent out in the new North Yorkshire report books to be signed by parents. Mrs Pringle returned to school with her new baby to attend morning assembly.

Extract from the Ragley School Logbook:
Friday, 10 April 1981

'Did you say *Murder at the Vicarage*?' whispered Vera.

'Yes. It's terrific,' said Sally softly.

'Surely not!' said Vera, picking up Sally's paperback novel.

'Did someone say *murder*?' asked a bemused Joseph, looking up from his assembly notices.

'Shush, Joseph!' said Vera.

As usual, Joseph didn't know what was going on around him. It was Friday, 10 April, the last day before the Easter holiday, and our bemused local vicar had agreed to lead our morning prayers. Meanwhile Sally had called in to introduce Grace, her beautiful two-month-old baby, to all the children during school assembly. It appeared she had been catching up with the novels of the world-famous crime writer Agatha Christie.

'You read it, Vera,' whispered Sally as she removed the baby's mittens. 'It's a wonderful novel. Really. I finished it this week in between feeding Grace. You could read it on tomorrow's coach trip to Harrogate.'

Vera nodded thoughtfully. Many of us were going on the Village Hall Committee's annual trip to the Harrogate Flower Show. It was a long journey and a good book would pass the time. 'But don't you think *Murder at the Vicarage* is an unfortunate title?' persisted Vera.

'Perhaps,' said Sally, 'but she's a wonderful writer and it's the first appearance of Miss Jane Marple in one of her crime novels.'

The mild-mannered spinster sleuth had quickly emerged as one of the nation's favourite detectives. In the sleepy quintessentially English village of St Mary Mead death and deception lurked, but, undeterred, Miss Marple, in her effortless and analytical style, assisted the plodding Inspector Slack to uncover the culprit.

'It's a real brain-teaser, Vera,' said Sally. 'You'd enjoy it.'

'Hmmm, possibly,' said Vera.

'Miss Marple and Hercule Poirot are the most wonderful creations, Vera,' said Valerie Flint.

'And did you know that Hercule Poirot actually got an obituary in *The Times* in 1976?' added Sally.

'Really?' said Vera. She was impressed. Perhaps this was *upper-class* detective literature.

'Miss Marple's just brilliant!' said the animated Jo, picking up the novel and eagerly scanning the back cover. 'She has such a sharp mind, Vera. In fact . . . she's a bit like you.'

'Well, I wouldn't go that far,' said Vera with slightly false modesty.

'Jo's got a point, Vera,' said Sally, 'so why not read it and see how she solves the murder?'

'Ah, so you *did* say murder,' said the distracted Joseph.

'Shush!' said Vera. 'You'll wake the baby.'

Grace Pringle was sleeping peacefully in a Moses basket on the staff-room coffee-table and we had all gathered round to admire this little miracle of nature.

'Sally's right, Vera,' said Valerie, lightly stroking little Grace's velvet cheek. 'Agatha Christie *is* the world's greatest crime writer.'

Jo was reading the synopsis on the cover. 'And it sounds a great plot,' she said. 'Colonel Lucius Protheroe has been murdered and everyone in St Mary Mead appears to be a suspect. So it has to be the unfaithful wife, her lover, the daughter who will inherit his fortune or the soppy vicar.'

'Soppy vicar!' exclaimed Vera. 'Surely not.'

'But it's got to be one of them,' replied Anne thoughtfully.

'I agree,' said Jo.

'But a vicar would never do such a thing,' said Vera.

Joseph looked up from his Easter assembly notices. 'What have I done now?'

'Shush, Joseph,' said Vera.

'Well, I'm afraid the vicar here did say that anyone who

259

murdered Colonel Protheroe would be doing the world a favour,' insisted Sally.

'Did I?' said Joseph.

'And he was waving a carving knife at the time,' added Sally, for good measure.

'Was I?' said Joseph, looking horrified at the thought.

'Well,' said Anne, 'what a strange vicar.'

'Oh dear,' said the perplexed Joseph.

'Oh, do be quiet, Joseph,' said Vera.

'Definitely odd behaviour for a vicar,' said Jo.

'I agree . . . and talking about murder like that is not very *Christian*,' said Vera, looking concerned.

Joseph looked up, horrified, a third custard cream held guiltily in his trembling hand. 'So you *did* say murder?' he mumbled through a mouthful of crumbs.

Vera slapped the lid on the biscuit tin.

'So do read it over the holidays, Vera,' said Sally.

'And I'll read it after you,' said Anne.

'Then me,' said Valerie.

'And me too,' added Jo.

Vera looked across the staff-room and shot a fierce glance at Joseph. 'And no more custard creams, Joseph. You've had quite enough.'

Joseph, deeply offended, considered giving his older sister his if-looks-could-kill glance but, after fingering his clerical collar, wisely said nothing.

We all sauntered back to our classrooms, Vera took out her late dinner money register, baby Grace remained in a deep slumber and Sally opened her April issue of *Cosmopolitan* magazine and wondered how Jerry Hall had poured herself into an astonishing bronze lamé figure-moulded sheath dress. Meanwhile, Joseph stared at Vera's Agatha Christie novel with a mixture of suspicion and curiosity. Then he picked it up rather guiltily and began to read. Finally, when the assembly bell rang he placed it reluctantly back on the coffee-table and walked into the hall with Sally and her sleeping baby.

The children loved meeting baby Grace, but at the end, when Joseph took over, the responses to his questions were predictably entertaining. 'What's the name of the first book of the Bible?' he asked.

Darrell Topper's hand shot up, which surprised me.

'Guinness,' he called out – which, of course, *didn't* surprise me.

Joseph's attempts to involve the smallest children in Anne's reception class, all seated cross-legged on the front row, met with similar confusion.

Five-year-old Benjamin Roberts had obviously formed his own view of the effort required in the act of creation. 'My dad says work is tiring,' he said, 'so he has Sundays off just like God.'

That evening Beth and I went to the York ABC cinema to watch Christopher Reeve in *Superman II*. Three prisoners from the planet Krypton had arrived on Earth, each with the same powers as Superman. Even though Terence Stamp as the evil General Zod stole the show, somehow good prevailed and we walked back to my car relaxed and looking forward to the Easter holiday. Much to my relief, nothing more was said about a new headship.

* * *

On Saturday morning in Ragley High Street, outside the village hall, April sunshine flashed on the shiny windows of William Featherstone's ancient cream and green Reliance bus. Although from an earlier age of sedate travel, William's bus was wonderfully maintained and perfectly reliable. 'You can rely on Reliance' had been painted in bright red letters under the rear window. As was the custom, William, in his neatly ironed brown bus driver's jacket, white shirt and ex-regimental tie, doffed his peaked cap and, with old-fashioned charm, welcomed each passenger as they boarded.

'G'morning, Mr Sheffield . . . and to you, Miss 'Enderson,' he said as Beth and I clambered aboard. To my surprise, Laura was sitting at the front, immediately behind the driver's seat. I knew she was intending to visit Beth during the Easter holiday but I hadn't expected to see her on this trip.

'Hello, Jack.'

'Oh, hello, Laura. How are you?'

She looked just as I remembered her, slim and beautiful, her long brown hair tumbling over a black leather jacket with padded shoulders. For a moment her eyes were soft and vulnerable, but an instant later her gaze was cautious and guarded. 'I'm fine,' she said.

I felt awkward, remembering our last meeting. There was still something special yet elusive about Laura. 'So how's London?'

'It's good, Jack – an exciting place to live.'

'So you decided to come after all,' said Beth.

Laura smiled at her sister. 'Last-minute decision,' she said. 'I've heard so much about Harrogate in the spring, I thought I'd come along.' Her green eyes flashed and she gave me that familiar mischievous look that brought back many memories. 'You don't mind, do you, Jack?'

'Of course not,' I said evenly. 'Lovely to see you again.' I leant over and gave her a peck on the cheek. Her perfume was just as I remembered it, Opium by Yves Saint Laurent, and for a moment I hesitated, recalling happier times.

We sat in the seat directly behind Laura and then Beth had a change of mind. 'I'd better sit with my sister,' she said apologetically and got up and settled down next to Laura.

Meanwhile, Joseph and Vera had climbed on board. Vera waved to Joyce Davenport and a few of her Women's Institute friends on the back seat and walked down the aisle to join them. Joseph grinned at me. 'May I?' he said.

'Of course, Joseph,' I replied, and he sat next to me and took Vera's *Daily Telegraph* from his pocket and settled into his seat. Soon he was frowning. Peter William Sutcliffe, a thirty-five-year-old Bradford lorry driver, known as the Yorkshire Ripper and accused of murdering thirteen women, was to be tried at the Old Bailey.

'Are you all right, Joseph?' I asked quietly.

'To be perfectly honest, Jack, I didn't really want to come. I would have preferred a quiet day at home with a glass of my peapod special and a good book, but you know what Vera's like.'

'Well, let's hope you enjoy it,' I said.

He gave me a resigned look and returned to his

newspaper. All was not well with the world. Customs and immigration workers at ports and airports were threatening to disrupt the Easter holidays over their fifteen per cent pay claim and Joseph sighed, folded the newspaper and stared out of the window.

Soon the vast plain of York that stretched from the Pennines to the Hambleton Hills was left behind us and our coach rumbled along the A59 Skipton road. The landscape rushed by, hedgerows were bursting into life and tiny lambs took their first faltering steps in fields of new grass.

We wound our way down into the Nidd valley and before us the large, wealthy spa town of Harrogate filled the skyline. As we drove along the Stray, wide gracious lawns studded with a mosaic of crocuses spread out on either side of us. It was an oasis of calm and elegance. Spring had come to Yorkshire in all its glory, breathing new life into the winter trees and lifting our spirits.

William slowed down to park on Montpelier Hill. Tourists were everywhere and, as we pulled up, he had to brake fiercely when an elderly lady stepped off the kerb in front of him. Books, newspapers, bags and coats fell on to the floor of the coach.

'Sorry, everybody,' shouted William.

Laura's handbag had burst open and keys, pens and assorted business cards scattered around her. There was a clatter as her lipstick fell into the aisle and rolled towards my size eleven Kickers shoes. I stretched down and picked it up just as Laura stooped to retrieve it. Our heads touched briefly and I stared into her soft green eyes. 'Sorry,' I said.

'Thanks, Jack. I'm all fingers and thumbs today.'

As she took the elegant metal tube from me our fingers touched briefly. Her hair brushed against my face and then she stood up and smoothed her skin-tight, stone-washed hipster jeans.

Beth picked up Laura's bunch of keys and Vera walked down the aisle to help. 'Here's your wallet,' she said.

'Oh, thanks, Vera,' said Laura, looking preoccupied.

'And the rest,' said Joseph, as he hastily gathered up her belongings and piled them on the seat.

When we got off the coach, everyone set off to join the crowds of tourists flocking to the annual Spring Flower Show. I stood with Laura, Vera and Joseph while Beth browsed through her Harrogate guidebook.

'How about starting at the Pump Room, the site of the old sulphur well?' she said. 'It looks interesting.'

'What about you, Joseph?' asked Vera.

He was staring in the opposite direction, deep in thought. 'Well, if you don't mind, I thought I might go and sit in the Montpelier Gardens and admire the lovely blooms and listen to the band, Vera,' said Joseph.

Vera looked quizzically at her brother. 'Very well, Joseph. We'll collect you from there a little later.' She fussed over his scarf for a moment and then stood back to admire her handiwork. 'There now, keep wrapped up and warm.'

He looked a little sheepish and, as he walked down the winding path of the gardens, he felt in his overcoat pocket, took out a book and smiled. 'Peace at last,' he murmured to himself and sat down on a secluded bench behind a high forsythia hedge. He settled back and began to read the next thrilling chapter.

As Beth had the guidebook, she became the impromptu guide and told us that the local springs possessed a sulphur and iron content that gave them a unique quality. 'It says they have the power to reinvigorate the body and heal ills,' she said.

'Just what I need,' said Laura.

When we came out we looked for Joseph but he was nowhere to be seen.

'Where *has* he gone?' asked Vera, scanning the crowds in the distant gardens. After a lifetime of looking after her absent-minded younger brother, she knew this was typical of him. 'Oh well, never mind, it's his loss . . . Where next, Beth?'

'The Royal Baths Assembly Rooms,' Beth announced, pointing to a photograph in her guidebook.

This was where Victorian health-conscious ladies and rheumatic gentlemen had bathed in the soothing waters. At the end of the nineteenth century, the opening of the Royal Baths Assembly Rooms with its mud baths and steam rooms was a masterstroke. Its pure spa waters became a veritable fountain of youth. By the early twentieth century, so many leading politicians sought the health-giving properties of the famous 'treatments' that it was almost possible to hold a Cabinet meeting in the opulent Turkish baths. Harrogate had become a health farm for the rich and the local economy boomed.

Again, when we came out, we looked for Joseph, who, unknown to us, was completely enthralled by his novel and had forgotten the time.

Vera shook her head in frustration. 'Silly man,' she said.

'How about a cup of tea in Bettys Café Tea Rooms?' said Beth.

'What a good idea,' said Laura.

'With fresh scones,' I said enthusiastically.

'And crumpets and curd tarts,' said Vera with a faraway smile.

Opposite the tall Cenotaph, at the head of Parliament Street, we paused under the impressive wrought-iron canopy of Bettys Café Tea Rooms, noticeably without the expected apostrophe in *Bettys* on the large ornate sign. In the window was a display of mouth-watering cakes, pastries and hand-made chocolates, as well as every blend of tea and coffee we could possibly imagine. We selected a table surrounded by Art Deco mirrors and oak panelling and with a large picture window overlooking the Montpelier Gardens.

The waitress who served us wore a starched white apron and neat little cap and looked as if she had just stepped out of the pages of one of Agatha Christie's novels. Vera ordered her favourite crumpets and curd tarts, while the rest of us tucked into a plateful of Yorkshire Fat Rascals – namely fruity scones filled with citrus peel, almonds and cherries. Vera poured the tea, which was served in a silver teapot with a matching sugar bowl, silver tongs and a delicate tea strainer. Everything looked superb. It was as if we had stepped back into a bygone era of white linen and impeccable silver service.

'Isn't this perfect?' said Vera.

Beth still had her nose in the guidebook. 'This is interesting,' she said. '"The North Yorkshire spa town of Harrogate will always be remembered for the strange occurrence of the third of December nineteen twenty-six",' she recited.

'Ah, you mean the strange story of Agatha Christie,' said Vera, putting down her teacup.

'What's that?' chorused Beth and Laura.

'Well,' said Vera, dabbing her mouth with a crisp linen napkin and replacing it on her lap, 'it all began after her husband revealed he was in love with another woman, Nancy Neele, and wanted a divorce.'

'Oh yes,' we all murmured. This had the makings of a good story and two blue-rinse ladies on the next table stopped speaking and listened in.

'Yes,' said Vera, 'Agatha Christie left a message for her secretary saying she was going to Yorkshire and then she carefully staged an accident. She drove her car to Sunningdale, left it hanging over the edge of a chalk pit and disappeared.'

'Disappeared!' exclaimed Beth.

'Where to?' said Laura.

'Over a thousand police and civilians searched for her to no avail,' said Vera, 'but eleven days later she re-appeared as a guest at the Hydropathic Hotel in Harrogate and no one could explain where she had been.'

'How strange,' I said.

'Some thought it was just a publicity stunt,' added

Vera, 'while others believed she had suffered from amnesia after the breakdown of her marriage and the death of her mother. She never revealed the true reason and the townspeople of Harrogate have discussed it ever since.'

The two ladies at the next table nodded knowingly.

'What a wonderful story, Vera,' I said.

'Almost better than one of her novels,' said Beth.

Laura just looked at me and said nothing.

We finished the last of the tea and Laura picked up her handbag. 'My treat,' she said. 'Please, no arguments. I'll pay on my card.'

'Card?' I looked puzzled.

'Yes, Jack, don't you remember? I've got a Barclay Visa card. It's great. If I keep fifty pounds in my personal cheque account I don't have to pay for cheques, standing orders or statements.'

'Even so, it's not really for me, Laura,' I said lamely.

She smiled. 'You really do need to knock him into shape, Beth.'

'Perhaps it could be worth considering, Jack,' said Beth. 'I've heard you can borrow up to five thousand pounds with no security as long as you are in a steady job.'

I was horrified at the thought of so much debt.

'And they're fitting cash-dispenser machines in the wall outside Barclay's bank,' added Laura, 'so you could draw out up to a hundred pounds per day and even order a statement.'

'Heavens,' said Vera.

'Well, I suppose it sounds impressive,' I said, but without conviction.

'Oh dear, Jack,' said Laura, 'I know that look so well.'

Beth gave her a glance but said nothing.

Laura began to rummage frantically in her handbag. 'Oh no,' she said, 'it's not here. My bank card's gone!'

We looked on helplessly as Laura continued to search to no avail.

While Vera and Beth were consoling her I paid the bill and we walked outside. I looked at my watch. 'Let's find Joseph on our way back to the coach,' I said.

'Where can he be?' asked Beth.

'We could split up, I suppose, and meet back here,' suggested Laura.

Vera didn't answer.

'What is it, Vera?' I asked.

'I'm just thinking back to the events of the day,' she said, staring thoughtfully, 'and it's just possible . . .'

'What's possible?' I asked.

'There has to be a simple solution to all this,' said Vera calmly. Her sharp brain missed nothing. In her cocoon of concentration, she was trying to unravel the mystery as if it were a game of three-dimensional chess. Ragley's very own Miss Marple was on the case!

She set off at a brisk pace back towards the coach, where we found Joseph sitting all alone, his head buried deep in his novel.

'I thought so!' said Vera.

Joseph looked up guiltily and hurriedly put the book in his jacket pocket.

'Sorry, Vera. I simply forgot the time.'

She leant over and tugged the paperback from Joseph's

pocket and held it up. It was Agatha Christie's *Murder at the Vicarage*.

'Oh,' said Joseph, 'I was just, well, you know . . . intrigued by the title.'

'And this, I presume, is what you've been using as a bookmark,' said Vera, holding up a plastic card, 'and you've obviously no idea what it is, have you, Joseph?'

'I'm afraid not,' mumbled Joseph, looking puzzled.

Vera turned the card over and showed him Laura's name printed across it.

'My bank card!' exclaimed Laura. 'Oh, thank you, Joseph, you've found it!'

'Have I?' said Joseph. 'It was under my seat and I thought it would be a useful bookmark.'

'What a relief,' said Laura.

'It's as we thought all along, I'm afraid,' said Vera. 'It was just a matter of a process of elimination.'

'Well done, Vera. What a detective you are,' said Laura.

'Just like Miss Marple,' said Beth.

Vera smiled modestly and held up *Murder at the Vicarage*. 'It was obvious from the beginning that it could only be one person,' said Vera.

'Oh, who's that?' asked Joseph.

She gave him an affectionate hug. 'The soppy vicar, of course!'

Chapter Sixteen

Grace, Hope and Chastity

The PTA agreed to lend their crockery to Mrs Pringle for the Christening party on Sunday, 26 April, at St Mary's Church Hall.

Extract from the Ragley School Logbook:
Friday, 24 April 1981

The chill of winter was forgotten and as I drove past the village hall on Ragley High Street the almond trees were in blossom and the closed buds on the cherry trees were waiting for the trigger of life as the season shifted on its axis with its message of the warm days to come.

However, when I slowed up at the school gate, the wonders of nature on this beautiful April morning were not being appreciated by everyone. A group of mothers was cheering something out of my eyeline. Suddenly Police Constable Dan Hunter came into sight, pedalling for all he was worth on a bright-red Raleigh bicycle. Even with the saddle extended as high as it would go, Dan's knees stuck out like Charlie Chaplin's. He gave the group of mothers a shy grin and, when he spotted me, he pulled up under the avenue of horse-chestnut trees and parked his bicycle against the school wall.

"Morning, Dan,' I called out. 'New transport?'

He was red in the face and clearly not very happy. 'The sergeant's borrowed my van because his has packed in,' said Dan breathlessly, 'so I'm stuck with the bike until Monday and it's not really . . . dignified.'

I suppressed a smile. 'I agree, Dan, but at least the weather looks fair for the next few days.'

The big policeman looked up at the sky and grinned. 'I suppose so, Jack.' He clambered back on the bicycle. 'By the way, I'm on duty on Sunday but I may be able to call in later at the christening, so I'm just praying for a peaceful weekend.'

'I'm sure it will be, Dan,' I called after him as he wobbled towards the village green. On reflection, I should have known better.

'Grace Eleanor Pringle,' said Sally proudly. Her cheeks were flushed as she put down the Moses basket on the staff-room coffee-table. Baby Grace was clearly putting on weight. At twelve pounds ten ounces, her days of floating down the Nile in this tiny basket were numbered.

It was the end of the first week of the summer term and Sally had called in to discuss Sunday's christening arrangements. 'So Colin and I settled on Grace, which was my maiden name, and then Eleanor after Colin's mother,' explained Sally.

'Grace is a beautiful name,' said Vera, 'and Eleanor is

so distinguished, but, of course, being born on a Tuesday, Grace is most appropriate.'

'Appropriate?' queried Jo.

Anne was quick on the uptake. 'Vera means the old rhyme, Jo,' she said: 'you know . . . Monday's child is fair of face, Tuesday's child is full of grace.'

'Oh, I see,' said Jo.

Joseph looked up from his assembly notices. 'And what's Wednesday?'

'My dear brother was born on a Wednesday,' announced Vera with a smile. 'Sorry, Joseph, but Wednesday's child is full of woe and Thursday's child has far to go.'

'Oh dear,' said Joseph. 'Not ideal for a vicar.'

Ruby was standing in the doorway, absent-mindedly polishing the cleanest door handle in Yorkshire. 'My Ronnie was born on a Thursday an' 'e never goes far enough – apart from t'bookie's in York.'

'What about you, Ruby?' I asked. 'On what day were you born?'

'Sat'day, Mr Sheffield.'

'And how about you, Vera?' asked Jo.

'I'm Friday,' said Vera. 'Friday's child is loving and giving,' she added with not quite sufficient modesty, 'and Saturday's child works hard for a living.'

'That's sounds reight t'me,' said Ruby. She looked at Vera and smiled. 'On both counts, ah reckon, Miss Evans.'

'But the child that is born on the sabbath day is bonny and blithe, good and gay,' recited Anne, completing the rhyme. 'That's me, I'm afraid, though I've never been too sure about *blithe*.'

Sally took a large flat cardboard box from her open-weave shopping bag. 'So what do you think of this, Vera? It's Grace's christening robe, the one my mother made for me when I was a baby.'

Vera took the lid off the box with great care. The material was wrapped in black paper. 'Ah, to keep the moths out of course,' she said. 'What a good idea.'

'My Ronnie uses mothballs, Miss Evans,' said Ruby suddenly.

Everyone looked surprised. 'What for?' asked Jo.

''E digs up mole 'ills an' shoves a 'andful down the 'ole. It's a smashing mole killer is mothballs. Put 'em down an' they never come back.' With that conversation-stopper, Ruby shut the door and there followed the muffled sound of a galvanized bucket being dragged across the entrance hall to the accompaniment of the first bars of 'Edelweiss'.

'It's beautiful,' said Vera softly and held up the delicate robe.

'It's made out of parachute silk,' said Sally, 'with eyelets for a coloured ribbon – blue for a boy, pink for a girl – and fringed with this beautiful lace.' She traced her finger along the delicate edges.

'Parachute silk?' I asked in surprise.

'My mother was in the air force during the war,' explained Sally. 'She worked as a radio operator in the Battle of Britain.'

Soon all the ladies were in animated conversation, so I slipped out for some fresh air before the morning bell for the start of school. In the playground children were bouncing tennis balls against the school wall, playing hopscotch and acting out the latest *Star Wars* adventure. Many of them were wearing the new light-blue polo shirts with a small, dark-blue Ragley-on-the-Forest logo in the shape of a tree on the left side of the chest. The PTA had bought these as a school 'uniform' to offset the growing trend for young girls to wear the new range of fashionable and expensive designer clothes that had begun to appear in the shops in York.

I walked back into school and stopped to look at our new library area. It was developing slowly but we urgently needed new books. Simon Nelson, one of our library monitors, was browsing through an old atlas with dog-eared pages.

'Mr Sheffield,' he said, 'why is most of the world coloured pink?'

I made a mental note to buy a new set of atlases that weren't a constant reminder of the demise of the British Empire.

On Saturday morning I drove to Ragley to do some shopping and called into Victor Pratt's garage for petrol.

'Ah 'ave t'tek tablets now, Mr Sheffield,' said Victor mournfully as he unscrewed my petrol cap.

'What for?' I asked.

''Cause Dr Davenport said I 'ad,' replied Victor with a shake of his head.

'Yes, but what's the matter, Victor?'

'Every time ah stand up quick, like, ah go proper dizzy.'

'Oh, I see . . . Well, maybe you should get up more slowly, Victor.'

He shambled back into his untidy garage to get my change and shouted over his shoulder, 'That's what Dr Davenport said,' and not for the first time I wondered if I might have made a good doctor.

In the villages of Ragley and Morton life was going on as normal. It was the time for spring cleaning. Vera was cutting out lavender-scented paper to line the drawers of her wardrobe; Ruby had slung the hearthrug over the washing line and was beating it with a ferocity that would have made Ronnie tremble; and Mrs Earnshaw was hanging out her bedroom curtains to dry alongside Dallas Sue-Ellen's nappies. Meanwhile, in the vicarage kitchen Joseph was preparing a new and subtle variation to his home-made greengage wine, happily oblivious to the fact it tasted like Domestos, while Maurice Tupham was walking across the High Street to Piercy's Butcher's Shop to collect his weekly order of two pig's trotters.

Kenny Kershaw and Anita Cuthbertson, who had been in my class when I first arrived at Ragley, were standing outside the General Stores.

'Kenny's gorra 'nother new bike, Mr Sheffield,' shouted Anita. Kenny smiled shyly. Anita always did most of the talking. 'It's a new Raleigh Grifter wi' three gears an' a twist-hand grip,' she said.

'It looks fantastic,' I said.

'Only thing is, Mr Sheffield,' said Kenny, 'it weighs a ton.'

I stared at this new addition to the Chopper family of bicycles.

'But it's the cool bike of the Eighties, Mr Sheffield,' said Anita with authority.

I stared at the chunky, cumbersome frame. With all that steel it must feel like a motorcycle. Also, sadly, the most innovative gear shift in bicycle technology, incorporated into the grips and controlled with a twisting motion, clearly had its drawbacks.

'An' ah've gorra blister on m'thumb 'cause of this rubber flange on t'handle grip,' said Kenny mournfully. He held up his thumb like a badge of honour and looked to Anita for some sympathy.

Anita, though, was made of harder stuff. 'C'mon, y'big softie,' she said, let's go t'Nora's. Ah've 'eard some big jammy doughnuts came in yesterday.'

Dorothy was standing in the open doorway of Nora's Coffee Shop with Little Malcolm, while the strains of 'Don't Stand So Close to Me' by the Police thundered out into the street. His 1250 cc bright-green, two-door Deluxe, 1973 Hillman Avenger was parked outside.

'There's a smashing new shop opened up called Next,' called out an excited Dorothy to Margery Ackroyd, who was passing by, 'an' Malcolm's gonna buy me a pastel top and a pair o' trendy pixie boots.'

Meanwhile, in Pratt's Hardware Emporium, Tidy Tim was using an anti-static cloth to clean the vinyl surface of his favourite record. He had heard that shopping to music was more relaxing and so it was that Albert Jenkins was about to purchase a bag of clout nails while humming along to a 1976 LP record of '100 Greatest Hits' by Max Bygraves.

After completing my shopping at Prudence Golightly's

General Stores I reflected how fortunate I was to work in this wonderful Yorkshire village.

Unfortunately, life wasn't proving quite so placid for PC Dan Hunter. Red-faced and panting, he had parked his bicycle outside the local police station and was reporting a surprising discovery.

'I've just found a donkey, sergeant,' said Dan somewhat lamely.

'A what?' yelled Sergeant Neil Grayson.

'A donkey with a red collar. It says it's called Hope.'

'You've found a donkey called Hope?' Sergeant Grayson had been brought up in Hull and was a fanatical Hull City supporter so he didn't suffer fools gladly. Watching his favourite team had given him enough grief to last a lifetime. He gave Dan a withering look. 'Ah don't care if it's called Bing bloody Crosby. Find out who owns it and get shut of it!'

These were tough times for Dan. After two years of probationary training, he had begun a year of study in York using *Moriarty's Police Law*, the police bible with its distinctive blue cover and gold-blocked lettering. It involved one evening per week in York, after which he would still be a police constable but officially 'qualified for promotion'. If, during the following year, a sergeant was absent from duty, then the 'most qualified PC' would be awarded two temporary stripes, not three, and become an acting sergeant.

He also had three promotion handbooks, *Road Traffic*, *Crime* and *General Police Duties*. The latter included important local information on the movement of livestock, which, he had just discovered to his cost, included fugitive donkeys.

On Sunday morning the breath of roses blessed the eastern sky with soft pink light. A new day had dawned and, in the vicarage garden, the rooks were building their nests high, the sign of a good summer.

Beth and I were outside the church, waiting for the others to arrive. Elsie Crapper, the church organist, always worked hard as a Friend of St Mary's and she had taken responsibility for the church noticeboard. Two large notices were displayed, each written in Elsie's recognizable script. The first read, in large capital letters, WHAT IS HELL? Next to it was COME EARLY TO HEAR THE CHOIR PRACTISE.

Beth and I were sharing the joke when, suddenly, a familiar figure appeared on his bicycle.

'Hello, Dan,' I shouted.

'I've lost bloody Hope,' gasped Dan as he pedalled past.

'Pardon?' said Beth.

'And I had it this morning!' he yelled frantically as he disappeared up Morton Road, head down and feet pumping on the pedals.

Soon everyone gathered, with baby Grace the centre of attention, and we walked into church. Elsie was also in charge of the monthly church magazine, although 'magazine' was rather a grand title for the single sheet of paper that comprised a list of births, marriages, deaths and church events. Beth and I read one as we sat quietly in one of the pews. In the April 1981 issue, Elsie had typed 'When the choir sang "I Will Not Pass This Way Again" it brought great pleasure to the congregation.' The advertisement at the bottom of the front page also raised a smile. It read: 'The ladies in the choir have cast off clothing. Please see them in the basement. Charge 10p.'

I smiled, leant back in my pew and, wrapped in the calm silence of this old church, looked around me. On the wall above a shelf of hymn-books and next to the old oak board on which the hymn numbers were displayed was a stone plaque. It had been placed there as a token of affection by fellow officers of Taverner Charles Weaver, Captain of the 43rd Light Infantry, who had died aged thirty-seven years at Madras on 18 September 1879. I was saddened by the thought of this young man who, a century ago, had fallen in battle so far from home. It occurred to me that he may have once stood on this very spot, full of life and with hopes of a bright future in a world where Queen Victoria reigned supreme.

Attached to the wall at the end of my pew were three ancient oak boxes next to a sign that read *For your offerings*. Above each box was a small brass plaque inscribed *Altar Fund*, *The Poor* and *Foreign Mission*, signs of an earlier age in the life of this church that had provided sanctuary and peace for many generations of villagers.

In the vestry of St Mary's Church, Joseph was going through his regular routine and, as always, Vera was in attendance. First he donned his black cassock, followed by his snow-white alb, a long, flowing cotton garment. Then Vera selected a loose sleeveless chasuble from their splendid collection designed for different festivals: purple for Lent and Advent, white and gold for Christmas, red for Palm Sunday and green for the rest of the year. Finally, around Joseph's neck Vera draped a beautiful white stole, intricately decorated with Christian emblems, butterflies and ancient symbols of resurrection.

Only then did Vera stand back and give her brother a gentle smile. Joseph knew all was well and, as was his custom, he lightly kissed the cross of pure silk before beginning the service.

Joseph opened his 1928 *Book of Common Prayer*, turned to page 352 and began in a sonorous voice, 'Almighty and everlasting God, who by the Baptism of thy well-beloved Son Jesus Christ, in the River Jordan, didst sanctify water to the mystical washing away of sin.'

Everyone was quiet and Sally was silently praying that Grace would not want feeding again in the middle of the service.

'The Lord be with you,' said Joseph.

'And with thy spirit,' we answered.

'Lift up your hearts,' he said.

Together we replied, 'We lift them up unto the Lord.'

'Let us give thanks unto our Lord God,' continued Joseph, without looking at his service book. It was clear that he knew all this off by heart.

'It is meet and right to do,' we replied and I wondered what the word 'meet' meant in that sentence.

Vera suddenly appeared like a genie with a lamp, except on this occasion it was a thermos flask full of hot water, which she poured into the font. Then she took the order of service book from Joseph and held it for him as he took Grace from Sally's arms.

The font was large enough to bathe a toddler in the days when children were fully immersed at a christening. Around its base was carved 'Heavenly Father, we thank thee for thy gift of children'.

Joseph sanctified the water and made the sign of the cross. Ruby was in the pew in front of me, alongside John and Anne Grainger. I imagined Ronnie was a reluctant churchgoer but would probably turn up for the reception in the church hall afterwards.

Ruby turned towards me and whispered, 'A good wedding an' a good christening, Mr Sheffield – y'can't beat 'em.'

'I agree,' I said.

'An' ah like this bit,' said Ruby. 'It's m'favourite.'

'What's that, Ruby?' I asked.

'Y'know . . . wi' t'constipated water,' said Ruby with a knowing look. 'It's allus very moving.'

'I imagine it is, Ruby,' I said with a smile.

Joseph turned to the godparents. Then, with a baptismal shell, he poured water over little Grace's forehead. 'In the name of the Father,' recited Joseph, 'the Son and the Holy Ghost.' With his thumb he made the sign of the cross on the baby's forehead. Happily Grace slept through it all and Sally breathed a sigh of relief.

Outside in the sunshine everyone relaxed and photographs were taken. I was talking to Joseph away from the crowd when Dan Hunter appeared, pushing his bicycle. He looked inconsolable.

'What is it, Daniel?' said Joseph. 'You look disturbed.'

Dan shook his head. 'I'm afraid I've lost Hope, vicar.'

Joseph looked concerned and put a hand on Dan's shoulder. 'Don't worry, my son,' he said with gravitas, 'we shall find hope together.'

'Thanks, vicar,' said Dan, propping his bike against the church wall. 'You look round the back and I'll check the outbuildings.'

Leaving a confused Joseph behind us, I followed Dan across the gravel forecourt of the vicarage and through the open gate that led to Vera's kitchen garden. There stood a donkey contentedly scratching his back against an apple tree.

'Hope!' shouted Dan.

'Pardon?' I said.

'Thank goodness,' said Dan. 'You keep him here and I'll get a rope.'

It had a bright-red halter and was apparently top of the Easington Police hit list of missing quadrupeds. Hope might have been *his* name but I was filled with despair. The donkey's manic stare was enough to freeze the blood. Joseph had recently told my class the epic Bible story of Daniel in the lion's den. However, if this donkey had walked in, it would have been debatable who would have got to the exit first – Daniel or the lion.

Dan returned with Vera's washing line and the donkey bared its teeth. Dan was six-feet-four-inches tall and a rugby second-row forward but there was something unnerving about this animal. Dan had also been expertly trained to deal with drunken football supporters, road-traffic accidents and elusive cat burglars, but this was different.

'Why don't you distract it, Jack?' asked Dan.

'What do you want, the Donkey Serenade?' I said, taking a step backwards.

'Do something to catch its eye and I'll lasso it,' he said.

While I waved my arms Dan dropped a noose over its head and secured the rope to a tree. Minutes later Hope was enjoying a welcome bucket of water and Jo had given Dan a lift back to the police station to make his report before going off duty.

An hour later, the donkey had been collected and the women were enjoying tea and cakes in the church hall and fussing over the baby. I was joined by Colin, John and a relieved Dan. We found a table in a quiet corner, munched on christening cake and drank strong tea.

'You're a bit quiet, Colin,' said Dan.

'Just thinking,' he said.

'About what?' said John.

'About Sally and the baby and where we go from here,' said Colin thoughtfully.

'How do you mean?' I asked.

'Well . . . you know . . . since the baby, Sally's kept herself to herself, if you take my meaning.'

Everybody did.

'Mind you, it's natural, I suppose – a bit of doing without, so to speak,' said Colin.

'Chastity,' added Dan.

Everyone nodded. It seemed the supportive thing to do.

'After all, it can't be much fun having a baby,' I said, eager to show solidarity.

'Thank God we don't have to do it,' said Dan, munching on his third slice of cake.

'Too true,' said John. 'It's probably like indigestion.'

'Really bad indigestion,' added Dan with feeling and through a mouthful of crumbs.

'And that's enough to bring tears to anyone's eyes,' said Colin.

In terms of the male pain threshold this was clearly close to the top of the scale and we all sat back, relieved we had shared these words of wisdom.

It was getting dark by the time Beth and I walked towards her front door and I stood there, reflecting on a busy day. Grace had been christened and Dan had finally found Hope. I smiled to myself as Beth fumbled for her keys in her handbag.

'So what do you think, Beth?'

'What about?' she said, unlocking the door and stepping inside.

'About chastity,' I said.

She pulled me inside the hallway, pushed me playfully against the wall and kissed me. 'I think it's a bit over-rated, don't you?'

Chapter Seventeen

Terry Earnshaw's Rainbow

Class 2 watched the National Geographic film 'Fish of the World' *at the University in York.*

Extract from the Ragley School Logbook:
Monday, 18 May 1981

'Now be good at school an' y'can tell me all about it when y'get 'ome.'

Heathcliffe and his brother Terry looked up at their mother and gave her a well-practised holier-than-thou look of complete innocence. They stood patiently in the doorway of the untidy, cramped house while Mrs Earnshaw tried to flatten their spiky blond hair with a damp floor cloth. Then, as they set off down the path, she lifted up Dallas Sue-Ellen, now eighteen months old, wiped the jam off her face and they both waved goodbye to the intrepid duo.

Pink petals from the cherry trees lay in a drift at the corner of School View. However, the usual five-minute walk to Ragley School held little interest for Heathcliffe and Terry. Pavements were boring. The Earnshaw brothers, both sons of Barnsley in South Yorkshire, still had the prerogative of the very young: imagination. So, for these two little boys, every day was a new opportunity to be a superhero and this didn't involve the pathways of normal mortals.

'Let's be Batman and Robin,' yelled Heathcliffe.

'OK, 'Eath',' said Terry. Resigned to be a perpetual Robin to his big brother's Batman, Terry nodded and they set off to the 'secret' gap in the hedgerow, recently shaped by Heathcliffe's bullet head and sturdy shoulders.

Once in the open fields at the back of Ragley School and with yells of 'Thwack!', 'Biff!' and 'Boom!', they ran with imaginary capes flowing behind them. It was Monday, 18 May, and the trees and hedgerows, just like the Earnshaw brothers, were full of new life.

'Let's mek bows 'n' arrers,' said Heathcliffe.

'OK, 'Eath',' said Terry.

Heathcliffe had 'borrowed' an ancient penknife from his father's garden shed and he emptied his trouser pockets. On to the grass tumbled an interesting collection of items, including a broken pencil, five pence, a piece of putty, two glass marbles, an ink-stained handkerchief, a ball of string, a dead worm and, of course, the penknife. He opened the rusty blade, spat on it and wiped it on the back of his sleeve. Terry watched intently, greatly impressed by the spitting part of the process. Heathcliffe cut two elder sticks from the hedgerow and, archery practice forgotten, an impromptu sword fight ensued.

'Wharrabout m'gobstopper?' asked Terry, after pretending to die for the umpteenth time.

Heathcliffe paused in his assault. With five pence he could buy a Milky Way and a huge penny gobstopper from the General Stores in the High Street and still have two pence left over to spend on the way home at the end of the day.

'Let's go, Robin,' said Heathcliffe.

'OK, 'Eath' . . . er, ah mean Batman,' said Terry.

Heathcliffe gathered up all the scattered treasures from the grass verge with the exception of the worm. He was not a sentimental boy and, after putting it in Elisabeth Amelia Dudley-Palmer's brand-new pencil case the previous day, it had now served its purpose. He tossed it into the bottom of the hedgerow, from where Terry retrieved it. After all, thought Terry, it might come in handy, particularly as Elisabeth Amelia's younger sister, Victoria Alice, was in his class.

The doorbell of the General Stores & Newsagent jingled wildly when the two little boys walked in. They liked the sound of the bell and, for good measure, they opened and closed the door again. Miss Prudence Golightly smiled at the dishevelled state of two of her favourite customers. While their impact on her profit margin was almost negligible, she enjoyed the schoolchildren coming into the shop. They reminded her of what might have been and, in quiet moments, she often wondered what *her* children would have been like if only Jeremy had returned from the war. Absent-mindedly, Miss Golightly turned to her ancient teddy bear and buttoned up his bright-red hand-knitted cardigan and placed a yellow bobble hat on his head. 'There, Jeremy, that's better,' she said. 'It's rather chilly today.'

She turned back to greet her two young customers. 'Good morning, boys.'

'Good morning, Miss. Good morning, Jeremy,' chorused Heathcliffe and Terry.

'Now, what would you like this morning?'

'Please can we 'ave a Milky Way an' a penny gob-stopper,' said Heathcliffe.

'Please,' echoed Terry.

Miss Golightly took the five pence and gave the Milky Way to Heathcliffe plus two pence change and the gob-stopper to Terry. 'I'm so glad you are remembering your manners, boys,' she said. It hadn't always been the case and she felt encouraged that these two little boys were learning their p's and q's. 'Here's a barley sugar each for being polite,' she said.

'Thank you, Miss,' they said.

'And are you going to work hard at school today?' asked Miss Golightly.

'Yes, Miss. Ah'm blackboard monitor,' said Heathcliffe proudly.

'That's wonderful, Heathcliffe,' she said, 'and what about you, Terry?'

'Ah'm frogspawn monitor, Miss,' said Terry.

'Oh . . . and what do you have to do?'

'Ah mek sure no one messes wi' 'em,' said Terry bluntly.

'I see,' said Miss Golightly dubiously, 'and what happens if they do?'

'Ah tell our 'Eath',' he replied darkly and wedged the

gobstopper in his mouth rendering future conversation impossible.

The two boys then ran up the High Street to the village green, where they climbed on to the lower branches of the weeping-willow tree alongside the duck pond. Coming towards them was Miss Amelia Duff, the local postmistress. She was carrying an enamel bucket.

'Be careful, you boys,' shouted Miss Duff. 'Don't fall in the pond.'

Heathcliffe and Terry jumped down. They knew Miss Duff was unaware that as superheroes they could swim like Mark Spitz.

'What's in the bucket, Miss Duff?' asked Heathcliffe politely.

'Ugh,' added Terry, whose lips could not yet meet over the huge gobstopper.

'Toads . . . well, baby ones,' said Miss Duff, peering at the frantic pondlife in the bucket with obvious affection. 'I'm helping them cross the road to get back to their favourite breeding pond.'

'Can ah put m'finger in, please?' asked Heathcliffe.

'Ugh,' echoed Terry.

'It's difficult being a frog or a toad,' said Miss Duff.

Heathcliffe and Terry peered in the bucket dubiously. After all, amphibians didn't have to go to school, be nice to girls or get washed every day.

'And frogspawn is a lovely meal for fish, rats, snakes and weasels,' said Miss Duff.

Suddenly, thought Heathcliffe and Terry, being a human being had its advantages.

'And it could be dangerous for them to cross this road.'

'Aagh,' agreed Terry.

'An' ah bet they don't know t'Green Cross Code,' added Heathcliffe.

Miss Duff and Terry both looked at Heathcliffe with deep appreciation of this meaningful insight.

I was standing on the stone steps in the entrance porch, the school bell was about to ring and the last stragglers were running in.

'Come on, Heathcliffe. Hurry up, Terry,' I yelled. 'It's nearly nine o'clock.' I looked at their red faces and muddy knees and smiled.

'We've been getting stuff for t'nature table, Mr Sheffield,' said Heathcliffe, holding up his elder stick and then nudging Terry, who did the same.

'Aagh,' said Terry.

'An' 'elping toads t'cross t'road.'

'Very well,' I said, 'I'll take the sticks and give them to Mrs Hunter and Miss Flint.'

They passed over their sticks like gunfighters giving up their Colt 45s to the sheriff. 'And Terry . . .'

'Ugh?'

'Put your gobstopper in your handkerchief until after school.'

Terry looked relieved. Breathing through his nose for the last ten minutes had been difficult. They hurried off to their classrooms and, with great care, Terry added his half-sucked gobstopper to the dead worm nestling serenely in his grubby handkerchief.

*   *   *

Outside the store cupboard in the entrance hall, Jo was sorting through a box of large plastic bottles of poster colours, and Ruby, Valerie and Anne were looking on.

'What are the colours of the rainbow again?' asked Jo.

'There's lots o' colours,' said Ruby, trying to be helpful.

'It's just that I've forgotten the sequence,' said Jo.

'It's really quite easy,' said Valerie. 'It's remembered by the mnemonic "Richard of York gave battle in vain".'

Ruby was puzzled. She thought mnemonic was an orchestra.

'Red, orange, yellow, green, blue, indigo, violet,' added Anne by way of explanation.

'Indigo?' said Jo, staring helplessly at our limited range of colours. The bottles were labelled red, yellow, blue, black and white.

'Don't worry,' said Anne, 'I know how to make indigo.' You didn't teach reception children for twenty-five years without picking up some useful knowledge along the way.

Jo had transformed an unlikely corner of her classroom into a 'secret garden'. She had draped a large sheet of oatmeal-coloured hessian over a high window ledge and an eighteen-drawer storage unit. This provided the background to a riot of colourful paintings and pastel drawings of flowers and animals. Alongside, the broken base of a swing bin, expertly covered in green crêpe paper, provided a perfect receptacle for a selection of bamboo canes, each with a bright cut-out sunflower pattern attached. Posters of plants, birds and fish were displayed under the heading 'Our Wonderful World' and, in front, each child was growing mustard and cress on damp cotton wool in individual saucers.

On the wall was a large chart divided into three columns headed CLOUD, SUNSHINE and RAINBOW. Every child's name was written in felt pen on a piece of white card and pinned in one of the columns. All the children began the day in the Sunshine column; however, if they misbehaved they became a Cloud, but if they excelled or showed a special kindness they became a Rainbow.

Having slipped the dead worm into Victoria Alice Dudley-Palmer's wax crayon tin, Terry was the first of the day to be demoted. 'Terry Earnshaw,' said Jo sternly, 'you will have to be on your best behaviour this afternoon when we go to the university.' Jo was taking her class to York University to see the film *Fish of the World* as part of Class 2's project.

Terry put his head in his hands and sighed deeply. It wasn't much fun being a cloud.

At morning break, in the staff-room, Vera was peering over her new half-moon spectacles at the front page of her *Daily Telegraph*.

'Doesn't she look beautiful,' she said, pointing to a photograph of Lady Diana Spencer.

The BBC had announced that its coverage of the marriage of the Prince of Wales and Lady Diana Spencer on 29 July would be the most comprehensive outside broadcast ever, at a cost of £150,000, with an audience of 500 million. Cliff Morgan, the head of outside broadcast, said the wedding in St Paul's Cathedral would be the biggest and most glamorous event since the 1937 Coronation of King George VI.

'The Women's Institute will be organizing a party on the village green,' said Vera.

'I've heard it will be like the 1977 Silver Jubilee celebrations,' said Anne.

'I missed those,' I said. 'I arrived here just after them but I heard they were wonderful.'

'They were,' said Valerie. 'We had bunting, party hats, jelly and ice cream, and Vera made some of her wonderful scones.'

Vera smiled at the memory and glanced back at the newspaper. A photograph of Captain Mark Phillips caught her eye. He was arriving at St Mary's Hospital, Paddington, to visit Princess Anne, who was about to give birth.

'Well, good luck to her,' she whispered almost to herself. 'At least we know she picks sensible names for her children.'

At lunchtime Shirley the cook looked worried. Instead of every child sitting down to a freshly cooked school dinner, ten children had brought packed lunch boxes and were sitting at a separate table.

'Where's it all going to end?' said Shirley, shaking her head in despair. 'I make good meals, but when they go up from thirty-five pence to fifty pence there'll be even more opting for pack-ups.'

Local authorities were now no longer committed to providing meals; they were only required to provide food for children having free meals, and a designated space to eat packed lunches. While Suffolk schools were experimenting with canteen music and in Hertfordshire they were rearing their own pigs, sheep and chickens, the message was clear. Government cuts were beginning to have an effect on school dinners.

'I'll do all I can to support you, Shirley,' I said, but the truth was that the tide was turning and we both knew we were powerless to resist it.

Meanwhile, Terry Earnshaw had finished his liver, onions, cabbage and mashed potato, followed by spotted dick and custard, and walked outside. It had rained during the morning and there were a few puddles on the playground.

'If y'jump off t'school wall it'll mek a bigger splash,' said Heathcliffe with the voice of experience. Terry followed his big brother's logic. After all, Heathcliffe was Ragley School's champion puddle-splasher.

Terry climbed on the wall and launched himself, but in mid-flight came a roar from the other side of the playground. 'Terry Earnshaw!' It was Mrs Critchley and she strode towards the two brothers.

Muddy water splashed everywhere as Terry landed and he looked round anxiously. He knew all too well that when a grown-up called you by your full name it meant trouble.

''E jus' slipped, Miss,' said Heathcliffe quickly.

'An' you're just as bad as y'brother,' said Mrs Critchley. 'Go inside, Terry, an' get dry,' she shouted, 'an' don't you think ah won't be 'aving words wi' your teacher, jus' you wait an' see if ah don't.'

Terry didn't understand double negatives, or even triple ones for that matter. He just knew that Mrs Critchley was very cross and he was in trouble. Through the office window I saw his forlorn figure walk into school.

'I'm sorry, Terry,' said Jo, 'but Mrs Critchley said you were naughty in the playground so you'll have to stay in the cloud column.' Even as she spoke, Jo looked sympathetically at the unhappy little figure and thought of ways he might become a rainbow or at least a ray of sunshine before the end of afternoon school.

Jo Hunter boarded William Featherstone's Reliance coach with the children in her class, along with three mothers who had volunteered to help, and travelled in to York University to watch the film.

On arrival, like any good primary school teacher, Jo sent all the children to the toilets. The little girls were supervised by the mothers, while Jo waited outside the gents. 'Off you go, boys,' she had said. However, unknown to Jo, a scene that would have made an entertaining Giles cartoon was being played out. The eleven small boys stared at the alien scene before them and considered the problem. All the wall-hung urinals were for adults and, therefore, above chest height. From outside came Jo's plaintive cry 'Don't be long,' so, following Terry's lead, the taller boys attempted to urinate like firemen hosing a tall building, while the smaller boys gave it up as a bad job and simply did what they had to do against the tiled walls. As the floor took on the appearance of a footbath they heard Jo Hunter's latest shouted instruction: 'And don't forget to wash your hands.' The washbasin taps were too high to reach, so once again they followed Terry's lead, spat on their hands and wiped them on their shorts. When they all rushed out after less than two minutes Jo Hunter said, 'Well done, boys.'

Anxious to give credit where credit was due, 'Terry showed us 'ow t'get our 'ands clean,' said Damian Brown, who was in Terry's debt. That morning, Terry had recovered his dead worm from the school dustbin at the back of the boiler house and given it to Damian.

Jo crouched down in front of Terry. 'I'm very pleased with you Terry,' she said. 'That was *very* thoughtful of you.'

Terry beamed. A cloudless afternoon might once again be on the distant horizon. Meanwhile, the boys lined up patiently, pleased to be praised but all silently wondering why it was that girls took so long to go to the toilet.

The film was enjoyed by everyone, with whales, dolphins and sharks drawing gasps of excitement from the large audience of children from all the local schools. However, on the coach on the way home, Terry was horrified at having to share a seat with a girl, namely Victoria Alice.

'Do you like me, Terry?' asked Victoria Alice.

Terry stared at her in horror. There was a long pause.

'I'll take that as a yes, then,' said Victoria Alice and stared out of the window.

In spite of the welcome distraction of the Buttle twins each filling a sick bag on the journey back to Ragley, Terry didn't enjoy the journey back to school.

*   *   *

Back in class, Terry pulled out all the stops. His writing had much improved in the past year and he could now manage lengthy and coherent sentences. At the end of the afternoon he was proud of his page of careful printing about 'Fishes of the World' – particularly the last two sentences, which read: 'Dolphins are clever. They breathe through an arsehole on the top of their head.'

Later, Jo told Terry how pleased she was that he had used his dictionary to look up 'dolphin', 'breathe' and 'through'. It was clear he already knew how to spell the other words.

Before final prayers at the end of the day, Jo made an announcement to the class. 'Boys and girls,' she said, 'Terry was very helpful during our visit today *and* he's using his dictionary, so . . . he's now a rainbow.'

Amid a smattering of applause led by Victoria Alice, Terry beamed from ear to ear.

On the way home, Heathcliffe and Terry called in at the General Stores once again and Heathcliffe spent the remaining two pence on two liquorice bootlaces.

Terry watched carefully as Heathcliffe expertly unrolled his long strand of liquorice and put one end in his mouth. Then, with a look of pure pleasure on his face, he began to suck slowly like a contented armadillo. Terry, a mirror image of his big brother, did exactly the same and together, in silence, they walked back through the ditches and fields and arrived home with happy pink faces and pitch-black tongues.

*　　*　　*

'So what did y'do today, boys?' asked Mrs Earnshaw when finally they sat down at the kitchen table.

Heathcliffe looked at Terry and remembered cutting hazel twigs with his dad's penknife; a Milky Way and a free barley sugar; a lesson in toad conservation; his brother being told off by Mrs Critchley and a liquorice bootlace.

Terry looked at Heathcliffe and remembered fighting with swords; sucking a gobstopper that changed colour until it resembled a small white pebble; Miss Duff's bright-red bucket; something that looked like a frog but with a different name; giving Victoria Alice his dead worm; making puddles on the tiled floor of the biggest toilet he had ever seen in his life; watching a film on a big screen with sixteen-foot-high sharks; recovering his dead worm and, best of all, becoming a rainbow.

'Well?' said Mrs Earnshaw as she shovelled two fish fingers on to each plate.

'Nowt,' said her sons in well-rehearsed unison.

She stood there, frying pan and spatula poised in mid-air. 'Y'must've done summat,' she said.

Heathcliffe relented. 'Well, ah cleaned t'blackboard,' he said.

Mrs Earnshaw put another fish finger on Heathcliffe's plate.

Terry observed this unexpected development and remembered the highlight of his day. 'Well, that's nowt: ah were a cloud an' then ah were a rainbow.'

His mother, thinking to herself that they taught them some peculiar things at school these days but it sounded as though they had learnt something useful, placed the remaining fish finger on Terry's plate.

It occurred to Terry that, in fish finger currency, rainbows ought to have more value, but he said nothing and waited his turn for the tomato ketchup.

At nine o'clock both boys were tucked up in bed.

'Mam, my bed's getting too small,' said Terry.

'Ah know, luv,' said Mrs Earnshaw. 'Don't worry, we'll get a bigger one one day.' She turned out the light.

'Mam!'

'What now, Terry?'

'Can ah tell y'summat?'

'No, Terry. Shut yer eyes and get some sleep.'

'Jus' one thing, Mam.'

'OK. What is it?'

'Ah liked being a rainbow, Mam . . . Ah started off as a cloud an' then ah did summat good . . . an' then ah were a rainbow.'

'That's lovely. Now, goodnight and God bless.'

There was silence in the boys' bedroom. Then, from the other side of the bedroom came the familiar click of Heathcliffe's three-colour torch and, under the covers, he began to read his *Superman* comic.

''Eath'?' whispered Terry.

'What?' muttered Heathcliffe.

'Are you gonna get married?'

'No!'

Long silence . . .

Heathcliffe was puzzled. 'Why? Are *you* gonna get married?'

'No!' said Terry.

Long silence . . .

'Why not?' asked Heathcliffe.

''Cause it'll be too much of a squash in this bed.'

Long silence . . .

''Eath',' whispered Terry.

'What?' mumbled Heathcliffe.

'Ah were a rainbow t'day.'

There was the sound of Heathcliffe turning the page of his comic. Then in a muffled voice he muttered, 'Better than being a bleedin' cloud.'

Terry nodded in acknowledgement, pulled the covers over his head, closed his eyes and, just before he fell asleep, he smiled.

He loved it when his big brother taught him new words.

Chapter Eighteen

Angel of Mercy

A PTA working party put up shelves in our new library resource centre. Class 4 will be leaving on Thursday, 4 June to take part in an outdoor activities weekend at Askrigg Low Mill Residential Youth Centre in Wensleydale.

Extract from the Ragley School Logbook:
Wednesday, 3 June 1981

'I believe everyone has a guardian angel, Mr Sheffield,' said Vera, 'so I'm sure all this work won't be wasted.'

'Let's hope so,' I said.

She put down a tray of North Yorkshire County Council glass tumblers filled with ice-cold home-made lemonade on the old pine table in the entrance hall. We all gathered round, grateful for the welcome refreshment.

'Thanks, Vera,' said John Grainger. 'I'm parched.' He put down his razor-sharp tenon saw, picked up two drinks and handed one to Anne.

She sipped hers gratefully and then stepped back to

admire our work. 'If they close us down after all this, it would break my heart,' she said.

There was a subdued acknowledgement and we knew that Anne had echoed all our thoughts. We needed something to lift our spirits.

It was Wednesday morning, 3 June, and high summer was upon us. School was closed for the spring bank holiday and a PTA working party had met to put up the new shelving in our library resource area. It had proved hot work. We were keen to finish because the next day we were leaving for our outdoor activities weekend in the Yorkshire Dales.

'Thanks, John,' said Sue Phillips. 'We couldn't have done this without you.'

John Grainger had taken a day off work to share his considerable expertise with us and the fitted pine shelving looked perfect for our book collection. He nodded modestly and Anne squeezed his hand.

'How about some fresh air?' said Dan Hunter.

'Good idea,' said Jo. They had arrived in their 'F' registered Wolseley Hornet and were proud of their first car, bought for the princely sum of £300. Married life seemed to be suiting them, I mused.

We took our drinks out to the playground and the welcome shade of the horse-chestnut trees. Beth had come along to help before leaving to spend a few days in Hampshire while I was in the Yorkshire Dales. She looked relaxed in her summer safari-style shirt with fashionable epaulettes and her Jaeger long-length shorts. Her legs were already tanned and her hair looked lighter in the summer sun.

We watched the busy comings and goings of thrushes, blackbirds, blue tits, coal tits and the occasional green-finch in the nearby hedgerow next to the cobbled school drive. It was a hive of activity alongside the stillness of the empty playground. We leant against the school wall and sipped our lemonade in silent reverie. There was a Victorian permanence to our beautiful little village school and, in the morning sunlight, the walls were like amber honey.

Anne Grainger walked over to join us. 'I love school at this time of the year,' she said quietly.

'Hmmm,' I murmured, 'I know what you mean – all the outdoor activities, summer fairs and sports days . . . Good times, Anne.'

Beth looked at the two of us curiously and then stared up at the high arched windows and the silent gothic bell tower.

Suddenly the spell was broken. Jo Hunter, with the energy of youth, hurried back towards the school entrance. 'Come on,' she said. 'Let's classify those non-fiction books.'

Valerie Flint gave us a knowing smile and followed on. With the help of some of the parents, she wrote Dewey decimal numbers on small white labels and stuck them on the spine of each book, while Jo began stacking the books on our new shelves. By lunchtime the job was completed but it was noticeable there were many gaps in our collection and there was a stark shortage of history, geography and poetry books. Our recent appeal for second-hand books had resulted in a good response from the villagers but there were few up-to-date reference books. We needed more but, after buying the shelving and the storage units, there were no spare funds.

After everyone had departed, Beth and I locked up the school and wandered out into the High Street. Nora Pratt had put a few tables and chairs outside her coffee shop and Petula Dudley-Palmer was sitting there with Elisabeth Amelia and Victoria Alice. They were eating ice cream from tall glasses.

'Oh, look, Jack,' said Beth, 'a knickerbocker glory. I've not had one of those in years.'

When we walked in, Nora was counting the plastic spoons and, on the juke-box, Leo Sayer was singing 'More Than I Can Say'.

'Hello, Nora,' I said. 'Two knickerbocker glories, please.'

She scooped various flavours of ice cream into two tall glasses, placed a cherry on top of each and served them accompanied by long spoons.

'Alexander the Gweat would never wun into battle without a knickerbocker glowy,' said Nora.

'Really? I didn't know that,' I said, while Beth gave me a wide-eyed stare.

'Ah were weally good at histowy, Mr Sheffield,' said Nora proudly.

I was always fascinated by the eclectic world of Nora Pratt.

We sat outside and Petula Dudley-Palmer lifted her Jodrell Bank sunglasses and glanced enviously at Beth's suntanned legs. Then she looked down at her Kayser's

15-denier smooth knit 'brevity-style' tights, guaranteed to make your legs look like a Mediterranean sun-worshipper until they were sufficiently tanned, and sighed deeply.

She had recently taken delivery from Torquay of a full-size Alpha Caribbean UVA sunbed. With its fast-tanning, six-inch Wotan tubes it was, she had told Geoffrey, a snip at £399 plus £12 delivery. However, she was still at the bright-red stage. It had also occurred to her that morning when she looked in the mirror that perhaps she shouldn't have worn goggles as she now looked like a panda.

After our ice creams I drove Beth back to Morton and arranged to meet her that evening for a farewell drink in The Royal Oak before we went our separate ways.

When I returned to Bilbo Cottage, the telephone rang in the hall.

'Hello. Jack Sheffield speaking.'

'Jack, Richard Gomersall here, at County Hall.'

'Oh hello, Richard. This is unexpected,' I said.

'Yes, well, we don't get school holidays like you, Jack.'

I didn't mention I had been in school all morning and was about to take a class of children on an outdoor education weekend.

'So what can I do to help?' I asked.

'Actually, Jack, I'm just following up our earlier conversation and I wondered if you had given the Scarborough headship any further thought.'

'I'm still considering it, Richard,' I said, stalling for time, 'and obviously appreciate your advice and support.' I felt

I was suddenly turning into a politician. The truth was I didn't know which way to turn.

'I understand, Jack, and, clearly, there's no pressure here, just a polite enquiry at this stage. You've obviously been earmarked as an up-and-coming headteacher who's doing a good job in one of our small village schools.'

'That's kind of you to say so,' I said cautiously.

'Fine. Let's leave it at that for the time being, Jack . . . and good luck in these uncertain times.'

'Yes, thank you,' I said.

'We'll talk again.'

And the line went dead.

I didn't mention the call to Beth when I met her in The Royal Oak. She had been shopping in York and had other things on her mind.

'Jack, I've bought a Betamax video recorder. It's brilliant, you'll love it. It's got over three hours' recording time and a three-day timer.'

Secretly, I would have preferred Beth to have saved her money for our wedding but I said nothing. In any case, she had changed into a sundress with narrow straps and a jade fabric belt and looked so beautiful. State-of-the-art video recorders held no interest for me.

'I'll miss you,' I said simply.

She sipped her gin and tonic and looked at me thoughtfully. 'It's only three days.'

Her hair tumbled over her suntanned shoulders and I just stared at her.

'And three nights,' I said with a wry grin.

Then she leant forward and took off my Buddy Holly

spectacles. 'Perhaps we ought to get you some new wire-rimmed spectacles,' she said, 'and maybe one of those black executive briefcases.'

'I'm happy as I am, Beth,' I said, retrieving my spectacles, 'and my old leather satchel has a few years left in it yet.'

'If you become a head of a big school, Jack, you'll need to look the part.'

I leant back in my chair and stared out of the bay window across the village green towards Ragley School. There were times when the life Beth seemed to want felt more than I could give her. Falling in love had been easy: what followed was proving more difficult.

On Thursday morning we boarded William Featherstone's Reliance bus and set off from outside school amid waving parents for our educational holiday. As well as myself and my class, the party consisted of Anne and John Grainger and Jo and Dan Hunter.

We left York on the A59 road, drove through Harrogate and on to Skipton, the 'Gateway to the Dales'. Then we headed north through a spectacular landscape of woods and waterfalls. I stared out of the window at the emerging panorama. Spread out before us, and shaped in the Ice Age, was a dale of carboniferous limestone, sandstone and shale. In the grazing land of the upland pastures lay isolated farmhouses and, beyond the hay meadows, the wild rugged moorland stretched out to the purple horizon. It was a perfect mix of natural and man-made beauty with its green fields criss-crossed with limestone walls. Sheep were everywhere on the distant canvas like tiny flecks of white paint flicked from a child's stiff-bristle paintbrush.

Soon we were in the heart of beautiful Wharfedale, with its green fields dotted with yellow buttercups, rugged limestone cliffs and the desolate cries of the curlews. Sudden splashes of sunlight illuminated the wild pink roses running riot through the prickly hedgerows, while a silent confusion of moving shadows darkened the winding River Wharfe in the valley below.

We drove into the cobbled main square of Grassington village to eat our packed lunches and parked next to an ancient stone horse trough surmounted by an old iron water pump. The air was familiar, sharp and cold and the passing of years had not changed the small shops in this timeless community. As I ate my sandwiches, I smiled at the rickety sign outside Mervyn the Barber's shop. It read, *'Gentleman's Barber, Clogger, Tonsorial Artist, Antiquarian, Poet, Chiropodist, Phrenologist and Botanist'*.

'Food tastes better 'ere, Mr Sheffield,' said Cathy Cathcart with her familiar Stonehenge smile and zest for life. She had put a pickled gherkin in a marmalade sandwich and was munching on it happily. New experiences were always a treat for Cathy.

Meanwhile William walked sedately up the narrow main street to the Devonshire Arms to partake of a more traditional Ploughman's lunch.

An hour later we were on our way again on the B6160 past the looming menace of Kilnsey Crag, the pretty village of Kettlewell and Aysgarth Falls. Finally our destination was in sight and the children were full of excitement. Here there were no traffic sounds, only birdsong, the whisper of the wind and the music of tumbling becks. Beyond, in the far distance, among limestone scars and gritstone crags, the brooding bulk of Addleborough lay like a sleeping giant. At its feet huddled the tall stone houses and winding cobbled streets of Askrigg village, centred round the thirteenth-century church of St Oswald. With its history of clock-making and hand-knitting, it already had its place in Yorkshire folklore but the television series *All Creatures Great and Small* had made it famous.

Askrigg Low Mill Residential Youth Centre was an old mill that had been superbly converted. Valerie Flint had told us it had won design awards for its innovative use of space and we soon realized it was the perfect base for a group of energetic children. After settling into our dormitories we set off up the steep hill to explore the village. Next to the cobbled marketplace and the stone market cross we found Skeldale House, the television home of James Herriot. A few paces further on was the King's Arms, a popular William Younger's public house known as the Drover's Arms in the television series.

It was fun recognizing the locations and, after a huge evening meal of shepherd's pie and fresh vegetables, we slept like logs under a starry Yorkshire sky.

Friday was a full and adventurous day. Across the river from Hawes village we scrabbled up the side of the beck until we reached the roaring waterfall of Hardraw Force, the highest single-drop waterfall in England. The bravest children, led by Darrell Topper and Katy Ollerenshaw, clambered fearlessly like mountain goats behind the cascading torrent while the others watched from a safe distance.

On the way back, we stopped in the beautiful village of Bainbridge, outside the white-fronted Rose and Crown Hotel. The children drank lemonade and played in the wooden stocks on the broad village green. Then the landlord invited us in to see the famous hunting horn hanging above the bar. He told the children that once this was a dense forest with deer and wild boar and that each evening, between Holy Rood and Shrovetide, the horn was blown to guide weary travellers to safety. Then, inevitably, the children took turns to blow it.

On school journeys, usually something happens that makes them memorable. Saturday was destined to be such a day.

Following a fascinating visit to the rope-makers in Hawes during the morning and a delicious fish-and-chips lunch in the marketplace, we drove through the high wild peaks up to Countersett, to the banks of Semerwater. The bearded, experienced warden of Low Mill was waiting for us with his huge trailer stacked high with two-person Canadian canoes. After a talk on safety, he gave everyone a life-jacket and we were off for a thrilling afternoon of canoe-racing. We took turns so that there was always an adult with a pupil in each canoe. Dan proved the most popular partner for the children as his boat always seemed to go the fastest and he rubbed it in by humming the theme tune from *Hawaii Five-O* as he raced past us. It was a group of happy, red-faced, slightly damp and very tired children who clambered back on to the bus for our return journey to Low Mill.

We were just outside Askrigg village when the unexpected happened. A dark-blue, open-top classic car with chromium wire wheels and a hugely powerful engine overtook us. The driver wore a checked flat cap and waved to William in acknowledgement for giving him space to pass. The lady next to him, with a silk headscarf to protect her hair in the stiff breeze, turned and smiled at the children.

Dan and I were on the front seat of our coach. 'Hey! Look at that,' he said, 'a 1964 Alvis TE21 drophead coupé . . . the car of my dreams.' Dan was a great classic-car enthusiast.

We watched it roar off into the distance, when, suddenly, a startled sheep appeared out of the ditch and ran headlong into the narrow road. There was a screech of brakes, the sheep bounded to safety, the car mounted the grass verge and crashed into the limestone wall with a crunch of metal and a burst of steam.

Seconds later we pulled up behind them and Dan leapt out and opened the passenger door of the sports car. He quickly assessed the situation.

'Are you hurt?' he asked.

'I think we're fine . . . No broken bones,' said the man behind the wheel.

'Oh, thank you for stopping,' gasped the woman in the passenger seat.

They were clearly shaken but, thankfully, unhurt. However, the car was in no fit state to continue their journey.

'It's not a write-off but it will take some time to repair,' said Dan, crouching down beside the damaged wing and burst tyre.

The smart, well-dressed couple, both, I guessed, in their fifties, looked concerned. 'I'm Edward and this is my wife, Dominique,' he said.

She was a strikingly beautiful woman with long dark hair and soulful eyes. 'We're so grateful,' she said. 'You really are an angel of mercy.' There was the merest hint of a French accent.

We shook hands. 'I'm Jack Sheffield, a headteacher from York, and we're staying in the next village,' I said, 'so why don't you come back with us and we can phone from there and get your car towed to the nearest garage?'

Edward smiled. 'An excellent idea,' he said and glanced up at the onrushing dark clouds, 'and not a moment too soon, by the look of the weather.'

Edward and Dominique stayed the night at Low Mill while their car was towed into Hawes village to be repaired. Outside, a fierce summer thunderstorm raged, but, happily, we were safe inside. Showered and changed and with spiky damp hair and dry clothes, the children enjoyed giant portions of steak-and-kidney pie followed by rhubarb crumble and custard and then settled down together in the common room to write up their daily diaries.

Dominique had made friends with Anne and they were sharing stories about school life, while Edward, who obviously knew much about the history of the area, began to tell a group of the children a fascinating story about Semerwater. He was clearly a well-read man and an experienced public speaker. Soon, the rest of the children gathered round and all became engrossed.

'An angel came down from heaven to a city of spires, fine buildings, large houses and busy shops,' said Edward in a dramatic voice. 'The angel was disguised as an old man and went from house to house, seeking shelter and food. At every house in the city he was turned away until at last he knocked on the door of an old cottage where the crofter, poor as he was, let him in and gave him food, water and a place to rest.'

Outside there was a flash of lightning, followed closely by the roar of thunder. The children snuggled closer together, eyes wide and full of interest.

'The angel suddenly appeared in a blaze of light,' said Edward, 'and shouted in a great voice to the valley below, "Semer Water rise, Semer Water sink, and swallow all save this little house that gave me meat and drink." And so a great flood came and covered up the whole village.'

The children stared in a mixture of horror and amazement. There was no doubt that Edward was a gifted storyteller and Dominique smiled quietly to herself and whispered something to Anne.

'All except for the crofter's cottage,' said Edward, 'and folk still say that beneath the dark waters the sound of the church bells can still be heard.'

There was silence and all of us were secretly glad we were safe and together in this warm room and away from the winds that howled mournfully across the lonely hillsides. Then everyone clapped, the spell was broken and tired children went off to their beds.

'Wonderful story, Edward. Thank you,' I said.

'No, Jack, thank *you* . . . The quality of mercy is not strained,' he said with a smile.

'It droppeth as the gentle rain from heaven,' I replied.

'Ah, good to meet a fellow lover of Shakespeare,' he said.

'And your children really do enjoy books,' said Dominique, gesturing towards our box of information books about bird life, wildflowers, geology and photographs of the Dales. 'They use them well . . . and Anne has told me all about your terrific library.'

It was a relaxing end to our visit to the Dales and the following week the children painted pictures of giant waterfalls and wrote dramatic stories about canoe-racing. One morning before the start of school I was in the office with Vera, who was opening the morning mail.

'Goodness me!' she exclaimed. 'Wonderful news, Mr Sheffield: we've received a cheque for five hundred pounds!'

'Pardon?'

'That's right, and the only stipulation is it must be spent on books for the school library.'

'It sounds like a dream come true, Vera,' I said, 'but who has sent it?'

'A Lord and Lady Stannington from Northumberland,' she said, scanning the crisp, headed writing paper with a distinctive coat of arms at the top of the page.

'Lord and Lady?'

She passed me the letter. It read:

Dear Mr Sheffield,

Thank you for being our angel of mercy. We wish success to everyone at Ragley School and trust the enclosed cheque will help to fill your library with further wonderful books – especially Shakespeare! Remember . . .

'The quality of mercy is not strained,
It droppeth as the gentle rain from heaven'.

With best wishes,
Edward and Dominique Stannington

I looked at Vera in disbelief and she smiled. 'As I said, Mr Sheffield, everyone has a guardian angel.'

Chapter Nineteen

The Guardians of Secrets

End-of-school-year reading tests were completed. Mrs Pringle wrote to the governing body to confirm she will return to full-time teaching in September 1981. All the children painted a picture for the annual Church Fête art competition entitled 'My Happiest Day at Ragley School'.

Extract from the Ragley School Logbook:
Friday, 26 June 1981

An early-morning mist covered the distant fields like a cloak of secrets.

I opened my bedroom window and breathed in the clean summer air. The scent of roses drifted up to greet me and wisteria clung to the window frame like a lover's embrace. Basking in the sunshine, bright-winged butterflies spread their lace wings on the sturdy stems of the buddleia bushes.

It was seven o'clock on Friday, 26 June, and there were

decisions to be made – decisions that would determine the rest of my life.

Over my breakfast cereal I opened the envelope once again and spread out the contents. The letter with the coat of arms of North Yorkshire County Council looked impressive and I scanned the first line: 'Headteacher required for Gorse Manor Primary School, Scarborough, to commence January 1982 . . .' Attached was a two-page application form requesting information about the schools I had attended, long-forgotten GCE results, degree classifications, details of my current post and a request for a handwritten letter in support of my application. The closing date was Friday, 3 July, only one week away. I gathered up the papers and the envelope and put them in my jacket pocket.

The playground was already full of early arrivals when I arrived at school. Boys were kicking a ball around the school field and pretending to be Liverpool beating Real Madrid in the European Cup Final, while on the tarmac playground the Buttle twins were winding a long skipping rope. Girls were taking turns to skip while chanting out a rhyme:

> *'One man went to mow,*
> *Went to mow a meadow.*
> *One man and his dog,*
> *Stop, bottle o' pop, fish an' chips,*
> *Ol' Mother Riley an' 'er cow,*
> *Went to mow a meadow.'*

I almost envied the children with their fantasy football and skipping rhymes. They were enjoying the long carefree summer days of a seemingly endless childhood and I wondered what would become of them. In our own way, and with an unwritten curriculum, we had taught them to read and write, share a box of crayons, eat with a knife and fork, recite their own poetry and be proud of their own precious gifts. We had uncovered the mysteries of long division, shared stories of magical lands, made colourful kites and flown them in a powder-blue sky.

There was a rhythm to the life of a village teacher, shaped by school terms and seasons. The autumn term had the bounty of a harvest festival and Bonfire Night, with its hot soup and sparklers, rockets and Roman candles. Then there was the excitement of Christmas with carols and cards, mulled wine and mince pies, parties and presents. The spring term brought with it the Jack Frost patterns on the school windows along with the smell of damp wellingtons lined up by the radiators. Summer term was always one of mixed emotions, with school trips, cricket matches, fêtes and fairs, followed inevitably by the final farewells to the school leavers.

I knew I loved teaching but what would it be like to manage a large school? My skills were in the classroom not in the unknown world of timetabling, political dog-fighting, financial management and education committees. I felt as if I was on an annual carousel where the children remained constant; only the faces changed year by year . . . So many children, so many faces.

'Penny for 'em, Mr Sheffield?'

'Oh, good morning, Ruby. What's that for?'

She was carrying a long window-pole and looked as if she was about to harpoon a whale. 'Balls, Mr Sheffield.'

'Pardon?'

'It's a full-time job in t'summer,' she grumbled. With an experienced flick of the pole she dislodged Jimmy Poole's tennis ball from the gutter above the entrance porch.

'Thank you, Mithuth Thmith,' said Jimmy and ran off to continue his game of Test Match cricket with Heathcliffe Earnshaw.

During morning school I completed our end-of-year reading tests to pass on to Easington Comprehensive School and I was pleased with Cathy Cathcart, who had worked hard and now had a reading age of eleven. Cathy had read seventy-six correct words out of one hundred on the Schonell Word Recognition Test, finally failing on the line 'oblivion, scintillate, satirical, sabre, beguile'.

At morning break Valerie was on playground duty and, when I walked into the staff-room, Joseph was sipping his milky coffee, reading Class 4's Religious Knowledge exercise books and wondering why Cathy Cathcart had written that the greatest miracle in the Bible was when Mary had an immaculate contraption.

Meanwhile Vera, Anne and Jo were huddled round Vera's *Daily Telegraph*.

'I wonder what her wedding dress will be like,' said Jo.

Vera scanned the text. 'It's being made by Emmanuel of London,' she said.

'I bet it will be beautiful,' said Anne.

Joseph looked up with a puzzled expression. 'Wedding dress?'

My thoughts were elsewhere and for a moment I was equally bemused. I thought they were talking about Beth.

'There's only *one* wedding dress, Joseph,' said Vera firmly.

'Lady Diana,' said Anne helpfully.

'Oh, yes, the future princess,' said Joseph. 'I'm sure it will be lovely.'

'Everything all right, Jack?' asked Anne, ever sensitive to my moods.

'Fine, thanks,' I said with a guarded smile and wondered if I should break the news. But, for the time being, I had decided to remain silent about the application.

'Well, this wedding dress is certainly the best-kept secret,' announced Anne.

Feeling guilty, I picked up my coffee and walked through to the office. I needed time to myself.

It was lunchtime when I saw my chance to speak to Joseph and I followed him out to the car park.

'Joseph, there's something on my mind I need to discuss with you.'

'Yes, Jack, what is it?'

I looked around. No one was in earshot, children were playing in the playground and we were alone. 'It's a confidential matter.'

He put his hand on my shoulder. 'You looked troubled, Jack. Let's sit in the car.'

We climbed into his little Austin A40 and I took out the application form.

'I'm thinking of applying for another headship. It's a large school in Scarborough,' I said quickly.

Joseph looked shocked. 'Oh, I see . . . This is un-expected.'

'I'm sorry, Joseph. You have always been so supportive, and I love it here at Ragley, but this is a good opportunity. Headships like this don't come up very often.'

'We should know the fate of Ragley School in a few weeks. Would that influence your decision?'

I pointed to the deadline date for the application. 'I need to decide this weekend and post my response on Monday if I'm to have a chance of getting this headship.'

He nodded. 'Yes. I can see the problem. The timing is not ideal.'

'So I really need your support, Joseph – and your bless-ing.'

He smiled gently and put his hand on my arm, but his eyes were troubled. 'You have it, Jack, and I wish you every success.'

'I haven't discussed this with anyone else.'

'Of course,' he said, 'and I won't say a word.'

'Only Beth knows,' I added.

'And is she supportive?'

'Yes, Joseph. She's very keen for me to secure a larger headship and then we can plan our marriage.'

'Ah, I see,' he said.

'I intend to discuss it with her tonight and I'll let you know the outcome over the weekend.'

When he drove off he looked sombre.

*   *   *

It was only when school was quiet at the end of the day and I was alone in the office that I decided to call Beth at Hartingdale.

'Beth, instead of the cinema, can we meet up tonight for a drink?' I said quickly.

'Fine, Jack. Everything OK?'

'It would be good to talk.'

'Well, I've got a huge pile of paperwork here, so . . .' I heard her give a big sigh, 'it would make sense for me to finish this first and then I can enjoy the weekend. Remember it's the church fête tomorrow.'

It was far from my mind. 'Yes. So I'll walk over to the Oak about seven and you come on when you can. We could have something to eat, if you like.'

'Fine, Jack. See you later.'

I stared at the receiver and then slowly replaced it in its cradle.

There was a time when I thought Beth would share my home and, perhaps one day, the patter of tiny feet might echo on the quarry-tiled floor of the kitchen of Bilbo Cottage. I had felt comfortable with my niche in the cluster of little villages at the foot of the Hambleton Hills in the vast and beautiful North Yorkshire countryside. Now, life seemed to be growing so complicated.

The Royal Oak was already busy. Most of the wooden tables and chairs outside were fully occupied by locals on this perfect summer evening.

''Ello, Mr Sheffield,' said Sheila. 'No Miss 'Enderson tonight?'

'She's coming later, Sheila,' I said in a distracted way.

'Usual, is it, Mr Sheffield? 'Alf o' Chestnut?'

'Make it a pint, please, Sheila.'

Sheila pulled on the pump and fluttered her false eye-lashes. 'Ah like a man who knows what 'e wants. She's a lucky woman, that fiancée o' yours.'

I put thirty pence on the bar. Don appeared at her elbow and collected some empty glasses from the bar.

'Thank you, Mr Sheffield, but let me tell y'summat f'nowt.' She leant over the bar and I averted my eyes from her colossal cleavage. 'Married life's not a bed o' roses.'

Don had a big grin on his stubbly face. 'Tek no notice,' he said. 'We've 'ad twenty 'appy years o' married life.' Then he ambled to the far end of the bar to serve two farmers.

Sheila looked after him and then winked at me. 'Only thing is, Mr Sheffield, 'e's 'ad nineteen and ah've 'ad one.'

When Beth sat down she immediately opened the *Times Educational Supplement* to the Primary Headships page. The advertisement for Gorse Manor was circled in red felt pen.

'You need to get your skates on, Jack,' she said. 'The closing date is next week.'

'I know,' I said. 'I'm still thinking about it.'

She sipped her gin and tonic and closed the paper. 'But you *must* go for it. We *have* discussed it.'

'Have we?'

'Yes. Don't you remember?' she said, leaning over the table. 'I told you about it.'

'Yes, you did.'

Suddenly, there was a sense of urgency in her voice. 'Jack, do you want to be a village teacher all your life?'

I put my head in my hands. 'I'm not sure . . .'

'If you get this, we could consider buying a bigger house somewhere between Scarborough and Hartingdale . . . And we ought to set a date for the wedding – say, next Easter.'

Beth seemed to have it all worked out.

I spent Saturday morning sitting at my garden table and filling in the application form. Another hot day was in store and, from far away, the bleating of sheep carried on the morning breeze. In the dense hedgerow of hazel and hawthorn, a blackbird's yellow beak could be seen, while wrens and starlings were all busy searching for their breakfast. On my Yorkshire stone pathway, a thrush was busy cracking a snail's shell with manic endeavour. Life lower down the food chain was clearly a hazardous business.

By lunchtime I had finished and I set off in my Morris Minor Traveller along the back road to Ragley village and then on towards Morton, where I parked outside Beth's cottage. Hand in hand we walked to the vicarage, where the church fête was in full swing. A host of colourful visitors in their straw hats and bright dresses had turned up in force to enjoy the ice cream and lemonade stall, the home-made cakes, the bowling for a pig competition, plus a bran-tub lucky-dip and the beautiful-baby competition.

Around us the villagers of Ragley were busy swapping

stories about Vera's excellent scones, the strange but compulsive taste of Joseph's home-made greengage wine and, of course, what Lady Diana's wedding dress might look like. There was laughter and chatter, colour and vivacity, alongside peace and tranquillity.

'Don't you just love all this, Beth – this village, the community, the characters?'

'You know I do, Jack, but I never imagined we would be here for ever.'

I stared at the scene around me. 'I like the feeling of . . . belonging.'

We walked in dappled shadow under the high elms and alongside tall, ageing gravestones.

'I know you do,' said Beth, 'but life moves on and you'd probably grow into this new headship.'

'I wouldn't have a class of my own.'

'You'll be able to teach lots of classes in a large school, if you wish.'

Ash-grey lichen had begun to encrust the gravestone beside me and, with my finger, I traced the carved letters. One day, they would disappear for ever and only the memory would remain. Time was irrepressible and, like the constant winds that circled the earth, it could turn our dreams to dust.

'I love Ragley School, Beth, and I would be sad to leave it all.'

'I know that, Jack, but . . .'

'But what?'

'Can't you see? It's *our* future as well.'

The gentle breeze blew a strand of honey-blonde hair across her face and I lifted it gently and tucked it behind her ear. She smiled at the gesture but her green eyes stared up at me with curiosity.

'I know,' I said quietly and we walked back together into the crowds.

Joyce Davenport beckoned to us. She was carrying a tray of scones filled with strawberry jam and fresh whipped cream. 'Mr Sheffield, Miss Henderson, perhaps you would like to join us for one of Vera's delicious scones and a cup of tea?'

We followed her to a nearby table and were soon deep in conversation with Valerie Flint and a group of ladies in the church choir about home baking.

'I wonder if we'll ever discover the secret art of Vera's scones,' said Joyce.

'There are secrets women take to their graves,' said Valerie Flint mysteriously.

The conversation ebbed and flowed and, occasionally, Beth glanced up at me, but I knew there was a lot left unsaid between us.

Later we walked into the marquee to see the results of the children's art competition, judged by Miss Tripps, the retiring headteacher of Morton School. Hazel Smith had won a Highly Commended certificate for a painting of Ruby winning the ladies egg-and-spoon race at a long-ago sports day.

Ruby was thrilled and was standing with Hazel outside the tent. She was also carrying a jar of humbugs with a winning tombola ticket attached.

"Umbug, Mr Sheffield, Miss 'Enderson?' said Ruby. 'Ah've jus' won 'em.' She nodded towards the high walls of the vicarage garden, where Vera was talking to the major. 'Nice t'see Miss Evans looking 'appy, Mr Sheffield,' she said. 'Ah once thought she were a bit hoity-toity, if y'tek m'meaning, but she's got 'eart o' gold.'

'I agree, Ruby,' I said.

Vera was standing with the major by a rickety gate that led to her secret garden. It was a time of plenty, none more so than in Vera's kitchen garden enclosed by tall red-brick walls. There, an abundance of potatoes, carrots, peas on twiggy sticks, lettuces, spring onions and tall runner beans waited to be harvested. George Hardisty, the retired school gardener, had recently become the vicarage gardener and he had surrounded the precious crops with wire netting to protect them from hungry rabbits.

'Oh, Rupert, how perfect. I simply love freesias,' said Vera. 'The scent is so wonderful.'

'Flowers for a lady,' said Rupert with a courteous bow.

'You are such a good friend,' she said.

Rupert bent and kissed her hand. One day he hoped to be more than just a friend, but for now that was his secret. Beth and I walked on, feeling we were intruding.

Meanwhile, at the ice-cream stall, Geoffrey Dudley-Palmer was standing with Elisabeth Amelia and Victoria Alice. The two beautifully dressed and coiffured little girls caught my eye and waved at me in delight.

Nearby, sitting alone at a picnic table, Petula Dudley-Palmer took out a small black-and-white photograph from a secret pocket in the lining of her handbag and recalled the days of her youth in a little council house in Withenshaw, on the outskirts of Manchester. The highlight of her life had been the Manchester Majorettes and the regular competitions had given her a colourful and exciting escape from her drab life. She looked with affection at the photograph of the youthful, pencil-slim Petula in her majorette costume. In a pair of white ankle socks, her legs looked skinny below a short skirt that had been lovingly decorated with pink pompons by her mother. Her ambition then was to be like the senior girls who wore distinctive waistcoats emblazoned with metal badges proclaiming their success as majorettes. As she scanned the youthful faces of her friends of long ago she wondered what had become of them. There was no doubt she had been fortunate in finding Geoffrey, the young business executive with the world at his feet, and she hurriedly replaced the photograph and smiled as he returned with her ice cream.

''Ello, Mr Sheffield,' shouted a cheerful voice. 'Ah'm gonna 'ave a candy-floss.' It was Darrell Topper with his mother and another elderly lady I had never seen before.

'Hello, Darrell,' I said.

'Ah don't think there is no candy-floss,' retorted the elderly lady.

'Yes, there is, Grandma. Look at t'sign. It says "Candy-floss for sale".'

I smiled. A year ago Darrell wouldn't have been able to read it.

As we walked on, Darrell's grandmother said, 'And who was that big feller wi' t'funny glasses?'

"'E's 'eadteacher, Mam,' said Mrs Topper. "'E taught our Darrell t'read.'

Beth turned back and looked at them thoughtfully and then squeezed my hand.

It was late when Beth and I arrived back at her cottage. She unlocked the door and turned to face me. It had been a lovely summer's day and now a vast purple sky spread to the far horizon over the plain of York. I held her in my arms, not wanting to let her go.

'What is it?' Beth asked. 'What's wrong?'

'It's fine, Beth. It's just me thinking about the future.'

Was it a backward step to say I was happy to be a village schoolteacher? Would Beth think me a man with no drive? My mother had once told me there were three types of people: those who simply take and then leave society all the poorer for it; those who tread water and leave society as they found it; and, finally, those who use their gifts to make society better. Ragley was such a place and I knew that with hard work I could make a difference in this little corner of Yorkshire I called my home.

'Jack, is everything . . . you know, all right?'

'Life just seems a little *uncertain* at present,' I said.

'I suppose the only certainty is uncertainty,' she said.

I stared into her green eyes as if seeing her for the first time. Perhaps happiness is always fragile and we have to take it while we can, before it breaks. 'Beth, sometimes I think I will never know you . . . But I will always love you.'

'Jack . . .'

'Yes?'

She stretched up and kissed me tenderly. 'Stay tonight,' and she took my hand and we stepped into the darkness of her silent hallway.

Chapter Twenty

Village Teacher

School closed today for the summer holidays with 88 children on roll. It was confirmed that Mrs Pringle will return to her post as full-time teacher of Class 3 in the autumn term and a presentation was made to Miss Flint in appreciation of her services. We were informed that County Hall will notify all schools in the area 'very soon' regarding proposed closures.

Extract from the Ragley School Logbook:
Friday, 24 July 1981

As I drove up the High Street, the village was coming alive. Diane Wigglesworth was putting a huge poster of Lady Diana in the window of her Hair Salon and Timothy Pratt was admiring his horizontal bunting. On the village green, Clint and Shane Ramsbottom were unpacking the Ragley scouts marquee from the back of a trailer and Major Rupert Forbes-Kitchener was holding a large flag of St George and supervising the erection of the village flagpole.

It was Friday, 24 July, the last day of the school year, and the villagers of Ragley were beginning their preparations for next week's national holiday. The royal wedding was drawing near – and so was my interview at County Hall.

I pulled into the school car park and sat there for a few moments, deep in my own thoughts. I took out the letter from my inside pocket and read it again.

Dear Mr Sheffield,
You are invited to attend for interview at County Hall,
Northallerton, at 10.00 a.m. on Thursday, 30 July 1981
for the post of Headteacher of Gorse Manor Primary
School, Scarborough, to commence January 1982 . . .

Then I stared up at the bell tower and wondered for how much longer it would ring out to announce the beginning of another school day.

The last day of the school year is always one of mixed emotions. The summer holidays stretched out before us but for the eleven-year-olds in my class it was time to say goodbye to Ragley School. The local comprehensive awaited them along with adolescence, a collar-and-tie uniform, blazers that they would grow into, teachers for every subject, a rigid timetable and, on a far-distant horizon, public examinations.

By ten o'clock, our school hall was full for the final 'Leavers' Assembly'. Predictably, it was a tearful one, particularly for the parents whose children were called out one by one to receive the gift of a book donated by the PTA. Saying goodbye to these children was hard enough but knowing that the school might close as well was almost heartbreaking.

The Revd Joseph Evans, as chair of governors, spoke of these 'uncertain times' in his final summary of the school year and there was silence when he said that our fate would soon be known. He thanked the teachers for all their hard work and, particularly, Valerie Flint, for taking over from Sally Pringle in Class 3.

Anne and Vera looked close to tears when Katy Ollerenshaw closed our last assembly of the academic year with our traditional school prayer:

Dear Lord,
This is our school, let peace dwell here,
Let the room be full of contentment, let love abide here,
Love of one another, love of life itself,
And love of God.
Amen.

At the end of school, Vera gave each pupil a sealed manila envelope containing a written report in an A5-size booklet for signing and eventual return by their parents. Once again, I had indulged in polite phrases: 'could do better' actually meant 'rather lazy' and 'a little more effort in mathematics would be helpful' really should have read 'struggles with long division'. Like most village teachers, I knew my pupils well and the after-school conversations with parents at the school gate were often far more valuable than the official communications.

Finally, the academic year 1980–1981 came to its close and I thanked Jo and Valerie Flint for all their hard work and wished them a happy holiday. Our school emptied for the last time and I watched the children of Ragley village walk down the drive and out of the school gates. For them there was always a tomorrow under a seemingly endless summer sun – a time of dreams and discoveries, of pigtails and promises. It was an image of childhood that was etched in my mind, forever constant but ever changing.

Now came the hard part. I wanted Anne and Vera to know about my interview.

Anne was clearing up the contents of her Home Corner when I walked into her classroom and shut the door behind me.

'Anne, I need to share something with you,' I said.

She sat down on one of the low plastic-topped tables and looked at me patiently.

I plunged in. 'I've got an interview for another headship.'

There was a long silence. 'Well, I hope it goes well for you,' said Anne. 'Which one is it?'

'Gorse Manor at Scarborough,' I said. 'The interview's next Thursday and, if I get it, the job would start after Christmas.'

She nodded. 'My guess is you'll have a good chance, Jack.'

'Thanks, Anne.'

'I presume this is confidential,' she said.

'Only Joseph knows at present, and I intend to tell Vera before she goes home, but no one else.'

Anne looked thoughtful. 'I understand . . . and Vera will appreciate being told.'

'It's been a difficult decision and not knowing Ragley's fate hasn't helped.'

Anne stood up and leant against her teacher's desk. 'Would it have made any difference?' she asked.

I hesitated. 'It's a good opportunity for Beth and me but, in reality, I'm unlikely to get it.'

She pondered my response for a moment. 'Well, I enjoy working with you, Jack, but obviously I'm a little sad.' She walked over and kissed me on the cheek. 'Good luck,' she said. 'It won't be the same without you.'

'Thanks,' I said and walked out.

Vera was putting on her coat when I walked into the school office. Once again, I shut the door behind me.

'Excuse me, Vera, may I have a word?' I said. 'It's important.'

'Of course, Mr Sheffield,' she said.

'Vera,' I began slowly, 'I spoke to Joseph a few weeks ago in confidence about applying for another headship. He agreed to support my application and I've got an interview at County Hall next Thursday for a school in Scarborough.'

'I see,' she said and sat down at her desk.

'I told Anne a few minutes ago, but I'm not mentioning it to anyone else at this stage.'

'Yes, that's wise,' she said and clasped her hands.

'I wanted you to know, Vera, and . . . I probably won't get it anyway.'

'Thank you for telling me,' she said. A knowing look crossed her face. 'Now I understand why Joseph has looked a little preoccupied lately.'

'He was *very* understanding,' I said.

'Yes, he would be – as I am.'

'Thank you, Vera.'

'I wish you luck, Mr Sheffield, and I'm sure you will do well in interview.' Her eyes scanned the office as if for the first time. 'I thought this might happen.'

'Did you?'

'Yes, once school closures became imminent. So I decided that, if you moved on, I should retire.'

'That would be a sad day for Ragley School,' I said.

She gave me a weak smile. 'Perhaps,' she said, 'but, even if the school remained open, I wouldn't want to start again with another headteacher.'

'I'm sorry to hear that, Vera,' I said. 'You're a marvellous secretary and I couldn't have managed without you.'

She stood up, took a tiny lace handkerchief out of her handbag and dabbed her eyes. 'I imagine Beth must be pleased,' she said.

'She's keen for everything to be settled so that we can get married.'

'I see,' she said and looked up at me curiously. Then she walked to the door and paused with her hand on the handle.

'What is it, Vera?' I asked.

'Jack . . . Thank you once again for your support and friendship.' She had called me by my first name.

'I should have been lost without you, Vera,' I said quietly.

'I know all good things come to an end,' she said, 'and I wish you luck . . .' she opened the door and looked back, 'but, remember, only *you* will know if you've made the right decision.'

When she had gone only the ticking of the school clock disturbed the silence. I sat down at my desk, opened my bottom drawer, took out the logbook and wrote my last entry of the academic year.

On Wednesday, 29 July, early-morning clouds were slow to clear. There wasn't a breath of wind and a hot, muggy day was in store. It seemed as though the world had slowed to a stop for the royal wedding and 700 million people were about to watch the day's events unfold.

At eight o'clock Vera switched on Radio 4 to listen to Wynford Vaughan-Thomas while she added chopped banana to Joseph's morning Weetabix. At that moment, in the village hall, Timothy Pratt arranged the chairs in perfectly straight lines and on the stage Albert Jenkins tuned in a huge television set to BBC 1 and Angela Rippon. Meanwhile, in the taproom of The Royal Oak, Don Bradshaw switched on the television set and selected ITV. He knew his customers: Big Dave and the Ragley cricket team preferred Selina Scott.

At half past ten Beth and I parked in the school car park and walked down Ragley High Street, which was lined with colourful bunting, and into the village hall. Shirley Mapplebeck and Doreen Critchley were serving tea and cake and the seats were filling up quickly. The front rows had been occupied for the last hour by the Ragley and Morton Women's Institute. Beth and I sipped our tea, munched on delicious Dundee cake and watched the television.

'Our turn next,' said Beth as Lady Diana waved to the crowds. Over half a million people had lined the streets of London.

I smiled and looked around the hall. 'And this hall would be perfect for our wedding breakfast,' I whispered.

'Not sure it's big enough, Jack,' said Beth.

I looked at her and realized she was serious.

Then there was a communal gasp from the ladies of the Women's Institute when the youthful twenty-year-old Lady Diana emerged from her glass coach.

'What a beautiful dress,' said Vera.

Designed by David and Elizabeth Emmanuel and made of ivory pure silk taffeta and old lace, it was a spectacular creation. The sweeping train, 25 feet long, cascaded down the steps of St Paul's.

'And such lovely flowers,' said Joyce Davenport, dabbing tears from her eyes. Lady Diana carried a bouquet of stephanotis, white orchids and lilies of the valley, with gold roses in memory of Lord Mountbatten. Everything was perfect.

When the Archbishop of Canterbury, Robert Runcie, began with the words 'Here is the stuff of which fairy tales are made,' Beth squeezed my hand.

There followed much discussion among Vera and her friends about Princess Margaret's deep-peach silk dress and the fact that Princess Anne had quickly regained her figure after giving birth to her daughter three months ago. Happily, the Queen Mother in sea green and the Queen in aquamarine passed the Women's Institute rigorous test of appropriate dress sense.

Discussion in The Royal Oak had a different emphasis. Dorothy was telling Little Malcolm that a copy of the bride's dress would shortly be on sale in Debenham's in London at the bargain price of £450. She was unaware that Little Malcolm's more immediate priority was that a pint of Tetley's was now costing him thirty pence.

"E's proper 'andsome is that Charlie-boy,' said Sheila, her voluptuous figure straining in her flag of St George blouse.

There was no doubt that thirty-two-year-old Prince Charles looked the part in the full dress uniform of a naval commander. Margery Ackroyd, who never missed a thing, spotted that, in the marriage ceremony, both Charles and Diana fluffed their lines. Charles omitted to mention that the goods with which he endowed her were worldly ones while Diana promised to take 'Philip Charles' instead of 'Charles Philip'.

As they walked back down the aisle, everyone in the taproom waved flags and York City scarves in time to Elgar's 'Pomp and Circumstance'.

Finally there was a communal 'aaaahh' when Charles kissed his bride on the balcony of Buckingham Palace. That was the signal for everyone to gather on the village green, where the ladies of the Women's Institute were serving glasses of home-made lemonade and Old Tommy Piercy's hog roast was doing a roaring trade. Soon, the children of Ragley were all seated at trestle tables, enjoying jelly and ice cream. The sights and sounds of the village in celebration were all around us as Beth and I relaxed with Anne and John Grainger on a line of hay bales under the weeping-willow tree by the duck pond.

Morris dancers went through their repertoire and Captain Fantastic amused the children with his Punch and Judy show, although it seemed Ruby and her grown-up daughters enjoyed it just as much.

Meanwhile in the beer tent, Big Dave was regaling the Ragley cricket team with a blow-by-blow account of England's victory over Australia at Headingley. Ian Botham had just scored 149 runs and the old foe couldn't score the 130 they needed for victory. England cricket was once again on top of the world and life for all of us was just that little bit sweeter.

I was standing in the queue for Old Tommy Piercy's hog roast when I overheard an interesting conversation. Deke Ramsbottom was helping out Old Tommy and supplying him with nips of whisky from his hip flask, while Ernie Morgetroyd and his son Rodney, the Morton village milkmen, were trying to score points off their Ragley neighbours.

'Ah 'eard your school might be closing,' said Ernie.

'Nay, not in my lifetime,' said Old Tommy.

'An' y'village teacher is from a long way off, so they say,' said Ernie.

'That's reight,' said Rodney. 'West Riding, ah were told.'

'Nay, 'e's one of us,' retorted Old Tommy. ''E's played

cricket f'Ragley an' 'e's marrying that nice-looking teacher from Morton.'

I smiled and looked back at Beth in her summer frock.

'An 'e taught my Wayne t'read,' added Deke.

'Bloody 'ell, that *is* summat,' said Ernie.

''Ow d'you mean?' asked Deke, looking puzzled.

'Ah thought your Wayne took after 'is dad,' said Ernie, with a chuckle: 'thick as chips.'

Deke roared with laughter and Old Tommy slapped another large piece of crackling on Ernie's plate.

By six o'clock the crowds had drifted home and Ruby and little Hazel settled down to watch *The Sound of Music* on BBC 1, while the older Smith sisters stayed in The Royal Oak to watch John Travolta strut his stuff in *Saturday Night Fever* and sing along with the Bee-Gees.

Later, when Beth kissed me goodnight, she whispered, 'Good luck tomorrow, Jack.'

Before I went to bed I looked through a copy of my letter of application and the information about the school. It didn't help and sleep was elusive.

On Thursday morning, under a beautiful summer sky, I set off in my Morris Minor Traveller. Dressed in my best suit and polished black shoes, I felt a little conspicuous when I called into the General Stores in Ragley High Street.

Nora Pratt was in front of me, clutching a *Woman's Own* in one hand and a twenty-pence piece in the other. 'A Woyal Wedding Souvenir, please, Pwudence,' said Nora. She looked at the photograph of Charles towering over

Diana on the front cover. ''E must be stood on a box,' said Nora in surprise, ''cause she's weally tall.'

'Here's your *Times*, Mr Sheffield,' said Prudence, 'and may I say how smart you are looking today.'

I put twenty pence on the counter, hurried out and glanced at the headline 'Day of romance in a grey world' over a photograph of the famous kiss on the balcony. It certainly felt like a grey world as I drove towards Northallerton and my date with destiny.

Once again I walked under vast Corinthian columns and my footsteps echoed on the wide marble stairs of County Hall. Richard Gomersall, the Senior Primary Adviser, greeted me. His sartorial elegance put my plain grey suit to shame.

Three men and two women were the other candidates. They all looked smart, calm and confident. There was little communication between us as we waited our turn to enter Room 109. The last time I had been in this room was when I was interviewed for the headship of Ragley School four years ago. So much had happened since.

The interview was chaired by Miss Barrington-Huntley and each member of the nine-strong panel asked two questions each. The chair of governors of Gorse Manor was clearly impressed that I actually *enjoyed* teaching. That apart, it was an unremarkable interview and I had little difficulty answering their questions about curriculum development, leadership and school discipline.

By lunchtime one of the candidates had decided the post was not for him and withdrawn. Lunch with the school governors was next, followed by an afternoon interview for those of us who had been selected to go forward to the next stage.

I was leaning against a marble pillar when Richard Gomersall tapped me on my shoulder.

'Can you come with me, please, Jack?' he said.

He opened a door, beckoned me to enter and then walked away. The office was spacious and beautifully furnished and Miss Barrington-Huntley was standing by the window and staring out. She held a sheet of paper in her hand.

'Come in, Jack.'

I shut the door. She walked to her desk and sat down.

'Please,' she said and gestured to one of the high-backed chairs that were arranged in an arc around her desk.

I sat down and she placed the sheet of paper on the leather-bound blotting pad in front of her. Then she stared at me and appeared to be weighing her words. 'Jack, you had a good interview this morning. There's no doubt the panel are aware of your strengths. How do *you* think it went?'

'From my point of view it went well,' I said. 'It appeared the chair of governors was interested in my willingness to take on a teaching commitment.'

'That's right. The present head has been very active in the classrooms and he's keen for this to continue.'

I said nothing but relaxed a little in my seat.

'You will be aware that it is at this stage I have a word with each candidate to confirm whether or not they would accept the post if it was offered . . . should they be invited to go forward to the afternoon. It may be, of course, that only one person will go forward.' She glanced down at the sheet of paper. 'However, I thought it wise to share a few thoughts with you before we go any further.'

I was curious. This was unexpected.

'Jack . . . I know how hard you have worked at Ragley School and we're all very grateful for your efforts.'

'Thank you,' I said and wondered what was coming next.

'There's no doubt that the post at Gorse Manor would be a much bigger challenge for you. Even so, you have shown that you have the appropriate leadership and management qualities required for a post such as this.'

I couldn't work out whether she was trying to let me down gently, although my instincts were telling me otherwise.

'I'm also aware of your personal circumstances and know that your career decisions also have an impact upon Beth.' She smiled. It had always been obvious that this formidable and powerful chair of the Education Committee had a soft spot for Beth. 'And, of course, Beth has made a good start at Hartingdale.'

'She's very happy there, Miss Barrington-Huntley,' I said, 'and, of course, we both want to stay in North Yorkshire.'

There was silence as she picked up the sheet of paper on her desk and stared at it. 'I have here a press statement that will be made available today to the governing body of every school in our area prior to it appearing in tomorrow's *Yorkshire Post* and local newspapers.'

She looked me squarely in the eyes. 'I thought it only fair to share this information before you progress further with the interview process for Gorse Manor. I know that it must have been difficult for you trying to plan your professional future, not knowing the fate of Ragley School.'

'Yes, it has,' I said simply.

'I'll give you a few minutes to read this,' she said and slid the neatly typed script towards me. Then she walked over to the window and stared out at the distant hills.

My hands were shaking as I read the press statement. It was written in cold hard clear language with no room for ambiguity.

When I had read it I stood up and walked over to her.

'Well?' she said very quietly.

We stood there side by side and I followed her gaze. In the far distance, the cluster of beautiful villages at the foot of the Hambleton Hills shimmered in a summer heat haze.

I handed her the letter and sighed deeply as I recalled Beth's words: *Do you want to be a village teacher all your life?*

For the first time the answer seemed clear.

And in a heartbeat I knew what I must do.

TEACHER, TEACHER!
by Jack Sheffield

Miss Barrington-Huntley took off her steel-framed spectacles and polished them deliberately. 'Mr Sheffield,' she said, 'after careful consideration we have decided to offer you the very challenging post of headmaster of Ragley School'.

It's 1977 and Jack Sheffield arrives at a small village school in North Yorkshire. Little does he imagine what the first year will hold in store as he has to grapple with:

Ruby, the 20 stone caretaker with acute spelling problem

Vera, the school secretary who worships Margaret Thatcher

Ping, the little Vietnamese refugee who becomes the school's best reader and poet

Deke Ramsbottom, a singing cowboy, father of Wayne, Shane and Clint,

and many other, including a groundsman who grows giant carrots, a barmaid parent who requests sex lessons, and a five-year-old boy whose language is colourful in the extreme. And then there's beautiful, bright Beth Henderson, a deputy head, who is irresistibly attractive to the young headmaster . . .

'*Heartbeat* for teachers'
Fay Yeomans, *BBC Radio*

9780552155281

MISTER TEACHER
by Jack Sheffield

It's 1978, and Jack Sheffield is beginning his second year as headmaster of a small village school in North Yorkshire. There are three letters on his desk – one makes him smile, one makes him sad and one is destined to change his life forever. This is from nine-year-old Sebastian, suffering from leukaemia in the local hospital, who writes a heartbreaking letter addressed to 'Mister Teacher'. So begins a journey through the seasons of Yorkshire life in which the school is the natural centre of the community.

Vera, the school secretary who worships Margaret Thatcher; Ruby, the 20-stone caretaker who sings like Julie Andrews; Dorothy, the coffee shop assistant who is desperate to be Wonder Woman; all these, and many more colourful characters, accompany Jack through the ups and downs of the school year. Most of all, there is the lovely Beth Henderson, a teacher from a nearby school, who with her sister Laura presents Jack with an unexpected dilemma.

'Take a dash of *Heartbeat*, add a sprinkling of *All Creatures Great And Small* . . . and you have *Mister Teacher*. It will have you crying tears of laughter and sadness. A joy to read'
Glasgow Evening Times

'A charming memoir'
Daily Express

9780552155274

DEAR TEACHER
by Jack Sheffield

It's 1979: *Dallas* is enthralling the nation on TV, Mrs
Thatcher has just become prime minister, Abba is top of
the pops, and in the small Yorkshire village of Ragley-
on-the-Forest, Jack Sheffield returns for his third
year as headmaster of the village school.

Jack and his staff struggle to keep a semblance of
normality throughout the turbulence of the school
terms, as once again the official School Log fails to
record what is really going on beneath the seemingly
quiet routine. Ruby the caretaker discovers her Prince
Charming; Vera the school secretary gets to meet her
hero, Nicholas Parsons; and Jack, to his astonishment,
finds himself having to stand in as a curiously
skinny Father Christmas.

Jack also finds himself, at last, having to choose between
vivacious sisters Beth and Laura Henderson . . .

'Jack Sheffield's charming Teacher series will
certainly put a smile on your face. Overflowing
with amusing anecdotes'
Daily Express

9780552157735